DANCE
DANCE
DANCE

Also by
Haruki Murakami

A WILD SHEEP CHASE

*HARD-BOILED WONDERLAND AND
THE END OF THE WORLD*

THE ELEPHANT VANISHES

DANCE DANCE DANCE

a novel by

HARUKI MURAKAMI

translated by

ALFRED BIRNBAUM

KODANSHA INTERNATIONAL
Tokyo • New York • London

Translated and adapted by Alfred Birnbaum with the approval of the author.

The translator wishes to acknowledge the indefatigable Elmer Luke, whose efforts above and beyond the call of common editorial duty really put *Dance* on its feet.

Originally published in Japanese under the title
Dansu Dansu Dansu
by Kodansha Ltd., 1988.

Distributed in the United States by Kodansha America, Inc.,
114 Fifth Avenue, New York, NY 10011.
Published by Kodansha International Ltd.,
1-17-14 Otowa, Bunkyo-ku, Tokyo 112, and
Kodansha America, Inc.

First edition, 1994.
94 95 96 10 9 8 7 6 5 4 3 2 1

Library of Congress Cataloging-in-Publication Data

Murakami, Haruki, 1949–
   [Dansu dansu dansu. English] *delete* 240
   Dance dance dance : a novel / by Haruki Murakami ; translated by
Alfred Birnbaum.—1st ed.
     p. cm.
   ISBN 4-7700-1683-2
   I. Title.
PL856.U673D3613   1994
895.6'35—dc20
93-14098
CIP

DANCE
DANCE
DANCE

1

I often dream about the Dolphin Hotel.

In these dreams, I'm there, implicated in some kind of ongoing circumstance. All indications are that I *belong* to this dream continuity.

The Dolphin Hotel is distorted, much too narrow. It seems more like a long, covered bridge. A bridge stretching endlessly through time. And there I am, in the middle of it. Someone else is there too, crying.

The hotel envelops me. I can feel its pulse, its heat. In dreams, I am part of the hotel.

I wake up, but where? I don't just think this, I actually voice the question to myself: "Where am I?" As if I didn't know: I'm here. In my life. A feature of the world that is my existence. Not that I particularly recall ever having approved these matters, this condition, this state of affairs in which I feature. There might be a woman sleeping next to me. More often, I'm alone. Just me and the expressway that runs right next to my apartment and, bedside, a glass (five millimeters of whiskey still in it) and the malicious— no, make that indifferent—dusty morning light. Sometimes it's raining. If it is, I'll just stay in bed. And if there's whiskey still left in the glass, I'll drink it. And I'll look at the raindrops dripping from the eaves, and I'll think about the Dolphin Hotel. Maybe I'll stretch, nice and slow. Enough for me to be sure I'm myself and not part of something else. Yet I'll remember the feel of the dream. So much that I swear I can reach out and touch it, and the whole of that *something* that includes me will move. If I strain my ears, I can hear the slow, cautious sequence of play take place, like droplets in an intricate water puzzle falling, step upon step, one after the other. I listen carefully. That's when I hear someone softly, almost imperceptibly, weeping. A sobbing from somewhere in the darkness. Someone is crying for me.

The Dolphin Hotel is a real hotel. It actually exists in a so-so section of Sapporo. Once, a few years back, I spent a week there. No, let me get that straight. How many years ago was it? Four. Or more precisely, four and a half. I was still in my twenties. I checked into the Dolphin Hotel with a woman I was living with. She'd chosen the place. *This is where we're staying,* was what she said. If it hadn't been for her, I doubt I'd ever have set foot in the place.

It was a tiny dump of a hotel. In the whole time we were there, I don't know if we saw another paying customer. There were a couple of characters milling around the lobby, but who knows if they were staying there? A few keys were always missing from the board behind the front desk, so I guess there were other hotel guests. Though not too many. I mean, really, you hang out a hotel sign somewhere in a major city, put a phone number in the business listings, it stands to reason you're not going to go entirely without customers. But granting there were other customers besides ourselves, they were awfully quiet. We never heard a sound from them, hardly saw a sign of their presence—with the exception of the arrangement of the keys on the board that changed slightly each day. Were they like shadows creeping along the walls of the corridors, holding their breath? Occasionally we'd hear the dull rattling of the elevator, but when it stopped the oppressive silence bore down once more.

A mysterious hotel.

What it reminded me of was a biological dead end. A genetic retrogression. A freak accident of nature that stranded some organism up the wrong path without a way back. Evolutionary vector eliminated, orphaned life-form left cowering behind the curtain of history, in The Land That Time Forgot. And through no fault of anyone. No one to blame, no one to save it.

The hotel should never have been built where it was. That was the first mistake, and everything got worse from there. Like a button on a shirt buttoned wrong, every attempt to correct things led to yet another fine—not to say elegant—mess. No detail seemed right. Look at anything in the place and you'd find yourself tilting your head a few degrees. Not enough to cause you any real harm, nor enough to seem particularly odd. Who knows? You might get used to this slant on things (but if you did, you'd never be able to view the world again without holding your head out of true).

That was the Dolphin Hotel. *Normalness,* it lacked. Confusion piled on confusion until the saturation point was reached, destined in the not-too-distant future to be swallowed in the vortex of time. Anyone could recognize that at a glance. A pathetic place, woebegone as a three-legged black dog drenched in December rain. Sad hotels existed everywhere, to be sure, but the Dolphin was in a class of its own. The Dolphin Hotel was conceptually sorry. The Dolphin Hotel was tragic.

It goes without saying, then, that aside from those poor, unsuspecting souls who happened upon it, no one would willingly choose to stay there.

A far cry from its name (to me, the "Dolphin" sobriquet suggested a pristine white-sugar candy of a resort hotel on the Aegean Sea), if not for the sign hung out front, you'd never have known the building was a hotel. Even with the sign and the brass plaque at the entrance, it scarcely looked the part. What it really resembled was a museum. A peculiar kind of museum where persons with peculiar curiosities might steal away to see peculiar items on display.

Which actually was not far from the truth. The hotel was indeed part museum. But I ask, would anyone want to stay in such a hotel? In a lodge-cum-reliquary, its dark corridors blocked with stuffed sheep and musty fleeces and mold-covered documents and discolored photographs? Its corners caked with unfulfilled dreams?

The furniture was faded, the tables wobbled, the locks were useless. The floorboards were scuffed, the light bulbs dim; the washstand, with ill-fitting plug, couldn't hold water. A fat maid walked the halls with elephant strides, ponderously, ominously coughing. And the sad-eyed, middle-aged owner, stationed permanently behind the front desk, had two fingers missing. The kind of a guy, by the looks of him, for whom nothing goes right. A veritable specimen of the type—dredged up from an overnight soak in thin blue ink, soul stained by misfortune, failure, defeat. You'd want to put him in a glass case and cart him to your science class: *Homo nihilsuccessus*. Almost anyone who saw the guy would, to a greater or lesser degree, feel their spirits dampen. Not a few would be angered (some folks get upset seeing miserable examples of humanity). So who would stay in that hotel?

Well, *we* stayed there. *This is where we're staying*, she'd said. And then later she disappeared. She upped and vanished. It was the Sheep Man who told me so. *Thewomanleft-alonethisafternoon*, the Sheep Man said. Somehow, the Sheep Man knew. He'd known that she had to get out. Just as I know now. Her purpose had been to lead me there. As if it were her fate. Like the Moldau flowing to the sea. Like rain.

When I started having these dreams about the Dolphin Hotel, she was the first thing that came to mind. She was seeking me out. Why else would I keep having the same dream, over and over again?

She. What was her name? The months we'd spent together, and yet I never knew. What *did* I actually know about her? She'd been in the employ of an exclusive call girl club. A club for members only; persons of less-than-impeccable standing not welcome. So she was a high-class hooker. She'd had a couple other jobs on the side. During regular business hours she was a part-time proofreader at a small publishing house; she was also an ear model. In other words, she kept busy. Naturally, she wasn't nameless. In fact I'm sure she went by a number of names. At the same time, practically speaking, she didn't have a name. Whatever she carried— which was next to nothing—bore no name. She had no train pass, no driver's license, no credit cards. She did carry a little notebook, but that was scrawled in an indecipherable code. Apparently she wanted no handle on her identity. Hookers may have names, but they inhabit a world that doesn't need to know.

I hardly knew a thing about her. Her birthplace, her real age, her birthday, her schooling and family background— zip. Precipitate as weather, she appeared from somewhere, then evaporated, leaving only memory.

But now, the memory of her is taking on renewed reality. A palpable reality. She has been calling me via that circumstance known as the Dolphin Hotel. Yes, she is seeking me once more. And only by becoming part of the Dolphin Hotel will I ever see her again. Yes, there is no doubt: it is she who is crying for me.

Gazing at the rain, I consider what it means to belong, to become part of something. To have someone cry for me. From someplace distant, so very distant. From, ultimately, a dream. No matter how far I reach out, no matter how fast I run, I'll never make it.

Why would anyone want to cry for me?

She is definitely calling me. From somewhere in the Dolphin Hotel. And apparently, somewhere in my own mind,

the Dolphin Hotel is what I seek as well. To be taken into
that scene, to become part of that weirdly fateful venue.

It is no easy matter to return to the Dolphin Hotel, not a
simple question of ringing up for a reservation, hopping on a
plane, flying to Sapporo, and mission accomplished. For the
hotel is, as I've suggested, as much circumstance as place, a
state of being in the guise of a hotel. To return to the Dolphin Hotel means facing up to a shadow of the past. The
prospect alone depresses. It has been all I could do these four
years to rid myself of that chill, dim shadow. To return to
the Dolphin Hotel is to give up all I'd quietly set aside during this time. Not that what I'd achieved is anything great,
mind you. However you look at it, it's pretty much the stuff
of tentative convenience. Okay, I'd done my best. Through
some clever juggling I'd managed to forge a connection to
reality, to build a new life based on token values. Was I now
supposed to give it up?

But the whole thing started there. That much was undeni-
able. So the story *had* to start back there.

I rolled over in bed, stared at the ceiling, and let out a
deep sigh. *Oh give in,* I thought. But the idea of giving in
didn't take hold. *It's out of your hands, kid. Whatever you
may be thinking, you can't resist. The story's already
decided.*

2

I got sent to Hokkaido on assignment. As work goes, it wasn't terribly exciting, but I wasn't in a position to choose. And anyway, with the jobs that come my way, there's generally very little difference. For better or worse, the further from the midrange of things you go, the less relative qualities matter. The same holds for wavelengths: Pass a certain point and you can hardly tell which of two adjacent notes is higher in pitch, until finally you not only can't distinguish them, you can't hear them at all.

The assignment was a piece called "Good Eating in Hakodate" for a women's magazine. A photographer and I were to visit a few restaurants. I'd write the story up, he'd supply the photos, for a total of five pages. Well, somebody's got to write these things. And the same can be said for collecting garbage and shoveling snow. It doesn't matter whether you like it or not—a job's a job.

For three and a half years, I'd been making this kind of contribution to society. Shoveling snow. You know, cultural snow.

Due to some unavoidable circumstances, I had quit an office that a friend and I were running, and for half a year I did almost nothing. I didn't feel like doing anything. The previous autumn all sorts of things had happened in my life. I got divorced. A friend died, very mysteriously. A woman

ran out on me, without a word. I met a strange man, found
myself caught up in some extraordinary developments. And
by the time everything was over, I was overwhelmed by a
stillness deeper than anything I'd known. A devastating
absence hovered about my apartment. I stayed shut-in for
six months. I never went out during the day, except to make
the absolute minimum purchases necessary to survive. I'd
venture into the city with the first gray of dawn and walk
the deserted streets, and when the streets started to fill with
people, I holed up back indoors to sleep.

Toward evening, I'd rise, fix something to eat, feed the
cat. Then I'd sit on the floor and methodically go over the
things that had happened to me, trying to make sense of
them. Rearrange the order of events, list up all possible alter-
natives, consider the right or wrong of what I'd done. This
went on until the dawn, when I'd go out and wander the
streets again.

For half a year that was my daily routine. From January
through June 1979. I didn't read one book. I didn't open one
newspaper. I didn't watch TV, didn't listen to the radio.
Never saw anyone, never talked to anyone. I hardly even
drank; I wasn't in a drinking frame of mind. I had no idea
what was going on in the world, who'd become famous,
who'd died, nothing. It wasn't that I stubbornly resisted
information, I simply had no desire to know anything. Even
so, I knew things were happening. The world didn't stop. I
could feel it in my skin, even sitting alone in my apartment.
Though little did it compel me to show interest. It was like a
silent breath of air, breezing past me.

Sitting on the floor, I'd replay the past in my head. Funny,
that's all I did, day after day after day for half a year, and I
never tired of it. What I'd been through seemed so vast, with
so many facets. Vast but real, very real, which was why the
experience persisted in towering before me, like a monument
lit up at night. And the thing was, it was a monument to me.
I inspected the events from every possible angle. I'd been
damaged, badly, I suppose. The damage was not petty. Blood

had flowed, quietly. After a while some of the anguish went away, some surfaced only later. And yet my half year indoors was not spent in convalescence. Nor in autistic denial of the external world. I simply needed time to get back on my feet.

Once on my feet, I tried not to think about where I was heading. That was another question entirely, to be thought out at a later date. The main thing was to recover my equilibrium.

I scarcely talked to the cat.

The telephone rang. I let it ring.

If someone knocked on the door, I wasn't there.

There were a few letters. A couple from my former partner, who didn't know where I was or what I was up to and was concerned. Was there anything he could do to help? His new business was going smoothly, old acquaintances had asked about me.

My ex-wife wrote, needing some practical affairs taken care of, very matter-of-fact. Then she mentioned she was getting married—to someone I didn't know, and probably never would. Which meant she'd split up with that friend of mine she'd gone off with when we divorced. Not surprising, them splitting up. The guy wasn't so great a jazz guitarist and he wasn't so great a person either. Never could understand what she saw in him—but none of my business, eh? About me, she said she wasn't worried. She was sure I'd be fine whatever it was I chose to do. She reserved her worries for the people I'd get involved with.

I read these letters over a few times, then filed them away.

And so the months passed.

Money wasn't a problem. I had saved plenty enough to live on, and I wasn't thinking about what came later. Winter was past.

And spring took hold. The scent of the wind changed. Even the darkness of night was different.

At the end of May, Kipper, my cat, died. Suddenly, without warning. I woke up one day and found him curled up on the kitchen floor, dead. He himself probably hadn't known it was happening. His body was cold and hard, like yesterday's roast chicken, sheen gone from the fur. He could hardly have claimed he had the best life. Never really loved by anyone, never seeming really to love anyone either. His eyes always had this uneasy look, like, *what now?* You don't see that look in a cat too often. But anyway, he was dead. Nothing more. Maybe that's the best thing about death.

I put his body in a Seiyu supermarket bag, placed him on the backseat of the car, and drove to the hardware store for a shovel. I turned off the highway a good ways up in the hills and found an appropriate grove of trees. A fair distance back from the road I dug a hole one meter deep and laid Kipper in his shopping bag to rest. Then I shoveled dirt on top of him. Sorry, I told the little guy, that's just how it goes. Birds were singing the whole time I was burying him. The upper registers of a flute recital.

Once the hole was filled in, I tossed the shovel into the trunk of the car, and got back on the highway. I turned the radio on as I drove home to Tokyo.

Which is when the DJ had to put on Ray Charles moaning about being *born to lose . . . and now I'm losing you.*

I felt like crying. Sometimes one little thing will do the trick. I turned the radio off and pulled into a service area. First, I washed the dirt from my hands, then went into the restaurant. I could only manage a third of a sandwich, but I put down two cups of coffee.

What was Kipper doing now? I wondered. Down there in the dark. The sound of the dirt hitting the Seiyu bag echoed in my brain. That's just how it goes, pal, for me the same as you.

I sat staring at my unfinished sandwich for an hour. Until a violet-uniformed waitress came by and nervously asked if she could clear the plate away.

That's that, I thought. So now, back to society.

3

It takes no great effort to find work in the giant anthill of an advanced capitalist society. That is, of course, so long as you're not asking the impossible.

When I still had my office, I did my share of editing and writing, and I'd gotten to know a few professionals in the field. So as I embarked on a free-lance career, there was no major retooling required. I didn't need much to live on anyway.

I pulled out my address book and made some calls. I asked if there was work available. I said I'd been laying back but was ready to take stuff on. Almost immediately jobs came my way. Though not particularly interesting jobs, mostly filler for PR newsletters and company brochures. Speaking conservatively, I'd say half the material I wrote was meaningless, of no conceivable use to anyone. A waste of pulp and ink. But I did the work, mechanically, without thinking. At first, the load wasn't much, maybe a couple hours a day. The rest of the time I'd be out walking or seeing a movie. I saw a lot of movies. For three months, I had an easy time of it. I was slowly getting back in touch.

Then, in early autumn, things began to change. Work orders increased dramatically. The phone rang nonstop, my mailbox was overflowing. I met people in the business and had lunch with them. They promised me more work.

The reason was simple. I was never choosy about the jobs
I did. I was willing to do anything, I met my deadlines, I
never complained, I wrote legibly. And I was thorough.
Where others slacked off, I did an honest write. I was never
snide, even when the pay was low. If I got a call at two-
thirty in the morning asking for twenty pages of text (about,
say, the advantages of non-digital clocks or the appeal of
women in their forties or the most beautiful spots in
Helsinki, where, needless to say, I'd never been) by six A.M.,
I'd have it done by five-thirty. And if they called back for a
rewrite, I had it to them by six. You bet I had a good reputation.

The same as for shoveling snow.

Let it snow and I'd show you a thing or two about efficient roadwork.

And with not one speck of ambition, not one iota of
expectation. My only concern was to do things systematically, from one end to the other. I sometimes wonder if this
might not prove to be the bane of my life. After wasting so
much pulp and ink myself, who was I to complain about
waste? We live in an advanced capitalist society, after all.
Waste is the name of the game, its greatest virtue. Politicians
call it "refinements in domestic consumption." I call it
meaningless waste. A difference of opinion. Which doesn't
change the way we live. If I don't like it, I can move to
Bangladesh or Sudan.

I for one am not eager to live in Bangladesh or Sudan.

So I kept working.

And soon enough, it wasn't just PR work. I got called to
do bits and pieces for regular magazines. For some reason,
mostly women's magazines. I started doing interviews, minor
legwork reportage. But really, the work wasn't much of an
improvement over PR newsletters. Due to the nature of these
magazines, most of the people I had to interview were in
show business. No matter what you asked them, they had
only stock replies. You could predict what they'd answer
before you asked the question. In the worst cases, the man-

ager would insist on seeing the questions in advance. So I always came with everything written out. Once I asked a seventeen-year-old singer something that wasn't on the list, which caused her manager to pipe up: "That wasn't what we agreed on—she doesn't have to answer that." That was a kick. I wondered if the girl couldn't answer what month followed October without this manager by her side. Still, I did my best. Before each interview I did my homework, surveyed available sources, tried to come up with questions others wouldn't think to ask. I took pains structuring the article. Not that these efforts received any special recognition. They never got me an appreciative word. I went the extra step because, for me, it was the simplest way. Self-discipline. Giving my disused fingers and head a practical—and if at all possible, harmless—dose of overwork.

Social rehabilitation.

After that, my days were busier than ever. Not only with double or triple my regular load, but with a lot of rush jobs too. Without fail, jobs that had no takers found their way to me. My role in those circles was the junkyard at the edge of town. Anything, particularly if complicated or a pain, would get hauled to me for disposal.

By way of thanks, my savings account swelled to figures I'd never seen the likes of, though I was too busy to spend much of it. So when a guy I knew offered me a good deal, I got rid of my nothing-but-headaches car and bought his year-old Subaru Leone. Hardly any miles on it, stereo and air-conditioning. A real first for me. And I moved to an apartment in Shibuya, closer to the center of town. It was a bit noisy—the expressway passing right outside my window—but you got used to it.

I slept with a few women I met through work.

Social rehabilitation.

I had a sense about which women I ought to sleep with. And which women I'd be able to sleep with, which not. Maybe even which I shouldn't sleep with. It's an intelligence that comes with age. I also knew when to call it quits, all

very nice and easy so no one got hurt. The only thing missing was those tugs on the heartstrings.

The deepest I got involved was with a woman who
worked at the phone company. I met her at a New Year's
party. Both of us were tipsy, we joked with each other, liked
each other, and ended up back at my place. She had a good
head on her shoulders and terrific legs. We went for rides in
my new-used Subaru. She'd call, whenever the mood struck,
and come over and spend the night. She was the only relationship with one foot in the door like that. Though both of
us knew there was no place this thing could go. Still, we quietly shared something approaching a pardon from life. I
knew days of peace for the first time in ages. We exchanged
tenderness, talked in whispers. I cooked for her, gave her
birthday presents. We'd go to jazz clubs and have cocktails.
We never argued, not once. We knew exactly what we
wanted in each other. And even so, it ended. One day it
stopped, as if the film simply slipped off the reel.

Her departure left me emptier than I would have sus-
pected. For a while, I stayed in again.

The problem was that I hadn't wanted her, really wanted
her. I'd liked her, liked being with her. She brought me back
to gentle feelings. But what it came down to was, *I never felt
a need for her*. Not three days after she got out of my life,
the realization hit home. That ultimately, all the time I'd
been next to her, I might as well have been on the moon. The
whole while I'd felt her breasts against me, I'd really wanted
something else.

It took four years to get my life back on steady ground. I
carefully dispatched each piece of work that came my way,
and people came to feel they could depend on me. Not
many, but a few, even became friendly. Though, it goes without saying, that wasn't enough. Not enough at all. Here I'd
spent all this time trying to get up to speed, and I was back
to where I started.

Okay, I thought, age thirty-four, square one. What do you
do now?

I didn't have to think much about that one. I knew already. The answer had been floating over my head like a dark, dense cloud. All I had to do was take action, instead of putting it off and putting it off. *I had to go to the Dolphin Hotel*. That's where it all started.

I also had to find *her*. The woman who'd first guided me to the Dolphin Hotel, *she* who'd been a high-class call girl in her own covert world of night. (Under astonishing circumstances, I was to learn this nameless woman's name sometime later, but, for reasons of convenience, unorthodox as it will seem, I'll tell it to you now. Pardon me, please. It was Kiki.) Yes, Kiki held the key. I had to call her back to me. To a life with me she'd left never to return. Was it possible? Who knew, but I had to try. From then would begin a new cycle.

I packed my bags, did double time to finish up outstanding work, then canceled all the jobs I'd penciled in for the next month. I said I was leaving Tokyo on family business. A couple of editors made noises, but what could they do? I'd never let them down before, and besides I was giving them plenty of advance notice to find other ways and means. In the end, it was fine. I'd be back in a month, I told them.

Then I took a flight to Hokkaido. This was the beginning of March 1983.

Of course, the family business wasn't over in anything near a month.

4

I booked a taxi for two days, and the photographer and I raced around Hakodate in the snow checking out eateries in the city.

I'm good at researching, very systematic, very efficient. The most important thing about this sort of job is to do your homework and set up a schedule. That's the key. When it comes to gathering materials beforehand, you can't beat organizations that compile information for people in the field. Become a member and pay your dues; they'll look up almost anything for you. So if by chance you're researching eating places in Hakodate, they can dig up quite a bit. They use mainframe computer retrieval, arrange the facts in file format, print out hard copy, even deliver to your doorstep. Granted, it's not cheap, but plenty worth the time it buys.

In addition to that, I do a little walking for information myself. There are reading rooms specializing in travel materials, libraries that collect local newspapers and regional publications. From all of these sources, I pick out the promising spots, then call them up to check their business hours. This much done, I've saved a lot of trouble on site. Then I draw lines in a notebook and plan out each day's itinerary. I look at maps and mark in the routes we'll travel. Trying to reduce uncertainties to a minimum.

Once we arrive in Hakodate, the photographer and I go

around to the restaurants in order. There are about thirty. We take a couple of bites—just enough to get the taste—then casually leave the rest of the meal uneaten. Refinements in consumption. We're still undercover at this stage, so no picture taking. Only after leaving the premises do the photographer and I discuss the food and evaluate it on a scale of one to ten. If it passes, it stays on the list; if not, it's out. We generally figure on dropping at least half. Taking a parallel tack, we also check the local papers for listings of places we've missed, selecting maybe five. We go to these too, and weed out the not-so-good. Then we've got our finalists. I call them up, give the name of the magazine, tell them we'd like to do a feature on them—text with photos. All that in two days. Nights, I stay in my hotel room, laying down the basic copy.

The next day, while the photographer does quick shots of the food and table settings, I talk to the restaurant owners. Saves on time. So we can call it a wrap in three days. True, there are those in our league who take even less time. But they don't do any research. They do a handful of the more well-known spots, cruise through without eating a thing, write brief comments. It's their business, not mine. If I may be perfectly frank, I doubt that many writers take as many pains as I do at this level of reportage. It's the kind of work that can break you if you're too serious about it, or you can kick back and do almost nothing. The worst of it is, whether you're earnest or you loaf, the difference will hardly show in the finished piece. On the surface. Only in the finer points can you find any hint of the distinction.

I'm not explaining this out of pride or anything.

I just wanted you to have a rough idea of the job, the sort of expendables I deal with.

On the third night, I finish writing.

The fourth day is left free, just in case.

But since the work has been completed and we don't have anything else in the tube, we rent a car and head off for a day of cross-country skiing. That evening, the two of us settle down to drinks over a nice, simmering hot pot. One day's relaxation. I turn over my manuscript to the photographer, and that's it. My job's done, the work's in someone else's hands.

But before turning in that evening, I rang up Sapporo directory assistance for the number of the Dolphin Hotel. I didn't have to wait long. I sat up in bed and sighed. Well, at least the Dolphin Hotel hadn't gone under. Relief, I guess. Because I wouldn't have been surprised if it had, a mysterious place like that. I took a deep breath, dialed the number —and someone answered immediately. As if they'd been just waiting for it to ring. So immediately, in fact, I was taken aback.

"Hello, Dolphin Hotel!" went a cheerful voice.

It was a young woman. A woman? What's going on? I don't remember a woman being there.

It didn't figure, so I checked if the address was the same. Yes, it was exactly where the Dolphin Hotel I knew used to be. Maybe the hotel had hired someone new, the owner's niece or something. Nothing so odd about that. I told her I wanted to make a reservation.

"Thank you very much, sir," she chirped. "Please wait a moment while I transfer you to our reservations desk."

Our reservations desk? Now I was really confused. I couldn't begin to digest that one. What the hell happened to the old joint?

"Sorry to keep you waiting. This is the reservations desk. How may I help you?" This time, a young man's voice. The brisk, friendly pitch of the professional hotel man. Curiouser and curiouser.

I asked for a single room for three nights. I gave him my name and my Tokyo phone number.

"Very well, sir. That's three nights, starting from tomorrow. Your single room will be waiting for you."

I couldn't think of anything to say to that, so I thanked him and hung up, completely disoriented. Shouldn't I have asked for an explanation? Oh well, it'd all become clear once I got there. And anyway, I couldn't *not* go. I didn't have an alternative.

I asked the concierge to check the schedule for trains to Sapporo. After that, I got room service to send up a bottle of whiskey and some ice, and I stayed up watching a late-night movie on TV. A Clint Eastwood western. Clint didn't smile once, didn't sneer. I tried laughing at him, but he never broke his deadpan. The movie ended and I'd had my fill of whiskey, so I turned out the light and slept straight through the night. If I dreamed, I don't remember.

All I could see outside the window of the early morning express train was snow. It was a bright, clear day, so the glare soon got to be too much. I didn't see another passenger looking out the windows. They all knew what snow looks like.

I'd skipped breakfast, so a little before noon I made my way to the dining car. Beer and an omelet. Across from me sat a fiftyish man in a suit and tie, having beer with a ham sandwich. He looked like a mechanical engineer, and that's just what he was. He spoke to me first, telling me he serviced jets for the Self-Defense Forces. Then he filled me in on how Soviet fighters and bombers invaded our airspace, though he didn't seem particularly upset about it. He was more concerned about the economics of F4 Phantoms. How much fuel they guzzled in one scramble, a terrible waste. "If the Japanese had made them, you can bet they'd be more efficient. And at no loss to performance either! There's no reason why we couldn't build a low-cost fighter if we wanted to."

That's when I proffered my words of wisdom, that waste is the highest virtue one can achieve in advanced capitalist society. The fact that Japan bought Phantom jets from America and wasted vast quantities of fuel on scrambles put an extra spin in the global economy, and that extra spin lifted capitalism to yet greater heights. If you put an end to all the waste, mass panic would ensue and the global economy would go haywire. Waste is the fuel of contradiction, and contradiction activates the economy, and an active economy creates more waste.

Well, maybe so, the engineer admitted, but having been a wartime child who had to live under deprived conditions, he couldn't grasp what this new social structure meant. "Our generation, we're not like you young folks," he said, straining a smile. "We don't understand these complex workings of yours."

I couldn't say I exactly understood things either, but as I wasn't eager for the conversation to drag on, I kept quiet. No, I'm not used to things; I just recognize them for what they are. There's a decisive difference between those two propositions. Which is just as well, I supposed, as I finished my omelet and excused myself.

I slept for thirty minutes, and the rest of the trip I read a biography of Jack London I'd bought near the Hakodate station. Compared to the grand sweep and romance of Jack London's life, my existence seemed like a squirrel with its head against a walnut, dozing until spring. For the time being, that is. But that's how biographies are. I mean, who's going to read about the peaceful life and times of a nobody employed at the Kawasaki Municipal Library? In other words, what we seek is some kind of compensation for what we put up with.

Arriving at Sapporo, I decided to take a leisurely stroll to the hotel. It was a pleasant enough afternoon, and I was carrying only a shoulder bag.

The streets were covered in a thin layer of slush, and people trained their eyes carefully at their feet. The air was exhilarating. High school girls came bustling along, their rosy red cheeks puffing white breaths you could have written cartoon captions in. I continued my amble, taking in the sights of town. It had been four and a half years since I was in Sapporo. It seemed like much longer.

Along the way I stopped into a coffee shop. All around me normal, everyday city types were going about their normal, everyday affairs. Lovers were whispering to each other, businessmen were poring over spread sheets, college kids were planning their next ski trip and discussing the new Police album. We could have been in any city in Japan. Transplant this coffee shop scene to Yokohama or Fukuoka and nothing would seem out of place. In spite of which—or, rather, all the more because—here I was, sitting in this coffee shop, drinking my coffee, feeling a desperate loneliness. I alone was the outsider. I had no place here.

Of course, by the same token, I couldn't really say I belonged to Tokyo and its coffee shops. But I had never felt this loneliness there. I could drink my coffee, read my book, pass the time of day without any special thought, all because I was part of the regular scenery. Here I had no ties to anyone. Fact is, I'd come to reclaim myself.

I paid the check and left. Then, without further thought, I headed for the hotel.

I didn't know the way exactly and part of me worried that I might miss the place. I didn't. How could anyone have? It had been transformed into a gleaming twenty-six-story Bauhaus Modern–Art Deco symphony of glass and steel, with flags of various nations waving along the drive-way, smartly uniformed doormen hailing taxis, a glass elevator shooting up to a penthouse restaurant. A bas-relief of a dolphin was set into one of the marble columns by the entrance, beneath which the inscription read:

l'Hôtel Dauphin

I stood there a good twenty seconds, mouth agape, staring up at it. Then I let out a long, deep breath that might as easily have been beamed straight to the moon. Surprise was not the word.

5

I couldn't stand around gawking at the façade forever. Whatever this building was, the address was correct, as was the name—for the most part. And anyway, I had a reservation, right? There was nothing to do but go in.

I walked up the gently sloped driveway and pushed my way through the shiny brass revolving door. The lobby was large enough to be a gymnasium, the ceiling at least two stories high. A wall of glass rose the full height, and through it cascaded a brilliant shower of sunlight. The floor space was appointed with a fleet of luxurious designer sofas, between which were stationed planters of ornamental trees. Lots of them. The overall decor focused on an oil painting—three tatami mats large—of some Hokkaido marshland. Nothing outstanding artistically, but impressive, if only for its size. At the far end of the lobby a posh coffee bar beckoned. The sort of place where you order a sandwich and they bring you four deviled ham dainties arrayed like calling cards on a silver tray with an embellishment of potato crisps and *cornichons*. Throw in a cup of coffee and you're spending enough to buy a frugal family of four a midday meal.

The lobby was crowded. Apparently a function was in progress. A group of well-dressed, middle-aged men sat on facing sofas, nodding and smiling magnanimously. Jaws thrust out, legs crossed, identically. A professional organization? Doctors or university professors? On their periphery—perhaps they were part of the same gathering—cooed a clutch of young women in formal dress, some of them in kimono, some in floor-length dresses. There were a few Westerners as well, not to mention the requisite salarymen in dark suits and harmless ties, attaché cases in hand.

In a word, business was booming at the new Dolphin Hotel.

What we had here was a hotel founded on a proper outlay of capital and now enjoying proper returns. But how the hell had this come about? Well, I could guess, of course. Having once put together a PR bulletin for a hotel chain, I knew the whole process. Before a hotel of this scale is built, someone first costs out every aspect of the venture in detail, then consultants are called in and every piece of information is input into their computers for a thorough simulation study. Everything including the wholesale price and usage volume of toilet paper is taken into account. Then students are hired to go around the city—Sapporo in this case—to do a market survey. They stop young men and women on the street and ask how many weddings they expect to attend each year. You get the picture. Little is left unchecked. All in an effort to reduce business risk.

So the Hôtel Dauphin project team had gone to great lengths over many months to draw up as precise a plan as possible. They bought the property, they assembled the staff, they pinned down flash advertising space. If money was all it took—and they were convinced they'd make that money back—there'd be no end of funds pouring in. It's big business of a big order.

Now, the only enterprises that could embark on such a big business venture were the huge conglomerates. Because even after paring away the risks, there's bound to be some hidden factor of uncertainty lurking around, which only a major player can conceivably absorb.

To be honest, this new Dolphin Hotel wasn't my kind of hotel.

Or at least, under normal circumstances, if I had to choose a place to stay, I wouldn't go for one that looked like this. The rates are too high; too much padding, too many frills. But this time the die had been cast.

I went to the front desk and gave my name, whereupon three light blue blazered young women with toothpaste-commercial smiles greeted me. This smile training surely figured into the capital outlay. With their virgin-snow white blouses and immaculate hairstyles, the receptionists were picture-perfect. Of the three, one wore glasses, which of course suited her nicely. When she stepped over to me, I actually felt a shot of relief. She was the prettiest and most immediately likable. There was something about her expression I responded to, some embodiment of hotel spirit. I half expected her to produce a tiny magic wand, like in a Disney movie, and tap out swirls of diamond dust.

But instead of a magic wand, she used a computer, swiftly typing in my name and credit card number, then verifying the details on the display screen. Then she handed me my card-key, room number 1523. I smiled as I accepted the hotel brochure from her. When had the hotel opened? I asked. Last October, she answered, almost in reflex. It was now in its fifth month of operation.

"You know," I began, donning *my* professional smile, "I seem to remember a small hotel with a similar name in this location a few years ago. Do you have any idea what became of it?"

A slight disturbance clouded her smile. Quiet ripples spread across her face, as if a beer bottle had been tossed into a sacred spring. By the time the ripples subsided, her reassumed smile was a shade less cheerful than before. I observed the changes with great interest. Would the sprite of the spring now appear to ask whether the item I disposed of had a gold or silver twist top?

"Well, now," she hedged, touching the bridge of her

glasses with her index finger. "That was before we opened
our doors, so I really couldn't—"

Her words cut off. I waited for her to continue, but she
didn't.

"I'm terribly sorry," she said.

"Oh," I said. Seconds went by. I found myself liking her. I
wanted to touch the bridge of my glasses as well, except that
I wasn't wearing any glasses. "Well, then, is there anyone
you can ask?"

She held her breath a second, thinking it over. The smile
vanished. It's exceedingly difficult to hold your breath and
keep smiling. Just try it if you don't believe me.

"I'm terribly sorry," she said again, "but would you mind
waiting a bit?" Then she retreated through a door. Thirty
seconds later, she returned with a fortyish man in a black
suit. A real live hotelier by the looks of him. I'd met enough
of them in my line of work. They are a dubious species, with
twenty-five different smiles on call for every variety of circumstance. From the cool and cordial twinge of disinterest
to the measured grin of satisfaction. They wield the entire
arsenal by number, like golf clubs for particular shots.

"May I help you, please," he said, sending a midrange
smile my way with a polite bow of the head. When he noted
my attire, however, the smile was quickly adjusted down
three notches. I was wearing my fur-lined hunting jacket
with a Keith Haring button pinned to the chest, an Austrian
Army–issue Alps Corps fur cap, a rough-and-ready pair of
hiking trousers with lots of pockets, and snow-tire treaded
work boots. All fine and practical items of dress, but just a
tad unsuitable for this hotel lobby. No fault of mine, only a
difference in life-style.

"You had a question concerning our hotel, I believe?" he
voiced most properly.

I put both hands on the counter and repeated my query.

The man cast a glance at my Mickey Mouse watch with
the same clinical unease a vet might direct at a cat's sprained
paw.

"Might I inquire," he regained his composure to speak, "why you wish to know about the previous hotel? If you don't mind my asking, that is?"

I explained as simply as I could: A good while back I had stayed at the old Dolphin Hotel and gotten to know the owner; now, years later, I visit and everything's completely changed. Which makes me wonder, what happened to the old guy?

The man nodded attentively.

"In all honesty, I'm not entirely clear on the details myself," he chose his words guardedly. "Nevertheless, my understanding of the history of this hotel is that our concerns purchased the property where the previous Dolphin Hotel stood and erected on the site what we now have before us. As you can see, the name was for all intents and purposes retained, but let me assure you that the management is altogether separate, with no relation whatsoever to its predecessor."

"Then why keep the name?"

"You must forgive me, I'm afraid I really don't . . ."

"And I suppose you wouldn't have any idea where I could find the former owner?"

"I *am* sorry, but no, I do not," he answered, moving on to smile number 16.

"Is there anyone else I could ask? Someone who might know?"

"Since you insist," the man began, straining his neck slightly. "We are merely employees here, and accordingly we are strictly out of touch with any goings on prior to when the current premises opened for business. So unfortunately, if someone such as yourself desires to know anything more specific, there's really very little . . ."

Certainly what he said made sense, yet something caught in the back of my mind. Something artificial, manufactured really, about the responses from both the young woman and the stiff now fielding my questions. I couldn't put my finger on anything exactly, yet I couldn't swallow the line. Do your share of interviews and you get this professional sixth sense. That tone of voice when someone's hiding something, that knowing expression of someone who's lying. No real evidence to go on. Only a hunch, that there was more here than being said.

Still, it was clear that nothing more would come from pushing them further. I thanked the man; he excused himself and withdrew. After his black suit had vanished from view, I asked the young woman about meals and room service, and she went on at length. While she spoke, I peered straight into her eyes. Beautiful eyes. I swear I almost began to see things in them. But when she met my gaze, she blushed. Which made me like her even more. Why was that? Was it that hotel spirit in her? Whatever, I thanked her, turned away, and took the elevator up to my floor.

Room 1523 proved to be quite a room. Both the bed and the bath were far too big for a single. A full complement of shampoo, conditioner, and after-shave was provided, as was a bathrobe. The refrigerator was chock-full of snacks. There was an ample writing desk, with plenty of stationery and envelopes. The closet was large, the carpet deep-piled. I took off my coat and boots and picked up the hotel brochure. Quite a production. They hadn't spared any expense on this job.

L'Hôtel Dauphin represents a wholly new development in quality city center lodgings, the brochure stated. *Complete with the latest conveniences and full twenty-four-hour services. Our guest rooms are spacious and sumptuously styled. Featuring the finest selection of products, a restful atmosphere, and a warm at-home feeling. "Professional space with a human face."*

In other words, they'd spent a lot of money, so the rates were high.

Indeed, this was a very well turned out hotel. A big shopping arcade in the basement, an indoor pool, sauna, and tanning salon. Tennis courts, a health club with training coaches and exercise equipment, conference rooms outfitted for simultaneous translation, five restaurants, three lounges, even a late-night café. Not to mention a limousine service, free work space, unlimited business supplies available to all guests. Anything you could want, they'd thought of—and then some. A rooftop heliport?

Intelligent facilities in an impeccable decor.

But what of the commercial group that owned and operated this hotel? I reread the brochure from cover to cover. Not one mention of the management. Odd, to say the least. It was unthinkable that any but the most experienced hotel chain could run a topflight operation like this, and any enterprise of such scale would be certain to stamp its name everywhere and take every opportunity to promote its full line of hotels. You stay at one Prince Hotel and the brochure lists every Prince Hotel in the whole of Japan. That's how it is.

And then there was still the question, why would a hotel of this class take on the name of a dump like the old Dolphin?

I couldn't come up with even a flake of an answer to that one.

I threw the brochure onto the table, fell back into the sofa with my feet kicked up, and looked out my fifteenth-story window. All I could see was blue sky. I felt like I was flying.

All this was fine, but I missed the old dive. There'd been a lot to see from those windows.

6

puttered around in the hotel, seeing what there was to see. I checked out the restaurants and lounges, took a peek at the pool and sauna and health club and tennis courts, bought a couple of books in the shopping arcade. I criss-crossed the lobby, then gravitated to the game center and played a few rounds of backgammon. That alone took up the afternoon. The hotel was practically an amusement park. The world is full of ways and means to waste time.

After that, I left the hotel to have a look around the area. As I strolled through the early evening streets, the lay of the town gradually came back to me. Back when I'd stayed at the old Dolphin Hotel, I covered this area with depressing regularity, day after day. Turn here, and there was this or that. The old Dolphin hadn't had a dining room—if it had, I doubt I would have been inclined to eat there—so we, Kiki and I, would always go someplace nearby for meals. Now I felt like I was visiting an old neighborhood and was content just to wander about, taking in familiar sights.

When the sun went down, the air grew cold. The streets echoed with the wet sounds of slush underfoot. There was no wind, so walking was not at all unpleasant. It was still crisp and clear. Even the piles of exhaust-gray snow plowed up on every corner looked positively enchanting beneath the streetlights.

The area had changed markedly from the old days. Of course, those "old days" were only four years back, as I've said, so most of the places I'd frequented were more or less the same. The local atmosphere was basically the same as well, but signs of change were everywhere. Stores were boarded up, announcements of development to come tacked over. A large building was under construction. A drive-through burger stand and designer boutiques and a European auto showroom and a trendy café with an inner courtyard of *sara* trees—all kinds of new establishments had popped up one after the next, pushing aside the dingy old three-story blockhouses and cheap eateries festooned with traditional *noren* entrance curtains and the sweetshop where a cat lay napping by the stove. The odd mix of styles presented an all-too-temporary show of coexistence, like the mouth of a child with new teeth coming in. A bank had even opened a new branch, maybe a spillover of the new Dolphin Hotel capitalization. Build a hotel of that scale in a perfectly ordinary—if a bit neglected—neighborhood, and the balance is upset. The flow of people changes, the place starts to jump. Land prices go up.

Or perhaps the changes were more cumulative. That is, the upheaval hadn't been wrought by the new Dolphin Hotel alone, but was a stage in the greater infrastructural changes of the area. Some long-term urban redevelopment program, for example.

I went into a small bar I remembered, and had a few drinks and a bite to eat. The place was dirty, noisy, cheap, and good. The kind of hole-in-the-wall I always look for when I have to eat out alone. Places like this put me at ease, never make me lonely. I can talk to myself and nobody listens or cares.

After eating, I still wanted something else, so I asked for some saké. As the warm brew seeped into my system, the question came to me: What on earth am I doing up here? The Dolphin Hotel, such that I was seeking, no longer existed. It didn't matter what it was I was looking for, the place was no more. And not merely gone, it'd been replaced by this idiotic

Star Wars high-tech hotel-a-thon. I was too late. My dreams of the once-Dolphin Hotel had been nothing more than dreams of Kiki, long vanished out the door. Perhaps there *was* someone crying for me. But that too was gone. Nothing was left. What could you possibly hope to find here, kid?

You said it, I thought. Or maybe I had my mouth open and actually said it to myself. *There's nothing left here. Not one thing left for you.*

I clamped my lips tight and stared at the bottle of soy sauce on the counter.

You live by yourself for a stretch of time and you get to staring at different objects. Sometimes you talk to yourself. You take meals in crowded joints. You develop an intimate relationship with your used Subaru. You slowly but surely become a has-been.

I left the bar and headed back to the hotel. I'd walked a fair bit, but it wasn't hard finding my way back. I had only to look up to see the new Dolphin Hotel towering above everything else. Like the three wise men guided by a star to Jerusalem or Bethlehem or wherever it was, I steered straight for the main attraction.

After a bath, toweling my hair dry, I gazed out over the Sapporo cityscape. When I stayed at the old Dolphin, hadn't there been a small office building outside my window? What kind of office, I never did figure out, but it was a company and people were busy. That had been my view day after day. What ever became of that company? There'd been a nice-looking woman working there. Where was she now?

I had nothing to do, so I shuffled around the room before flicking on the TV. It was the same old nausea-inducing fare. Not even original nausea-inducing fare. It was phony, synthetic, but being synthetic, it wasn't entirely repugnant. If I didn't turn the thing off, though, I felt sure I'd be seeing the results of some real nausea.

I pulled on some clothes and went up to the lounge on the twenty-sixth floor. I sat at the bar and ordered a vodka-and-soda with lemon. One whole wall of the lounge was win-

dow, providing a sweeping panorama of Sapporo at night. A
Star Wars alien city set. Otherwise, it was a comfortable,
quiet place, with real crystal glasses that had a nice ring.

Besides myself, there were only three other customers.
Two middle-aged men talking in a hush at a back table.
Some very important matter by the look of things. A plot to
assassinate Darth Vader? And sitting at a table directly to
their right, a girl of twelve or thirteen, plugged in to a Walkman, sipping a drink through a straw. She was a pretty girl.
Her long hair, unnaturally straight, draped silkily against the
edge of the table. She tapped her fingers on the tabletop,
keeping time to the rhythm she was hearing. Her long fingers made a more childlike impression than the rest of her.
Not that she was trying to act like an adult. No, not dis-
agreeable or arrogant, but aloof.

Yet, in fact, the girl wasn't looking at anything. She was
completely oblivious to her surroundings. She was wearing
jeans and white Converse All Stars and a sweatshirt embla-
zoned with GENESIS, sleeves rolled up to her elbows, and she
seemed to be concentrating entirely on the music. Sometimes
she'd move her lips to form fragments of lyrics.

"Lemonade," the bartender volunteered, as if to excuse
the presence of a minor. "The girl's waiting for her mother."

"Hmm," I answered, noncommital. Certainly, you don't
go into a hotel bar after ten at night and expect to find a
young girl sitting by herself with a drink and a Walkman.
But if the bartender hadn't broached the subject, I probably
wouldn't have thought anything was out of the ordinary.
The girl just seemed a part of the place.

I ordered another drink and made small talk with the bartender. The weather, the view, assorted topics. Then nonchalantly I dropped the line that, hey, this place sure has
changed, hasn't it? To which the bartender strained a smile
and admitted that, until recently, he'd been working at a
hotel in Tokyo, so he scarcely knew anything about Sapporo. And at that point, a new customer walked in, termi-
nating our fruitless conversation.

I drank a total of four vodka-and-sodas. I could have drunk any number more but decided to call it quits. The girl was still in her seat, grafted to the Walkman. Her mother hadn't shown, and the ice in her glass had melted, which she didn't seem to notice. Yet when I got up from the counter, she looked up at me for two or three seconds, and smiled. Or perhaps it was the slightest trembling of her lips. But to me, it looked like she smiled. Which—I know it sounds strange—really shook me up. I felt as if I'd been chosen. A charge shot through me; my body seemed to lift up a few centimeters.

A bit disarmed, I boarded the elevator and returned to my room. A smile from a twelve-year-old girl? How could anything so innocent have set me off so much? She could have been my daughter.

And Genesis—what a stupid name for a band.

But because the girl had that sweatshirt on, the name seemed somehow symbolic. *Genesis.*

Why do rock groups have overblown names like that?

I fell back onto the bed with my shoes still on. Closed my eyes and the young girl's image came to me. Walkman. White fingers tapping tabletop. Genesis. Melted ice.

Genesis.

With my eyes shut, I could feel the alcohol swimming around inside me. I pulled off my work boots, got out of my clothes, and crawled under the covers. I was too tired, too drunk, to feel much of anything. I waited for the woman next to me to say, "Had a bit too much, have we?" But there was no such conversation.

Genesis.

I reached out to turn out the light. Will my dreams take me to the Dolphin Hotel? I wondered in the dark.

When I awoke the next morning, I felt a hopeless emptiness. No dream, no hotel. Zilch.

My work boots lay at the foot of the bed where they'd fallen. Two tired puppies.

Outside my window the sky hung low and gray. It looked

like snow, which added to my malaise. The clock read five
after seven. I punched the remote control and watched the
morning news as I lay in bed. Something about an upcoming
election. Fifteen minutes later I got up and went to the bathroom to wash and shave, humming the overture to *The
Marriage of Figaro* as a wake-me-up. Or was it the overture
to *The Magic Flute*? I racked my brain, but couldn't get it
straight. I cut my chin shaving, then popped a button from
my cuff getting into my shirt. The signs for the day were not
good.

At breakfast, I saw the young girl I'd seen in the bar, sitting with a woman I took to be her mother. Wearing the
same GENESIS sweatshirt but at least without the Walkman.
She'd hardly touched her bread or scrambled eggs, seemed
absolutely bored drinking her tea. Her mother was a smallish woman in her early forties. Hair pulled into a tight bun,
eyebrows exactly like her daughter's, slender, refined nose,
camel-colored sweater that looked like it was cashmere over
a white blouse. She wore her clothes well, clothes that suit a
woman accustomed to the attentions of others. There was a
touching world-weariness in the way she buttered her toast.

As I passed by their table, the girl glanced up at me. Then
smiled. A more definitive smile than last night's. Unmistak-
ably, a smile.

I ate my breakfast alone and tried to think, but after that
smile I couldn't focus. No matter what came to mind, the
thoughts spun around uselessly. In the end, I stared at the
pepper shaker and didn't think at all.

7

There was nothing for me to do. Nothing I should do, and nothing I wanted to do. I'd come all this way to the Dolphin Hotel, but the Dolphin Hotel that I wanted had vanished from the face of the earth. What to do?

I went down to the lobby, planted myself in one of the magnificent sofas, and tried to come up with a plan for the day. Should I go sightseeing? Where to? How about a movie? Nah, nothing I wanted to see. And why come all the way to Sapporo to see a movie? So, what to do?

Nothing to do.

Okay, it's the barbershop, I said to myself. I hadn't been to a barber in a month, and I was in need of a cut. Now that's making good use of free time. If you don't have anything better to do, go to the barber.

So I made tracks for the hotel barbershop, hoping that it'd be crowded and I'd have to wait my turn. But of course the place was empty, and I was in the chair immediately. An abstract painting hung on the blue-gray walls, and Jacques Rouchet's *Play Bach* lilted soft and mellow from hidden speakers. This was not like any barbershop I'd been to—you could hardly call it a barbershop. The next thing you know, they'll be playing Gregorian chants in bathhouses, Ryuichi Sakamoto in tax office waiting rooms. The guy who cut my hair was young, barely twenty. When I mentioned that there used to be a tiny hotel here that went by the same name, his response was, "That so?" He didn't know much about Sapporo either. He was cool. He was wearing a Men's Bigi designer shirt. Even so, he knew how to cut hair, so I left there pretty much satisfied.

What next?

Short of other options, I returned to my sofa in the lobby and watched the scenery. The receptionist with glasses from yesterday was behind the front desk. She seemed tense. Was my presence setting off signals in her? Unlikely. Soon the clock pushed eleven. Lunchtime. I headed out and walked around, trying to think what I was in the mood for. But I wasn't hungry, and no place caught my fancy. Lacking will, I wandered into a place for some spaghetti and salad. Then a beer. Outside, snow was still threatening, but not a flake in sight. The sky was solid, immobile. Like Gulliver's flying island of Laputa, hanging heavily over the city. Everything seemed cast in gray. Even, in retrospect, my meal—gray. Not a day for good ideas.

In the end, I caught a cab and went to a department store downtown. I bought shoes and underwear, spare batteries, a travel toothbrush, nail clippers. I bought a sandwich for a late-night snack and a small flask of brandy. I didn't need any of this stuff, I was just shopping, just killing time. I killed two hours.

Then I walked along the major avenues, looking into windows, no destination in mind, and when I tired of that, I stepped into a café and read some Jack London over coffee. And before long it was getting on to dusk. Talk about boring. Killing time is not an easy job.

Back at the hotel, I was passing by the front desk when I heard my name called. It was the receptionist with glasses. She motioned for me to go to one end of the counter, the car-rental section actually, where there was a display of pamphlets. No one was on duty here.

She twirled a pen in her fingers a second, giving me a I've-got-something-to-tell-you-but-I-don't-know-how-to-say-it look. Clearly, she wasn't used to doing this sort of thing.

"Please forgive me," she began, "but we have to pretend we're discussing a car rental." Then she shot a quick glance out of the corner of her eye toward the front desk. "Management is very strict. We're not supposed to speak privately to customers."

"All right, then," I said. "I'll ask you about car rates, and you answer with whatever you want to say. Nothing personal."

She blushed slightly. "Forgive me," she said again. "They're real sticklers for rules here."

I smiled. "Still, your glasses are very becoming."

"Excuse me?"

"You look very cute in those glasses. Very cute," I said.

She touched the frame of these glasses, then cleared her throat. The nervous type. "There's something I've been wanting to ask you," she regained her composure. "It's a private matter."

If I could have, I would have patted her on the head to comfort her, but instead I kept quiet and looked into her eyes.

"It's what we talked about last night, you know, about there having been a hotel here," she said softly, "with the same name as this one. What was that other hotel like? I mean, was it a *regular* hotel?"

I picked up a car-rental pamphlet and acted like I was studying it. "That depends on what you mean by 'regular.'"

She pinched the points of her collar and cleared her throat again. "It's . . . hard to say exactly, but was there anything strange about that hotel? I can't get it out of my mind."

Her eyes were earnest and lovely. Just as I'd remembered. She blushed again.

"I guess I don't know what you mean, but I'm sure it will take a little time to talk about and we can't very well do it here. You seem like you're pretty busy."

She looked over at the other receptionists at the front desk, then bit her lower lip slightly. After a moment's hesitation, she spoke up. "Okay, could you meet me after I get off work?"

"What time is that?"

"I finish at eight. But we can't meet near here. Hotel rules. It's got to be somewhere far away from here."

"You name the place. I don't care how far, I'll be there."

She thought a bit more, then scribbled the name of a place and drew me a map. "I'll be there at eight-thirty."

I pocketed the sheet of paper.

Now it was her turn to look at me. "I hope you don't think I'm strange. This is the first time I've done something like this. I've never broken the rules before. But this time I don't know what else to do. I'll explain everything to you later."

"No, I don't think you're strange. Don't worry," I said. "I'm not so bad a guy. I may not be the most likable person in the world, but I try not to upset people."

She twirled her pen again, not quite sure how to take that. Then she smiled vaguely and pushed up the bridge of her glasses. "Well, then, later," she said, and gave me a businesslike bow before returning to her station at the front desk. Charming, if a little insecure.

I went up to my room and pulled a beer from the refrigerator to wash down my department-store roast beef sandwich. Okay, at least we have a plan of action. We may be in low gear, but we're rolling. But where to?

I washed and shaved, brushed my teeth. Calmly, quietly, no humming. Then I gave myself a good, hard look in the mirror, the first time in ages. No major discoveries. I felt no surge of valor. It was the same old face, as always.

I left my room at half past seven and grabbed a taxi. The driver studied the map I showed him, then nodded without a word, and we were off. It was a-thousand-something-yen distance, a tiny bar in the basement of a five-story building. I was met at the door with the warm sound of an old Gerry Mulligan record.

I took a seat at the counter and listened to the solo over a nice, easy J&B-and-water. At eight-forty-five she still hadn't shown. I didn't particularly mind. The bar was plenty comfortable, and by now I was getting to be a pro at killing time. I sipped my drink, and when that was gone, I ordered another. I contemplated the ashtray.

At five past nine she made her entrance.

"I'm sorry," she said in a flurry. "Things started to get busy at the last minute, and then my replacement was late."

"Don't worry. I was fine here," I said. "I had to pass the time anyway."

At her suggestion we moved to a table toward the back. We settled down, as she removed her gloves, scarf, and coat. Underneath, she had on a dark green wool skirt and a lightweight yellow sweater—which revealed generous volumes I'm surprised I hadn't noticed before. Her earrings were demure gold pinpoints.

She ordered a Bloody Mary. And when it came, she sipped it tentatively. I took another drink of my whiskey and then she took another sip of her Bloody Mary. I nibbled on nuts.

At length, she let out a big sigh. It might have been bigger than she had intended, as she looked up at me nervously.

"Work tough?" I asked.

"Yeah," she said. "Pretty tough. I'm still not used to it. The hotel just opened so the management's always on edge about something."

She folded her hands and placed them on the table. She wore one ring, on her pinkie. An unostentatious, rather ordinary silver ring.

"About the old Dolphin Hotel . . . ," she began. "But wait, didn't I hear you were a magazine writer or something?"

"Magazine?" I said, startled. "What's this about?"

"That's just what I heard," she said.

I shut up. She bit her lip and stared at a point on the wall.

"There was some trouble once," she began again, "so the

management's very nervous about media. You know, with property being bought up and all. If too much talk about this gets in the media, the hotel could suffer. A bad image can ruin business."

"Has something been written up?"

"Once, in a weekly magazine a while ago. There were these suggestions about dirty dealings, something about calling in the *yakuza* or some right-wing thugs to put pressure on the folks who were holding out. Things like that."

"And I take it the old Dolphin Hotel was mixed up in this trouble?"

She shrugged and took another sip. "I wouldn't be surprised. Otherwise, I don't think the manager would have acted so nervous talking to you about the old hotel. I mean, it was almost like you sounded an alarm. I don't know any of the details, but I did hear once about the Dolphin name in connection with an older hotel. From someone."

"Someone?"

"One of the blackies."

"Blackies?"

"You know, the black-suit crowd."

"Check," I said. "Other than that, you haven't heard anything about the old Dolphin Hotel?"

She shook her head and fiddled with her ring. "I'm scared," she whispered. "I'm so scared I . . . I don't know what to do."

"Scared? Because of me and magazines?"

She shook her head, then pressed her lip against the rim of her glass. "No, it's not that. Magazines don't have anything to do with it. If something gets printed, what do I care? The management might get all bent out of shape, but that's not what I'm talking about. It's the whole place. The whole hotel, well, I mean, there's always something a little weird about it. Something funny . . . something . . . warped."

She stopped and was silent. I'd finished my whiskey, so I ordered another round for the both of us.

"What do you mean by 'warped'?" I tried prompting her. "Do you mean anything specific?"

"Of course I do," she said sharply. "Things have happened, but it's hard to find the words to describe it. So I never told anyone. I mean, it was really real, what I felt, but if I try to explain it in words, then it sort of starts to slip away."

"So it's like a dream that's very real?"

"But this *wasn't* a dream. You know dreams sort of fade after a while? Not this thing. No way. It's always stayed the same. It's always real, right there, before my eyes."

I didn't know what to say.

"Okay, this is what happened," she said, taking a drink of her Bloody Mary and dabbing her lips with the napkin. "It was in January. The beginning of January, right after New Year's. I was working the late shift, which I don't generally like, but on that day it was my turn. Anyway, I didn't get through until around midnight. When it's late like that, they send you home in a taxi because the trains aren't running. So after I changed clothes, I realized that I'd left my book in the staff lounge. I guess I could have waited until the next day, but the girl I was going to share the taxi with was still finishing up, so I decided to go get it. I got in the employee elevator and punched the button for the sixteenth floor, which is where the staff lounge and other staff facilities are—we take our coffee break there and go up there a lot.

"Anyway I was in the elevator and the door opened and I stepped out like always. I didn't think anything of it, I mean, who would? It's something that you do all the time, right? I stepped out like it was the most natural thing in the world. I guess I was thinking about something, I don't remember what. I think I had both hands in my pockets and I was standing there in the hallway, when I noticed that everything around me was dark. I mean, like absolutely pitch black. I turned around and the elevator door had just shut. The first thing I thought was, uh-oh, the power's gone out. But that's impossible. The hotel has this in-house emergency generator,

so if there's a power failure, the generator kicks on automat-
ically. We had these practice sessions during training, so I
know. So, in principle, there's not supposed to be anything
like a blackout. And if on the million-to-one chance something goes wrong with the generator, then emergency lights
in the hallway are supposed to come on. So what I'm saying
is, it wasn't supposed to be pitch black. I should have been
seeing green lamps along the hall.

"But the whole place was completely dark. All I could see
were the elevator call buttons and the red digital display that
says what floor it's on. So the first thing I did was press the
call buttons, but the elevator kept going down. I didn't
know what to do. Then, for some reason, I decided to take a
look around. I was really scared, but I was also feeling really
put out.

"What I was thinking was that something was wrong with
the basic functions of the hotel. Mechanically or structurally
or something. And that meant more hassle from the
management and no holidays and all sorts of annoying stuff.
So, the more I thought about these things, the more annoyed
I got. My annoyance got bigger than my fear. And that's how
I decided to, you know, just have a look around. I walked
two or three steps and—well, something was really strange. I
mean, I couldn't hear the sound of my feet. There was no
sound at all. And the floor felt funny, not like the regular carpet. It was hard. Honest. And then the air, it felt different,
too. It was . . . it was moldy. Not like the hotel air at all. Our
hotel is supposed to be fully air-conditioned and management
is very fussy about it because it's not like ordinary air-conditioning, it's supposed to be *quality* air, not the dehumidified
stuff in other hotels that dries out your nose. Our air is like
natural air. So the stale, moldy air was really a shock. And it
smelled like it was . . . old—you know, like when you go to
visit your grandparents in the country and you open up the
old family storehouse—like that. Stagnant and musty.

"I turned around and now even the elevator call buttons
had gone out. I couldn't see a thing. Everything was out, com-

pletely, which was really frightening. I mean, I was entirely alone in total darkness, and it was utterly quiet. *Utterly*. There wasn't a single sound. Strange. You'd think that in a power failure, at least one person would be calling out. And this was when the hotel was almost full. You'd've thought a lot of people would be making noise. Not this time."

Our drinks arrived, and we each took sips. Then she set hers down and adjusted her glasses.

"Did you follow me so far?"

"Pretty much," I said. "You got off the elevator on the sixteenth floor. It's pitch black. It smells strange. It's too quiet. Something funny is going on."

She let out a sigh. "I don't know if it's good or bad, but I'm not especially a timid person. At least I think I'm pretty brave. I'm not the type who screams her head off when the lights go out. I get scared but I don't freak out. I figure that you ought to go check things out. So I started feeling my way blind up the hallway."

"In which direction?"

"To the right," she said, raising her right hand. "I felt my way along the wall, very slowly, and after a bit the hallway turned to the right again. And then, up ahead, I could see a faint glow. Really faint, like candlelight leaking in from far away. My first thought was that someone had found some emergency candles and lit them. I kept going, but when I got closer, I saw that the light was coming from a room with the door slightly ajar. The door was pretty strange too. I'd never seen an old door like that in the hotel before. I just stood there in front of it, not knowing what to do next. What if somebody was inside? What if somebody weird came out? What was this door doing here in the first place?

"So I knocked on the door softly, very softly. It was hardly a knock at all, but it came out sounding really loud —maybe because the hallway was dead quiet. Anyway, no response. I waited ten seconds, and during those ten seconds, I was just frozen. I hadn't the slightest idea what I was going to do. Then I heard this muffled noise. I don't know, it was like a person in heavy clothing standing up, and then there were these footsteps. Really slow, *shuffle . . . shuffle . . . shuffle . . .* , like he was wearing slippers or something. The footsteps came closer and closer to the door."

She stared off into space and was shaking her head.

"*That* was when I started to freak out. Like maybe these footsteps weren't human. I don't know how I came to that conclusion. It was just this creepy feeling I got, because human feet don't walk like that. Chills ran up my spine, I mean seriously. I ran. I didn't even look where I was going. I must have fallen once or twice, I think, because my stockings were torn. This part I don't remember very well. All I can remember is that I ran. I panicked. Like what if the elevator's dead? Thank god, when I finally got back there, the red floor-number light and call buttons were lit up and everything. The elevator was on the ground floor. I started pounding the call buttons and then the elevator started coming back up. But much slower than usual. Really, it was like this incredible slug. Like, *second . . . third . . . fourth . . .* I was praying, *c'mon, hurry up, oh come on,* but it didn't do any good. The thing took forever. It was like somebody was jamming the controls."

She let out a deep breath and sipped her drink again. Then she played with her ring a second longer.

I waited for her to continue. The music had stopped, someone was laughing.

"I could still hear those footsteps, *shuffle . . . shuffle . . . shuffle . . .* , getting closer. They just didn't stop, *shuffle . . . shuffle . . . shuffle . . .* , moving down the hall, coming toward me. I was terrified! I was more terrified than I'd ever been in my whole life. My stomach was practically squeezed up into my throat. I was sweating all over, but I was cold. I had the chills. The elevator wasn't anywhere near. *Seventh . . . eighth . . . ninth . . .* The footsteps kept coming."

She paused for twenty or thirty seconds. And once again, she gave her ring a few more turns, almost as if she were tuning a radio. A woman at the counter said something, which drew another laugh from her companion. If only they'd hurry up and put on a record.

"I can't really describe how I felt. You just have to experience it," she spoke dryly.

"Then what happened?"

"The next thing I knew, the elevator was there," she said, shrugging her shoulders. "The door opened and I could see that nice, familiar light. I fell in, literally. I was shaking all over, but I managed to push the button for the lobby. When it got there, I must've scared everyone silly. I was all pale and speechless and trembling. The manager came over and shook me, and said, 'Hey, what's wrong?' So I tried to tell him about the strange things on the sixteenth floor, but I kept running out of breath. The manager stopped me in the middle of my story and called over one of the staff boys, and all three of us went back up to the sixteenth floor. Just to check things out. But everything was perfectly normal up there. All the lights were shining away, there was no old smell, everything was the same as always, as it was supposed to be. We went to the staff lounge and asked the guy who was there if he knew anything about it, but he swore up and down he'd been awake the whole time and the power hadn't gone out. Then, just to be sure, we walked the entire sixteenth floor from one end to the other. Nothing was out of the ordinary. It was like I'd been bewitched or something.

"We went back down and the manager took me into his office. I was sure he was going to scream at me, but he didn't even get mad. He asked me to tell him what happened again in more detail. So I explained everything as clearly as I could, from the beginning, right down to those footsteps coming after me. I felt like a complete idiot. I was sure he was going to laugh at me and say I'd dreamed the whole thing up.

"But he didn't laugh or anything. Instead, he looked dead serious. Then he said: 'You're not to tell anyone about this.' He spoke very gently. 'Something must have gone wrong, but we shouldn't upset the other employees, so let's keep this completely quiet.' And let me tell you, this manager is not the type to speak gently. He's ready to fly off the handle at any second. That's when it occurred to me—that maybe I wasn't the first person this happened to."

She now sat silent.

"And you haven't heard anybody talk about something like this? Weird experiences, or strange happenings, or anything mysterious? What about rumors?"

She thought it over and shook her head. "No, not that I'm aware of. But there really is something funny about the place. The way the manager reacted when I told him what happened and all those hush-hush conversations going on all the time. I really can't explain any better, but something isn't right. It's not at all like the hotel I worked at before. Of course, that wasn't such a big hotel, so things were a little different, but this is *real* different. That hotel had its own ghost story—every hotel's probably got one—but we all could laugh at it. Here, it's not like that at all. Nobody laughs. So it's even more scary. The manager, for example, if he made a joke of it, or even if he yelled at me, it wouldn't have seemed so strange. That way, I would've thought there was just a malfunction or something."

She squinted at the glass in her hand.

"Did you go back to the sixteenth floor after that?" I asked.

"Lots of times," she said matter-of-factly. "It's still part of my workplace, so I go there when I have to, whether I like it or not. But I only go during the day. I never go there at night, I don't care what. I don't ever want to go through *that* again. That's why I won't work the night shift. I even told my boss that."

"And you've never mentioned this to anyone else?"

She shook her head quickly. "Like I already said, this is the first time. No one would've believed me anyway. I told you about it because I thought maybe you'd have a clue about this sixteenth-floor business."

"Me?"

She gazed at me abstractedly. "Well, for one thing, you

knew about the old Dolphin Hotel and you wanted to hear what happened to it. I couldn't help hoping you might know something about what I'd gone through."

"Nope, afraid not," I said, after a bit. "I'm not a specialist on the hotel. The old Dolphin was a small place, and it wasn't very popular. It was just an ordinary hotel."

Of course I didn't for a moment think the old Dolphin was just an ordinary hotel, but I didn't want to open up that can of worms.

"But this afternoon, when I asked you about the Dolphin Hotel, you said it was a long story. What did you mean by that?"

"That part of it's kind of personal," I said. "If I start in on that, it gets pretty involved. Anyway, I don't think it has anything to do with what you just told me."

She seemed disappointed. Pouting slightly, she stared down at her hands.

"Sorry I can't be of more help," I said, "especially after all the trouble you took to tell me this."

"Well, don't worry, it's not your fault. I'm still glad I could tell you about it. These sort of things, you keep them all to yourself and they really start to get to you."

"Yup, you gotta let the pressure out. If you don't, it builds up inside your head." I made an over-inflated balloon with my arms.

She nodded silently as she fiddled with her ring again, removing it from her finger, then putting it back.

"Tell me, do you even believe my story? About the sixteenth floor and all?" she whispered, not raising her eyes from her fingers.

"Of course I believe you," I said.

"Really? But it's kind of *peculiar*, don't you think?"

"That may be, but peculiar things do happen. I know that much. That's why I believe you. It all links up somewhere, I think."

She puzzled over that a minute. "Then you've had a similar experience?"

"Yeah, at least I think I have."

"Was it scary?" she asked.

"No, it wasn't like your experience," I answered. "No, what I mean is, things connect in all kinds of ways. With me . . ." But for no reason I could understand, the words died in my throat. As if someone had yanked out the telephone line. I took a sip of whiskey and tried again. "I'm sorry. I don't know how to put it. But I definitely have seen my share of unbelievable things. So I'm quite prepared to believe what you've told me. I don't think you made up the story."

She looked up and smiled. An individual smile, I thought, not the professional variety. And she relaxed. "I don't know why," she said, "but I feel better talking to you. I'm usually pretty shy. It's really hard for me to talk to people I don't know, but with you it's different."

"Maybe we have something in common," I laughed.

She didn't know what to make of that remark, and in the end didn't say anything. Instead, she sighed. Then she asked, "Feel like eating? All of a sudden, I'm starving."

I offered to take her somewhere for a real meal, but she said a snack where we were would do.

We ordered a pizza. And continued talking as we ate. About work at the hotel, about life in Sapporo. About herself. After high school, she'd gone to hotelier school for two years, then she worked at a hotel in Tokyo for two years, when she answered an ad for the new Dolphin Hotel. She was twenty-three. The move to Sapporo was good for her; her parents ran an inn near Asahikawa, about 120 kilometers away.

"It's a fairly well-known inn. They've been at it a long time," she said.

"So after doing your job here, you'll take over the family business?" I asked.

"Not necessarily," she said, pushing up the bridge of her glasses. "I haven't thought that far ahead. I just like hotel work. People coming, staying, leaving, all that. I feel comfortable there in the middle of it. It puts me at ease. After all, it's the environment I was raised in."

"So that's why," I said.

"Why what?"

"Why standing there at the front desk, you looked like you could be the spirit of the hotel."

"Spirit of the hotel?" she laughed. "What a nice thing to say! If only I really could become like that."

"I'm sure you can, if that's what you want," I smiled back.

She thought that over a while, then asked to hear my story.

"Not very interesting," I begged off, but still she wanted to hear. So I gave her a short rundown: thirty-four, divorced, writer of odd jobs, driver of used Subaru. Nothing novel.

But still she was curious about my work. So I told her about my interviews with would-be starlets, about my piece on restaurants in Hakodate.

"Sounds like fun," she said, brightening up.

"'Fun' is not the word. The writing itself is no big thing. I mean I like writing. It's even relaxing for me. But the content is a real zero. Pointless in fact."

"What do you mean?"

"I mean, for instance, you do the rounds of fifteen restaurants in one day, you eat one bite of each dish and leave the rest untouched. You think that makes sense?"

"But you couldn't very well eat everything, could you?"

"Of course not. I'd drop dead in three days if I did. And everyone would think I was an idiot. I'd get no sympathy whatsoever."

"So what choice have you got?" she said.

"I don't know. The way I see it, it's like shoveling snow. You do it because somebody's got to, not because it's fun."

"Shoveling snow, huh?" she mused.

"Well, you know, cultural snow," I said.

We drank a lot. I lost track of how much, but it was past eleven when she eyed her watch and said she had an early

morning. I paid the bill and we stepped outside into flurries
of snow. I offered to have my taxi drop her at her place,
about ten minutes away. The snow wasn't heavy, but the
road was frozen slick. She held on tight to my arm as we
walked to the taxi stand. I think she was more than a little
inebriated.

"You know that exposé about how the hotel got built," I
asked as we made our way carefully, "do you still remember
the name of the magazine? Do you remember around when
the article came out?"

She knew right off. "And I'm sure it was last autumn. I
didn't see the article myself, so I can't really say what it said."

We stood for five minutes in the swirling snow, waiting
for a cab. She clung to my arm.

"It's been ages since I felt this relaxed," she said. The
same thought occurred to me too. Maybe we really did have
something in common, the two of us.

In the taxi we talked about nothing in particular. The
snow and chill, her work hours, things in Tokyo. Which left
me wondering what was going to happen next. One little
push and I could probably sleep with her. I could feel it. Naturally I didn't know whether she wanted to sleep with me.
But I understood that she wouldn't mind sleeping with me. I
could tell from her eyes, how she breathed, the way she
talked, even her hand movements. And of course, I knew I
wouldn't mind sleeping with her. There probably wouldn't
be any complications either. I'd have simply happened
through and gone off. Just as she herself had said. Yet, somehow, the resolve failed me. The notion of fairness lingered
somewhere in the back of my mind. She was ten years
younger than me, more than a little insecure, and she'd had
so much to drink she couldn't walk straight. It'd be like calling the bets with marked cards. Not fair.

Still, how much jurisdiction does fairness hold over sex?
If fairness was what you wanted, your sex life would be as

exciting as the algae growing in an aquarium.

The voice of reason.

The debate was still raging when the cab pulled up to her plain, reinforced-concrete apartment building and she briskly swept aside my entire dilemma. "I live with my younger sister," she said.

No further thought on the matter needed or wanted. I actually felt a bit relieved.

But as she got out, she asked if I would see her to her door. Probably no reason for concern, she apologized, but every once in a while, late at night, there'd be a strange man in the hall. I asked the driver to wait for a few minutes, then accompanied her, arm in arm, up the frozen walk. We climbed the two flights of stairs and came to her door marked 306. She opened her purse to fish around for the key. Then she smiled awkwardly and said thanks, she'd had a nice time.

As had I, I assured her.

She unlocked the door and slipped the key back into her purse. The dry snap of her purse shutting resounded down the hall. Then she looked at me directly. In her eyes it was the old geometry problem. She hesitated, couldn't decide how she wanted to say good-bye. I could see it.

Hand on the wall, I waited for her to come to some kind of decision, which didn't seem forthcoming.

"Good night," I said. "Regards to your sister."

For four or five seconds she clamped her lips tight. "The part about living with my sister," she half whispered. "It's not true. Really, I live alone."

"I know," I said.

A slow blush came over her. "How could you know?"

"Can't say why, I just did," I said.

"You're impossible, you know that?"

The driver was reading a sports newspaper when I got back to the cab. He seemed surprised when I climbed back into the taxi and asked him to take me to the Dolphin.

"You really going back?" he said with a smirk. "From the look of things, I was sure you'd be paying me and sending me on. That's the way it usually happens."

"I bet."

"When you do this job as long as I have, your intuition almost never misses."

"When you do the job that long, you're bound to miss sometime. Law of averages."

"Guess so," the cabbie answered, a bit nonplussed. "But still, kinda odd, aren'tcha pal?"

"Maybe so," I said, "maybe so."

Back in my room, I washed up before getting into bed. That was when I started to regret what I'd done—or didn't do—but soon fell fast asleep. My bouts of regret don't usually last very long.

First thing in the morning, I called down to the front desk and extended my stay for another three days. It was the off-season, so they were happy to accommodate me.

Next I bought a newspaper, headed out to a nearby Dunkin' Donuts and had two plain muffins with two large cups of coffee. You get tired of hotel breakfasts in a day. Dunkin' Donuts is just the ticket. It's cheap and you get refills on the coffee.

Then I got in a taxi and told the driver to take me to the biggest library in Sapporo. I looked up back numbers of the magazine the Dolphin Hotel article was supposed to be in and found it in the October 20th issue. I xeroxed it and took it to a nearby coffee shop to read.

The article was confusing to say the least. I had to read it several times before I understood what was going on. The reporter had tried his best to write a straightforward story, but his efforts had been no match for the complexity of the details. Talk about convolution. You had to sit down with it before the general outline emerged. The title, "Sapporo Land Dealings: Dark Hands behind Urban Redevelopment." And printed alongside, an aerial photograph of the nearly completed new Dolphin Hotel.

The long and the short of the story was this: Certain parties had bought up a large tract of land in one section of the city of Sapporo. For two years, the names of the new property holders were moved around, under the surface, in surreptitious ways. Land values grew hot for no apparent reason. With very little else to go on, the reporter started his investigation. What he turned up was this: The properties were purchased by various companies, most of which existed only on paper. The companies were fully registered, they paid taxes, but they had no offices and no employees. These paper companies were tied into still other paper companies. Whoever they were, their juggling of property ownership was truly masterful. One property bought at twenty million yen was resold at sixty million, and the next thing you knew it was sold again for two hundred million yen. If you persisted in tracing each paper company's holdings back through this maze of interconnecting fortunes, you'd find that they all ended at the same place: B INDUSTRIES, a player of some renown in real estate. Now B INDUSTRIES was a real company, with big, fashionable headquarters in the Akasaka section of Tokyo. And B INDUSTRIES happened to be, at a less-than-public level, connected to A ENTERPRISES, a massive conglomerate that encompassed railway lines, a hotel chain, a film company, food services, department stores, magazines, . . . , everything from credit agencies to damage insurance. A ENTERPRISES had a direct pipeline to certain political circles, which prompted the reporter to pursue this line of investigation further. Which is how he found out something even more interesting. The area of Sapporo that B INDUSTRIES was so busily buying up was slated for major redevelopment. Already, plans had been set in motion to build subways and to move governmental offices to the area. The greater part of

the moneys for the infrastructural projects was to come from
the national level. It seems that the national, prefectural, and
municipal governments had worked together on the planning and agreed on a comprehensive program for the zoning
and scale and budget. But when you lifted up this "cover," it
was obvious that every square meter of the sites for redevelopment had been systematically bought up over the last few
years. Someone was leaking information to A ENTERPRISES,
and, moreover, the leak existed well before the redevelopment plans were finalized. Which also suggested that, politi-
cally speaking, the final plans had been a fait accompli
probably from the very beginning.

And this is where the Dolphin Hotel entered the picture.
It was the spearhead of this collusive cornering of real estate.
First of all, the Dolphin Hotel secured prime real estate.
Hence, A ENTERPRISES could set up offices in this new
chrome-and-marble wonder as its local base of operations.
The place was both a beacon and a watchtower, a visible
symbol of change as well as a nerve center which could redi-
rect the flow of people in the district. Everything was pro-
ceeding according to the most intricate plans.

That's advanced capitalism for you: The player making
the maximum capital investment gets the maximum critical
information in order to reap the maximum desired profit
with maximum capital efficiency—and nobody bats an eye.
It's just part of putting down capital these days. You demand
the most return for your capital outlay. The person buying a
used car will kick the tires and check under the hood, and
the conglomerate putting down one hundred billion yen will
check over the finer points of where that capital's going, and
occasionally do a little fiddling. Fairness has got nothing to
do with it. With that kind of money on the line, who's going
to sit around considering abstract things like that?

Sometimes they even force hands.

For instance, suppose there's someone who doesn't want
to sell. Say, a long-established shoe store. That's when the
tough guys come out of the woodwork. Huge companies

have their connections, and you can bet they count everyone from politicians and novelists and rock stars to out-and-out *yakuza* in their fold. So they just call on the boys with their samurai swords. The police are never too eager to deal with matters like this, especially since arrangements have already been made up at the top. It's not even corruption. That's how the system works. That's capital investment. Granted, this sort of thing isn't new to the modern age. But everything before is nothing compared to the exacting detail and sheer power and invulnerability of today's web of capitalism. And it's megacomputers that have made it all possible, with their inhuman capacity to pull every last factor and condition on the face of the earth into their net calculations. Advanced capitalism has transcended itself. Not to overstate things, financial dealings have practically become a religious activity. The new mysticism. People worship capital, adore its aura, genuflect before Porsches and Tokyo land values. Worshiping everything their shiny Porsches symbolize. It's the only stuff of myth that's left in the world.

Latter-day capitalism. Like it or not, it's the society we live in. Even the standard of right and wrong has been subdivided, made sophisticated. Within good, there's fashionable good and unfashionable good, and ditto for bad. Within fashionable good, there's formal and then there's casual; there's hip, there's cool, there's trendy, there's snobbish. Mix 'n' match. Like pulling on a Missoni sweater over Trussardi slacks and Pollini shoes, you can now enjoy hybrid styles of morality. It's the way of the world—philosophy starting to look more and more like business administration.

Although I didn't think so at the time, things were a lot simpler in 1969. All you had to do to express yourself was throw rocks at riot police. But with today's sophistication, who's in a position to throw rocks? Who's going to brave what tear gas? C'mon, that's the way it is. Everything is rigged, tied into that massive capital web, and beyond this web there's another web. Nobody's going anywhere. You throw a rock and it'll come right back at you.

The reporter had devoted a lot of energy to following the paper trail. Still, despite his outcry—or rather, all the more because of his outcry—the article curiously lacked punch. A rallying cry it wasn't. The guy just didn't seem to realize: Nothing about this was suspect. It was a *natural* state of affairs. Ordinary, the order of the day, common knowledge. Which is why nobody cared. If huge capital interests obtained information illegally and bought up property, forced a few political decisions, then clinched the deal by having *yakuza* extort a little shoe store here, maybe beat up the owner of some small-time, end-of-the-line hotel there, so what? That's life, man. The sand of the times keeps running out from under our feet. We're no longer standing where we once stood.

The reporter had done everything he could. The article was well researched, full of righteous indignation, and hopelessly untrendy.

I folded it, slipped it into my pocket, and drank another cup of coffee.

I thought about the owner of the old Dolphin. Mister Unlucky, shadowed by defeat since birth. No way he could have made the cut for this day and age.

"Untrendy!" I said out loud.

A waitress gave me a disturbed look.

I took a taxi back to the hotel.

8

From my room I rang up my ex-partner in Tokyo. Somebody I didn't know answered the phone and asked my name, then somebody else came on the line and asked my name, then finally my ex-partner came to the phone. He seemed busy. It had been close to a year since we'd spoken. Not that I'd been consciously avoiding him; I simply didn't have anything to talk to him about. I'd always liked him, and still did. But the fact was, my ex-partner was for me (and I for him) "foregone territory." Again, not that we'd pushed each other into that position. We'd just gone our own separate ways, and those two paths didn't seem to cross. No more, no less.

So how's it going? I asked him.

Well enough, he said.

I told him I was in Sapporo. He asked me if it was cold.

Yeah, it's cold, I answered.

How's work? was my next question.

Busy, his one-word response.

Not hitting the bottle too much, I hoped.

Not lately, he wasn't drinking much these days.

And was it snowing up here? His turn to ask.

Not at the moment, I kept the ball in the air.

We were almost through with our polite toss-and-catch.

"Listen," I broke in, "I've got a favor to ask." I'd done

him one a long while back. Both he and I remembered it.
Otherwise, I'm not the type to go asking favors of people.

"Sure," he said with no formalities.

"You remember when we worked on that in-house news-
letter for that hotel group?" I asked. "Maybe five years ago?"

"Yeah, I remember."

"Tell me, is that connection still alive?"

He gave it a moment's thought. "Can't say it's kicking,
but it's alive as far as alive goes. Not impossible to warm it
up if necessary."

"There was one guy who knew a lot about what was
going on in the industry. I forget his name. Skinny guy,
always wore this funny hat. You think you can get in contact
with him?"

"I think so. What do you want to know?"

I gave him a brief rundown on the Dolphin scandal article. He took down the date the piece appeared. Then I told
him about the old, tiny Dolphin that was here before the
present monster Dolphin and said I'd like to know more
about the following things: First, why had the new hotel
kept the old Dolphin name? Second, what was the fate of the
old owner? And last, were there any recent developments on
the scandal front?

He jotted it all down and read it back to me over the
phone.

"That's it?"

"That'll do," I said.

"Probably in a hurry, too, huh?" he asked.

"Sorry, but—"

"I'll see what I can do today. What's your number up
there?"

I gave it to him.

"Talk to you later," he said and hung up.

I had a simple lunch in a café in the hotel. Then I went
down to the lobby and saw that the young woman with

glasses was behind the counter. I took a seat in a corner of the lobby and watched her. She was busy at work and didn't seem to notice me. Or maybe she did, but was playing cool. It didn't really matter, I guess. I liked seeing her there. As I thought to myself, I could have slept with her if I wanted to.

There are times when I need to chat myself up like that.

After I'd watched her enough, I took the elevator back to my room and read a book. The sky outside was heavy with clouds, making me feel like I was living in a poorly lit stage set. I didn't know when my ex-partner would call back, so I didn't want to go out, which left me little else to do but read. I soon finished the Jack London and started in on the Spanish Civil War.

It was a day like a slow-motion video of twilight. Uneventful, to put it mildly. The lead gray of the sky mixed ever so slowly with black, finally blending into night. Just another quality of melancholy. As if there were only two colors in the world, gray and black, shifting back and forth at regular intervals.

I dialed room service and had them send up a sandwich, which I ate a bite at a time between sips of a beer. When there's nothing to do, you do nothing slowly and intently. At seven-thirty, my ex-partner rang.

"I got ahold of the guy," he said.

"A lot of trouble?"

"Mmm, some," he said after a slight pause, making it obvious that it had been extremely difficult. "Let me run through everything with you. I suppose you could say the lid was shut pretty tight on this one. And not just shut, it was bolted down and locked away in a vault. No one had access to it. Case closed. No dirt to be dug up anymore. Seems there might have been some small irregularities in government or city hall. Nothing important, just fine tuning, as they say. Nobody knows any more than that. The Attorney's Office snooped around, but couldn't come up with anything incriminating. Lots of lines running through this one. Hot stuff. It was hard to get anything out of anyone."

"This concern of mine is personal. It won't make trouble for anyone."

"That's exactly what I told the guy."

Still holding the receiver, I reached over to the refrigerator to get another beer, and poured it into a glass.

"At the risk of sounding like your mother, a word to the wise: If you're going to pry, you're going to get hurt," my ex-partner said. "This one, it seems, is big, real big. I don't know what you've got going there, but I wouldn't get in too deep if I were you. Think of your age and standing, you ought to live out your life more peaceably. Not that I'm the best example, mind you."

"Gotcha," I said.

He coughed. I took another sip of beer.

"About the old Dolphin owner, seems the guy didn't give in until the very last, which brought him a lot of grief. Should've walked right out of there, but he just wouldn't leave. Couldn't read the big picture."

"He was that type," I said. "Very untrendy."

"He got the bad end of the business. A bunch of *yakuza* moved into the hotel and had a field day. Nothing so bad as to bother the law. They set up court in the lobby, and stared down anyone who walked into the place. You get the idea, no? Still, the guy held out for the count."

"I can see it," I said. The owner of the Dolphin Hotel was well acquainted with misery in its various forms. No small measure of misfortune was going to faze him.

"In the end, the Dolphin came out with the strangest counteroffer. Your guy told them he'd pack up shop on one condition. And you know what that was?"

"Haven't a clue," I said.

"Take a guess. Think, man, just a bit. It's the answer to one of your other questions."

"On the condition that they kept the Dolphin Hotel name. Is that it?"

"Bingo," he said. "Those were the terms, and that's what the buyers agreed to."

"But c'mon, why?"

"It's not such a bad name. 'Dolphin Hotel' sounds fair enough, as names go."

"Well, I guess," I said.

"What's more, this hotel was supposed to be the flagship for a whole new chain of hotels that A ENTERPRISES was planning. Luxury hotels, not their usual top-of-the-middle class. And they didn't have a name for it yet."

"Voilà! The Dolphin Hotel Chain."

"Right. A chain to rival the Hiltons and Hyatts of the world."

"The Dolphin Hotel Chain," I tried it out one more time. A heritage passed on, a dream unfurled. "So then what happened to the old Dolphin owner?"

"Who knows?"

I took another sip of my beer and scratched my ear with the tip of my pen.

"When he left they gave him a good chunk of money, so he could be doing almost anything. But there's no way to trace him. He was a bit player, just passing through."

"I suppose."

"And that's about it," said my ex-partner. "That's all I could find out. Nothing more. Will that do you?"

"Thanks. You've been loads of help," I said.

He cleared his throat.

"You out some dough?" I asked.

"Nah," he said. "I'll buy the guy dinner, then take him to a club in Ginza, pay his carfare home. That's not a lot, so forget about it. I can write it off as expenses anyway. Everything's deductible. Hell, my accountant tells me all the time to spend more. So don't worry about it. If you ever feel like going to a Ginza club, let me know. It'll be on me. Seeing as you've never been to any of those places."

"And what's the attraction of a Ginza club?"

"Booze, girls," he said. "Kind words from my tax accountant."

"Why don't you go with him?"

"I did, not so long ago," he said, sounding absolutely bored.

We said our good-byes and hung up.

I started to think about my ex-partner. He was the same age as me, and already he was getting a paunch. All kinds of prescription drugs in his desk. Actually concerned about who won elections. Worried about his kids' education. He was always fighting with his wife, but basically he was a real family man. He had his weaknesses to be sure, he was known to drink too much, but he was a hardworking, straightforward kind of guy. In every sense of the word.

We'd teamed up right after college and gotten on pretty well. It was a small translation business, and it gradually expanded in scale. We weren't exactly the closest of friends, but we made a fine enough partnership. We saw each other every day like that, but we never fought once. He was quiet and well-mannered, and I myself wasn't the arguing type. We had our differences, but managed to keep working together out of mutual respect. But when something unforeseen came up, we split up, perhaps at the best time too. He got started again, kept up both ends of the business, maybe better than when we were together, honestly. That is, if his client list is anything to go on. The company got bigger, he got a whole new crew. Even psychologically, he seemed a lot more secure.

More likely I was the one with problems. And I probably exerted a not-so-healthy influence over him. Which helps to explain why he was able to find his way after I left. Fawning and flattering to get the best out of his people, cracking stupid jokes with the woman who keeps the books, dutifully taking clients out to Ginza clubs no matter how dull he found it. He might have been too nervous to do that if I were still around. He was always aware of how I saw him, worried about what I would think. That was the kind of guy he was. Though, to tell the truth, I didn't pay a lot of attention to what he was doing next to me.

Good he's his own man now. In every way.

That is, by my leaving, he wasn't afraid to act his age, and he came into his own.

So where did that leave me?

At nine o'clock the phone rang. I wasn't expecting a call —nobody besides my ex-partner knew I was here—so at first the sound of the phone ringing didn't register. After four rings I picked up the receiver.

"You were watching me in the lobby today, weren't you?" It was my receptionist friend. She didn't seem angry, but then she wasn't exactly happy either. Her voice was without equivocation.

"Yes, I was," I admitted.

Silence.

"I don't like it when people watch me while I'm working. It makes me nervous and I start making mistakes. I could feel your eyes on me the whole time."

"Sorry, I won't stare at you again," I said. "I was only watching you to give myself confidence. I didn't think you'd get so nervous. From now on I'll be more careful. Where are you calling from?"

"Home," she answered. "I'm just about to take a bath and go to bed. You extended your stay, didn't you?"

"Uh-huh. Business got postponed a bit."

Another short silence.

"Do you think I'm too nervous?" she asked.

"I don't know. It's a different thing for everybody. But in any case, I promise not to stare again. I don't want to ruin your work."

She thought it over a second, then we said good night.

I hung up the phone, took a bath, and stretched out on the sofa reading until eleven-thirty. Then I dressed and stepped out into the hall. I walked it from one end to the other. It was like a maze. At the farthest recess was the staff elevator, a little hidden from view, next to the emergency staircase. If you followed the signs pointing past the guest rooms, you came to an elevator marked FREIGHT ONLY. I stood before it, noting that the elevator was stopped on the ground floor. No one seemed to be using it. From speakers in the ceiling came the strains of "Love Is Blue." Paul Mauriat.

I pressed the button. The elevator roused itself and started to ascend. The digital display registered the floors—1, 2, 3, 4, 5, 6—slowly but surely advancing, to the rhythm of the music. If someone was in the elevator, I could always plead ignorance. It was a mistake guests were probably making all the time. 11, 12, 13, 14—and rising steadily. I took one step back, dug my hands in my pockets, and waited for the doors to open.

15—the count stopped. There was a moment's pause, and not a sound, then the door slid open. The elevator was empty.

Awfully quiet, I thought to myself. A far cry from that wheezing contraption in the old hotel. I got in and pressed 16. The door shut, soundlessly, again, I felt a slight movement, and the door opened. The sixteenth floor. Bright, fully lit, with "Love Is Blue" flowing out of the ceiling. No darkness, no musty odor. For good measure, I walked the entire floor from end to end. It proved to have the exact same layout as the fifteenth. Same winding hallways, same interminable array of guest rooms, same vending machine alcove midway along, same bank of guest elevators.

The carpet was deep red, rich with soft pile. You couldn't hear your own footsteps. In fact, everything was resoundingly hushed. There was only "A Summer Place," probably by Percy Faith. After getting to the end, I turned around and walked back halfway to where the guest elevators were and took one down to the fifteenth floor. Then I went through the whole routine all over again. Staff elevator to the sixteenth floor, where there was the same, perfectly ordinary, well-lit floor as before. And it was still "A Summer Place."

I gave up and went down to the fifteenth floor again, had two sips of brandy and hit the sack.

At dawn, the black changed back to gray. It was snowing. Well now, I thought, what do I do today?

As usual, there wasn't anything to do.

I walked in the snow to Dunkin' Donuts, chewed on a couple doughnuts, and read the morning paper as I sipped my coffee. I skimmed through an article about local elections. I looked through the movie listings. Nothing I particularly wanted to see, but there was this one film featuring a former junior high school classmate of mine. A teen angst movie by the title of *Unrequited Love*, with an up-and-coming teenage actress and an up-and-coming teenage singer. I could guess the sort of role my classmate would play: handsome, young teacher with his wits about him, tall, slim, all-around athlete, girls swooning all over him. Naturally the lead girl has a crush on him. So she spends Sunday baking cookies and takes them to his apartment. But there's a boy who's got his eyes on her. Average boy, kind of shy, . . . Typical. I could see the movie without seeing it.

When this classmate of mine became an actor, I went to see his first few films, partly out of curiosity. But before long I didn't bother. Every movie was straight out of the same mold, and every role he had was basically the same: tall, handsome, athletic, clean-cut, often a student at first, then later teacher or doctor or young elite salaryman, adored by the girls around him. He had perfect teeth, a charming smile. Very suave. Though still not anything you'd want to pay money to see. Now I'm not a snob who only goes to see Fellini or Tarkovsky. No, not by any means. But this guy's films were the pits. Low-budget productions with cliché plots and mediocre dialogue, movies you could tell even the directors didn't care about.

Although, come to think of it, in real life the guy had been pretty much like the parts he played. He was nice enough, but who actually knew anything about him? We were in the same class during junior high school, and once we shared the same lab table on a science experiment. We were friendly. But even back then he was too nice to be real—just like in his movies. Girls were already falling all over him. If he talked to them, their eyes would go moist. If he lit a Bunsen burner with those graceful hands of his, it was like the opening ceremony of the Olympics. None of the girls ever noticed I was alive.

His grades were good too, always first or second in the class. Kind, sincere, friendly. It didn't matter what kind of clothes he wore, he always looked neat and clean. Even when he took a leak, there was something elegant about him. And there's hardly a male around who looks elegant when pissing. Of course, he was good at sports, active in school government. There was talk that he had a thing going with the most popular girl in the class, but no one knew for sure. All the teachers thought he was great, and on Parents' Day all the mothers would be enchanted with him too. He was just that type. Though, like I said, it was hard to know what the guy was thinking.

His life was practically right out of the movies.

Why the hell would I pay money to go see a movie like that?

I tossed the newspaper into the trash and walked back to the hotel in the snow. In the lobby, I glanced at the front desk, but my friend was nowhere to be seen. I went over to the video game corner and played a couple rounds of Pacman and Galaxy. Nerve-racking. Games like those bring out the aggression in people. But they do kill time.

After that I went back to my room and read.

The day was impossible to get a handle on. When I got tired of reading, I looked out the window at the snow. It snowed the entire day. I found it inspiring that a sky could actually snow this much. At twelve o'clock I went down to the café for lunch. Then I returned to my room and read and watched the snow.

But the day wasn't a complete loss. Around four o'clock, while I lay in bed reading, there was a knock on the door. It was my receptionist friend, standing there in glasses and light blue blazer. Without waiting for me to open the door any wider, she slipped into the room like a shadow and shut the door.

"Hotel policy. If they catch me here, I'm fired," she said quickly.

She looked around the room and sat down on the sofa, straightening the hem of her skirt at her knees. Then she breathed a sigh. "I'm on my break now," she said.

"I'm going to have a beer. Want something to drink?" I asked.

"No thanks. I don't have too much time. You've been holed up inside here all day, haven't you?"

"I didn't have anything special to do. I'm just whiling away the hours, reading and watching the snow," I said.

"What's the book?"

"It's about the Spanish Civil War. The whole history, from beginning to end. Full of innuendo." To be sure, the Spanish Civil War was rich in historical suggestion. It was a real old-fashioned war.

"Listen, don't take this wrong," she interrupted me.

"Don't take what wrong?" I asked.

Pause.

"You mean, your coming to my room?" I asked.

"Uh-huh."

I sat down on the edge of the bed, beer in hand. "Don't worry. I was surprised to see you standing at my door, but pleasantly surprised. I'm happy for some company. It's been pretty boring."

She stood up and in the middle of the room removed her blazer. She draped it over the back of a chair, carefully so it wouldn't wrinkle. Then she walked over to me at the edge of the bed and sat down, her legs neatly aligned. Without the blazer, she seemed vulnerable, defenseless. I put my arm around her and she rested her head on my shoulder. Her white blouse was pressed crisply, and she smelled nice. We stayed in this position for five minutes. Me just holding her, her just sitting there, head on my shoulder, eyes closed, breathing softly, almost as if she were asleep. Out in the street, the snow kept falling, without end, swallowing all sound.

She was tired. She needed somewhere to roost. I was the nearest tree branch. I understood. It seemed unreasonable, unfair, that a woman so young and beautiful should be so exhausted. Of course, it was neither unreasonable nor unfair. Exhaustion pays no mind to age or beauty. Like rain and earthquakes and hail and floods.

Then she raised her head, stood up, and slipped her blazer back on. She walked over to the sofa, sat down, and fiddled with the ring on her pinkie. In her uniform, she seemed stiff and distant.

I kept sitting on the edge of the bed.

"You know that weird experience you had on the sixteenth floor?" I began, "did you do anything special or was there something out of the ordinary? Like before you got into the elevator, or while you were going up?"

She cocked her head quizzically. "Hmm . . . let me think. No, I don't think so. But I can't really remember."

"There wasn't a hint of anything odd?"

"Everything was like always," she shrugged. "There was nothing unusual at all. And, really, it was a completely normal elevator ride, but when the door opened everything was pitch black. That's all."

"I see," I said. "How about dinner somewhere tonight?"

She shook her head. "I'm sorry. I've made other plans for tonight."

"How about tomorrow?"

"I have swim club tomorrow."

"Swim club?" I said, smiling. "Did you know they had swim clubs in ancient Egypt?"

"No," she said, "but I find it awfully hard to believe, don't you?"

"No, it's the truth. I learned that from some research I had to do once," I explained. A token from the department of useless facts.

She looked at her watch and got up. "Well, thanks," she said. And slid out the door, as noiselessly as when she entered. So much for my only handle on the day. It left me wondering how the ancient Egyptians filled their days, what little pleasures they enjoyed as they whiled their weary way to death. Learning to swim, wrapping mummies. And the sum accomplishment of that you call a civilization.

9/

By eleven o'clock that night I was out of things to do. I'd pretty well done everything. I'd trimmed my nails, taken a bath, cleaned my ears, even watched the news on TV. Did push-ups, sit-ups, stretched, ate dinner, finished my book. But I wasn't sleepy. I thought about checking out the staff elevator one more time, but it was too early for that. I had to wait until after midnight for the comings and goings of the employees to fall off.

In the end I decided to go up to the lounge on the twenty-sixth floor. I nursed a martini while gazing out blankly at the flecks of white swirling down through the void. I thought about the ancient Egyptians, tried to imagine what kind of lives they led. Who were the ones that joined the swim club? No doubt, it was the Pharaoh's clan, aristocrats, the upper classes. Trendy, jet-set ancient Egyptians. They probably had their own private section of the Nile or built special pools to teach their chic strokes in. Complete with handsome, likable swim instructor, like my friend the movie star, who'd say things like, "Excellent, Your Highness, only perhaps Thou might extend Thy right arm a little further for the crawl."

The sky-blue waters of the Nile, the scintillating sun (thatched cabañas and palm fronds a must), spear-bearing soldiers to beat back the crocodiles and commoners, swaying reeds, the Pharaoh's crowd. Princes, sure, but what about princesses? Did women learn to swim? Cleopatra, for instance. In her younger days looking like Jodie Foster, would she have swooned over my classmate, the swim instructor? Most likely. That's what he was there for.

Somebody ought to make a film like that. I, for one, would pay to see it.

No, the swim instructor couldn't be of poor birth. He'd be the son of the King of Israel or Assyria or somewhere like that, captured in battle and dragged back to Egypt, a slave. But he doesn't lose an iota of his good-naturedness, even if he is a slave. That's where he differs from Charlton Heston or Kirk Douglas. He flashes his brilliant white teeth in a smile and takes a leak, aristocratically. Then, standing on the banks of the Nile, he takes out a ukulele and bursts into a chorus of "Rock-a-Hula Baby." Obviously he's the only man for the part.

Then, one day, the Pharaoh and entourage happen by. The swim instructor's out scything reeds when he sees a barge capsize. Without the least hesitation, he dives into the river, swims a magnificent crawl out and rescues a little girl and races the crocodiles back to shore. All with powerful grace. As gracefully as he'd lit the Bunsen burner in science class. The Pharaoh is most impressed and thinks, that's it, I'll get this youth to teach my princes how to swim. The previous swim instructor had proven insubordinate and was thrown into the bottomless pit just the week before. Thus my classmate becomes the Royal Swim Instructor. And he's so likable everyone adores him. At night, the ladies-in-waiting anoint their bodies with oils and perfumes and hasten to his bed. The princes and princesses are all devoted to him.

Cut to a spectacle scene on the order of *The Bathing Beauty* or *The King and I*. My classmate and the princes and princesses in a grand synchronized swim routine in celebration of the Pharaoh's birthday. The Pharaoh is overjoyed, which further boosts the youth's stock. Still, he doesn't let it go to his head. He's a paragon of humility. He smiles the same as ever, and pisses elegantly. When a lady-in-waiting slips under the covers with him, he spends a full one hour on foreplay, brings her all the way to climax, then afterward strokes her hair and says, "You're the best." He's a good guy.

For a moment, I tried to picture sleeping with an Egyptian court lady, but the image wouldn't gel. The more I forced it, the more everything turned into 20th Century Fox's *Cleopatra*. Very epic. Elizabeth Taylor, Richard Burton, Rex Harrison. The "Hollywood Exotic" mode—olive-skinned, long-legged slave girls waving long-handled fans over Liz, who strikes various glamorous poses to seduce my classmate. A specialty of the Egyptian femme fatale.

But the Jodie Foster Cleopatra has fallen head-over-heels for him.

Mediocre fare, admittedly, but that's the movies.

He's pretty much gone on Jodie Cleopatra, too.

But he's not the only one who's crazy about Jodie Cleopatra. There's a dark, dark Arabian prince who's burning with passion for her. He's so in love with her that just thinking about her is enough to make him dance. The role is tailormade for Michael Jackson. He's crossed the Arabian sands all the way to Egypt for her love. We see him dancing around the caravan camp fire, shaking a tambourine, singing "Billie Jean." His eyes gleam in the starlight. So of course there ensues a major face-off between Michael and my classmate, our swim instructor. A rivalry between lovers. . . .

I'd gotten this far when the bartender came over and said sorry, closing time. It was a quarter past twelve; I was the last customer in the lounge, glasses were already drying on towels, the bartender almost through cleaning up. Had I been tweaking this nonsense all this time? What an idiot! I signed the bill, downed the last of my martini, and walked out, shuffling my way to the elevators, hands useless in my pockets.

Still, wasn't Jodie Cleopatra obliged to marry her younger brother? My dream scenario had a life of its own. I couldn't get it out of my head. The scenes kept on coming. Her shiftless and crooked younger brother. Now who'd be good for the part? Woody Allen? Gimme a break. This isn't a comedy! We don't need a court jester cracking stupid jokes and hitting himself over the head with a plastic mallet.

We'll work on the brother later. The Pharaoh's got to go to Laurence Olivier. Always got a migraine, always pressing fingers to his temples. Throws anyone who gets on his nerves into the bottomless pit or makes them swim the Nile with the crocs. Intelligent, cruel, and high-strung. Digs out people's eyes and throws the poor souls into the desert.

Oh, the casting, the casting, and then the elevator arrived. The door opened, ever so silently. I got in and pressed 15. And went back to my Egyptian movie. Not that I really wanted to, but there was no way to stop it.

The scene changes to the desert wastelands. Unbeknownst to all, in a cave in the wilderness lives a solitary prophet-recluse, cast out of society by the Pharaoh. With his eyes gouged out, he has miraculously survived his long trek across the desert. A sheepskin shields him from the merciless sun. He dwells in total darkness, eating locusts and wild grasses. He gains inner vision and sees the future. He sees the fall of the Pharaoh, Egypt's twilight, a world shifting on its foundations.

It's the Sheep Man, I think. *The Sheep Man?*

The elevator door opened silently, and I exited without thought. The Sheep Man? In ancient Egypt? Isn't this all meaningless pastiche anyway? I reasoned these things out, standing, hands in my pockets, in total darkness.

Total darkness?

Only then did I notice the complete absence of light. Not one speck of light. As the elevator door shut behind me, I was enveloped in lacquer black darkness. I couldn't see my own hands. The Muzak was gone too. No "Love Is Blue," no "A Summer Place." And the air was chill and moldy.

I stood there alone, abandoned in utter nothingness.

10

The darkness was deathly absolute.

I could not distinguish one shape or object. I could not see my own body. I could not get any sense of anything *out there*. I was in a great black vacuum.

I was reduced to pure concept. My flesh had dissolved; my form had dissipated. I floated in space. Liberated of my corporeal being, but without dispensation to go anywhere else. I was adrift in the void. Somewhere across the fine line separating nightmare from reality.

I stood. But I could not move. My arms and legs felt paralyzed. I was at the bottom of the sea, the pressure dense, crushing, inexorable. Dead silence strained against my eardrums. The darkness was without reprieve. No mental adjustment could make it less absolute. It was impenetrable—black painted over black painted over black.

Unconsciously I groped around in my pockets. On the right was my wallet and key holder, on the left my room card-key and handkerchief and small change. All useless now. Now if I hadn't quit smoking, I'd at least be carrying a lighter or some matches. As if that would make a difference. I pulled my hands out of my pockets and reached out to touch a wall. I found one all right, alarmingly slick and chill, not exactly a wall you'd expect to find in the climate-controlled Dolphin Hotel.

Easy now. Think it through.

Okay, this is exactly what happened to my receptionist friend. I am merely retracing her steps. There is no need for alarm. She survived; I will too. Calm down; do what she did. Now, something funny is definitely going on here. Maybe it has something to do with me? With the old Dolphin Hotel? That's why I came here, isn't it? Yes. So go through the motions and finish the job.

Scared?

Damned straight.

I was scared, scared witless. I felt naked. Cast into the midst of violent particle drifts of intense black, thrashing about me like blind eels. I was overcome with my helplessness. My shirt was drenched in cold sweat, my throat felt raspy, dry.

Where the hell was I? I wasn't *here*, at l'Hôtel Dauphin, that's for sure. I had crossed a line and I had entered this world in limbo. I shut my eyes and breathed deeply.

I know it sounds ridiculous, but I found myself longing for "Love Is Blue." The sound of Muzak—any Muzak—would give me strength. I'd have settled for Richard Clayderman. Or Los Indios Tabajaras, José Feliciano, Julio Iglesias, Sergio Mendes, The Partridge Family, 1910 Fruitgum Company, Mitch Miller and chorus, Andy Williams in duet with Al Martino . . . , anything.

But enough. My mind went blank. From fear? Could fear lurk in empty space?

Michael Jackson dancing around the camp fire with his tambourine singing "Billie Jean." The camels entranced by the song.

I must be getting a little confused.

I must be getting a little confused.

Seems like an echo inside my head. An echo inside my head.

I took another deep breath, and tried to drive meaningless images from my mind.

I braced myself and turned right, arms extended. But my

legs would not move, as if they were not mine. The muscles
and nerves would not respond. I was sending the signals, but
nothing was happening. I was immersed in fluid darkness. I
was trapped, I was immobilized.

The darkness was without end. I was being propelled
toward the center of the earth. I would never resurface.
Think of something else, kid. Think, or fear will take over
your whole being. How about that Egyptian film scenario?
Where were we? The Sheep Man enters. Move on from
desert wilderness back to palace of the Pharaoh. Tinsel tow-
ers aglitter with the treasures of Africa. Nubian slaves everywhere. Dead center, the Pharaoh. Music, by Miklos Rozsa.
The Pharaoh is pissed off. *Something is rotten in the state of
Egypt*, he thinks. *I smell a plot in the palace. I can feel it in
my bones. I must set it right.*

One foot at a time, I stepped forward, carefully. That was
when it occurred to me. What my receptionist friend had
been able to do. Amazing! Thrown into some crazy black
hole and she's able to go check out everything for herself.

And now she's wearing her black racing swimsuit, doing
her laps at the swim club. And who's there but my movie
star classmate. Sure enough, she goes gaga at the sight of
him. He gives her pointers on the right arm extension for the
crawl. She gazes at him, her eyes aglow. And that very night,
she slips into his bed. I'm crushed. I can't let this happen.
She doesn't know a thing. Oh, he's nice and kind all right.
He says sweet things and he gets her juices going. But that's
as far as the kindness goes. That's just foreplay.

The hallway bent to the right.

Just like she said.

But she's in bed with my classmate. Gently he takes off
her clothes, lavishing compliments on her about each part of
her body. And he's being sincere. Great, just great. Got to
hand it to the guy. But little by little the anger mounts inside
me. This was wrong!

The hallway bends to the right.

I turned right, feeling my way along the wall. Far off up

ahead there was a faint light. As if filtered through layers and layers of veils.

Just like she said.

My classmate is kissing her all over. Slowly, with such finesse, from the nape of her neck to her shoulders to her breasts. Camera angle shows his face and her back. Then the camera dollies around to reveal her face. But it isn't my receptionist friend, no. It's Kiki! My high-class call-girl friend with the world's most beautiful ears, who was with me at the old Dolphin. Kiki, who disappeared without a word, without a trace. And here she is, sleeping with my classmate.

It's a real scene from a real movie. Every shot and cut according to plan. Maybe a little too planned—it looks so commonplace. They are making love in an apartment, the light shining in through the blinds. Kiki. What's she doing here? Time and space must be getting out of whack.

Time and space must be getting out of whack.

I kept walking toward the light. As my feet took the lead, the image in my head evaporated.

FADE OUT.

I proceeded along the wall. No more thinking. Concentrate on moving feet forward. Carefully, surely. The dim light ahead begins to leak and spread, from a door. But I still don't know where I am. And I can barely tell that it's a door. It isn't like anything I saw when I made the rounds earlier. On the door, a metal plate, a number engraved on it. I can't read the number. It's dark, the plate's tarnished. But, at the very least, I *know* this isn't the Dolphin Hotel. The doors are different. The air is wrong too. That smell, what is it? Like old papers. The light sways from time to time. Candlelight.

I thought about my receptionist friend again. I should have slept with her when I could have. Who knew if I'd ever return to the real world? Would I ever get another chance to see her? I was jealous of the real world and her swim club. Or maybe I wasn't jealous. Maybe it was a matter of regret, an overblown, distorted sense of regret, although maybe

what it came down to, plunged in this darkness, was I was
jealous. It'd been years. I'd forgotten what it felt like to be
jealous. It's such a personal emotion. Maybe I was feeling
jealous now. Maybe, but toward a swim club?

This is stupid.

I swallowed. It sounded like a metal baseball bat striking
a barrel drum. That was saliva?

Then a strange vibration, a half sound. I had to knock.
That's right, like she said. I summoned up my courage and
let go with a tiny rap. Something that didn't necessarily
demand to be heard. But it was a huge, booming noise. Cold
and heavy as death.

I held my breath.

Silence. Just like with her. How long it lasted, I couldn't
tell. It might have been five seconds, it might have been a
minute. Time wasn't fixed. It wavered, stretched, shrank. Or
was it me that wavered, stretched, and shrank in the silence?
I was warped in the folds of time, like a reflection in a fun
house mirror.

Then that sound. A rustling, amplified, like fabric. Something getting up from the floor. Then footsteps. Coming
toward me. The scuffling of slippers. Something, but not
human. Like she said. Something from another reality—a
reality that existed *here*.

There was no escape. I did not move. Sweat streamed
down my back. Yet, as the footsteps grew closer and closer,
unaccountably my fears began to subside. It's all right, I said
to myself. Whatever it is, it is not evil. I knew. I knew there
was nothing to fear. I could let it happen.

I felt aswirl with warm secretions. I gripped the doorknob, I shut my eyes, I held my breath. You're all right,
you're fine. I heard a tremendous heartbeat through the
darkness. It was my own. I was enveloped in it, I was a part
of it. There was nothing to fear. It was all connected.

The footsteps halted. They were beside me. *It* was beside
me. My eyes were shut. *It is beginning to come together*. I
knew. I knew I was connected to this place. The banks of the

Nile and the perfumed Nubian court ladies and Kiki and the Dolphin Hotel and rock 'n' roll, everything, everything, everything! An implosion of time and physical form. Old light, old sound, old voices.

"Beenwaitingforyou. Beenwaitingforages. Comeonin."

I knew who it was without opening my eyes.

11

We faced each other across a small table, talking. The table was very old, round, set with one candle in the middle. The candle had been stuck directly onto a saucer. And that was the entire inventory of furnishings in the room. There weren't any chairs. We sat on piles of books.

It was the Sheep Man's room.

Narrow and cramped. The walls and ceiling had the feeling of the old Dolphin Hotel, but it wasn't the old hotel either. At the far end of the room was a window, boarded up from inside. Boarded up a long time ago, if the rusty nails and gray dust in the cracks of the boards were any indication. The room was a rectangular box. No lights. No closet. No bath. No bed. He must've slept on the floor, wrapped in his sheep costume.

There was barely enough room to walk. The floor was littered with yellowing old books and newspapers and scrapbooks filled with clippings. Some were worm-eaten, falling apart at their bindings. All, from what I could tell, having to do with the history of sheep in Hokkaido. All, probably, from the archive at the old Dolphin Hotel. The sheep reference room, which the owner's father, the Sheep Professor, pretty much lived in. What ever became of him?

The Sheep Man looked at me across the flickering candle

flame. Behind him, his disproportionately enormous shadow played over a grimy wall.

"Beenalongtime," he spoke from behind his mask. "Let'sussee, youthinnerorwhat?"

"Yeah, I might have lost some weight."

"Sotellus, what'stheworldoutside? Wedon'tgetmuchnews, notinhere."

I crossed my legs and shook my head. "Same as ever. Nothing worth mentioning. Everything's getting more complicated. Everything's speeding up. No, nothing's really new."

The Sheep Man nodded. "Nextwarhasn'tbegunyet, wetakeit?"

Which was the Sheep Man's last war? I wasn't sure. "Not yet," I said.

"Butsoonerorlateritwill," he voiced, uninflected, folding his mitted hands. "Youbetterwatchout. War'sgonnacome, nothreewaysaboutit. Markourwords. Can'ttrustpcople. Won'tdoanygood. They'llkillyoueverytime. They'llkilleachother. They'llkilleveryone."

The Sheep Man's fleece was dingy, the wool stiff and greasy. His mask looked bad too, like something patched together at the last minute. The poor light in the damp room didn't help and maybe my memory was wrong, but it wasn't just the costume. The Sheep Man was worn-out. Since the last time I'd seen him four years ago, he'd shrunk. His breathing came harder, more disturbing to the ears, like a stopped-up pipe.

"Thoughtyou'dgetheresooner," said the Sheep Man. "Webeenwaiting, allthistime. Meanwhile, somebodyelsecame-'round. Wethought, maybe, butwasn'tyou. Howdoyoulikethat? Justanybody, comewanderinginhere. But anyway, wasexpectingyousooner."

I shrugged my shoulders. "I always thought I would come back, I guess. I knew I had to, but I didn't have it together. I dreamed about it. About the Dolphin Hotel, I mean. Dreamed about it all the time. But it took a while to make up my mind to come back."

"Triedtoputitoutofmind?"

"I guess so, yes," I said. Then I looked at my hands in the flickering candlelight. A draft was coming in from somewhere. "In the beginning I thought I should try to forget what I could forget. I wanted a life completely dissociated from this place."

"Becauseyourfrienddied?"

"Yes. Because my friend died."

"Butyoucameback," said the Sheep Man.

"Yes, I came back," I said. "I couldn't get this place out of my mind. I tried to forget things, but then something else would pop up. So it didn't matter whether I liked it or not, I sort of knew I belonged here. I didn't really know what that meant either, but I knew it anyway. In my dreams about this place, I was . . . part of everything. Someone was crying for me here. Someone wanted me. That's why I came back. What *is* this place anyway?"

The Sheep Man looked me hard in the face and shook his head. "'Fraidwedon'tknowmuch. It'srealbig, it'srealdark. All-weknow'sthisroom. Beyondhere, wedon'tknow. Butanyway, you'rehere, somust'vebeentime. Timeyoufoundyourwayhere. Wayweseeit, atleast. . . ." The Sheep Man paused to ruminate. "Maybesomebody'scryingforyou, throughthisplace. Somebodywhoknewyou, knewyou'dbeheadinghereanyway. Likeabird, comingbacktothenest. . . . Butlet'sussayitdifferent. Ifyouweren'tcomingbackhere, thisplacewouldn'texist." The Sheep Man wrung his mitts. The shadow on the wall exaggerated every gesture on a grand scale, a dark spirit poised to seize me from above.

Like a bird returning to the nest? Well, it did have that feel about it. Maybe my life had been following this unspoken course all this time.

"Sonow, yourturn," said the Sheep Man. "Tellus'bout-yourself. Thishere'syourworld. Noneedstandingoncere-mony. Takeyourtime. Talkallyouwant."

There in the dim light, staring at the shadow on the wall, I poured out the story of my life. It had been so long, but slowly, like melting ice, I released each circumstance. How I

managed to support myself. Yet never managed to go anywhere. Never went anywhere, but aged all the same. How
nothing touched me. And I touched nothing. How I'd lost
track of what mattered. How I worked like a fool for things
that didn't. How it didn't make a difference either way. How
I was losing form. The tissues hardening, stiffening from
within. Terrifying me. How I barely made the connection to
this place. This place I didn't know but had this feeling that I
was part of. . . . This place that maybe I knew instinctively I
belonged to. . . .

The Sheep Man listened to everything without saying a
word. He might even have been asleep. But when I was
through talking, he opened his eyes and spoke softly.
"Don'tworry. Youreallyarepartofhere, really. Alwayshave-
been, alwayswillbe. Itallstartshere, itallendshere. Thisisyour-
place. It'stheknot. It'stiedtoeverything."

"Everything?"

"Everything. Thingsyoulost. Thingsyou'regonnalose.
Everything. Here'swhereitalltiestogether."

I thought about this. I couldn't make any sense of it. His
words were too vague, fuzzy. I had to get him to explain.
But he was through talking. Did that mean explanation was
impossible? He shook his woolly head silently. His sewed-on
ears flapped up and down. The shadow on the wall quaked.
So massively I thought the wall would collapse.

"It'llmakesense. Soonenough, it'llallmakesense. Whenthe-
timecomes, you'llunderstand," he assured me.

"But tell me one thing then," I said. "Why did the owner
of the Dolphin Hotel insist on the name for the new hotel?"

"Hediditforyou," said the Sheep Man. "Theyhadtokeep-
thename, soyou'dcomeback. Otherwise, youwouldn'tbehere.
Thebuildingchanges, theDolphinHotelstays. Likewesaid,
it'sallhere. Webeenwaitingforyou."

I had to laugh. "For me? They called this place the Dolphin Hotel just for me?"

"Darntootin'. Thatsostrange?"

I shook my head. "No, not strange, just amazing. It's so

out-of-the-blue, it's like it's not real."

"Oh, it'sreal," said the Sheep Man softly. "RealastheDol-
phinHotelsigndownstairs'sreal. Howrealdoyouwant?" He
tapped the tabletop with his fingers, and the flame of the
candle shuddered. "Andwe'rereallyhere. Webeenwaiting.
Foryou. Wemadearrangements. Wethoughtofeverything.
Everything, soyoucouldreconnect, witheveryone."

I gazed into the dancing candle flame. This was too much
to believe. "I don't get it. Why would you go to all the trouble? For *me*?"

"Thisisyourworld," said the Sheep Man matter-of-factly.
"Don'tthinktoohardaboutit. Ifyou'reseekingit, it'shere. The-
placewasputhereforyou. Special. Andweworkedspeciallhard-
togeyoubackhere. Tokeepthingsfromfallingapart. Tokeep-
youfromforgetting."

"So I really am part of something here?"

"'Courseyoubelonghere. Everybody'sallinhere, together.
Thisisyourworld," repeated the Sheep Man.

"So who are you? And what are you doing here?"

"WearetheSheepMan," he chortled. "Can'tyoutell?
Wewearthesheepskin, andweliveinaworldhumanscan'tsee.
Wewerechasedintothewoods. Longtimeago. Long, longtimeago. Canhardlyrememberwhatwewerebefore. Butsince-
thenwebeenkeepingoutofsight. Easytodo, ifthat'swhatyou-
want. Thenwecamehere, tolookaftertheplace. It'ssomewhere,
outoftheelements. Thewoodsgotwildanimals. Knowwhatwe-
mean?"

"Sure," I said.

"Weconnectthings. That'swhatwedo. Likeaswitchboard,
weconnectthings. Here'stheknot. Andwetieit. We'rethelink.
Don'twantthingstogetlost, sowetietheknot. That'sourduty.
Switchboardduty. Youseekforit, weconnect, yougotit. Getit?"

"Sort of," I said.

"So," resumed the Sheep Man, "sonowyouneedus. Else,
youwouldn'tbehere. Youlostthings, soyou'relost. Youlostyour-
way. Yourconnectionscomeundone. Yougotconfused, think-
yougotnoties. Buthere'swhereitalltiestogether."

I thought about what he said. "You're probably right. As you say, I've lost and I'm lost and I'm confused. I'm not anchored to anything. Here's the only place I feel like I belong to." I broke off and stared at my hands in the candlelight. "But the other thing, the person I hear crying in my dreams, is there a connection here? I think I can feel it. You know, if I could, I think I want to pick up where I left off, years ago. That must be what I need you here for."

The Sheep Man was silent. He didn't seem to have more to say. The silence weighed heavily, as if we'd been plunged to the bottom of a very deep pit. It bore down on me, pinning my thoughts under its gravity. From time to time, the candle sputtered. The Sheep Man turned his gaze toward the flame. Still the silence continued, interminably. Then slowly, the Sheep Man raised his eyes toward me.

"We'lldowhatwecan," said the Sheep Man. "Thoughwe'regettingoninyears. Hopewestillgotthestuffinus, hehheh. We'lltry, butnoguarantees, nopromisesyou'regonnabehappy." He picked at a snag in his fleece and searched for words. "Wejustcan'tsay. Inthatotherworld, mightnotbeanyplaceanymore, notanywhereforyou. You'restartingtolookprettyfixed, maybetoofixedtopryloose. You'renotsoyounganymore, either, yourself."

"So where does that leave me?"

"Youlostlotsofthings. Lostlotsofpreciousthings. Notanybody'sfault. Buteachtimeyoulostsomething, youdroppedawholestringofthingswithit. Nowwhy? Why'dyouhavetogoanddothat?"

"I don't know."

"Hardtododifferent. Yourfate, orsomethinglikefate. Tendencies."

"Tendencies?"

"Tendencies. Yougottendencies. Soevenifyoudideverythingoveragain, yourwholelife, yougottendenciestodojustwhatyoudid, alloveragain."

"Yes, but where does that leave me?"

"Likewesaid, we'lldowhatwecan. Trytoreconnectyou,

towhatyouwant," said the Sheep Man. "Butwecan'tdoit-alone. Yougottaworktoo. Sitting'snotgonnadoit, thinking's-notgonnadoit."

"So what do I have to do?"

"Dance," said the Sheep Man. "Yougottadance. Aslong-asthemusicplays. Yougotta dance. Don'teventhinkwhy. Start-tothink, yourfeetstop. Yourfeetstop, wegetstuck. Wegetstuck, you'restuck. Sodon'tpayanymind, nomatterhowdumb. You-gottakeepthestep. Yougottalimberup. Yougottaloosenwhat-youbolteddown. Yougottauseallyougot. Weknowyou're tired, tiredandscared. Happenstoeveryone, okay? Justdon't-letyourfeetstop."

I looked up and gazed again at the shadow on the wall.

"Dancingiseverything," continued the Sheep Man. "Danceintip-topform. Dancesoitallkeepsspinning. Ifyoudo-that, wemightbeabletodosomethingforyou. Yougottadance. Aslongasthemusicplays."

Dance. As long as the music plays, echoed my mind.

"Hey, what is *this world* you keep talking about? You say that if I stay fixed in place, I'm going to be dragged from *that world* to *this world,* or something like that. But isn't this world meant for me? Doesn't it exist for me? So what's the problem? Didn't you say this place really exists?"

The Sheep Man shook his head. His shadow shook a hurricane. "Here'sdifferent. You'renotready, notforhere. Here's-toodark, toobig. Hardtoexplain. Likewesaid, wedon't-knowmuch. Butit'sreal, allright. Youandustalkinghere'sreal-ity. Butit'snottheonlyonereality. Lotsofrealitiesoutthere. Wejustchosethisone, because, well, wedon'tlikewar. Andwe-hadnothingtolose. Butyou, youstillgotwarmth. Sohere'stoo-cold. Nothingtoeat. Nottheplaceforyou."

No sooner had the Sheep Man mentioned the cold than I noticed the temperature in the room. I burrowed my hands in my pockets, shivering.

"Youfeelit, don'tyou?" asked the Sheep Man.

Yes, I nodded.

"Time'srunningout," warned the Sheep Man. "Themoretimepasses, thecolderitgets. Youbetterbegoing."

"Wait, one last thing. I guess you've been around all this time, except I haven't seen you. Just your shadow every-where. You're just sort of always *there*."

The Sheep Man traced an indefinite shape with his finger. "That'sright. We'rehalfshadow, we'reinbetween."

"But I still don't understand," I said. "Here I can see your face and body clearly. I couldn't before, but now I can. Why?"

"Youlostsomuch," he bleated softly, "thatnowyoucan-seeus."

"Do you mean . . . ?" And bracing myself, I asked the big question: "Is this the world of the dead?"

"No," replied the Sheep Man. His shoulders swayed as he took a breath. "Youandus, we'reliving. Breathing. Talking."

"I don't get it."

"Dance," he said. "It'stheonlyway. Wishwecouldex-plainthingsbetter. Butwetoldyouallwecould. Dance. Don't-think. Dance. Danceyourbest, likeyourlifedependedonit. Yougottadance."

The temperature was falling. I suddenly seemed to remember this chill. A bone-piercing, damp chill. Long ago and far away. But where? My mind was paralyzed. Fixed and rigid.

Fixed and rigid.

"Youbettergo," urged the Sheep Man. "Stayhere, you'll-freeze. Butifyouneedus, we'rehere. Youknowwheretofind us."

The Sheep Man escorted me out to the bend in the hall-way, dragging his feet along, *shuffle . . . shuffle . . . shuffle*. We said good-bye. No handshake, no special salutations. Just good-bye, and then we parted into the darkness. He returned to his tiny room and I continued to the elevator. I pressed the call button. When the elevator arrived, the door opened without a sound. Bright light spilled out over me into the hallway. I got in and collapsed against the wall. The door closed. I did not move.

Well . . . , I thought to myself. Well what? Nothing came after. My mind was a huge vacuum. A vacuum that went on and on endlessly nowhere. Like the Sheep Man said, I was tired and scared. And alone. And lost.

"Yougottadance," the Sheep Man said.

You gotta dance, echoed my mind.

"Gotta dance," I repeated out loud.

I pressed the button for the fifteenth floor.

When the elevator got there, "Moon River" greeted me from the ceiling speakers. The real world—where I probably could never be happy, and never get anywhere.

I glanced at my watch. Return time, three-twenty A.M.

Well now, I thought. *Well now well now well now well now well now well now . . .* , echoed my mind.

12

Back in my room, I ran a bath. I undressed, then slowly sank in. But strangely, I couldn't get warm. My body was so chilled, sitting in the hot water only made me shiver. I considered staying in the tub until I stopped shivering, but before that happened, the steam made me woozy, so I climbed out. I pressed my forehead against the window to clear my head, then poured myself a brandy which I downed in one gulp before dropping into bed. I wanted to sleep without the taint of a thought in my head, but no such luck. I lay in bed, conscious beyond control. Eventually morning came, heavy, overcast. It wasn't snowing, but clouds filled the sky, thick and seamless, turning the whole town gray. All I saw was gray. A sump of a city slushed with sunken souls.

Thinking wasn't what kept me awake. I hadn't been thinking at all. I was too tired to think. Except that one hardened corner of my head insisted on pushing my psyche into high gear. I was on edge, irritable, as if trying to read station signs from a speeding train. A station approaches. The letters blur past. You can almost read something, but you're traveling too fast. You try again, when the next station careens into view, but you fly by before you can make anything out. And then the next station . . . Backwater flags in the middle of nowhere. The train sounds its whistle. High, shrill, piercing.

This routine went on until nine, when I got out of bed. I shaved, but had to keep telling myself *I'm shaving now* to get me through. I dressed and brushed my hair and went down to the hotel restaurant. I sat at a table by the window and ordered coffee and toast. It took me an eternity to get through the toast, which tasted like lint and was gray from the sky. The sky foretold the end of the world. I drank my coffee and read and reread and reread the menu. My head was too hard. Nothing would register. The train raced on. The whistle screamed. I felt like a dried lump of toothpaste. All around me, people were devouring their breakfasts, stirring their coffee, buttering their toast, forking up their ham and eggs. Plates and cutlery *clink-clink-clinking*. A regular train yard.

I thought about the Sheep Man. He existed at this very moment. Somewhere, in a small time-space warp of this hotel. Yes, he was here. And he was trying to tell me something. But it was no good. I couldn't read it. I was speeding by too fast for the message to register. My head was too thick to make out the words. I could only read what wasn't moving: *(A) Continental Breakfast—Juice (choice of orange, grapefruit, or tomato), Toast or . . .*

Someone was talking to me. Seeking my response. But who? I looked up. It was the waiter. Immaculate in his white uniform, coffee pot in both hands, like a trophy. "Care for more coffee, sir?" he asked politely. I shook my head. He moved on and I got up to go. Leaving the train yard behind.

Back in my room, I took another bath. No shivers this time. I took a long stretch in the tub, softening my stiff joints. I got my fingers moving freely again. Yes, this was my body all right. Here I am now. Back in a real room, in a real tub. Not aboard some superexpress train. No whistle in my ears. No need to read station signs. No need to think at all.

Out of the bath, I crawled into bed. Ten-thirty. Great, just great. I half considered canning the sleep and going out for a walk, but before I could focus, sleep overtook me. The house-lights went down and suddenly everything went dark. It happened quickly. I can remember the instant I fell asleep. As if a giant, gray gorilla had sneaked into the room and whacked me over the head with a sledgehammer. I was out cold.

My sleep was hard, tight. Too dark to see anything. No background Muzak. No "Moon River" or "Love Is Blue." A simple no-frills sleep. Someone asks me, "What comes after 16?" I answer, "41." The gray gorilla steps in and says, "He's out." That's right, I was asleep. All rolled up in a tight little squirrel ball inside a steel sphere. A solid steel wrecking ball, fast asleep.

Something is calling me.

A steam whistle?

No, something else, the gulls inform me.

Somebody's trying to cut open the steel ball with a blow-torch. That's the sound.

No, not that, chant the gulls. Like a Greek chorus.

It's the phone, I think.

The gulls vanish.

I reach out and grope for the bedside telephone. "Yes?" I hear myself saying. But all I hear is a dial tone. *Beeeeeeee eeeeeeee*, comes a noise from somewhere else. The doorbell! Somebody's ringing the doorbell! *Beeeeeeeeeeeeeeee*.

"The doorbell," I mumbled.

Gone are the gulls. No one applauds. No "bingo," no nothing.

Beeeeeeeeeeeeeeee.

I threw on a bathrobe and went to the door. Without asking who it is, I opened up.

My receptionist friend. She slipped inside and shut the door.

The back of my head was numb. Did that ape have to whack me so hard? It feels like there's a dent in my skull.

She noted my bathrobe, and her brows knitted. "Sleeping at three in the afternoon?" she said in disbelief.

"Three in the afternoon?" I repeated. It didn't make much sense even to me. "Why?" I asked myself.

"What time did you get to bed? Really!"

I tried to think. It took real effort. Nothing came.

"It's okay, don't bother," she said, shaking her head. Then she plopped down on the sofa, adjusted the frame of her glasses, and looked at me straight in the face. "You look terrible."

"Yeah, I bet I do," I said.

"You're pale and puffed up. Are you okay? Do you have a fever?"

"I'm okay. I just need some sleep. Don't worry. I'm generally pretty healthy. Are you on break?"

"Yes," she said. "I wanted to see you. I hope I'm not intruding."

"Not at all," I said, sitting down on the bed. "I'm zonked, but no, you're not intruding."

"You won't try anything funny?"

"I won't try anything funny."

"Everyone says they won't, but they all do."

"Maybe everyone does, but I don't," I said.

She thought it over and tapped her finger on her temple as if to verify the mental results. "Well, I guess probably not. You're kind of different from other people."

"Anyway, I'm too sleepy right now," I added.

She stood up and peeled off her light blue blazer, draping it over the back of the chair like the day before. This time, though, she didn't sit next to me. She walked over to the window and stood, gazing out at the sky. Maybe she was surprised to find me in such a haggard state, in only a bathrobe—but you can't have everything. I don't make my living looking great all the time.

"Listen," I spoke up. "I didn't tell you, but I think we have a few things in common."

"Oh?" she said without emotion. "For instance?"

"For instance—," I began, but right then my mental transmission stalled. I couldn't think of a thing. I couldn't get words to come. Maybe it was only a feeling. But if it was a feeling between the two of us, however slight, that at least meant something. No *for instance* or *even so*. Knowing it was enough.

"I don't know," I picked up again. "I need to put my thoughts in order. A method to the madness. First organize, then ascertain."

"Wow, that's really something," she addressed the windowpane. While her voice didn't ring entirely cynical, it didn't quite have the ring of enthusiasm either.

I got into bed, leaned back against the headboard, and observed her. That wrinkle-free white blouse. Navy blue tight skirt. Stockinged legs. Yet, even she was tinged gray, like an old photograph. Actually quite wonderful. I felt like I'd connected to something. Next thing I knew I had an erection. Not bad. Gray sky, exhaustion, hard-on at three in the afternoon.

I continued to watch her. Even when she turned around and saw me looking, I kept looking.

"Why are you staring at me like that?" she demanded.

"I'm jealous of your swim club," I said.

She shook her head, then broke into a smile. "You're a strange guy, you know?"

"Not strange," I said. "Confused. I need to put my thoughts in order."

She drew close and felt my forehead.

"Well, no fever," she said. "You should get some sleep. Pleasant dreams."

I wanted her to stay here with me. By my bedside, while I slept. But I knew that was impossible, so I didn't say anything. I watched her put on her light blue blazer and leave. And then the gray gorilla entered the room with his sledgehammer again. "That's okay, I was falling asleep anyway," I started to tell him. But the words weren't out of my mouth before another blow fell.

"What comes after 25?" somebody asks. "71," I answer. "He's out," says the gray gorilla. Surprise, surprise, I thought. Hit me that hard and I'm not going to be in a coma? Darkness overcame me once again.

13

Knots.

It was nine P.M. I was eating dinner alone, having awakened from a deep sleep at eight. I got up and was awake, about as abruptly as I'd fallen asleep. There was no middle ground between sleeping and waking. And my head seemed to be back in working order. All postcranial gray gorilla lesions had vanished. I wasn't drowsy or sluggish and I had no shivers. I remembered everything with great clarity. I had an appetite—I was ravenous. So I headed out to the local watering hole I'd gone to the first night and had a few nibbles with drinks. Drinks and grilled fish and simmered vegetables and crab and potatoes. The place was packed, thick with smoke and smells and noise, everybody and his neighbor screaming at each other.

Need to organize, I thought.

Knots? I queried myself in the midst of the chaos. I brought the words softly to my lips: You have but to seek and the Sheep Man shall connect.

Not that I completely understood what that meant. It was a bit too figurative, metaphoric. But maybe it was the sort of thing you *had* to express metaphorically. For one thing, I could hardly believe the Sheep Man had chosen to speak that way for his amusement. Maybe it was the only way.

Through that world of the Sheep Man—via his switchboard—all sorts of things were connected. Some connections led to confusion, he'd said. Because I lost track of what I wanted. So were all my ties meaningless?

I drank and stared at the ashtray in front of me.

What had become of Kiki? I'd felt her presence very strongly in dreams. It was she who'd called me here. It was she who needed me. She was the reason I'd come to the Dolphin Hotel. But I had yet to hear her voice. Her message was cut off. As if someone had pulled the plug.

Why was everything so vague?

Perhaps the lines were crossed. I had to get clear what it was she wanted from me. Enlist the help of the Sheep Man and link things up one by one. No matter how out of focus the picture, I had to unravel each strand patiently. Unravel, then bind all together. I had to recover my world.

But where to begin? Not a clue. I was flat against a high wall. Everything was mirror-slick. No place for the hand, no place to reach out and grab. I was at wit's end.

I paid my bill and left. Big flakes of snow tumbled down from the sky. It wasn't really coming down yet, but the sound of the town was different because of the snow. I walked briskly around the block to sober up. Where to begin? Where to go? I didn't know. I was rusting, badly. Alone like this, I would gradually render myself useless. Great, just great. Where to begin? My receptionist friend? She seemed nice. I did like her. I did feel a bond between us. I could sleep with her if I tried. But then what? Where would I go from there? Nowhere, probably. Just another thing to lose. *I don't know what I want.* And, if that's the case, as my ex-wife said, I'd only hurt people.

Once more around the block. Snow quietly coming down. Sticking to my coat, lingering a brief instant, then disappearing. I tried to put my thoughts in order. People walked past, puffing white breaths into the air. It was so cold the skin of my face hurt. Still, I kept going around the block, kept trying to think. My ex-wife's words stuck in my head like a curse. Worse, because it was true. I hurt everybody. If I kept going like this, I'd go on losing them too.

"Go home to the moon!" were my last girlfriend's parting words. No, not departing—*returning*. She was braving it back to the big, bad, real world.

Then along comes Kiki. Yes! Kiki's got to be the touchstone. But her message had vaporized midway.

So where to begin?

I closed my eyes and struggled for an answer. But in my head no one was at home. No Sheep Man, no gulls, no gray gorilla. I was abandoned, sitting in a vast empty chamber, alone. No one could give me the answer. I'd sit, grow old, and shrivel in that room. No dancing here. Very sad.

Why couldn't I read the station signs?

The answer was to come the following afternoon. As usual, with no prior warning, out of nowhere. Like a gorilla whack out of the gray.

14

Strangely enough—but not that strangely, I suppose—when I hit the sack at midnight, I fell asleep immediately. And I didn't wake until eight in the morning. Precisely at eight, as if I'd come full cycle. I felt rested—and hungry. So I went back to Dunkin' Donuts, and then went for a walk around town. The streets were frozen solid, feather-soft snow drifting quietly down. As ever, the sky was heavy with clouds. Not exactly weather for a care-free stroll, but getting out was good for my spirits. The cold was bracing and cleared my head. I hadn't resolved a thing, so why a simple stretch should make a difference was curious.

After an hour, I made my way back to the hotel. My receptionist friend was on duty at the front desk, together with a colleague busy with a guest. My friend was on the phone, smiling her professional smile, unconsciously twirling a pen between her fingers. I walked up and waited until she finished her call.

She shot me a look of reproach, but she didn't let it interfere with her manual-perfect professional smile. "How may I help you?" she asked politely.

I cleared my throat. "Excuse me," I began, "but I heard that two girls were tragically attacked by an alligator at the swim club last night. Do you know if there's any truth to that story?"

"Well, one never knows about these things, does one?" she replied, the fastidious artificial flower of her smile pinned in place. Her cheeks blushed slightly, her nostrils taut. "I can't say I know anything about it, sir. Excuse me, but are you certain that was the story you heard?"

"It was a huge alligator, by all accounts, the size of a Volvo station wagon. It came flying through the skylight, shattering glass everywhere, and it swallowed the two girls in one bite. Then it had half a potted palm for dessert. I was wondering if the creature was still at large. Do you think it's safe to go out?"

"Forgive me," she broke in, without a flicker of change in her expression, "but have you considered contacting the police yourself, sir? I'm sure they could provide you with the most recent developments on the case. There's a police station not far from here. You might try asking there."

"Thank you. I'll do that," I said. "May the Force be with you."

"Not at all, sir," she said coolly, adjusting her glasses.

Not long after I returned to my room, she called.

"Would you care to tell me what that was all about?" Her calm monotone scarcely disguised her anger. "You weren't going to do anything funny during business hours. Didn't I ask you that? I hate pranks like that when I'm working."

"I just had to talk to you," I said apologetically. "I wanted to hear your voice. It was a dumb joke. I'm sorry. I only wanted to say hello. I really didn't mean to bother you."

"It's very upsetting. I told you that. When I'm on duty, I get tense. So please, don't do anything like that again. You promised not to stare too."

"I wasn't staring. I was just trying to talk to you."

"Well, then, from now on, no more talking like that. *Please*."

"I promise, I promise. No talking. No staring and no

talking. I'll be as quiet as granite. But you know, while I've got you on the line, are you free this evening? Or do you have mountain-climbing lessons tonight?"

There was the sound of a dry laugh, half of it silence, and then she hung up.

I waited for thirty minutes, but she didn't call back. I'd pissed her off. Sometimes people don't know when I'm kidding, any more than when I'm being serious. At a loss for something better to do, I went out walking again. With luck, I might run into something new. Anyway, the idea of exercise seemed more appealing than sitting and doing nothing. May the Force be with me.

I walked for an hour and succeeded only in getting cold. The snow kept coming down. At twelve-thirty I popped into a McDonald's for a cheeseburger and coke and fries. I didn't even know why. For reasons that escape me, I sometimes just find myself eating the stuff. Maybe my physical make-up's been programmed for periodic ingestion of junk food. Maybe I did "need a break today."

After McDonald's, I walked for another thirty minutes. Still no major revelations. The snow picked up. The storm was getting fierce. I zipped my coat all the way to the collar and wrapped my scarf around over my nose. Even then I was cold. And I had to take a leak. Why'd I have to go and drink a coke on a day like this? I scanned the area for a place where I could use the toilet, but the only possibility was a movie theater. A real deadbeat establishment, but they had to have a toilet. And it was probably warm in there. Why not? I had time to kill anyway. So what was playing? A domestic double bill, one of which was *Unrequited Love*, that movie starring my former classmate. Well, fancy that.

After relieving myself at length, I bought a hot coffee and took it into the theater. The place was empty, as expected, and warm. It was thirty minutes into the film, but it was hardly like walking into a complicated plot. My classmate played a tall, handsome biology teacher, the object of a young girl's adoration. Predictably, she was gaga over him, practically fainting at the sight of him. And of course, there was this other guy—who did kendo in his spare time— earnestly in love with her. Talk about an original concept. Hell, *I* could've written this movie.

Even so, I had to admit, my classmate—whose real name was Ryoichi Gotanda, not exactly the stuff for making girls swoon, so he'd been given some dashing screen pseudo- nym—played his role with a little bit of complexity. Not only was he handsome and nice, etc., but he also exuded traces of a troubled past. Common garden-variety wounds, to be sure—maybe he'd been a student radical or maybe he'd gotten a girl pregnant and abandoned her—but better than nothing. From time to time, the film would have these flash- backs—CUT TO ACTUAL FOOTAGE OF STUDENT TAKEOVER OF TOKYO UNIVERSITY—inserted with all the subtlety of a mon- key lobbing clay against a wall.

Anyway, Gotanda played his part to the hilt. But the film was ludicrous and the director such an obvious zero talent and the script so embarrassingly infantile, with an endless succession of breathtakingly meaningless scenes and close- ups of the girl, that Gotanda was doomed from the start. No matter how much real acting he did, you couldn't bear to watch.

Then, at one point in the film, Gotanda's in bed in his apartment on a Sunday morning with some woman when the girl who's in love with him shows up with homemade cookies or something. Good grief, I *did* write this movie. Gotanda's oh-so sweet and slow and sincere in bed, close to what I'd imagined. It's very nice sex. And he probably has very nice-smelling armpits too. His hair has been mussed sensuously. He's caressing the woman's back. She's naked. The camera dollies around to zoom in on her. And suddenly I see her face—

It's Kiki!

I froze in my seat. I could hear the sound of an empty bottle rolling down the aisle. Unbelievable! This was the exact same image I'd seen in that dark corridor of the

Dolphin. Gotanda sleeping with *her*!

That's when I knew: *We were all connected.*

That's the only scene Kiki appears in. Sunday morning, in bed with Gotanda. That's it. Gotanda had gone to a bar on Saturday night, picked her up, and brought her home. Then they fuck one more time in the morning. That's when his love-smitten pupil, the girl lead, enters. He's forgotten to lock the door. That's the whole scene. Kiki has only one line. And it's a pretty awful line at that. This is how it goes:

KIKI
What was that all about?

After the girl lead runs out in shock and Gotanda's all in a daze, that's the line Kiki says.

I wasn't even sure if it was her own voice. My memories of her weren't very clear, nor were the movie theater speakers too sharp on audio fidelity. I could remember her body, though. The shape of her back, the feel of her neck, her silky breasts—yes, it was *she* all right. I sat there riveted to my seat, staring at the screen. The scene couldn't have lasted more than a couple of minutes. Kiki's in Gotanda's embrace, she flows to his caresses, she closes her eyes in a state of bliss, her lips tremble slightly. She lets out a little sigh. I can't tell whether she's acting or not—but let's suppose it's acting. This is a movie, after all. Not that I believe for a moment that Kiki could act. Which poses definite phenomenological problems.

Suppose Kiki wasn't acting, then that meant she really was coming on to Gotanda's lovemaking. But if she was acting, then that meant she wasn't the woman I knew. She didn't believe in acting. She wasn't meant to act. Either way, though, I was burning with jealousy.

First a swim club, now a stupid movie. Was I capable of getting jealous of *any*thing? Was this a good sign?

Now the girl lead opens the door. She catches sight of the two naked bodies embracing. She swallows her breath. She shuts her eyes. She turns and runs.

Gotanda is stunned. Kiki says: "What was that all about?" Close-up of Gotanda's dazed face. FADE OUT.

Aside from that cameo, Kiki appeared in no other scene. Forget the dumb plot, I was all eyes at the screen, and I know she wasn't anywhere. She was destined to be a one-night stand, witness to one fleeting scene in Gotanda's life, before vanishing forever. That was her role. The same as with me. Suddenly she's there, she sees what there is to see, then she's gone.

The movie ended. The lights came up. Music played. I remained in my seat, transfixed by the blank white screen. Was this reality? The film was over, but I didn't get it. What was Kiki doing in a movie? And together with Gotanda, no less. Absurd. I must have been mistaken. Got the wrong circuit. Got my wires crossed somewhere. How else could I explain it?

I walked around again for a while after leaving the theater. Thinking about Kiki the whole time. "What was that all about?" she whispered into my ears.

What *was* that all about?

It *had* to have been her. It *couldn't* be a mistake. She'd made the same face when I made love to her, her lips trembled like that, she'd sighed like that. That wasn't acting. No way. But this was a movie.

It didn't make sense.

The more I walked, the less I trusted my memory. Maybe the movie was a hallucination.

An hour and a half later, I went back to the same movie theater. And I watched *Unrequited Love* again from the beginning. Sunday morning, Gotanda is making love to a woman. The woman's back is to the camera. The camera dollies around. The woman's face comes into view. It's Kiki! Plain as day. Enter the girl lead. Who swallows her breath. Shuts her eyes. Runs. Gotanda, dazed and confused. KIKI: "What was that all about?" FADE OUT.

Exactly the same, down to the last detail.

I'd seen it a second time and I still didn't believe it. Not at all. There had to be something wrong here. Why would Kiki be sleeping with Gotanda?

The following day, I went to the movies again. I sat stiffly through *Unrequited Love* another time, waiting for that one scene. Antsy and impatient. At last the scene came up. Sunday morning, Gotanda is making love to a woman. The woman's back is to the camera. The camera dollies around. The woman's face comes into view. It's Kiki! Plain as day. Enter the girl lead. Who swallows her breath. Shuts her eyes. Runs. Gotanda, dazed and confused. KIKI: "What was that all about?" FADE OUT.

There in the dark, I let out a deep sigh.

Okay, okay. You win. This is real. There's no mistake. *We are connected.*

15

I sank back into my seat, folded my hands in front of my nose, and asked the old familiar: What to do?

The same question. But now I knew I really needed to think things over calm and collected. Needed to put things in order. Needed to sort through the confused connections.

Something was confused here, that was for sure. Something was amiss. Kiki and Gotanda and I were all connected, in a tangle, but why? I had to untangle us. I had to recover my own sense of reality. But maybe the connections weren't confused, maybe this was a totally unrelated, new connection. Still, I had to untangle the entangled threads. In order not to break any.

Here was a clue. I had to get moving. I couldn't stand still. I had to dance. So light on my feet that it all keeps spinning.

You gotta dance, the Sheep Man said.

Gotta dance, echoed my mind.

Time to return to Tokyo. Nothing more for me here. The Dolphin Hotel had fulfilled its purpose. Once I got back to Tokyo, I'd have a lot of knots to untie.

I bundled myself up and left the theater. Snow was falling thicker than ever, nearly obscuring my way. The entire city was as icy as a corpse, and every bit as depressing.

Back at the hotel, I rang up All Nippon Airways and

booked a flight to Tokyo that evening.

"Because of the snow, there's a good chance of delay or even cancellation," the reservation lady informed me. I didn't care. I'd made up my mind and the sooner I got back to Tokyo the better. Then I packed and went down to settle my bill. My friend with the glasses was on duty at the front desk. I asked to speak to her at the car-rental desk.

"Urgent business came up and I have to go back to Tokyo," I explained.

"Thank you very much. Please come again," she said with a professional smile. Could she have been hurt that I was giving her so little notice?

"I plan to be back soon," I said. "When I do get back, we'll go to dinner and talk things over. There's a lot I want to tell you. First I have things to straighten out in Tokyo. But when I'm done, I'm coming back. I don't know how many months it'll take, but I'm coming back. There's something—I don't know how to put it—special about this place. So sooner or later I know I'll be here again."

"Hmm," she said, rather dubiously.

"Hmm," I countered, rather positively. "I'm sure what I'm saying sounds phony."

"Not at all," she said, expressionless. "One can't be sure about things so many months down the road."

"It won't be so many months. We'll meet again. I really feel that we share something special too," I said, as sincerely as I meant it. "Don't you have that feeling?"

She tapped her pen on the countertop in lieu of a response. "And I suppose you're going to tell me you're taking the next flight out?"

"Well, uh, yes, I planned to. If they're flying, that is. But with this weather, we may not get off the ground."

"Well, if you do leave by the next plane, I have a request."

"Of course."

"There's a thirteen-year-old girl who has to get back to Tokyo. Her mother had to leave suddenly on business, and the girl's been left here in the hotel. I realize it's a terrible imposition, but could the girl possibly accompany you down to Tokyo? She's got a lot of luggage, and I'm afraid to send her off on a plane by herself."

"I don't really understand," I said. "Isn't it kind of off-the-wall for a mother to run off somewhere and leave her child behind?"

My friend shrugged. "I suppose, but she *is* off-the-wall. She's an artist, a famous photographer, and she can be quite eccentric. An idea popped into her head, and she was off and running. She completely forgot about the child. Later on, we got this call from her, about her daughter being somewhere around the hotel, and could we please put her on a flight back to Tokyo. That was it."

"Shouldn't she come and get the girl herself?"

"That's not for me to say. Besides, she's in Kathmandu on this job, and she said she'd be busy for another week. She's very famous and she's a regular guest at the hotel, so who am I to contradict her? She said that if I got her daughter to the airport, she'd be fine by herself the rest of the way. Maybe so, but really, the girl's a child, and if anything were to happen to her, it'd be our responsibility."

"Great," I said. Then the thought occurred to me. "It wouldn't happen to be a kid with long hair and rock 'n' roll sweatshirts and a Walkman, would it?"

"The very same. How did you know?"

"Fun for the whole family."

My friend snapped into action immediately. She phoned ANA and reserved a seat for the girl on my flight. She buzzed the girl and told her that someone—someone she knew—was going to take her back to Tokyo and that she should gather her things together right away. She called the bellboy and sent him up to the girl's room for the bags. She summoned the hotel limousine service. I couldn't help expressing my admiration.

"I told you I liked my job. I'm cut out for it."

"But if someone gives you a hard time, you'd rather cut out."

She tapped her pen. "That's different. I don't like being the butt of jokes."

"I didn't mean it that way. Please believe me," I said. "I was only trying to be funny. No offense intended, honest. I only joke around because I need to relax."

She pursed her lips slightly and looked me in the face. With the look of someone surveying the lowlands from a hill after the floodwaters have subsided. Then she spoke in a voice that was almost a sigh, almost a snort. "By the way, could I ask you for your business card, please? As a professional measure, of course, seeing as how I'm entrusting a young girl to your care."

"As a professional measure," I muttered and pulled out a card for her. For what it's worth, I do carry business cards. For what it's worth, at least a dozen people have told me how necessary for business they are. She eyed my card as if it were a dust rag.

"And could I ask what your name is?" I had to try.

"Next time, maybe," she said, pushing up her glasses with her middle finger. "*If* we meet again."

"Of course we will," I said.

Soft and silent as a new moon, a smile drifted across her face.

Ten minutes later the bellboy and the girl appeared in the lobby. The bellboy was lugging two huge Samsonite suitcases. Each could have held a full-grown German shepherd, standing. A bit much for a thirteen-year-old girl to haul to the airport all by herself, to be sure. She was wearing tight jeans and boots, and her sweatshirt of the day read TALKING HEADS. Over which she wore an expensive-looking fur stole. There was the same transparent sense about her as before. A beauty that was so vulnerable, so high-strung. A balance too delicate to last.

Talking Heads. Not bad, for a band name. Like something out of Kerouac.

The girl looked me over, blasé. She didn't smile. But she did raise an eyebrow, then turned to my receptionist friend with glasses.

"Don't worry, he's all right," my friend said.

"I'm not as bad as I look," I declared.

The girl looked at me again. Then she made an *oh-well-I-suppose* sort of nod.

"Really, you'll be fine," my friend went on. "The old man tells funny jokes—"

"*Old man!*" I gasped.

"He throws in a nice word from time to time," she continued, paying me no attention, "he's a real gentleman to us ladies. Besides, he's a friend of mine. So you'll be just fine."

The two of them proceeded to the limousine at the entrance of the hotel. I followed, dignity deflated, quietly behind.

The weather was terrible. The road to the airport all ice and snow. Antarctica.

"What's your name?" I asked the girl.

The girl stared at me, then shook her head briefly. *Gimme a break.* Then she slowly looked around as if searching for something, but all there was to see was the blizzard outside. "*Yuki*," she said. *Snow.*

"You can say that again."

"It's my *name!*" she hissed.

Then she pulled her Walkman out of her pocket and plugged in to her own private pop music microcosm. The rest of the way to the airport she never gave me so much as a glance.

Snow, eh? Such a charming character, so full of social grace. You'd think she'd at least offer me a stick of gum every time she helped herself to some. Not that I wanted any, but hadn't she heard of polite? It would have made me feel like I was riding in the same car with her. I sank into my seat, aging by the minute, and shut my eyes.

Only later did I learn that "Yuki" actually was her name.

I thought about when I was her age. I used to collect pop records myself. Singles. Ray Charles' "Hit the Road, Jack," Ricky Nelson's "Travelin' Man," Brenda Lee's "All Alone Am I." I owned maybe a hundred 45s. I used to listen to them day in and day out. I knew all the lyrics by heart. The things kids can memorize. Always the most meaningless, idiotic lines. Stuff about a *China doll down in old Hong Kong,* waiting for my return. . . .

Not quite Talking Heads. But okay, the times they are a-changin'.

I stationed Yuki in the waiting room and went to purchase our tickets. The flight was running an hour late, but the ticket agent warned that the chances were it'd be delayed even longer. "Please listen for the announcement," she said. "At the moment, visibility is extremely bad."

"Do you think the weather will improve?" I asked.

"That's what the forecast says, but it may take some time," she said grimly. She probably had to say the same thing two hundred times. Enough to depress anyone.

I returned to Yuki with the news. She glanced up at me with a *hmmph* sort of look, but didn't say a word.

"Who knows when we'll get on, so let's not check in yet. It might be a disaster trying to get our luggage back," I said.

A *whatever-you-say* look. Again, not a word.

"I guess there's nothing we can do but wait. No fun getting stuck at an airport for hours, though." No one could accuse me of not keeping up my end of the non-conversation. "Have you eaten?"

She nodded.

"What do you say we go to the coffee shop anyway? We could get something to drink. Whatever you want."

An *I-don't-know-about-this* look. She had a whole repertoire of expressions.

"Okay, let's go," I said, rising to my feet. And off we went, rolling her Samsonites along.

The coffee shop was crowded. All flights out of Sapporo were delayed, and everyone looked uniformly on edge. We waded through waves of irritability. I ordered a sandwich and coffee. Yuki asked for hot chocolate.

"How long were you staying at the hotel?" Well, somebody had to try to be civil.

After a moment's thought, a real live answer: "Ten days."

"And when did your mother leave?"

She looked out the window at the snow a bit, then: "Three days ago."

I felt like we were practicing a Beginning English language drill.

"So your school's been on vacation all this time?"

That did the trick. "No, my school hasn't been on vacation all this time. Don't bug me," she snapped. She retrieved her Walkman from her pocket and plugged her ears in.

I finished my coffee and read the paper. Was every female in the world out to give me a hard time? Was it just my luck or a fundamental flaw in me?

If I had a choice, I'd rather it be just my luck, I decided, folding up my newspaper and pulling out a paperback of *The Sound and the Fury*. Faulkner, and Philip K. Dick too. When besieged by groundless fatigue, there's something about them you can always relate to. That's why I always pack a novel—for times like these.

Yuki went to the restroom, came back, changed the batteries in her Walkman. Thirty minutes later the announcement came: The flight to Tokyo, Haneda Airport, was delayed four hours due to continued poor visibility. Great, just great. More agony sitting here.

Look on the bright side, I tried cheering myself up. Use the power of positive thinking. Give yourself five minutes to consider how you can turn a miserable situation to your benefit and that little light bulb is going to click on. Maybe it will, and then again maybe it won't. But something had to beat sitting and killing time in this noisy, smoke-filled hole.

I told Yuki to stay put while I went back into the lobby. I walked over to a car rental and the woman behind the counter quickly did the paperwork for a Toyota Corolla Sprinter, complete with stereo. A microbus gave me a lift to the lot, where I was handed the keys to a white car with brand-new snow tires. I drove ten minutes back to the airport and went to fetch Yuki in the coffee shop. "Let's go for a three-hour ride."

"In the middle of a blizzard? What are we going to see? And where are we going anyway?"

"Nowhere. Just around," I said. "But the car's got a stereo and you can play your music as loud as you want. Better for your ears than listening to that Walkman."

A *you-gotta-be-kidding* shake of the head this time. All the same, as I got up to go, she stood up too.

I got her suitcases into the trunk, then pointed the car out into the snow-swept no-man's-land. Yuki fished a cassette tape out of her bag, popped it into the stereo, and David Bowie was singing. Followed by Phil Collins, Jefferson Starship, Thomas Dolby, Tom Petty & the Heartbreakers, Hall & Oates, Thompson Twins, Iggy Pop, Bananarama. Typical teenage girl's stuff.

Then the Stones came on with "Goin' to a Go-Go." "I know this one," I boasted. "The Miracles did it ages ago. Smokey Robinson and the Miracles. Years ago when I was fifteen or sixteen."

"Oh," said Yuki with not a flicker of interest.

Next it was Paul McCartney and Michael Jackson singing "Say Say Say."

The wipers were going full force, batting away at the flakes. Few cars on the road. Almost none in fact. We were warm, riding around in the car, and the rock music pleasant. I even didn't mind Duran Duran. Singing along, I kept our wheels on the straight roads. We did this for ninety minutes, when she noticed the cassette I'd borrowed from the car rental.

"What's that?" she asked.

"Oldies," I said.

"Put it on."

"Can't guarantee you'll like it."

"That's okay. I can handle it. I've been listening to the same tapes for the last ten days."

No sooner had I punched the PLAY button than Sam Cooke's "Wonderful World" came on. *Don't know much about history* . . . Sam the Man, killed when I was in ninth grade. Then it was "Oh Boy," by Buddy Holly, another dead man. Airplane crash. Bobby Darin, "Beyond the Sea." He was gone, too. Elvis "Hound Dog" Presley. A drugged stiff. Everyone dead and gone. Everyone except maybe Chuck Berry with his "Sweet Little Sixteen." And me, singing along.

"You really remember the words, don't you!" Yuki said, genuinely impressed.

"Who wouldn't? I was just as crazy about rock as you are," I said. "I used to be glued to the radio every day. I spent all my allowance on records. I thought rock 'n' roll was the best thing ever created."

"And now?"

"I still listen sometimes. I like some songs. But I don't listen so carefully, and I don't memorize all the lyrics anymore. They don't move me like they used to."

"How come?"

"*How come?*"

"Yeah, *how come?* Tell me."

"Maybe it's because after all this time I think that really good songs—or really good anything—they're hard to find," I said. "Like if you listen to the radio for a whole hour, there's maybe one decent song. The rest is mass-produced garbage. But back then I never thought about it, and it was great just listening. Didn't matter what it was. I was a kid. I was in love. And when you're a kid you can relate to anything, even if it's silly. Am I making sense to you?"

"Kind of."

The Del Vikings' "Come Go with Me" came on, and I sang along on the chorus. "Are you bored?" I asked Yuki.

"Uh-uh, not so much," she answered.

"Not so much at all," I threw in.

"Now that you're not young anymore, do you still fall in love?" asked Yuki.

I had to think about that one. "Difficult question," I said finally. "You got any boy you like?"

"No," she said flatly. "But there sure are a lot of creeps out there."

"I know what you mean," I said.

"I'd rather just listen to music."

"I know what you mean."

"You do?" she said, surprised.

"Yeah, I really do," I said. "Some people say that's escapism. But that's fine by me. I live my life, you live yours. If you're clear about what you want, then you can live any way you please. I don't give a damn what people say. They can be reptile food for all I care. That's how I looked at things when I was your age and I guess that's how I look at things now. Does that mean I have arrested development? Or have I been right all these years? I'm still waiting on the answer to that one."

Jimmy Gilmer's "Sugar Shack." I whistled the riff during the refrain. A huge expanse of pure white snow spread out to the left of the road. *Just a little shack made out of wood. Espresso coffee tastes mighty good . . . .* 1964.

"You know," remarked Yuki, "anyone ever tell you you're . . . different?"

"Hmmph." My response.

"Are you married?"

"I was once."

"So you're not married now?"

"That's right."

"Why?"

"Wife walked out on me."

"Are you telling the truth?"

"Yeah, I'm telling the truth. She went to live with someone else."

"Oh."

"You can say that again," I said.

"But I think I can see how your wife must've felt."

"What do you mean?"

She shrugged her shoulders but didn't say anything. I made no effort to probe further.

"Want some gum?" she asked after a bit.

"No thanks."

By now, the two of us were chiming in on the back chorus of the Beach Boys' "Surfin' U.S.A." All the dumb parts. *Inside—outside—U.S.A.* Maybe I wasn't entirely relegated to the dustheap of "old men" after all.

The snow was starting to lighten. We headed back to the airport, turned in the keys at the car rental, checked in, and thirty minutes later were at the gate.

In the end, the plane took off five hours late. Yuki fell asleep as soon as we left the ground. She was beautiful, sleeping next to me. Finely made, exquisite, and fragile. The stewardess brought around drinks, looked over at Yuki, and smiled broadly at me. I had to smile too. I ordered a gin and tonic. And as I drank, I thought about Kiki. The scene played over and over again in my head. Kiki and Gotanda are in bed, making love. The camera pans around. And there she is. "What was that all about?" she says.

Yes, *what was that all about?*

16

After collecting our bags at Haneda, Yuki told me where she lived.

Hakone.

"That's a pretty long haul," I said. It was already past eight in the evening, and even if I got a taxi to take her, she'd be wiped out by the time she reached there. "Do you know anybody in Tokyo? A relative or a friend?"

"No one like that, but we have a place in Akasaka. It's small, but Mama uses it when she comes to town. I can stay there. Nobody's there now."

"You don't have any family? Besides your mother?"

"No," answered Yuki. "Just Mama and me."

"Hmm," I said. Unusual family situation, but what business was it of mine? "Why don't we go to my place first? Then we can eat dinner somewhere. Then afterward, I'll drive you to your Akasaka apartment. That okay with you?"

"Anything you say."

We caught a cab to my apartment in Shibuya, where I got out of my Hokkaido clothes. Leather jacket, sweater, and sneakers. Then we got in my Subaru and drove fifteen minutes to an Italian restaurant I sometimes go to. Call it an occupational skill; I do know how to locate good eating establishments.

"It's like those pigs in France," I told her, "trained to grunt when they find a truffle."

"Don't you like your work?"

"Nah. What's to enjoy? It's all pretty meaningless. I find a good restaurant. I write it up for a magazine. Go here, try this. Why bother? Why shouldn't people just go where they feel like and order what they want? Why do they need someone to tell them? What's a menu for? And then, after I write the place up, the place gets famous and the cooking and service go to hell. It always happens. Supply and demand gets all screwed up. And it was me who screwed it up. I do it one by one, nice and neat. I find what's pure and clean and see that it gets all mucked up. But that's what people call information. And when you dredge up every bit of dirt from every corner of the living environment, that's what you call enhanced information. It kind of gets to you, but that's what I do."

She eyed me from across the table, as if she were looking at some rare species in the zoo.

"But still you do it," she said.

"It's my job," I replied, then suddenly I remembered that I was with a thirteen-year-old. Great. What did I think I was doing, shooting my mouth off like that to a girl not half my age? "Let's go," I said. "It's getting late. I'll take you to your apartment."

We got in the Subaru. Yuki picked up one of my cassettes and put it on to play. Driving music. The streets were empty, so we made it to Akasaka in no time.

"Okay, point the way," I said.

"I'm not telling," Yuki answered.

"What?" I said.

"I said I'm not telling you. I don't want to go home yet."

"Hey, it's past ten," I tried reasoning with her. "It's been a long, hard day. And I'm dog-tired."

This made little impression on her. She was unbudgeable. She just sat there and stared at me, while I tried to keep my eyes on the road. There was no emotion whatsoever in her stare, but it still made me jumpy. After a while, she turned to look out the window.

"I'm not sleepy," she began. "Anyway, once you drop me off, I'll be all alone, so I want to keep driving and listening to music."

I thought it over. "All right. We drive for one hour. Then you're going home to bed. Fair?"

"Fair," said Yuki.

So we drove around Tokyo, music playing on the stereo. It's because we let ourselves do these things that the air gets polluted, the ozone layer breaks up, the noise level increases, people become irritable, and our natural resources are steadily depleted. Yuki lay her head back in her seat and gazed silently at the city night.

"Your mother's in Kathmandu now?" I asked.

"Yeah," she answered listlessly.

"So you'll be on your own until she returns?"

"We have a maid in Hakone."

"Hmm, this sort of scene happens all the time?"

"You mean Mama up and leaving me?"

"Yeah."

"All the time. Work is the only thing Mama thinks of. She doesn't mean to be mean or anything, that's just how she is. She only thinks about herself. Sometimes she forgets I'm around. Like an umbrella, you know, I just slip her mind. And then she's outa there. If she gets it into her head to go to Kathmandu, that's it, she's off. She apologizes later. But then the same thing happens the next time. She dragged me up to Hokkaido on a whim—and that was kind of fun—but she left me alone in the room all the time. She hardly ever came back to the hotel and I usually ate by myself. . . . But I'm used to it now, and I guess I don't expect anything more. She says she'll be back in a week, but maybe from Kathmandu she'll fly off to somewhere else."

"What's your mother's name?" I asked.

I'd never heard of her.

"Her professional name," she tried again, "is Amé. *Rain.*

That's why I'm Yuki. *Snow*. Dumb, huh? But that's her idea
of a sense of humor."

Of course I'd heard of Amé. Who hadn't? Probably the
most famous woman photographer in the country. She was
famous, but she herself never appeared in media. She kept a
low profile. She only accepted work that she liked. Well-
known for her eccentricity. Her photos were known for the
way they startled you and stuck in your mind.

"So that means your father's the novelist, Hiraku Makimura?" I said.

Yuki shrugged. "He's not such a bad person. No talent
though."

Years back I'd read a couple of his early novels and a collection of short stories. Pretty good stuff. Fresh prose, fresh
viewpoint. Which is what made them best-sellers. He was
the darling of the literary community. He appeared on TV,
was in all the magazines, expressed an opinion on the full
spectrum of social phenomena. And he married an up-and-
coming photographer who went by the name of Amé. That
was his peak. After that, it was downhill all the way. He
never wrote anything decent. His next two or three books
were a joke. The critics panned them, they didn't sell.

So Makimura underwent a transformation. From naïf
novelist he was suddenly avant-garde. Not that there was
any change in the lack of substance. Makimura modeled his
style on the French *nouvelle vague*, rhetoric for rhetoric's
sake. A real horror. He managed to win over a few brain-
dead critics with a weakness for such pretensions. But after
two years of the same old stuff, even they got tired of him.
His talent was gone, but he persisted, like a once-virile
hound sniffing the tail of every bitch in the neighborhood.
By that time, he and Amé had divorced. Or more to the
point, Amé had written him off. At least that was how it
played in the media.

Yet that wasn't the end of Hiraku Makimura. Early in the
seventies, he broke into the new field of travel writing as a
self-styled adventurer. Good-bye avant-garde, time for action

and adventure. He visited exotic and forbidden destinations in far corners of the globe. He ate raw seal meat with the Eskimos, lived with the pygmies, infiltrated guerrilla camps high in the Andes. He cast aspersions on armchair literarians and library shut-ins. Which wasn't so bad at first, but after ten years, the pose wore thin. After all, we're no longer living in the age of Livingstone and Amundsen. The adventures didn't have the stuff they used to, but Makimura's prose was pompous as ever.

And the thing of it was, they'd ceased to be real adventures. By now he was dragging around whole entourages, coordinators and editors and cameramen. Sometimes TV would get into the act and there'd be a dozen crew members and sponsors tagging along. Things got to be staged, more and more. Before long, everyone had his number.

Not such a bad person perhaps. But like his daughter said, no talent.

Nothing more was said about Yuki's father. She obviously didn't want to talk about the guy. I was sorry I brought him up.

We kept quiet and listened to the music. Me at the wheel, eyes on the lights of the blue BMW in front of us. Yuki tapped her boot along with Solomon Burke and watched the passing scenery.

"I like this car," Yuki spoke up after a while. "What is it?"

"A Subaru," I said. "I got it used from a friend. Not many people look twice at it."

"I don't know much about cars, but I like the way it feels."

"It's probably because I shower it with warmth and affection."

"So that makes it nice and friendly?"

"Harmonics," I explained.

"What?"

"The car and I are pals. We help each other out. I enter its space, and I give off good vibes. Which creates a nice atmosphere. The car picks up on that. Which makes me feel good, and it makes the car feel good too."

"A machine can feel good?"

"You didn't know that? Don't ask me how, though. Machines can get happy, but they can get angry too. I have no logical explanation for it. I just know from experience."

"You mean, machines are like humans?"

I shook my head. "No, not like humans. With machines, the feeling is, well, more finite. It doesn't go any further. With humans, it's different. The feeling is always changing. Like if you love somebody, the love is always shifting or wavering. It's always questioning or inflating or disappearing or denying or hurting. And the thing is, you can't do anything about it, you can't control it. With my Subaru, it's not so complicated."

Yuki gave that some thought. "But that didn't get through to your wife? Didn't she know how you felt?" she asked.

"I guess not," I said. "Or maybe she had a different perspective on the matter. So in the end, she split. Probably going to live with another man was easier than adjusting her perspective."

"So you didn't get along like with your Subaru?"

"You said it." Of all the things to be talking about to a thirteen-year-old.

"And what about me?" Yuki suddenly asked.

"What about you? I hardly know you."

I could feel her staring at me again. Much more of this and pretty soon she'd bore a hole in my left cheek. I gave in. "Okay, of all the women I've gone out with, you're probably the cutest," I said, eyes glued on the road. "No, not probably. Without question, absolutely, the cutest. If I were fifteen, I'd fall in love with you just like that. But I'm thirty-four, and I don't fall in love so easily. I don't want to get hurt anymore. So it's safer with the Subaru. All right?"

Yuki gave me a blank look. "Pretty weird," was all she could say.

Which made me feel like the dregs of humanity. The girl probably didn't mean anything by it, but she packed a punch.

At eleven-fifteen we were back in Akasaka.

Yuki kept her part of the bargain and told me how to get to the apartment. It was a smallish redbrick condo on a quiet back street near Nogi Shrine. I pulled up to the building and killed the engine.

"About the money and all," she said before opening the door, "the plane and the dinner and everything—"

"The plane fare can wait until your mother gets back. The rest is on me. Don't worry about it. I don't go dutch on dates."

Yuki shrugged and said nothing, then got out and dropped her wad of gum into a convenient potted plant.

Thank you very much. You're quite welcome. I bandied with myself. Then I took a business card out of my wallet. "Give this to your mother when she returns. And in the meanwhile, if you need anything, you can call me at this number. Let me know if I can help out."

She snapped up the card, glared at it a second, then buried it in her coat pocket.

I pulled her overweight suitcases out of the car, and we took the elevator to the fourth floor. Yuki unlocked the door, and I brought the suitcases in. It was a dinette-kitchen-bedroom-bath studio. Practically brand-new, spick-and-span as a showroom, complete with neatly arrayed furniture and appliances, all tasteful and expensive and without sign of use. The apartment had the unlived-in charm of a glossy magazine spread. Very chic, very unreal.

"Mama hardly ever uses this place," Yuki declared, as she watched me scan the place. "She has a studio nearby, and she usually stays there when she's in Tokyo. She sleeps there, and she eats there. She only comes here between jobs."

"I see," I said. Busy woman.

Yuki hung up her fur coat and turned on the heater. Then she brought out a pack of Virginia Slims and lit up with a cool flick of the wrist. I couldn't say I thought much of a thirteen-year-old smoking. Yet there was something positively attractive about that pencil-thin filter poised on her sharp knife-cut lips, her long lashes luxuriating on the updraft. Picture perfect. I held my peace. If I were fifteen years old, I really would have fallen for her. As fatefully as the snow on the roof comes tumbling down in spring. I would have lost my head and been terribly unhappy. It took me back years. Made me feel helpless, a teenage boy pining away again for a girl who could almost have been Yuki.

"Want some coffee?"

I shook my head. "Thanks, but it's late. I'm heading home."

Yuki deposited her cigarette in an ashtray and showed me to the door.

"Mind the cigarette and heater before you turn in."

"Yes, Dad," she replied.

Back in my own apartment at last, I collapsed on the sofa with a beer. I glanced through my mail. Nothing but business and bills. File under: later. I was dead, didn't want to do anything. Still, I was on edge, too pumped up with adrenaline to sleep. What a day!

How long had I stayed in Sapporo? The images jumbled together in my head, crowding into my sleep time. The sky had been a seamless gray. Implicating events and dates. Date with receptionist with glasses. Call to ex-partner for background on Dolphin Hotel. Talk with Sheep Man. Movie showing Gotanda and Kiki. Beach Boys, thirteen-year-old girl, and me. Tokyo. So how many days altogether?

You tell me.

Tomorrow, I told myself. *It can wait.*

I went into the kitchen and poured myself a whiskey. Straight, neat, and otherwise unadulterated. Plus some crackers. A bit damp, like my head, but they'd have to do. I put on an old favorite of the Modernaires singing Tommy Dorsey numbers. Nice and low. A bit out-of-date, like my head. A bit scratchy, but not enough to bother anyone. A perfection of sorts. That didn't go anywhere. Like my head.

What was that all about? Kiki repeated in my brain.

The camera pans around. Gotanda's able fingers sail gently down her back. Seeking for that long-lost sea passage.

What was going on here? I was thoroughly confused. Gone was my self-confidence. Love and used Subarus were two different things. Weren't they? I was jealous of Gotanda's fingers. Had Yuki put out her cigarette? Had she turned off the heater? *Yes, Dad.* You said it. No confidence at all. Was I doomed to rot, muttering away to myself like this in this elephants' graveyard of advanced capitalist society?

Leave it to tomorrow. Everything.

I brushed my teeth, changed into my pajamas, then polished off the last of the whiskey in my glass. The moment I got into bed, the phone rang. At first I just stared at the thing ringing there in the middle of the room, and finally I picked it up.

"I turned off the heater," Yuki began. "Put out my cigarette. Everything's okay. Sleep easier now?"

"Yes, thank you," I replied.

"Nighty-night then," she said.

"Good night," I said.

"Hey," Yuki started, then paused, "you saw that guy in the sheepskin up at the Sapporo hotel, didn't you?"

I sat down on the bed, holding the telephone to my chest as if keeping a cracked ostrich egg warm.

"You can't fool me. I know you saw him. I knew that right away."

"You saw the Sheep Man?" I blurted out.

"Mmm," Yuki skirted the question, then clicked her tongue. "But we can talk about that later. Next time, huh? We'll have a long talk. I'm beat right now."

And she hung up, just like that. *Click.*

I had a pain in my temples. I went to the kitchen and poured myself another whiskey. I was trembling all over. A roller coaster was rumbling under me. *It's all connected*, the Sheep Man had said.

Connected.

All sorts of strange connections were starting to come together.

leaned up against the sink in the kitchen and downed the whiskey. What should I do? How could Yuki have known about the Sheep Man? Should I ring her back? But I really was exhausted. It'd been one long day. Maybe I should wait for her to call. Did I know her phone number?

I climbed into bed and stared at the phone. I had a feeling that Yuki might call. If not Yuki, somebody else. At times like this, the telephone becomes a time bomb. Nobody knows when it's going to go off. But it's ticking away with possibility. And if you consider the telephone as an object, it has this truly weird form. Ordinarily, you never notice it, but if you stare at it long enough, the sheer oddity of its form hits home. The phone either looks like it's dying to say something, or else it's resenting that it's trapped inside its form. Pure idea vested within a clunky body. That's the telephone.

Now the phone company. All those lines coming together. Lines stretching all the way from this very room. Connecting me, in principle, to anyone and everyone. I could even call Anchorage if I wanted. Or the Dolphin Hotel, for that matter, or my ex-wife. Countless possibilities. And all tied together through the phone company switchboard. Computer-processed these days of course. Converted into strings of digits, then transmitted via telephone wires to underground cable or undersea tunnel or communications satellite, ultimately finding its way to us. A gigantic computer-controlled network.

But no matter how advanced the system, no matter how precise, unless we have the will to communicate, there's no connection. And even supposing the will is there, there are times like now when we don't know the other party's number. Or even if we know the number, we misdial. We are an imperfect and unrepentant species. But suppose we clear those hurdles, suppose I manage to get through to Yuki, she could always say, "I don't want to talk now. Bye." *Click!* End of conversation, before it ever began. Talk about one-way communication.

Actually, the telephone looked rather irritated.

It—or let's call it a "she"—seemed pissed off at being less than pure idea. Angered at the uncertain and imperfect grounds upon which volitional communication must necessarily base itself. So very imperfect, so utterly arbitrary, so wholly passive.

I propped myself up on my pillow and watched the telephone fume. A perfectly pointless exercise. *It's not my fault,* the phone seemed to be telling me. Well, that's communication. Imperfect, arbitrary, passive. The lament of the not-quite-pure idea. But I'm not to blame either. The phone probably tells this to all the boys. It's just that being part of these quarters of mine makes her—it—all the more irritable. Which makes me feel responsible. As if I'm aiding and abetting all the imperfection.

Take my ex-wife, for example. She'd just sit there and, without a word, put me in my place. I'd loved her. We'd had some really good times. Traveled together. Made love hundreds of times. Laughed a lot. But sometimes, she'd give me the silent treatment. Usually at night, subtle, but unrelenting. As punishment for my imperfection, my arbitrariness and passiveness.

I knew what was eating her. We got along well, but what she was after, the image in her mind, was somewhere else, not where I was. She wanted a kind of autonomy of communication. A scene where the hero—whose name was "Communication"—led the masses to a bright, bloodless revolution, spotless white flags waving. So that perfection could swallow imperfection and make it whole. To me, love is a pure idea forged in flesh, awkwardly maybe, but it had to connect to somewhere, despite twists and turns of underground cable. An all-too-imperfect thing. Sometimes the lines get crossed. Or you get a wrong number. But that's nobody's fault. It'll always be like that, so long as we exist in this physical form. As a matter of principle.

I explained it to her. Over and over again.

Then one day she left.

Or else I'd magnified that imperfection, and helped her out the door.

I looked at the telephone and replayed scenes of me getting it on with my wife. For the three months before she left, she hadn't wanted to sleep with me once. Because she was sleeping with the other guy. At the time, I didn't have the least idea.

"Sorry dear, but why don't you go sleep with someone else? I won't be mad," she'd said. And I thought she was joking. But she was serious. I told her I didn't want to sleep with another woman, which was true. But she wanted me to, she said. Then we could think things over from there.

In the end, I didn't sleep with anyone. I'm not a prude, but I don't go sleeping with women just to think things over. I sleep with someone because I want to.

Not long after that, she walked out on me. But say I had gone and slept with someone like she wanted me to, would that have kept her from leaving? Did she really believe that that would've put our communication on even slightly more autonomous grounds? Ridiculous.

Already past midnight, but the drone of the expressway showed no sign of letting up. Every now and then a motorcycle would blast by. The soundproof glass dampened the noise, but not much. It was right out there, up against my life, oppressing me. Circumscribing me to this one patch of ground.

I grew tired of looking at the phone and closed my eyes.

And as soon as I did, the surrender I must have been waiting for silently filled the void. Very deftly and ever so quick. Sleep came over me.

After breakfast, I thumbed through my address book for the number of a guy in talent management I'd met when I needed to interview young stars. It was ten in the morning when I rang him up, so naturally he was still asleep. That's showbiz. I apologized, then told him I had to find Gotanda. He moaned and groaned, but eventually came across with the goods. The number for Gotanda's agency, a midsize entertainment production firm.

I called up and got his manager on the line. I said I was a magazine writer and wanted to talk with Gotanda. Was I doing a piece on him? Not exactly, this was personal. How personal? Well, I happened to be a junior high school classmate of his, and this was urgent. Fine, he'd pass the message on. No, I had to talk to Gotanda directly. Me and how many others?

"But this is very important," I insisted. "So if you'd be so kind as to put us in touch, I'm sure I can return the favor on a professional level."

The manager considered my proposition. Of course it was a lie. I didn't have any strings to pull. My whole claim to editorial sway consisted of going out and doing the interview I was assigned to do. A glorified gofer. But the manager didn't know that.

"And you're sure this isn't coverage?" he said. "Because all media have to go through me. Out front and official."

No, this was one-hundred-percent personal.

The guy asked for my number. "Junior high school classmate, eh?" he said with a sigh. "He'll call tonight or tomorrow. *If* he feels like it."

"Of course," I said.

The guy yawned and hung up. Couldn't blame him. It was only ten-thirty.

Before noon I drove to Aoyama to do my shopping at the fancy-schmancy Kinokuniya supermarket. Parking my Subaru among the Saabs and Mercedes in the lot, I almost felt as if I were exposing myself, the twin of this narrow-shouldered old chassis of mine. Still, I admit it: I enjoy shopping at Kinokuniya. You may not believe this, but the lettuce you buy there lasts longer than lettuce anywhere else. Don't ask me why. Maybe they round up the lettuce after they close for the day and give them special training. It wouldn't surprise me. This is advanced capitalism, after all.

At home, there were no messages on my answering machine. No one had called. I put away the vegetables to the "Theme from *Shaft*" on the radio. *Who's that man? Shaft! Right on!*

Then I went to see *Unrequited Love* yet again. That made four times. I couldn't *not* see it. I concentrated on the critical scene, trying to catch every detail.

Nothing had changed. It was Sunday morning. Everything bathed in peaceful Sunday light. Window blinds drawn. A woman's bare back. A man's caressing fingers. Le Corbusier print on wall. Bottle of Cutty Sark on table at side of bed. Two glasses, ashtray, pack of Seven Stars. Stereo equipment. Flower vase. Daisies. Peeled-off clothes on floor. Bookshelf. The camera pans. It's Kiki. I shut my eyes involuntarily. Then I open them. Gotanda is embracing her. Gently, softly. "No way," I say. Out loud. A young kid four seats away shoots me a look. The girl lead comes into frame. Hair in a ponytail. Yachting windbreaker and jeans. Red Adidases. She's holding a container of cookies. She walks right in, then dashes out. Gotanda is dumbfounded. He sits up in bed, squinting into the light, following the girl with his eyes. Kiki rests a hand on his shoulder, her words drenched with world-weariness. "What was that all about?"

After I left the theater, I walked around the streets of Shibuya.

I walked, through the swarming crowds of school kids, as Gotanda's slender, well-mannered fingers played over her back in my mind. I walked to Harajuku. Then to Sendagaya past the stadium, across Aoyama Boulevard toward the cemetery and over to the Nezu Museum. I passed Café Figaro and then Kinokuniya and then the Jintan Building back toward Shibuya Station. A bit of a hike. It was getting late. From the top of the hill, I could see the neon signs coming on as the dark-suited masses of salarymen crossed the intersection like instinct-blinded salmon. When I got back to my apartment, the red message lamp on my answering machine was blinking. I switched on the room lights, took off my coat, and pulled a beer out of the fridge. I sat down on my bed, took a sip, and pushed PLAY.

"Well, been a long time." It was Gotanda.

18

"Well, been a long time."

Gotanda's voice came through bright and clear. Not too fast, not too slow. Not too loud, not too soft. Not tense, not inordinately relaxed. A perfect voice. I knew it was Gotanda in a second. It's not the sort of voice you forget once you've heard it. Any more than his smiling face, his sparkling white teeth, his finely sculpted nose. Actually, I'd never paid any attention to Gotanda's voice before, couldn't really recall it either, but obviously it'd stuck subconsciously to the inside of my skull, and it came back to me immediately, as vivid as the tolling of a bell on a still night. Amazing.

"I'm going to be at home tonight, so call. I don't go to bed until morning anyway," he said, then enunciated his telephone number, twice. "Be talking to you."

From the exchange, his place couldn't have been so far from here. I wrote the number down, then carefully dialed. At the sixth ring, an answering machine kicked on. A woman's voice saying, "I'm out right now, but if you'd care to leave a message." I left my name and the time and said that I'd be in all evening. Complicated world we live in. I hung up and was in the kitchen when the phone rang.

It was Yuki. What was I up to? My response: Chewing

on a stalk of celery and having a beer. Hers: Yuck. Mine: It's
not so bad. She wasn't old enough to know things could be a
lot worse.

"So where are you calling from?" I asked.

"Akasaka," she said. "How about going for a drive?"

"Sorry, I can't today," I said. "I'm waiting for an important business call. How about another time? But first I got a
question. When we talked yesterday, you said you'd seen a
man in a sheep suit? Can you tell me more about that? I
need to know."

"How about another time?" she said, then slammed the
phone down.

I munched on the celery and thought about what to have
for dinner. Spaghetti.

*First slice two cloves of garlic and brown in olive oil. Tilt
the frying pan on its side just so, to pool the oil, and cook
over a low flame. Toss in dried red peppers, fry together but
remove before oil gets too spicy. Touch-and-go. Then cut
thin slices of ham into strips and sauté until crisp. Last, add
to al dente spaghetti, toss, sprinkle with chopped parsley.
Serve with salad of fresh mozzarella and tomatoes.*

Okay, let's do it.

The water for the spaghetti was just about to boil when
the telephone rang. I turned off the gas and went to pick up
the phone.

It was Gotanda. "He–ey, long time. Takes me back.
How're you doing?"

"All right, I guess."

"So what's up? My manager said you had something
urgent. Hope we don't have to dissect a frog again," he
laughed.

"No, nothing like that. I know this call is out of the blue,
but I just needed to ask you something. Sorry, I know you're
busy. Anyway, this may sound kind of strange, but—"

"Listen, are you busy right now?" Gotanda interrupted.

"No, not at all. I had some time on my hands, so I was about to fix dinner."

"Perfect. How about a meal? I was just thinking about looking for a dinner partner. You know how it is. Nothing tastes good when you eat alone."

"Sure, but I didn't mean to . . . I mean, I called so suddenly and—"

"No problem. We all get hungry whether we like it or not, and a man's got to eat. I'm not forcing myself to eat on your account. So let's go have a good meal somewhere and talk about old times. Haven't seen you in ages. I really want to see you. I hope I'm not imposing. Or am I?"

"C'mon, I'm the one who wanted to talk to you."

"Well, then, I'll swing by and pick you up. Where are you?"

I told him where my apartment building was.

"Not so far from here. Maybe twenty minutes. So get yourself ready to go. I don't know about you, but I'm starving."

I'd hop to it, I said, and hung up. Old times?

What old times could Gotanda possibly have to talk about? We weren't especially close back then. He was the bright boy of the class, I was a nobody. It was some kind of miracle that he even remembered who I was.

I shaved and put on the classiest items in my wardrobe: an orange striped shirt and Calvin Klein tweed jacket, an Armani knit tie (a birthday present from a former girlfriend), just-washed jeans, and brand-new Yamaha tennis shoes. Not that he'd ever think this was classy. I'd never eaten with a movie star before. What was one supposed to wear anyway?

Twenty minutes later on the dot, my doorbell rang. It was Gotanda's chauffeur, who politely informed me that Gotanda was downstairs. In a metallic silver Mercedes the size and shape of a motorboat. The glass was also silvered so you couldn't see in. The chauffeur opened the door with a smart, professional snap of the wrist and I got in. And there was Gotanda.

"Who—oa, been a while, eh?" he flashed me his smile. He didn't shake my hand, and I guess I was glad.

"Yeah, it has, hasn't it?" I said.

He wore a dark blue windbreaker over a V-neck sweater and faded cream corduroy slacks. Old Asics jogging shoes. Impeccable. Perfectly ordinary clothes, but the way he wore them was perfect. He gave my outfit a once-over and offered, "*Trés chic.*"

"Thanks," I said.

"Just like a movie star." No irony, just kidding. We both laughed. Which let us relax.

I sized up the interior of the car.

"Not bad, eh?" he said. "The agency lets me use it whenever I want. Complete with driver. This way there're no accidents, no drunken driving. Safety first. They're happy, I'm happy."

"Makes sense," I said.

"But if it were up to me, I would never drive this baby. I don't like cars this big."

"Porsche?"

"Maserati."

"I like cars even smaller," I said.

"Civic?"

"Subaru."

"Subaru," he repeated, nodding. "You know, the first car I ever bought was a Subaru. With the money I made on my first picture, I bought a used Subaru. Boy, I loved that car. I used to drive it to the studio when I had my second supporting role. And someone got on my case right away. *Kid, if you want to be a star, you can't drive a Subaru.* What a business. So I traded it in. But it was a great car. Dependable. Cheap. Really terrific."

"Yeah, I like mine too."

"So why do you think I drive a Maserati?"

"I haven't the foggiest."

"I have this expense account I got to use up," he said with a tilt of his eyebrow. "My manager keeps telling me, spend more, more. I'm never using it up fast enough. So I went and bought an expensive car. One high-priced automobile can write off a big chunk of earnings. It makes everybody happy."

Good grief. Didn't anyone have anything else on their mind but expense account deductions?

"I'm really hungry," he said, running his hand through his hair. "I feel like a nice, thick steak. Are you up for something like that?"

"Whatever you say."

He gave directions to the driver, and we were off. Gotanda looked at me and smiled. "Don't mean to get too personal," he said, "but since you were fixing a meal for yourself, I take it you're single."

"Correct," I said. "Married and divorced."

"Just like me," he said. "Married and divorced. Paying alimony?"

"Nope."

"Nothing?"

"Nothing. She didn't want a thing."

"You lucky bastard," he said, grinning. "I don't pay alimony either, but the marriage broke me. I suppose you heard about my divorce?"

"Vaguely."

It'd been in all the magazines. His marriage four or five years ago to a well-known actress, then the divorce a couple years later. But as usual, who knew the real story? The rumor was that her family didn't like him—not so unusual a thing—and that she had this cordon of relatives who muscled in on every move she made, public and private. Gotanda himself was more the spoiled, rich-kid type, used to the luxury of living life at his own pace. So there was bound to be trouble.

"Funny, isn't it? One minute we're doing a science experiment together, the next thing you know we're both divorced. Funny," he forced a smile, then lightly rubbed his eyes. "Tell me, how come you split up?"

"Simple. One day the wife up and walked out on me."

"Just like that?"

"Yup. No warning, not a word. I didn't have a clue. I thought she'd gone out to do the shopping or something, but she never came back. I made dinner and I waited. Morning came and still no sign of her. A week passed, a month passed. Then the divorce papers came."

He took it all in, then he sighed. "I hope you don't mind my saying this, but I think you got a better deal than I did."

"How's that?"

"With me, the wife didn't leave. I got thrown out. Literally. One day, I was thrown out on my ear." He gazed out through the silvered glass. "And the worst part about it was, she planned the whole thing. Every last detail. When I wasn't around, she changed the registration on everything we owned. I never noticed a thing. I trusted her. I handed everything over to her accountant—my official seal, my IDs, stock certificates, bankbooks, everything. They said they needed it for taxes. Great, I'm terrible at that stuff, so I was happy for them to do it. But the guy was working for her relatives. And before I knew it, there wasn't a thing to my name left. They stripped me to the bone. And then they kicked me out. A real education, let me tell you," he forced another smile. "Made me grow up real fast."

"Everybody has to grow up."

"You're right there. I used to think the years would go by in order, that you get older one year at a time," said Gotanda, peering into my face. "But it's not like that. It happens overnight."

The place we went to was a steak house in a remote corner of Roppongi. Expensive, by the looks of it. When the Mercedes pulled up to the door, the doorman and maître d' and staff came out to greet us. We were conducted to a secluded booth in the back. Everyone in the place was very fashionable, but Gotanda in his corduroys and jogging shoes was the sharpest dresser in the place. His nonchalance oozed style. As soon as we entered, everyone's eyes were on him. They stared for two seconds, no longer, as if it were some unwritten law of etiquette.

We sat down and ordered two scotch-and-waters. Gotanda proposed the toast: "To our ex-wives."

"I know it sounds stupid," he said, "but I still love her. She treated me like dirt and I still love her. I can't get her out of my mind, I can't get interested in other women."

I stared at the extremely elegant ice cubes in the crystal tumblers.

"What about you?" he asked.

"You mean how do I feel about my ex-wife? I don't know. I didn't want her to go. But she left all right. Who was in the wrong? I don't know. It sure doesn't matter now. I'm used to it, though I suppose 'used to it' is about the best I can do."

"I hope I'm not touching a sore spot?"

"No, not really," I said. "Fact is fact, you can't run away from it. You can't really call it painful, you don't really know what to call it."

He snapped his fingers. "That's true. You really can't pin it down. It's like the gravity's changed on you. You can't even call what you're feeling pain."

The waiter came and took our orders. Steak, both medium rare, and salad and another round of scotch.

"Oh yeah, wasn't there something you wanted to talk to me about? Let's get that out of the way first. Before we get too plastered."

"It's kind of a strange story," I began.

He floated me one of his pleasant smiles. Well-practiced, but still, without malice.

"I like strange stories," he said.

"Well, here goes. The other day I went to see the movie you have out."

"*Unrequited*?" he said with a grimace, his voice dropping to a whisper. "Terrible picture. Terrible director, terrible script, it's always like that. Everybody involved with the thing wishes they could forget it."

"I saw it four times," I said.

His eyes widened, as if he were peering into the cosmic void. "I'd be willing to bet there's not a human alive in this galaxy who's sat through that movie four times."

"Someone I knew was in the film," I said. "Besides you, I mean."

Gotanda pressed an index finger into his temple and squinted. "Who?"

"The girl you were sleeping with on the Sunday morning."

He took a sip of whiskey. "Oh yeah," he said, nodding. "Kiki."

"Kiki," I repeated.

Kiki. Kiki. Kiki.

"That was the name I know her by anyway. In the film world, she went by Kiki. No last name, that was it."

Which is how, finally, I learned *her* name.

"And can you get in touch with her?" I asked.

"Afraid not."

"Why not?"

"Let's take it from the top. First of all, Kiki wasn't a professional actress. Actors, famous or not, all belong to some production company. So you get in contact with them through their agents. Most of them live next to their phones, waiting for the call, you know. But not Kiki. She didn't belong to any production group I knew of. She just happened through that one time."

"Then how did she land that part?"

"I recommended her," he said dryly. "I asked her if she wanted to be in a picture, and I introduced her to the director."

"What for?"

He took a sip of whiskey. "The girl had—maybe not talent exactly—she had the makings of . . . presence. She had *something*. She wasn't really beautiful. She wasn't a born actress. But you got the feeling that if she ever got on film, she could pull the whole frame into focus. And that's talent, you know. So I asked the director to put her in the picture. And she *made* that scene. Everyone thought she was great. I don't mean to brag, but that scene was the best thing in the movie. It was real. Didn't you think so?"

"Yeah, I did," I had to agree. "Very real."

"So I thought the girl would go into movies. She could've cut the ice. But then she disappeared. Vanished. Like smoke, like morning dew."

"Vanished?"

"Like literally. Maybe a month ago. I'd been telling everyone she was exactly what we needed for this new part, and she was set. All the girl had to do was to show up, and it was hers. I even called her up the day before to remind her. But she never showed. That was the last time we ever talked."

He raised a finger to call over the waiter and ordered two more scotches.

"One question, though it's none of my business," Gotanda said. "Did you ever sleep with her?"

"Uh-huh."

"So then, well, if I were to say, supposing I slept with her too, would that bother you?"

"Not especially," I said.

"Good," said Gotanda, relieved. "I'm a terrible liar. So I'll come right out with it. We slept together a few times. She was a good kid. A little mixed-up maybe, but really a good person. She should've become an actress. Could've done some good things. Too bad."

"And you really don't know where to contact her? Or what her real name is?"

"Afraid not. I don't know of any way to find her. Nobody knows. 'Kiki' is all there is to go on."

"Weren't there any pay slips in the film company accounting department?" I asked. "They've got to put your real name and address on those things. For the tax office and all."

"Don't you think I checked? Not a clue. She didn't bother

to pick up her pay. No money accepted, so no record, nothing."

"She didn't pick up her pay?"

"Don't ask me why," said Gotanda, well into his third drink. "The girl's a mystery. Maybe she wanted to keep her name and address a secret. Who knows? But whatever, now we have three things in common. Science lab in junior high. Divorce. And Kiki."

Presently our steaks and salads arrived. Beautiful steaks. Magazine-perfect medium rare. Gotanda dug in with gusto. His table manners were less than finishing-school polished, but he did have a casual ease that made him an ideal dining companion. Everything he ate looked appetizing. He was charming. He had a grace you don't encounter every day. A woman would be snowed.

"So tell me, where did you meet Kiki?" I asked, cutting into my steak.

"Let's see, where was it?" he thought out loud. "Oh yeah, I called for a girl and she showed up. You know what I mean, there are these numbers you call. Right?"

"Uh-huh."

"After my divorce, for a while there I would call up and these girls would come and spend the night. No fuss, no muss. I wasn't up for an amateur and if I was sleeping with someone in the industry it'd be splashed all over the magazines. So that's the companionship I had. They weren't cheap, but they kept quiet about it. Absolutely confidential. A guy at the agency gave me an introduction to this club, and all the girls were nice and easy. Professional, but without the attitude. They enjoy themselves too."

He brought a forkful of steak to his mouth and slowly savored the juiciness.

"Mmm, not bad," he said.

"Not bad at all," I seconded. "This is a great place."

"Great, but you get tired of it six times a month."

"You come here six times a month?"

"Well, I'm used to the place. I can walk right in and no

onc bats an eye. The employees don't whisper. They're used to famous people, so they don't stare. No one coming to ask for your autograph when you've got your mouth full. It's hard to relax and eat in other places. Really."

"Rough life," I kidded. "Plus you can't slack off on that expense account."

"You said it! So where were we?"

"Up to the part about call girls."

"Oh right," said Gotanda, wiping his mouth with his napkin. "So, one time I call for the usual girl. But she's not available. Instead, they send these two other girls. I get to choose, because I'm such a special customer. Well, one of the girls was Kiki. It was tough to decide, so I slept with both of them."

"Hmm," I said.

"That bother you?"

"If I were still in high school, maybe. But not now, no."

"I never did anything like that in high school, that's for sure," chuckled Gotanda. "But anyway, I slept with both of them. It was a funny combination. I mean, one girl was absolutely gorgeous. I'm talking stunning. Some expensive work on that body, let me tell you. Every square millimeter of her dripping with money. In my business you run into plenty of beautiful women, and this girl was no slouch. She had a nice personality, intelligent too. And then there was Kiki. Not a real beauty. Pretty enough, but no pizzazz, not like the typical club girl. She was more, well, . . ."

"Ordinary?" I offered.

"Yeah, ordinary. Regular clothes, hardly any makeup, not a super conversationalist either. She didn't seem to care a lot about what people thought of her. No one you'd give a second look. And the strange thing about her was, somehow she was more attractive, she interested me more. After the three of us got it on, we were sitting on the floor, drinking and listening to music and talking. I hadn't enjoyed myself like that in ages. Not since college. I felt so relaxed with them that the three of us got together a few more times after that."

"When was this?"

"This was about six months after I got divorced, so that makes maybe a year and a half ago," he said. "We had this threesome five or six times. I never slept with Kiki alone. I wonder why. I really should have."

"Yeah, why not?"

He set his knife and fork down on his plate, then pressed at his temple again. Seemed to be a mannerism of his. And a charming one too.

"Maybe I was scared," Gotanda said.

"What do you mean?"

"Scared to be alone with her," he said, picking up his cutlery. "There was something challenging about her, almost threatening. At least that was the feeling I got. No, not exactly threatening."

"Sort of suggestive? Or leading?"

"Yeah, maybe. I can't really say. But whatever it was, I got only a hint of it. I never got the full frontal effect. So anyway, I never felt like sleeping with just her. Despite the fact that she attracted me more. Does this make any sense to you?"

"I guess."

"Somehow, if I'd slept with Kiki, just the two of us, I wouldn't have been able to relax. I'd have wanted to go a lot deeper with her. Don't ask me why. But that wasn't what I was after. I only wanted to sleep with girls as a kind of release. Even though I really did like Kiki."

We ate in silence for a moment or two.

"When Kiki didn't show for the audition, I rang up her club," Gotanda went on, as if he'd just remembered. "I specifically asked for her, but she wasn't there. They told me they didn't know where she was. True, she could've told them to say that if I called. Who knows? But in any case, she evaporated, just like that."

The waiter cleared the table and asked if we wanted coffee.

"No, but I'd like another drink," said Gotanda. "How about you?"

"I'm in your hands."

And so we were brought our fourth round.

"What do you think I did today?" Gotanda asked out of nowhere.

I told him I had no idea.

"I assisted a dentist, all afternoon. Background study for a role. Right now I'm doing this series where I play a dentist. Ryoko Nakano's an optometrist, and we have clinics in the same neighborhood. We've known each other since childhood, but something's always conspiring to keep us apart. Pretty harmless stuff. But, well, TV dramas are all the same. You ever seen it?"

"No, can't say I have," I said. "I don't watch TV. Except the news. And I only watch it twice a week."

"Smart," said Gotanda. "It's a stupid program anyway. If I wasn't in it, I wouldn't watch it myself. But it's a popular show. The ratings are pretty high. You know how the public loves this kind of stuff. And you wouldn't believe the mail I get every week. Dentists writing in, complaining about how such-and-such a procedure wasn't rendered right or the treatment for such-and-such a toothache should have been something else. And then there are these jokers who say they never saw such a poor excuse for a show. Well, if you don't like it, don't watch."

"Nobody's forcing them to."

"The funny thing is, I always get stuck playing a doctor or a teacher or somebody wholesome and respectable like that. I've played more doctor roles than I can count. The only thing I haven't been is a proctologist! Imagine how much fun that would be! But I've been a vet and a gynecologist and of course I've been a teacher of every curriculum in the book. I've even taught home economics. What do you make of all this?"

"Well, obviously, you radiate trust," I laughed.

"Yes, a fatal flaw," Gotanda laughed back. "Once, I played

this crooked used-car salesman. A bullshit artist with one glass eye. Boy, I had fun with that. The role had some bite to it, and I wasn't bad either. But no way. The letters came pouring in. It was too mean a role for the noble likes of me. Somebody even threatened to boycott the sponsor! Toothpaste, if I remember correctly. So my character got scratched in the middle of the season. Written right out. A pretty important part, killed by natural selection. And ever since then, it's been doctors and teachers, doctors and teachers."

"Complicated life."

"Or a truly simple one," he laughed again. "Anyway, today I was doing time as a dental assistant, studying technique. I've been doing this for a while now, and I swear, I can probably do a simple procedure myself. The dentist—the real live dentist—even praised the way I handle the tools. I have this gauze mask on, and none of the patients knows it's me. But still, they all relax when I talk to them."

"Can't stop radiating that trust, can you?"

"Yup, that's what I'm beginning to think. Matter of fact, *I* get to feeling so relaxed I wonder if I wasn't cut out to be a *real* dentist or a doctor or a teacher or something. I could've done that, you know. Maybe I'd be happier doing something like that."

"You're not happy now?"

"Don't know," said Gotanda, finger in the middle of his forehead this time. "It's this trust business I'm such a pro at. I don't know whether *I* trust myself. Everybody else trusts me, sure, but, really, I'm nothing but this image. A push of the button and—*brrp!*—I'm gone. Right?"

"Hmm."

"If I really was a doctor or a teacher, no one could switch me off. I'm always there."

"True, but even with acting, you always have to be there."

"Sometimes I just get tired," said Gotanda. "I get headaches, and I just lose track. I mean, it's like which is me and which the role? Where's the line between me and my shadow."

"Everybody feels that way, not just you."

"I know that. Everybody loses track of themselves. Only in me, the slant is too strong. It's, well, fatal. I've always been this way, since I don't know when. To be honest, I was always envious of you."

"Of me?" I was incredulous. "Why the hell would *you* be envious of *me*?"

"I don't know, you always seemed to get along just fine doing your own thing. Didn't matter what others thought, you didn't really care. You did what you wanted, how you wanted. You were solid." He raised his glass and looked through it. "I, on the other hand, was the eternal golden boy. I never did anything wrong, I got the best grades, I won elections, I was a star athlete. Girls liked me. And teachers and parents *believed* in me. How do things like this happen? I never really understood what was going on, but you sort of get into a groove, you know. You probably can't even imagine what I'm talking about."

No, not really, I told him.

"After junior high, I went to this school that was big in soccer. We almost made it to the nationals. So it was like an extension of junior high. I kept on being *good*. I had a girlfriend. She was gorgeous. Used to come cheer for me at the soccer matches. That's how we met. But we didn't go all the way, as we used to say. We only fooled around. We'd go to her place when her folks weren't home and we'd fool around. We'd have dates at the library. High school days right out of NHK Teen Playhouse."

Gotanda took a sip of whiskey.

"Things changed a bit in college. There was all this campus unrest, the United Student Front. I got put in a leading role again. And I played the role all right. I did everything. Put up barricades, slept around, smoked dope, listened to Deep Purple. The riot squad broke in and we got dragged off to jail. After that, there wasn't much for us to do.

"That was when the girl I was living with talked me into doing underground theater. So I tried out, partly as a joke,

but gradually it got interesting. I was this beginner, and I
lucked into a couple decent roles. Pretty soon I realized I had
a talent for that kind of thing. I'd have this role and I could
actually make it work. After a couple years, people started
to know who I was. Even if I was a real mess in those days. I
drank a lot, slept around all the time. But that's how everyone was.

"One day a guy from the movies came around and asked
if I'd ever considered acting on-screen. Of course I was interested, so I tried out and I landed a bit part. It wasn't a bad
part—I was this sensitive young man—and that led to something else. There was even talk of TV. Things got busy, and I
had to quit the theater group. I was sorry to leave but, you
know how it is, you think, there's a big, wide world out
there, gotta move on. And, well, you know the rest. I'm a
doctor and a teacher and I hustle antacid lozenges and
instant coffee in between. Real big, wide world, eh?"

Gotanda sighed. A charming sigh, but a sigh no less.

"Life straight out of a painting, don't you think?"

"Not such a bad painting, though," I said.

"You got a point. I haven't had it bad. But when I think
back on my life, it's like I didn't make one choice. Sometimes
I wake up in the middle of the night and it scares me.
Where's the first-person 'I'? Where's the beef? My whole life
is playing one role after another. Who's been playing the lead
in my life?"

I didn't say anything.

"I guess I'm running off at the mouth."

"Doesn't bother me," I told him. "If you want to talk,
you ought to talk. I won't spread it around."

"I'm not worried about that," said Gotanda, looking me
in the eye. "Not worried in the least. There's something
about you—I don't know what it is—somehow I know I can
trust you. I trust you from the word go. But it's hard to be
open with people. I could talk—well, maybe I could—to my
ex-wife. For a while there, until everyone around us screwed
up the works, we really understood and loved each other. If

it was just the two of us, things might have worked out. But she was too insecure. She needed her family too much, couldn't get out from under them. So that's when I . . . No, I'm getting ahead of myself. That's a whole other story. What I want to know is, is all this talk a drag?"

Nope, I said, not a drag at all.

After that he talked about our science lab unit. How he was always uptight, having to see to it that the experiment came out right, having to explain things to the slow girl. How, again, he envied my puttering along at my own pace. I, however, could scarcely recall what we'd done in science class. So I was at a total loss what there'd been to envy. All I remember was that Gotanda was good with his hands. Setting up the microscope, things like that. Meanwhile, I could relax precisely because he tended to all the hard tasks.

I didn't say that to him. I just listened.

At some point, a well-appointed man in his forties came up to our table and tapped Gotanda on the shoulder. They exchanged greetings and talked show business. The fellow glanced at me, pegged me immediately as a nobody, and continued his conversation. I was invisible.

When the fellow left, after a promise of lunch and golf, Gotanda fretted one eyebrow a few millimeters, raised two fingers to gesture for a waiter, and asked for the check. Which he signed, with no ceremony whatsoever.

"It's all expenses," he said. "It's not money, it's expenses."

19

Then we rode in the Mercedes to a bar down a back street in Azabu. We took seats at one end of the counter and had a few more drinks. Gotanda could hold his liquor; he didn't show the least sign of inebriation, not in his color or his speech. He went on talking. About the inanity of the TV stations. About the lamebrained directors. About the no-talents who made you want to throw up. About the so-called critics on news shows. He was a good storyteller. He was funny, and he was incisive.

He wanted to hear about me. What sorts of turns my life had taken. So I proceeded to relate snippets of the saga. The office I set up with a friend and then quit, the personal life, the free-lance life, the money, the time, . . . Taken in gloss, an altogether sedate, almost still life. It hardly seemed to be my own story.

The bar began to fill up, making conversation difficult. People were ogling Gotanda's famous face. "Let's get out of here. Come over to my place," he said, rising to his feet. "It's close by. And empty. And there's drink."

His condo proved to be a mere two or three turns of the Mercedes away. He gave the driver the rest of the night off, and we went in. Impressive, with two elevators, one requiring a special key.

"The agency bought me this place when I got thrown out

of my house," he said. "They couldn't have their star actor broke and living in a dump. Bad for the image. Of course, I pay rent. On a formal level, I lease the place from the office. And the rent gets deducted from expenses. Perfect symmetry."

It was a penthouse condo, with a spacious living room and two bedrooms and a veranda with a view of Tokyo Tower. Several Persian rugs on the hardwood floor. Ample sofa, not too hard, not too soft. Large potted plants, post-modern Italian lighting. Very little in the way of decorator frills. Only a few Ming dynasty plates on the sideboard, *GQ* and architectural journals on the coffee table. And not a speck of dust. Obviously he had a maid too.

"Nice place," I said with understatement.

"You leave things to an interior designer and it ends up looking like this. Something you want to photograph, not live in. I have to knock on the walls to make sure they're not props. Antiseptic, no scent of life."

"Well, you've got to spread your scent around."

"The problem is, I haven't got one," he voiced expressionlessly.

He put a record on a Bang & Olufsen turntable and lowered the cartridge. The speakers were old-favorite JBL P88s, the music an old Bob Cooper LP. "What'll you have?" he asked.

"Whatever you're drinking," I said.

He disappeared into the kitchen and returned with vodka and soda and ice and sliced lemons. As the cool, clean West Coast jazz filtered through this glorified bachelor pad, I couldn't help thinking, antiseptic or not, the place was comfortable. I sprawled on the sofa, drink in hand, and felt utterly relaxed.

"So out of all the possibilities, here I am," Gotanda addressed the ceiling light, drink in hand also. "I could have been a doctor. In college I got my teaching credentials. But this is how I end up, with this life-style. Funny. The cards were laid out in front of me, I could have picked any one. I could've done all right whatever I chose. Not a doubt in my mind. All the more reason not to make a choice."

"I never even got to see the cards," I said in all honesty. Which elicited a laugh from Gotanda. He probably thought I was joking.

He refilled our glasses, squeezed a lemon, and tossed the rind into the trash. "Even my marriage was by default, almost. We were in the same film and went on location together. We got friendly and went on drives. Then after the filming was over, we dated a couple of times. Everyone thought what a nice couple we made, so we thought, yeah, what a nice couple we make, let's get married. Now I don't know if you realize it, but the film industry's a small world. It's like living in a tenement at one end of a back alley. Not only do you see everybody's dirty laundry, but once rumors start, you can't stop 'em. All the same, I did like her, truly. She was the best thing I ever laid hands on. That really came home to me after we got married. I tried to make it last, but it was no go. The second I make a conscious choice, I chase the thing away. But if I'm on the receiving end, if it's not me that's making the decision, it seems like I can't lose."

I didn't say anything.

"I'm not looking on the dark side," he said. "I still love her. Maybe that's the problem. I still think of her. How it might have been if we both had given up acting and settled down to a quiet life. Wouldn't need a condo that looked like this. Wouldn't need a Maserati. None of that. Only a decent job and our own little place. Kids. After work I'd stop somewhere for a beer and let off steam. Then home to the wife. A Civic or Subaru on installment. That's the life. That would be everything I needed—if she was there. But it's not going to happen. She wanted something different. And her family —don't get me started on them. Anyway, I guess some things just don't work out. But you know what? I slept with her last month."

"With your former wife?"

"Yup. Do you think that's normal?"

"I don't think it's abnormal," I said.

"She came here, I couldn't figure out what for. She rings up, wants to drop by. Of course, I say. So we're drinking, the two of us, just like old times, and we end up in bed together. It was great. She told me she still liked me and I told her how I wished we could start all over again. But she didn't say anything to that. She just listened and smiled. I started going on about having a normal life, a regular home, like I was telling you now. And she listened and smiled, but she wasn't really listening. She didn't hear a word of it. It was like talking to a wall. Futile. She was feeling lonely and wanted to be with someone. I happened to be available. Not a nice thing to say about yourself, but it's true. She's a world apart from somebody like you or me. For her, loneliness is something you have others remove for you. And once it's gone, everything's okay. Doesn't go any further. I can't live that way."

The record finished. He raised the cartridge and stood thinking in silence for a moment.

"What do you think about calling in some girls?" he asked.

"Fine by me. Whatever you want," I said.

"You never bought a woman?" he asked.

Never, I told him.

"How come?"

"Never occurred to me," I said, honestly.

Gotanda shrugged his shoulders. "Well tonight, I think you should. Play along with me, okay?" he said. "I'll ask for the girl who came with Kiki. She might know something about her."

"I leave it up to you," I said. "But don't tell me you can write it off as expenses."

He laughed as he refilled his glass. "You won't believe it, but I can. There's a whole system. This place has this front as a party service, so they can make out these very legitimate receipts. Sex as 'business gifts and entertainment.' Amazing, huh?"

"Advanced capitalism," I said.

While waiting for the girls to arrive, Kiki and her fabulous ears came to mind. I asked Gotanda if he'd ever seen them.

"Her ears?" he said, puzzled. "No, I don't think so. Or if I did, I don't remember. What about her ears?"

Oh, nothing, I told him.

It was past twelve when the girls arrived. One was Gotanda's stunningly beautiful companion to Kiki. And really, she was stunning. The sort of woman who'd linger in your memory even if she never spoke a word to you. Not glitter and glamour, but refinement. Under her coat she wore a green cashmere sweater and an ordinary wool skirt. Simple earrings, no other adornment. Very well-bred university girl.

The other woman wore glasses and a soft-colored dress. She wasn't beautiful like her companion. She was more what you would call appealing and fresh. With long legs and slender arms, and tan as if she'd spent the last week on the beach in Guam. Her hair was short and neatly pinned up. She wore silver bangles that played on her wrists with her brisk movements, her flesh trim and taut, like a sleek carnivore.

Memories of high school came to mind. These two distinct types were to be found in any class. The elegant beauty and the quick-witted mink. It was like being at a reunion. Especially with Gotanda there, so relaxed and effervescent. He seemed to have slept with both of them before, so it was all, "Hey there, how's it going?" Gotanda introduced me as a former schoolmate, now a writer. Both smiled warmly, fine-we're-all-friends-here smiles.

We sat on the floor with brandy-and-sodas, Joe Jackson and the Alan Parsons Project playing in the background. Gotanda put on his dentist act for the girl with the glasses. Then he whispered something to her and she giggled. Then the Beauty was leaning on my shoulder and holding my hand. Her scent was lovely. She was every man's, every boy's dream. The high school girl you'd always wanted, now come back years later. *I always liked you though I didn't know how to tell you at the time. Why didn't you try to reach me?* I put my arm around her, and she gently closed her eyes, seeking out my ear with the tip of her nose. She kissed me lightly on the neck, breathing softly. Then I noticed that Gotanda and his girl weren't around. Why didn't I turn the lights down a bit? my coed cooed. I got up and switched off the overhead lights, leaving only a low table lamp on. Bob Dylan was droning *it's all over now, baby blue.*

"Undress me nice and slow," she whispered into my ear. So I took off first her sweater, then her skirt, then her blouse and stockings. Out of reflex I almost started to fold her things, but then realized that in this scene there was no need to do that. She in turn undressed me. Armani tie, Levi's, T-shirt.

She stood before me in scanty bra and panties. "Well, what do you think?" she asked with a smile.

"Super," I said. She had a beautiful body. Full, brimming with life, clean and sexy.

"*How* super?" she wanted to know. "If you tell me better, I'll do you the best ever."

"It's like old times. Takes me back to high school." I was being honest.

She squinted curiously, then smiled. "Unique, I'll say that."

"Did I say something wrong?"

"Not at all," she said. Then she came over next to me and did things nobody in my thirty-four years had ever done for me. Delicate, yet daring, things you wouldn't think of so readily. But somebody obviously had. The tension slipped out of my body as I closed my eyes, giving myself over to the flow of sensations. This was utterly different from any sex I'd known before.

"Not bad, huh?" she said, whispering again.

"Not bad," I agreed.

It put my mind at ease, like the best music, released the pockets of tension from my being, sent my temporal senses into limbo. Instead, there was a quiet intimacy, a blending of time and space, a perfect self-contained form of communication. And to think it was tax deductible! "Not bad," I said again. What was Dylan going on about now? "A Hard Rain's A-Gonna Fall." She snuggled into the crook of my arm. What a world, where you can sleep with gorgeous women while listening to Bob Dylan and then write off the whole works! Unthinkable in the sixties.

It's all just images, I found myself thinking. Pull out the plug and it'll all go away. A 3-D sex scene. Complete with eau de cologne, soft touchie-feelies, hot breath.

I followed the expected course, I came, then we took a shower. We returned to the living room, wrapped in over-sized towels, to listen to Dire Straits and sip some brandy.

She asked me about my work, what kind of things I wrote. I explained briefly and she said, how uninteresting. Well, it depends, I told her. What I did was shovel cultural snow. To which she responded that her work was to shovel sensual snow. I had to laugh. But wouldn't I like to shovel some more snow, right about now? And so we rolled over on the carpet and made love again, this time very simply, very slowly. And she knew just how to please me. Uncanny.

Later, both lying full-length in Gotanda's luxurious tub, I asked her about Kiki.

"Kiki?" she said. "Now there's a name I haven't heard in a while. You know Kiki?"

She pursed her lips like a child and tried to think. "She's not anywhere now. She just disappeared, all of a sudden. We were pretty close too. Sometimes we'd go out shopping or drinking together. Then, without warning, she was gone. A month, maybe two months ago. But that's not so unusual. You don't need to hand in a formal resignation in this line of work. If you want to quit, you quit. You don't have to tell anyone. I'm sorry she left. We were friends, but that's how it goes. We're not girl scouts, after all," she said, stroking my thighs and cock with her long graceful fingers. "Have you slept with Kiki?"

"There was a time we lived together. Four years ago."

"Four years ago?" she said with a smile. "That's ancient history. Four years ago, I was still in high school."

"Hmm." I let it pass. "You know of any way I could get to see Kiki?"

"Pretty difficult, I'd say. I honestly don't have any idea where she went. It's like I told you, she just up and left. Practically vanished into a blank wall. Haven't a clue how you'd go about looking for her. So, you still got a thing for her?"

I stretched out in the tub and looked up at the ceiling. Was I still in love with Kiki?

"I don't know. But that's almost beside the point now. I just have to see her. Something's been telling me Kiki wants to see me. I keep dreaming about her."

"Strange," she said, looking me in the eye. "I sometimes dream about Kiki, too."

"What sort of dreams?"

She didn't reply. She only smiled and said she'd like another drink. She rested against my chest and I threw my arm around her naked shoulder. Gotanda and his girl showed no sign of emerging from the bedroom. Asleep, I supposed.

"I know you won't believe me," she then said, "but I like being with you like this. I enjoy it, no business, no acting. It's the truth."

"I believe you," I said. "I'm enjoying myself, too. I feel really relaxed. It's like a class reunion."

"Unique, again," she giggled.

"About Kiki," I pressed on, "isn't there anyone who'd know? Her real name, her address, that sort of thing?"

She shook her head slowly. "We almost never talk about those things. Why else would we bother with these names?

She was Kiki. I'm Mei, the other girl's Mami. Everyone's four letters or less. It's our cover. Private life is out-of-bounds. We don't know and we don't ask. Manners, you know. We're all real friendly and we go out together sometimes. But it's not really us. We don't actually know each other. Mei, Kiki. These names don't have real lives. We're all image. Signs tacked up in empty air. That's why we respect each other's illusions. Does that make sense?"

"Perfect sense," I said.

"Some of our customers take pity on us. But we don't do this just for the money. Me, for example, I do it 'cause it's fun. And because the club is strictly for members only, we don't have to worry about crazies, and everyone wants to have fun with us. After all, we're all in this made-up world together."

"Shoveling snow for the fun of it," I threw in.

"Right, shoveling snow for fun," she laughed. Then putting her lips to my chest, "Sometimes even snowball fights."

"Mei." I said her name over again. "I once knew a girl whose name really was Mei. She worked as a receptionist at the dentist's next to my office. From a farming family up in Hokkaido. Skinny, dark. Everyone called her Mei the Goat Girl."

"Mei the Goat Girl," she repeated. "And your name?"

"Winnie the Pooh," I said.

"Our own little fairy tale."

I drew her to me and kissed her. It was a heady kiss, a nostalgic kiss. Then we drank our umpteenth brandy-and-soda, and snuggled together while listening to the Police. Soon Mei had drifted off to sleep, no longer the beautiful dream woman, but only an ordinary, brittle young girl. A class reunion. The clock read four o'clock and everything was still. Mei the Goat Girl and Winnie the Pooh. Images. Deductible fairy tales. What a day! Connections that almost connected but didn't. Follow the string until it snaps. I'd met Gotanda after all these years, even come to like him, really.

Through him I'd met Mei the Goat Girl. We made love. Which was wonderful. Shoveled sensual snow. But none of it led anywhere.

I made some coffee, and at half past six the others woke up. Mei had on a bathrobe. Mami came in wearing a paisley pajama top and Gotanda the bottom. I was in my jeans and T-shirt. We all took seats at the dining table and passed around the toast and marmalade. The FM station was playing "Baroque for You." A Henry Purcell pastoral.

"Morning at camp," I said.

Cuck–koo, sang Mei.

At seven-thirty Gotanda called a taxi for the girls. Mei kissed me good-bye. "If you find Kiki, give her my best," I said. I handed her my card and asked her to call if she learned anything.

"Hope we can meet again and shovel some more snow," she winked.

"Shovel snow?" Gotanda asked.

Gotanda and I sat down to another cup of coffee. It was like a commercial. A quiet morning, sun rising, Tokyo Tower gleaming in the distance. *Tokyo begins its mornings with Nescafé.*

Time for normal people to be starting their day. Not for us though. Like it or not, we two were excluded.

"Find out anything about Kiki?" asked Gotanda.

I shook my head. "Only that she'd disappeared. Just like you said. No leads, not a clue. Mei didn't even know her real name."

"I'll ask around the film company," he said. "Maybe somebody knows something."

He pouted slightly and pressed at his temple with the handle of his coffee spoon. He sure was good at it.

"But tell me, what do you plan to do if you find her?" he

asked. "Try to win her back? Or is it just for old times?"

I told him I didn't know. I hadn't thought that far.

Gotanda saw me home in his spotless brown Maserati.

"Mind if I call you again soon?" he said. "It really was terrific seeing you. Don't know anyone else I can talk to like we did. That is, if it's okay by you."

"Of course," I said. And I thanked him again for the steak and drinks and girls and . . .

He gave a quiet shake of his head. Without a word, I understood everything he meant to say.

20

The next few days passed uneventfully. The phone rang, but the whole time I kept the answering machine on and didn't bother picking up. Nice to know that my services were still in demand, though. I cooked meals, went into Shibuya, and saw *Unrequited Love* every day. It was spring break, so the theater was always packed with high school students. It was like an animal house. I wanted to burn the place down.

Now that I knew what to look for, I was able to find Kiki's name, in fine type, in the opening credits.

Then after her scene, I'd leave the theater and walk my usual course. From Harajuku to the Jingu Stadium, Aoyama Cemetery, Omotesando, past the Jintan Building, back to Shibuya. Sometimes I'd stop for a coffee along the way. Spring had surely come, bringing its familiar smells. The earth persisted in its measured orbit of the sun. I always find it a cosmic mystery that spring knows when to follow winter. And how is it that spring always brings out the same smells? Year after year, however subtle, exactly identical.

The town was plastered with election posters. Ugly and repugnant. Trucks were making the rounds, blaring out speeches by politicians. So loud you couldn't tell what they were saying. Noise.

I walked and I thought about Kiki. And before long I

noticed I'd regained my stride, a lift had come back to my step. My awareness of things around me had sharpened. I was moving forward intently, one step at a time. I had focus, a goal. Which somehow, quite naturally, lightened my step, almost gave me soft-shoe footwork. This was a good sign. *Dance*. Keep in step, light but steady. Freshen up, maintain the rhythm, keep things going. I had to pay careful attention where this was leading me to next. Had to make sure I stayed in *this world*.

The last four or five days of March passed in this way. On the surface, there was no progression at all. I'd do the shopping, make meals in the kitchen, see *Unrequited*, go for long walks. I'd play back the answering machine when I got home—inevitably calls about work. At night, I'd read and drink alone. Every day was a repeat of the day before.

Drinking alone at night, I fixated on sex with Mei the Goat Girl. Shoveling snow. An oddly isolated memory, unconnected to anything. Not to Gotanda, not to Kiki. But ever so real. Down to the smallest details, in some sense even more vivid than waking reality, though ultimately unconnected. I liked it that way. A self-bound meeting of souls. Two persons joined together respecting their illusions and images. That fine-we're-all-friends-here smile. Morning at camp. *Cuck–koo*.

I tried to picture Kiki and Gotanda sleeping together. Did she give him the same ultra-sexy service as Mei gave me? Were all the girls at the club drilled in such professional know-how? Or was Mei strictly her own technician? I had no idea, and I couldn't very well ask Gotanda. All the time Kiki was living with me, she was, if anything, rather passive about sex. Sure, she warmed up and responded, but she never made the first move, never had demands of her own. Not that I ever had any complaints. She was wonderful when she relaxed. Her soft inviting body, quiet easy breath, hot vagina. No, I had no complaints. I just couldn't picture her delivering professional favors to anyone—to Gotanda, for instance. Maybe I lacked the imagination.

How do prostitutes keep their private sex separate from their professional sex? Before Mei, I'd never slept with a call girl. I'd slept with Kiki. And Kiki was a call girl. But I didn't sleep with Kiki the call girl, I slept with Kiki. And conversely I'd slept with Mei the call girl, but not Mei. There probably was nothing to gain from correlating these two circumstances. That would only make matters more complicated. And anyway, where does sex stop being a thing of the mind? Where does technique begin? How far does the real thing go, how much is acting? Was sufficient foreplay a spiritual concern? Did Kiki actually enjoy sex with me? Was she really acting in the movie? Were Gotanda's graceful fingers sliding down her back turning her on?

Caught in the cross hair of the real and the imaginary.

Take Gotanda. His doctor persona was all image. Yet he looked more like a real doctor than any doctor I knew. All the dependability and trust he projected.

What was *my* image? Did I even have one?

Dance, the Sheep Man said. *Dance in tip-top form. Dance so it all keeps spinning.*

Did that mean I would then have an image? And if I did, would people be impressed? Well, more than they'd be impressed by my real self, I bet.

When I awoke the following morning, it was April. As delicately rendered as a passage from Truman Capote, fleeting, fragile, beautiful. April, made famous by T.S. Eliot and Count Basie.

I went to Kinokuniya for some overpriced groceries and well-trained vegetables. Then I picked up two 6-packs of beer and three bottles of bargain wine.

When I got back home, there was a message from Yuki, her voice totally disinterested. She said she'd call again around twelve. Then she slammed down the receiver. A common phrasing in her body language.

I dripped some coffee, then sat down with a mug and the

latest 87th Precinct adventure, something I've failed to quit for ten years now. Then a little past noon, the phone rang.

"How's it going?" It was Yuki.

"Okay."

"What are you doing?" she asked.

"Thinking about lunch. Smoked salmon with pedigreed lettuce and razor-sharp slices of onion that have been soaked in ice water, brushed with horseradish and mustard, served on French butter rolls baked in the hot ovens of Kinokuniya. A sandwich made in heaven!"

"It sounds okay."

"It's not okay. It's nothing less than uplifting. And if you don't believe me, you can ask your local bee. You could also ask your friendly clover. They'll tell you—it really is great."

"What's this bee and clover stuff? What're you talking about?"

"Figure of speech."

"You know," said Yuki, "you ought to try growing up. I'm only thirteen, but even so I sometimes think you're kind of dumb."

"You mean I should become more conventional? Is that what you're telling me? Is that what growing up means?"

"I want to go for a drive," she ignored my question. "How about tonight?"

"I think I'm free," I said.

"Well, then, be here at five in Akasaka. You remember how to get here, don't you?"

"Yeah, but don't tell me you've been alone all this time?"

"Uh-huh. Nothing's happening in Hakone. I mean, the place is on top of a mountain. Who wants to go there to be alone? More fun in town."

"What about your mother? She hasn't returned?"

"Not that I know of. I can't keep track of her. I'm not *her* mother, you know. She hasn't called or anything, so maybe she's still in Kathmandu."

"What about money?"

"I'm okay for money. I've got a cash card that I pinched

from her purse. One less card, she'll never notice. I mean, if I don't look out for myself, I'll die. Mama's such a space cadet, as you know."

My turn to ignore her. "You been eating healthy?"

"I'm eating. What did you think? I'd die if I didn't."

"That's not what I asked. I said, are you eating *healthy*?"

Yuki coughed. "Let's see. First there was Kentucky Fried Chicken, then McDonald's, then Dairy Queen, . . . And what else?"

"I'll be there at five," I said. "We'll go somewhere decent to eat. You can't survive on the garbage you've been putting down. An adolescent girl needs nourishment. You're at a very delicate time of life, you know. Bad diet, bad periods."

"You're an idiot," she muttered.

"Now, if it's not too much to ask, would you give me your phone number?"

"Why?"

"Because one-way communication isn't fair. You know my number, I don't know yours. You call me when you feel like it, I can't call you. It's one-sided. Besides, suppose something came up suddenly, I wouldn't be able to reach you."

She paused, muttered some more, then gave me her number.

"But don't think you can change plans anytime you feel like it," said Yuki. "Mama's so good at it already, you wouldn't stand a chance."

"I promise. I won't change plans. Cross my heart and hope to die. You can ask the cabbage moth, you can ask the alfalfa. There's not a human alive who keeps promises better than me. But sometimes the unexpected happens. It's a big, complicated world, you know. And if it happens, don't you think it'd be nice if I could get through to you? Got it?"

"Unforeseeable circumstances," she said.

"Out of the clear blue sky."

"Nice if they didn't happen," said Yuki.

"Nice if they didn't," I echoed.

But of course they did.

21

They showed up a little past three in the afternoon.

I was in the shower when the doorbell started ringing. By the time I got there, it was on ring number eight. I opened up, and there stood two men.

One in his forties, one in his thirties. The older guy was tall, with a scar on his nose. A little too well-tanned for this time of the year, a deep, tried-and-true bronze of a fisherman, not the precious color you get from the beach or ski slope. He had stiff hair, obscenely large hands, and a gray overcoat. The younger guy was short with longish hair and narrow, intense eyes. A generation ago he might have been called bookish. The fellow at the literary journal meeting who ran his hands through his hair as he declared, "Mishima's our man." He had on a dark blue trench coat. Both guys in regulation black shoes, cheap and worn-out. The sort you wouldn't glance at twice if you saw them lying by the side of the road. Nor were the fellas the type you'd go out of your way to make friends with.

Without a word of introduction, Bookish flashed his police ID. Just like in the movies. I'd never actually seen a police ID before, but one look convinced me it was the real thing. It fit with the worn-out shoes. Something in the way he pulled it out of his pocket, he could have been selling his literary journal door-to-door.

"Akasaka precinct," Bookish announced, and asked if I was who I was.

Uh-huh.

Fisherman stood by silently, both hands in the pockets of his overcoat, nonchalantly propping the door open with his foot. Just like in the movies. Great!

Bookish filed away his ID, then gave me the once-over. Me in bathrobe and wet hair.

"We need you to come down to headquarters for questioning," said Bookish.

"Questioning? About what?"

"Everything in due time," he said. "We have formal procedures to follow for this sort of thing, so why don't we get going right away."

"Huh? Okay, but mind if I get into some clothes?"

"Certainly," said Bookish flatly, without the slightest change of expression. If Gotanda played a cop, he'd do a better job. That's reality for you.

The fellas waited in the doorway while I got some clothes on and turned off switches. Then I stepped into my blue topsiders, which the two cops stared at as if they were the trendiest thing on the market.

A patrol car was parked near the entrance to my building, a uniformed cop behind the wheel. Fisherman got into the backseat, then me, then Bookish. Again, like in the movies. Bookish pulled the door shut and the car took off.

The streets were congested, but did they turn on the siren? No, they made like we were going for a ride in a taxi. Sans meter. We spent more time stopped in traffic than moving, which gave everybody in all the cars and on the street plenty of opportunity to stare at me. No one uttered a word. Fisherman looked straight ahead, arms folded. Bookish looked out the window, grimacing like he was laboring over a literary exercise. The school of dark-and-stormy metaphors. *Spring as concept raged in upon us, a somber tide of longing. Its advent roused the passions of those nameless multitudes fallen between the cracks of the city, sweeping them noiselessly toward the quicksands of futility.*

I wanted to erase the whole passage from my head. What the hell was "spring as concept"? Just where were these "quicksands of futility"? I was sorry I started the whole dumb train of thought.

Shibuya was full of mindless junior high students dressed like clowns, same as ever. No passions, no quicksand.

At police headquarters, I was taken to an interrogation room upstairs. Barely three meters square with one tiny window. Table, two steel office chairs, two vinyl-covered stools, clock on the wall. That was it. On the table, a telephone, a pen, ashtray, stack of folders. No vase with flowers. The gumshoes entered the room and offered me one of the steel office chairs. Fisherman sat down opposite me, Bookish stood off to the side, notepad open. Lots of silent communication.

"So what'd you do last night?" Fisherman finally got going after a lengthy wait. Those were the first words I'd heard out of his mouth.

Last night? What was I doing? I could hardly think last night was any different from any other night. Sad but true. I told them I'd have to think about it.

"Listen," Fisherman said, coughing, "legal rigmarole takes a long time to spit out. We're asking you a simple question: From last evening until this morning what did you do? Not so hard, is it? No harm in answering, is there?"

"I told you, I have to think about it," I said.

"You can't remember without thinking? This was yesterday. We're not asking about last August, which maybe you don't remember either," Fisherman sneered.

Like I told you before, I was about to say, then I reconsidered. I doubted they would understand a temporary memory loss. They'd probably think I had some screws loose.

"We'll wait," said Fisherman. "Take all the time you need." He pulled a pack of cigarettes from his jacket pocket and lit up with a Bic. "Smoke?"

"No thanks," I said. According to *Brutus* magazine,

today's new urbanite doesn't smoke. Apparently these two guys didn't know about this, Fisherman with his Seven Stars, Bookish with his plain Hopes, chain-smoking.

"We'll give you five minutes," said Bookish, very deadpan. "After that you will tell us something simple, such as, where you were last night and what you were doing there."

"Don't rush the guy. He's an intellectual," Fisherman said to Bookish. "According to his file here, this isn't his first time talking to the law. University activist, obstruction of public offices. We have his prints. Files sent to the prosecutor's office. He's used to our gentle questioning. Steel-reinforced will, it says here. He doesn't seem to like the police very well. You know, I bet he knows all about his rights, as provided for in the constitution. You think he'll be calling for his lawyer next?"

"But he came downtown with us of his own volition and we merely asked him a simple question," Bookish said to Fisherman. "I haven't heard any talk of arrest, have you? I don't think there's any reason for him to call his lawyer, do you? Wouldn't make sense."

"Well, if you ask me, I think it's more than an open-and-shut case of hating cops. The gentleman has a negative psychological reaction to anything that resembles authority. He'd rather suffer than cooperate," Fisherman went on.

"But if he doesn't answer our questions, what can we do but wait until he answers. As soon as he answers, he can go home. No lawyer's going to come running down here just because we asked him what he was doing last night. Lawyers are busy people. An intellectual understands that."

"Well, I suppose," said Fisherman. "If the gentleman can grasp that principle, then we can save each other a lot of time. We're busy, he's busy. No point in wasting valuable time when we could be thinking deep thoughts. It gets tiresome. We don't want to wear ourselves out unnecessarily."

The duo kept up their comic routine for the allotted five minutes.

"Well, it looks like time's up," Fisherman smiled. "How

about it? Did you remember anything?"

I hadn't. True, I hadn't been trying very hard. Current situation aside, the fact was, I couldn't remember a thing. The block wouldn't budge. "First of all, I'd like to know what's going on," I spoke up. "Unless you tell me what's going on, I'm not saying a thing. I don't want to say anything that may prove inopportune. Besides, it's common courtesy to explain the circumstances before asking questions. It's a breach of good manners."

"He doesn't want to say anything that may prove *inopportune*," Bookish mocked me. "Where is our *common courtesy*? We don't want to have a—what did he call it?— *breach of good manners*."

"I told you the gentleman was an intellectual," said Fisherman. "He looks at everything slanted. He hates cops. He subscribes to *Asahi Shimbun* and reads *Sekai*."

"I do not subscribe to newspapers and I do not read *Sekai*," I broke in. Had to put my foot down somewhere. "And as long as you don't tell me why I'm here, I'm not going to feel a lot like talking. If you want to keep insulting me, go ahead. I've got as much time to sit around shooting the breeze as you guys do."

The two detectives looked at each other.

Fisherman: "Are you telling us that if we're polite and explain these circumstances to you, you'll cooperate and give us some answers?"

Me: "Probably."

Bookish, folding his arms and glancing high up the wall: "The guy's got a sense of humor."

Fisherman rubbed the horizontal scar on his nose. Probably a knife gash, and fairly deep, judging from how it tugged at the surrounding flesh. "Listen," he got serious. "We're busy, and this isn't a game. We all want to finish up and go home in time to eat dinner with the family. We don't have anything against you, and we got no axes to grind. So if you'll just tell us what you did last night, there'll be no more demands. If you got a clear conscience, what's the grief in telling us? Or is it you got guilty feelings about something?"

I stared at the ashtray.

Bookish snapped his notepad shut and slipped it into his pocket. For thirty seconds, no one said a word. During which time, Fisherman lit up another Seven Stars.

"Steel-reinforced will," said Fisherman.

"Want to call the Committee on Human Rights?" asked Bookish.

"Please," Fisherman and his partner were at it again, "this is not a human rights issue. This is the duty of the citizen. It's written, right here in your favorite *Statutes of Law*, that citizens are obliged to cooperate to the fullest extent with police investigations. So what do you have against us officers of the law? We're good enough to ask for directions when you're lost, we're good enough to call if a robber breaks into your home, but we're not good enough to cooperate with just a little bit. So let's try this again. Where were you last night and what were you doing?"

"I want to know what's going on," I repeated.

Bookish blew his nose with a loud honk. Fisherman took a plastic ruler out of the desk drawer and whacked it against the palm of his hand.

"Listen, guy," pronounced Bookish, tossing a soiled tissue into the trash, "you do realize that your position is becoming worse and worse?"

"This is not the sixties, you know. You can't keep carrying on with this antiestablishment bullshit," said Fisherman, disgruntled. "Those days are over. You and me, we're hemmed in up to here in society. There's no such thing as establishment and antiestablishment anymore. That's passé. It's all the same big-time. The system's got everything sewed up. If you don't like it, you can sit tight and wait for an earthquake. You can go dig a hole. But getting sassy with us won't get you or us anywhere. It's a dead grind. You understand?"

"Okay, we're beat. And maybe we've not shown you proper respect. If that's the case, I'm sorry. I apologize."

Bookish's turn again, notepad open again. "We've been working on another job and hardly even slept since yesterday. I haven't seen my kids in five days. And although you have no respect for me, I'm a public servant. I try to keep society safe. So when you refuse to answer a simple question, you can bet it rubs us the wrong way. And when I say things are looking worse for you, it's because the more tired we get, the worse our temper gets. An easy job ends up being not so easy after all. Of course you got rights, the law's on your side, but sometimes the law takes a long time to kick in and so it gets put in the hands of us poor suckers on duty. You get my drift?"

"Don't misunderstand, we're not threatening you," Fisherman interjected. "He was just giving you a friendly warning. He doesn't want anything bad to happen to you."

I kept my mouth shut and looked at the ashtray. A plain old dirty glass ashtray without markings. How many decades had it sat here on this desk?

Fisherman kept slapping his hands with the ruler. "Very well," he gave in. "I'll explain the circumstances. It's not the procedure we follow when asking questions, but since we want your respect, we'll try things your way."

He picked up a folder, removed an envelope and produced three large photographs. Black-and-white site photos, without much in the way of artistry. That much was clear at a glance. The first photo showed a naked woman lying facedown on a bed. Long legs, tight ass, hair fanned out from the neck up. Her thighs were parted just enough to reveal what was between them. Her arms flung out to the sides. She could have been sleeping.

The second photo was more graphic. She was turned over, her pubic area, breasts, face exposed. Her legs and arms arranged stiffly at attention. Her eyes open wide, glassy, her mouth contorted out of shape. The woman was not sleeping. The woman was dead.

The woman was Mei.

The third photo was a close-up of Mei's face. Mei. No

longer beautiful. Cold, ice cold. Chafe marks around her neck.

My mouth went dry, I couldn't swallow. My palms itched. Mei. So full of life and sex. Now cold, dead.

I stopped myself from shaking my head, from showing any reaction. I knew the two guys were watching my every move. I restacked the three photos and casually handed them back to Fisherman. I tried to look unaffected.

"Do you know this woman?" asked Fisherman.

"No." I could've said yes, of course, but then I would've had to tell them about Gotanda, who was my link to Mei, and his life would be ruined if this got out to the media. True, he might have been the one who coughed up my name. But I didn't know that. I'd have to risk it. *They* weren't about to bring up Gotanda's name.

"Take another look," Fisherman said slowly. "This is extremely important, so do look again carefully before you answer. Have you ever seen this woman before? Don't bother lying to us. We're not babes in the woods. We catch you lying, you'll *really* be in trouble. Understand?"

I took a lengthy look at the three photographs. I didn't want to look at all, but that would have given me away.

"I don't know her," I said. "But she's dead, right?"

"Dead," Bookish repeated after me. "Very dead. Extremely dead. Completely dead. As you can see for yourself. This fox is naked and dead. Once a very fine specimen, but now that she's dead it cuts no ice. She's dead, like all dead people. You let her decay, her skin starts to crack and shrivel, the rot oozes out. And the stink! And the bugs. Ever see that?"

Never, I said.

"Well, we've seen it plenty. It gets to where you can't even tell that it was a woman. It's dead meat. Rotten steak. And once the smell gets in your nose, you don't think of food, let me tell you. It's a smell you never forget. True, if you let things go for a long, long, long time, then all you got are bones. No smell. Everything's all dried up. White, beautiful, clean bones. Needless to say, this lady didn't make it that far. And she wasn't rotting either. Just dead. Just stiff. You could tell she had to be some piece when she was warm. But seeing her like this, I didn't even twitch.

"Somebody killed this woman. She had the right to live. She was barely twenty. Somebody strangled her with a stocking. Not a very quick way to go. It's painful and it takes time. You know you're going to die. You're thinking why do I have to die like this? You want to go on living. But you can feel the oxygen drying up. Your head goes foggy. You piss. You lose the feeling in your legs. You die slow. Not a nice way to die. We'd like to catch the son of a bitch who killed this gorgeous young thing. And I think you're going to help us.

"Yesterday at noon, the lady reserved a double room in a luxury hotel in Akasaka. At five P.M., she checked in, alone," Fisherman recounted the facts. "She told the desk her husband would show up later. Phony name, phony telephone number. At six P.M., she called room service for dinner for one. She was alone at the time. At seven P.M., the empty tray was put out in the hall. The DO NOT DISTURB sign was hanging on the door. Checkout time was twelve noon. When the lady didn't check out, the front desk called her room at twelve-thirty. No answer. The DO NOT DISTURB sign was still on the door. There was no response. When hotel security unlocked the door, the lady was naked and dead, exactly as you see in this first photograph. No one saw the lady's 'husband.' The hotel has a restaurant on the top floor, so there's a lot of people going in and out. Very popular place to rendezvous."

"There was no identification in her handbag," said Bookish. "No driver's license, address book, credit cards, no bank card. No initials on her clothing. Besides cosmetics, birth-control pills, and thirty thousand yen, the only item in her possession, tucked, almost hidden, in her wallet, was a business card. *Your* business card."

"You're going to say you really don't know her?" Fisherman tried again.

I shook my head. I wanted to give these guys all the cooperation I could. I really did. I wanted to see her killer caught as much as anyone. But I had the living to think about.

"Well, then, now that you know the circumstances, why don't you tell us where you were last night and what you were doing," Bookish drummed on.

My memory came rushing back. "At six o'clock I ate supper at home by myself, then I read and had a couple of drinks, then before midnight I went to bed."

"Did you see anyone?" asked Fisherman.

"I didn't see anyone. I was alone the entire time."

"Any phone calls to anyone? Anyone call you?"

I told them I didn't take any calls. "A little before nine, one came in on the machine. When I played it back, it was work-related."

"Why keep the answering machine on, if you're at home?"

"I'm on a break. I don't want to have to talk business."

They asked for the name of the caller, and I told them.

"So you ate dinner alone, and you read all evening?"

"After washing the dishes, yes."

"What was the book?"

"You may not believe it, but it was Kafka. *The Trial.*"

Kafka. *The Trial.* Bookish made note.

"Then, you read until twelve," Fisherman kept going. "And drank."

"First beer was around sundown. Later brandy."

"How much did you drink?"

"Two cans of beer, and then I guess a quarter of a bottle of brandy. Oh, and I also ate some canned peaches."

Fisherman took everything down. *Also ate canned peaches.* "Anything else?"

I tried, but it really had been a night without qualities. I'd quietly read my book, while somewhere off in the still of the night Mei was strangled with a stocking. I told them there was nothing else.

"I'd advise you to try harder," said Bookish with a cough.

"You realize what a vulnerable position you're in, don't you?"

"Listen, I didn't do anything, so how can I be in a vulnerable position? I work free-lance, so I hand my business card out all over the place. I don't know how this girl got ahold of my card. Just because she had it on her doesn't mean I killed her."

"People don't carry around business cards that don't mean anything to them in the safest corner of their wallets," Fisherman said. "We have two hypotheses. One, the lady arranged to meet one of your business associates in the hotel and that person killed her. Then the guy dumped something into her bag to throw us off the track. Except the card, that single card, was wedged too deep in her wallet for that. Hypothesis number two, the lady was a professional lady of the night. A prostitute. A high-class prostitute. The kind that fulfills her duties at luxury hotels. The kind that doesn't carry any identification on her person. But for some reason the john kills her. He doesn't take any money, so it's possible he's a psycho, a nut case. Those are our angles. What do you think?"

I cocked my head to the side and kept silent.

"Your business card is the central piece of evidence in this case," said Fisherman leadingly, rapping his pen on the desk.

"A business card is just a piece of paper with a name printed on it," I said. "It's not evidence. It doesn't prove anything."

"Not yet it doesn't." He kept rapping on the desk. "The Criminal ID boys are going over the room for traces. There's an autopsy going on right now. By tomorrow we'll know a lot more. So you know what? You're going to wait with us. Meanwhile, be a good idea if you start remembering more details. It might take all night. Take your time, you'll be surprised at what you can remember. Why don't we start from the beginning? What did you do when you woke up in the morning?"

I looked at the clock on the wall. Ten past five. I suddenly remembered my date with Yuki.

"I need to call somebody first, okay?" I said to Fisherman. "I was supposed to meet someone at five. It was important."

"A girl?" questioned Fisherman.

"Right."

He held out the phone to me.

"You're going to tell me that something came up and you can't come," Yuki said immediately, beating me to the punch.

"Something unforeseen. Really," I explained. "I'm sorry, it's not my fault. I've been hauled down to the Akasaka police station for questioning. It'll take too long to tell you about it now, but it looks like they're going to hold onto me for a while."

"Police? What'd you do?"

"I didn't do anything. There was a murder, and the cops wanted to talk to me. That's all."

"What a drag," Yuki remarked, unmoved.

"I'll say."

"You didn't kill anyone, did you?"

"Of course I didn't kill anyone. I'm a bungler, not a murderer. They're just asking about, you know, circumstances. But I'm sorry I'm going to let you down. I'll make it up to you."

"What a drag," said Yuki, then slammed down the receiver in her inimitable fashion.

I passed the phone back to Fisherman. They had been straining to listen in, but didn't seem to come away with much. If they knew it was a thirteen-year-old girl, you can be sure their opinion of me wouldn't have shot up.

They had me go over the fine points of my movements all day yesterday. They wrote everything I said down. Where I'd gone, what I ate. I gave them the full rundown on the *konnyaku* yam stew I'd eaten for dinner. I explained how I shaved the bonito flakes. They didn't think I was being humorous at all. They just wrote everything down. The pages were mounting fast.

At half past six they sent out for food—salty, greasy, tasteless, terrible—which we all ate with relish. Then we had some lukewarm tea, while they smoked. Then we got back to questions and answers.

At what time had I changed into pajamas? From what page to what page of *The Trial* had I read? I tried to tell them what the story was about, but they didn't show much interest.

At eight o'clock I had to take a leak. Which they let me do alone, happily. I breathed deeply. Not the ideal place to breathe deeply, but at least I could breathe. Poor Mei.

When I got back, Bookish wanted to know about my solitary telephone caller that evening. Who was he? What did he want? What was my relationship with him? Why didn't I call him back? Why was I taking a break from work? Didn't I need to work for a living? Did I declare my taxes?

My question, which I didn't ask, was: Did they actually think all this was helpful? Maybe they *had* read Kafka. Were they trying to wear me down so that I'd let the truth escape? Well, they'd succeeded. I was so exhausted, so depressed, I was answering everything they asked with a straight face. I was under the mistaken impression that I'd get out of here quicker that way.

By eleven, they hadn't stopped. And they showed no sign of stopping. They'd been able to take turns, leave the room and take a nap while the other kept at me. I hadn't had that luxury. Instead, they offered me coffee. Instant coffee, with sugar and white powder mixed in.

At eleven-thirty I made my declaration: I was tired and wasn't going to answer any more questions.

"Aww, c'mon, *pul–eeze*," Bookish said lamely, drumming his fingers on the table. "Listen, we're going as fast as we can, but this investigation is very important. We have a dead lady on our hands, so I'm afraid you're going to have to stick it out."

"I find it hard to believe these questions have any importance at all," I said.

"Petty details serve their purpose. You'd be surprised how many cases are solved by petty details. What looks like petty isn't always petty, especially when it comes to homicide. Murder isn't petty. Sorry, but why don't you just hang around a while. To be perfectly frank, if we felt like it, we could designate you a prime witness and you'd be stuck here as long as we liked. But that would take a lot of paperwork. Bogs everything down. That's why we're being nice, asking you to go through this with us nice and easy. If you cooperate, we won't have to get rough."

"If you're sleepy, there's a bunk downstairs," Fisherman said. "Catch a few hours of shut-eye, you might remember something."

Okay, a few hours sleep would be nice. Anywhere was better than this smoke-filled hole.

Fisherman walked me down a dark corridor, down an even darker stairwell, to another corridor. This was not boding well. Indeed, the bunk room was a holding tank.

"Nice place, but can I get something with a better view?"

"All due apologies. It's our only model," said Fisherman without expression.

"No way. I'm going home. I'll be back tomorrow."

"Don't worry, we're not locking you in," said Fisherman. "A cell is just a room if you don't lock the door."

I was too tired to argue. I gave up. I stumbled in and fell onto the hard cot. Damp mattress, cheap blanket, smell of piss. Love it.

"It won't be locked," Fisherman repeated as he shut the door with a cold, solid *thunk*.

I sighed and pulled the blanket over me. Someone somewhere was snoring loudly. It seemed to come from far off, but it could've been in the next cell. Very disturbing.

But Mei, Mei! You were on my mind last night. I don't know if you were alive at the time, but you were on my mind. I was slowly taking off your clothes, and then we were

making love. It was our little class reunion. I was so relaxed,
I thought someone had loosened the main screw of this
world. But now, Mei, there's nothing I can do for you. Not a
damned thing. I'm sorry. We lead such tenuous lives. I don't
want Gotanda to get caught up in a scandal. I don't want to
ruin his image. He wouldn't get work after that. Trashy
work in a trashy world of trashy images. But he trusted me,
as a friend. So it's a matter of honor. But Mei, my little Goat
Girl Mei, we did have a good time together. It was so wonderful. Like a fairy tale. It's no comfort to you, Mei, but I'll
never forget you. Shoveling snow until dawn. Holding you
tight in that world of images, making love on deductible
expenses. Winnie the Pooh and Mei the Goat Girl. Strangling is a horrible way to die. And you didn't want to die, I
know. But there's nothing I can do for you now. I don't
know what's right or wrong. I'm doing all I can. This is how
I live. It's the system. I bite my lip and do what I got to.
Good night, Mei, my little Goat Girl. At least you'll never
have to wake again. Never have to die again.

Good night, I voiced the words.

Good night, echoed my mind.

Cuck–koo, sang Mei.

22

The next day wasn't much different than the previous. In the morning the three of us reassembled in the interrogation room over a silent breakfast of coffee and bread. Then Bookish loaned me an electric razor, which was not exactly sharp. Since I hadn't planned ahead and brought my toothbrush, I gargled as best I could.

Then the questioning started. Stupid, petty legal torture. This went on at a snail's pace until noon.

"Well, I guess that about does it," said Fisherman, laying his pen down on the desk.

As if by prior agreement, the two detectives sighed simultaneously. So I sighed too. They were obviously stalling for time, but obviously they couldn't keep me here forever. One business card in a dead woman's wallet does not constitute sufficient cause for detention. Even if I didn't have an alibi. They'd have to strap me down—at least until the fingerprinting and autopsy yielded a more plausible suspect.

"Well," said Fisherman, pounding the small of his back as he stretched. "About time for lunch."

"As you seem to have finished your questions, I'll be going home," I told them.

"I'm afraid that's not possible," Fisherman said with fake hesitation.

"And why not?" I asked.

"We need to have you sign the statement you've made."

"I'll sign, I'll sign."

"But first, read over the document to verify that the contents are accurate. Word by word. It's extremely important you know what you're signing your name to."

So I read those forty-odd sheets of official police transcriptions. Two hundred years from now, I couldn't help but think, they might be of some value in reconstructing our era. Pathologically detailed, faultlessly accurate. A real boon to research. The daily habits of an average, thirty-four-year-old, single male. A child of his times. The whole exercise of reading it through in this police interrogation room was depressing. But read it I did, from beginning to end. Now I could go home. I straightened the stack of papers and said that everything looked in order.

Playing with his pen, Fisherman glanced over at Bookish. Bookish pulled a single cigarette from his box of Hope Regulars on top of the radiator, lit up and grimaced into the smoke. I had an awful feeling.

"It's not that simple," Bookish spoke in that slow professional tone reserved for elucidating matters to the unordained. "You see, the statement's got to be in your own hand."

"In my own *hand*?"

"Yes, you have to copy everything over. In your own handwriting. Otherwise, it's not legally valid."

I looked at the stack of pages. I didn't have the strength to be angry. I wanted to be angry, I wanted to fly into a rage, I wanted to pound on the desk and scream, *You jerks have no right to do this!* I wanted to stand up and walk out of there. And strictly speaking, I knew they had no right to stop me. Yes, but I was too tired. Too tired to say a word, too tired to protest. If I wasn't going to protest, I'd be better off doing what I was told. Faster and easier. *I'm wimping out,* I

confessed to myself. *I'm worn out and I'm wimping out.*
Used to be, they'd have to tie me down. But then again, their
junk food and cigarette smoke and razor that chewed up my
face wouldn't have gotten to me either. I was getting weak in
my old age.

"No way," I surprised myself by saying. "I'm going
home. I have the right to go home. You can't stop me."

Bookish sputtered something indecipherable. Fisherman
stared up at the ceiling and rapped his pen on the desk. *Tap-
tap-tap, tap, tap-tap, tap-tap, tap.*

"You're making things difficult," said Fisherman succinctly. "But very well. If that's the way it's going to be, we'll
get a summons. And we'll forcibly hold you here for investigation. Next time won't be such a picnic. We don't mind
that, you know. It'll be easier for us to do our job that way
too. Isn't that right?" he tossed the question over to Bookish.

"Yes sir, that's going to be even easier in the long run.
That's what we should've done earlier. Let's get a summons," he declared.

"As you like," I said. "But I'm free until the summons is
issued. If and when the summons comes through, you know
where to find me. Otherwise, I don't care. I'm outa here."

"We can place a temporary hold on your person until the
summons is issued."

I almost asked them to show me where it said that in
Statutes of Law, but now I *really* didn't have the energy. I
knew they were bluffing, but it didn't matter.

"I give up. I'll write out my statement. But I need to make
a phone call first."

Fisherman passed me the telephone. I dialed Yuki's number.

"I'm still at the police station," I said. "It looks like this'll
take all night. So I guess I won't make it over today either.
Sorry."

"You're still in the clink?"

"A real drag." This time I beat her to the punch.

"That's not fair," she came back. There's a lot of descrip-
tive terms out there.

"What have you been doing?"

"Nothing special," she said. "Just lying around, listening to music, reading magazines, eating cake. You know."

The two detectives tried to listen in again.

"I'll call you as soon as I get out of here."

"*If* you get out of there," said Yuki flatly.

"Well, okay then, lunchtime," announced Fisherman, soon as I hung up.

Lunch was *soba*, cold buckwheat noodles. Overcooked and falling apart. Hospital food, practically a liquid diet. An aura of incurable illness hovered over it. Still, the two of them wolfed the stuff down, and I followed suit. To wash down the starch, Bookish brought in more of his famous lukewarm tea.

The afternoon passed as slowly as a silted-up river. The ticking of the clock was the only sound in the room. A telephone rang in the next room. I did nothing but write and write and write and write. Meanwhile the two detectives took turns resting. Sometimes they'd go out into the corridor and whisper.

I kept the pen moving. *At six-fifteen I decided to make dinner, first taking the yam cake out of the refrigerator . . .*

By evening I'd copied twenty pages. Wielding a pen for hours on end is hard work. Definitely not recommended. Your wrist starts to go limp, you get scribe's elbow. The middle finger of your hand begins to throb. Drift off in your thoughts for a second and you get the word wrong. Then you have to draw a line through it and thumbprint your mistake. It could drive a person batty. It was driving *me* batty.

For dinner, we had generic take-out food again. I hardly ate. The tea was still sloshing around in my gut. I felt woozy, lost the sense of who I was. I went to the toilet and looked in the mirror. I could barely recognize myself.

"Any findings yet?" I asked Fisherman. "Fingerprints or traces or autopsy results?"

"Not yet," he said. "These things take time."

I kept at it until ten. I had five more pages to go, but I'd reached my limit. I couldn't write another word and I told them so. Fisherman conducted me to the tank and I dozed right off.

In the morning, it was the same electric razor, coffee, and bread. The five pages took two hours. Then I signed and thumbprinted each sheet. Then Bookish checked the whole lot.

"Am I free to go now?" I asked hopefully.

"If you answer a few more questions, yes, you can go," said Bookish.

I heaved a sigh. "Then you're going to have me do more paperwork, right?"

"Of course," answered Bookish. "This is officialdom. Paperwork is everything. Without the paper and your prints, it doesn't exist."

I pressed my fingers into my temples. It felt as if some loose object were lodged inside. As if something had found its way into my head and ballooned up to where it was impossible to remove.

"This won't take too long. Be over before you know it."

More mindless answers to more mindless questions. Then Fisherman called Bookish out into the corridor. The two stood whispering for I don't know how long. I leaned back in my chair and studied the patterns of mildew on the ceiling. The blackened patches could have been photographs of pubic hair on dead bodies. Spreading down along the cracks in the wall like a connect-the-dots picture. Mildew, cultured in the body odor of the poor fools ground down in this room the last several decades. From a systematic effort to undermine a person's beliefs, dignity, and sense of right and wrong. From psychological coercion that fed on human insecurity and left no visible scars. Where far removed from sunlight and stuffed with bad food, you sweat uncontrollably. Mildew.

I placed both hands on the desk and closed my eyes,

thinking of the snow falling in Sapporo. The Dolphin Hotel and my receptionist friend with glasses. How was she getting along? Standing behind the counter, flashing that professional smile of hers? I wanted to call her up this very second. Tell her some stupid joke. But I didn't even know her name. *I didn't even know her name.*

She sure was cute. Especially when she was working hard. Imbued with that indefinable hotel spirit. She loved her work. Not me. I never once enjoyed mine. I do good work, but I have never *loved* my work. Away from her work, she was vulnerable, uncertain, fragile. I could have slept with her if I'd felt like it. But I didn't.

I want to talk to her again.

Before someone killed her too.

Before she disappeared.

23 ———

The two detectives came back into the room to find me still lost in the mildew. They both stood.

"You can go home now," Fisherman told me, expressionless. "Thanks for your cooperation."

"No more questions. You're done," Bookish added his comments.

"Circumstances have changed," Fisherman said. "We can't keep you here any longer. You're free to go. Thank you again."

I got up from my chair and pulled on my jacket, which reeked of cigarette smoke. I didn't have a clue what had happened, but I was happy to get the hell out of there. Bookish accompanied me to the entrance.

"Listen, we knew you were clean last night," he said. "We got the results from the coroner and the lab. You were clean. Absolutely clean. But you're hiding something. You're biting your tongue. You're not so hard to read. That's why we figured we'd hold you, until you spit it out. You know who that woman is. You just don't want to tell us. For some reason. You know, that's not playing ball. We're not going to forget that."

"Forgive me, but I don't know what you're talking about," I said.

"We might call you in again," he said, digging into his cuticle with a matchstick. "And if we do, you can be sure we'll work you over good. We'll be so on top of things that lawyer of yours won't be able to do a damn thing."

"Lawyer?" I asked, all innocence.

But by then he'd disappeared into the building. I grabbed a taxi back home.

I ran a bath and took a nice, long soak. I brushed my teeth, washed my face, shaved. I couldn't get rid of the smoke on me. What a hole that place was!

Refreshed, I boiled some cauliflower, which I ate along with a beer. I put on Arthur Prysock backed by the Count Basie Orchestra. An unabashedly gorgeous record. Bought sixteen years before. Once upon a time.

After that I slept. Just enough sleep to say I'd been somewhere and back, maybe thirty minutes. When I woke up, it was one in the afternoon. Still time in the day. I packed my gear, threw it into the Subaru, and drove to the Sendagaya Pool. After an hour's swim I was almost feeling human again. And I was hungry.

I called Yuki. When I reported that I'd been released, she gave me a cool *that's nice*. As for food, she'd eaten only two cream puffs all day, sticking to her junk-ridden regimen. If I came over now, though, she'd be ready and waiting, and probably pleased.

I tooled the Subaru through the outer gardens of Meiji Shrine, down the tree-lined avenue before the art museum, and turned at Aoyama-Itchome for Nogi Shrine. Every day was getting more and more like spring. During the two days I'd spent inside the Akasaka police station, the breeze had become more placid, the leaves greener, the sunlight fuller and softer. Even the noises of the city sounded as pleasant as Art Farmer's flügelhorn. All was right with the world and I was hungry. The pressure lodged behind my temples had magically vanished.

Yuki was wearing a David Bowie sweatshirt under a brown leather jacket. Her canvas shoulder bag was a patchwork of Stray Cats and Steely Dan and Culture Club buttons. Strange combination, but who was I to say?

"Have fun with the cops?" asked Yuki.

"Just awful," I said. "Ranks up there with Boy George's singing."

"Oh," she remarked, unimpressed with my cleverness.

"Remind me to buy you an Elvis button for your collection," I said, pointing at her bag.

"What a nerd," she said. Such a rich vocabulary.

We went to a restaurant where we each had a roast beef sandwich on whole wheat and a salad. I made her drink a glass of wholesome milk too. I skipped the milk for myself, got coffee instead. The meat was tender and alive with horseradish. Very satisfying. *This* was a meal.

"Well then, where to from here?" I asked Yuki.

"Tsujido," she said without hesitation.

"Okay by me," I said. "To Tsujido we shall go. But what's there to see in Tsujido?"

"Papa lives there," said Yuki. "He says he wants to meet you."

"Me?"

"Yeah, you. Don't worry, he's not such a bad guy."

I sipped my second cup of coffee. "You know, I never said he was a bad guy. Anyway, why would he want to meet me? You told him about me?"

"Sure. I phoned him and told him how you'd helped me get back from Hokkaido and how you got picked up by the cops and might never come out. So Papa had one of his lawyer friends make inquiries about you. He's got all kinds of connections. He's real practical that way."

"I see," I said. "So that's what it was."

"He can be handy sometimes."

"I'll say."

"Papa said that the police had no right to hold you there like that. If you didn't want to stay there, you were free to go. Legally, that is."

"I knew that myself," I said.

"Why didn't you just go home then? Just up and say, I'm going. *Sayonara*."

"That's a difficult question," I said after some moments' thought. "Maybe I was punishing myself."

"Not normal," she said, propping up her chin.

It was late in the afternoon and the roads to Tsujido were empty. Yuki had brought a bagful of tapes with her. A complete travel selection, from Bob Marley's "Exodus" to Styx's "Mister Roboto." Some were interesting, some not. Which was pretty much all you could say about the scenery on the way. It all sped past. Yuki sank into her seat silently listening to the music. She tried on the pair of sunglasses I'd left on the dashboard, and at one point she lit up a Virginia Slim. I concentrated on driving. Methodically shifting gears, eyes fixed on the road ahead, carefully checking each traffic sign.

I was jealous of Yuki. Here she was, thirteen years old, and everything, including misery, looked, if not wonderful, at least new. Music and places and people. So different from me. True, I'd been in her place before, but the world was a simpler place then. You got what you worked for, words meant something, things had beauty. But I *wasn't* happy. I was an impossible kid at an impossible age. I wanted to be alone, felt good being alone, but never had the chance. I was locked in these two frames, home and school. I had this crush on a girl, which I didn't know what to do about. I didn't know what love meant. I was awkward and introverted. I wanted to rebel against my teachers and parents, but I didn't know how. Whatever I did, I bungled. I was the exact opposite of Gotanda.

Even so, there were times that I saw freshness and beauty. I could smell the air, and I really loved rock 'n' roll. Tears were warm, and girls were beautiful, like dreams. I liked movie theaters, the darkness and intimacy, and I liked the deep, sad summer nights.

"Hey," I said to Yuki. "Could you tell about that man in

the sheepskin? Where did you meet him? And how did you know I'd met him too?"

She looked at me, placing the sunglasses back on the dashboard, then shrugged. "Okay, but first, will you answer something for me?"

"I guess so," I agreed.

Yuki hummed along with a hangover-heavy Phil Collins song for a moment, then picked up the sunglasses again and played with them. "Do you remember what you said after we got back from Hokkaido? That I was the prettiest girl you ever dated?"

"Uh-huh."

"Did you mean that? Or were you just trying to make me like you? Tell me honestly."

"Honestly, it's the truth," I said.

"How many girls have you dated, up to now?"

"I haven't counted."

"Two hundred?"

"Oh, come on," I laughed. "I'm not that kind of a guy. I may play the field, but my field's not that big. I'd say fifteen, max."

"That few?"

I nodded. This gave her something to puzzle over.

"Fifteen, huh?"

"Around there," I said. "Twenty on the outside."

"Twenty, huh?" sighed a disappointed Yuki. "But out of all of them, I'm the prettiest?"

"Yes, you are the prettiest," I said.

"You never liked the beautiful type?" she asked, lighting up her second Virginia Slim. I spotted a policeman at the intersection ahead, grabbed the cigarette out of her hand, and flung it out the window.

"I dated some pretty girls," I went on. "But none of them was as pretty as you. I mean that. You probably will take this wrong, but you're pretty in a different way. Nothing like most girls. But please, no smoking in the car, okay? You'll stink it up. And I don't want cops poking their nose in.

Besides, don't you know that girls who smoke too much when they're young get irregular periods?"

"Gimme a break," she cried.

"Now tell me about the guy in the sheepskin," I said.

"The Sheep Man?"

"How do you know that was his name?"

"You said it over the phone. *The Sheep Man.*"

"Did I?"

"Uh-huh."

We were stopped at an intersection, waiting for the light to change. Traffic, as we neared Tsujido, had picked up, and the light had to change twice before we could move on.

"So about the Sheep Man. Where did you see him?"

Yuki shrugged. "I never saw him. He just came into my head, when I saw you," she said, winding a strand of her fine straight hair around her finger. "I just had this feeling. About a guy dressed in a sheepskin. Like a hunch. Whenever I ran into you at the hotel, I had this . . . feeling. So I brought it up. That was it."

I tried to make sense of that. I had to think, had to wrack my brains.

"What do you mean by *like a hunch*?" I pressed her. "You mean you didn't really see him? Or you only caught a *glimpse* of him?"

"I don't know how to put it," she said. "It wasn't like I saw him with my own eyes. It was more this feeling that *someone* had seen him, even though he was invisible. I couldn't see anything, but inside, the feeling I had had a kind of shape. Not a definite shape. Something like a shape. If I had to show it to someone, they probably wouldn't know what it was. It could only make sense to me. I'm not explaining this very well. Am I coming through at all?"

"Vaguely."

Yuki raised her eyebrows and nibbled at the frame of my sunglasses.

"Let me go over this again," I tried. "You sensed something in me, some kind of feeling, or ideation—"

"Ideation?"

"A very strong thought. And it was attached to me and you visualized it, like you do in a dream. You mean something like that?"

"Yeah, something kind of like that. A strong thought, but not only that. There was some *thing* behind it. Something powerful. Like energy that was creating the thinking. I could just feel that it was out there. They were like vibes that I could see. But not like a dream. Like an *empty dream*. That's it, an empty dream. Nobody's there, so you don't see anybody. You know, like when you turn the contrast on the TV real low and the brightness way up. You can't see a thing. But there's an image in the picture, and if you squint real hard, you can *feel* what the image is. You know what I mean?"

"Uh-huh."

"Anyway, I could sort of see this man in a sheepskin. He didn't seem evil or anything like that. Maybe he wasn't even a man. But the thing is, he wasn't bad. I don't know how to put it. You can't see it, but it's like a heat rubbing, you know it's something, like a form without a shape." She clicked her tongue. "Sorry, awful explanation."

"You're explaining just fine."

"Really?"

"Really," I said.

We continued our drive along the sea. Beside a pine grove, I pulled the car over and suggested we go for a short walk. The afternoon was pleasant, hardly any wind, the surf gentle. Just a rippling sheet of tiny waves drawing in toward shore. Perfect peaceful periodicity. The surfers had all given up and were sitting around on the beach in their wet suits, smoking. The white smoke trail from burning trash rose nearly straight up into the blue, and off to the left drifted the island of Enoshima, faint and miragelike. A large black dog trotted across the breakers from right to left. In the distance fishing boats dotted the deeper waters, while noiseless white clouds of sea gulls swirled above them. Spring had come even to the sea.

Yuki and I strolled the path along the shore, passing joggers and high school girls on bicycles going the other way. We ambled in the direction of Fujisawa, then we sat down on the sand and looked out to sea.

"Do you often have experiences like that?" I asked.

"Sometimes," said Yuki. "Rarely, actually. I get these feelings from very few people. And I try to avoid them if I can. If I get a feeling, I try not to think about it, I try to close it off. That way I don't have to feel it so deep. It's like if you close your eyes, you don't have to see what's in front of you. You know something's there, like with a scary part in the movies, but you don't have to see it if you shut your eyes and keep them shut until the scary part is over."

"But why should you close yourself up?"

"Because it's horrible to see it," she said. "When I was small, I didn't close up. At school, if I felt something, I just came right out and told everybody about it. But then, it made everyone sick. If someone was going to get hurt, I'd say, so-and-so is going to get hurt, and sure enough, she would. That happened over and over again, until everyone started treating me like a weird spook. That's what they called me. 'Spook.' That was the kind of reputation I had. It was terrible. So ever since then, I decided not to say anything. And now if I feel like I'm going to feel anything, I just close myself up."

"But with me you didn't close up."

She shrugged. "It was an accident. There wasn't any warning. Really, suddenly, the image just popped up. The very first time I saw you. I was listening to music . . . Duran Duran or David Bowie or somebody . . . and I wasn't on guard. I was relaxed. That's why I like music."

"Then you're kind of clairvoyant?" I asked. "Like when, say, you knew beforehand that a classmate was going to get hurt."

"Maybe. But kind of different. When something's going to happen, there's this atmosphere that gives me the feeling it's going to happen. I know it sounds funny, for instance, with someone who's going to get injured on the high bar, there's this carelessness or this overconfidence that's in the air, almost like waves. People who are sensitive can pick up these waves. They're like pockets in the air, maybe even solid pockets in the air. You can tell that there's danger. That's when those empty dreams pop up. And when they do . . . Well, that's what they are. They aren't like premonitions. They're more unfocused. But they appear and I can see them but I'm not talking about them anymore. I don't want people calling me a spook. I just keep my mouth shut. I might see that that person over there is maybe going to get burned. And maybe he does get burned. But he can't blame me. Isn't that horrible? I hate myself for it. That's why I close up. If I close myself, I don't hate myself."

She scooped up sand and sifted it through her fingers.

"Is there really a Sheep Man?" she asked.

"Yes, there really is," I said. "There's a place in that hotel where he lives. A whole other hotel in that hotel. You can't see it most of the time. But it's there. That's where the Sheep Man lives, and all sorts of things connect to me through there. The Sheep Man is kind of like my caretaker, kind of like a switchboard operator. If he weren't around, I wouldn't be able to connect anymore."

"Huh? Connect?"

"Yeah, when I'm in search of something, when I want to connect, he's the one who does it."

"I don't get it."

I scooped up some sand and let it run through my fingers too.

"I still don't really understand it myself. But that's how the Sheep Man explained it to me."

"You mean, the Sheep Man's been there from way back?"

"Uh-huh, for ages. Since I was a kid. But I didn't realize he had the form of the Sheep Man until not so long ago.

Why is he around? I don't know. Maybe I needed him. Maybe because as you get older, things fall apart, so something needs to help hold things together. Put the brakes a little on entropy, you know. But how do I know? The more I think about it, the stranger it seems. Stupid even."

"You ever tell anybody else about it?"

"No. If I did, who would believe me? Who would understand what the hell I was talking about? And anyway, I can't explain it very well. You're the first person I've told."

"I've never talked to anybody about this thing I have either. Mama and Papa know about it a little, but we never discussed it or anything. After what happened in school, I just clamped up about it."

"Well, I guess I'm glad we had this talk," I said.

"Welcome to the Spook Club," said Yuki.

"I haven't gone to school since last summer vacation," Yuki told me as we strolled back to the car. "It's not because I don't like to study. I just hate the place. I can't stand it. It makes me sick, physically sick. I was puking every day and every time I puked, they'd gang up on me some more. Even the teachers were picking on me."

"Why would anyone want to pick on someone as pretty as you?"

"Kids just like to pick on other kids. And if your parents are famous, it can be even worse. Sometimes they treat you special, but with me, they treat me like trash. Anyway, I have trouble getting along with people to begin with. I'm always tense because I might have to close myself up any moment, you know. So I developed this nervous twitch, which makes me look like a duck, and they tease me about that. Kids can be really mean. You wouldn't believe how mean . . ."

"It's all right," I said, grabbing for Yuki's hand and holding it. "Forget about them. If you don't feel like going to school, don't. Don't force yourself. School can be a real nightmare. I know. You have these brown-nosing idiots for classmates and these teachers who act like they own the world. Eighty percent of them are deadbeats or sadists, or both. Plus all those ridiculous rules. The whole system's designed to crush you, and so the goodie-goodies with no imagination get good grades. I bet that hasn't changed a bit."

"Was it like that for you too?"

"Of course. I could talk a blue streak about how idiotic school is."

"But junior high school is compulsory."

"That's for other people to worry about, not you. It's not compulsory to go someplace where you're miserable. Not at all. You have rights too, you know."

"And then what do I do after that? Is it always going to be like this?"

"Things sure seemed that way when I was thirteen," I said. "But that's not how it happens. Things can work out. And if they don't, well, you can deal with that when the time comes. Get a little older, you'll fall in love. You'll buy brassieres. The whole way you look at the world will change."

"Boy, are you a dolt!" she turned to me and shook her head in disbelief. "For your information, thirteen-year-old girls already wear bras. You're half a century behind, I swear!"

"I'm only thirty-four," I reminded her.

"Fifty years," said Yuki. "Time flies when you're a dolt."

And at that, she walked to the car ahead of me.

24

By the time we reached Yuki's father's house near the beach, it was dusk. The house was big and old, the property thick with trees. The area exuded the old charm of a Shonan resort villa. In the grace of the spring evening all was still. Cherry trees were beginning to fill out with buds, a prelude to the magnolias. A masterful orchestration of colors and scents whose change day to day reflected the sweep of the seasons. To think there were still places like this.

The Makimura villa was circumscribed by a high wooden fence, the gate surmounted by a small, traditional gabled roof. Only the nameplate was new. We rang the doorbell and soon a tall youth in his mid-twenties came to let us in. With short-cropped hair and a pleasant smile, he was clean-cut and amiable—not unlike Gotanda but without the refinement. Apparently Yuki had met him several times before. Leading us around to the back of the house, he introduced himself as Makimura's assistant.

"I act as his chauffeur, deliver his manuscripts, research, caddy, accompany him overseas, whatever," he explained eagerly. "I am what in times past was known as a gentleman's valet."

"Ah," I said.

I felt sure Yuki was about to come out with something

rude, but to my surprise she said nothing. Apparently she could be discreet if she wanted to.

Makimura was practicing his golf swing in the backyard. A green net had been stretched between the trunks of two pines. The famous writer was trying to hit the target in the center with little white balls. When his club sliced through the air, you'd hear this *whoosh*. One of my least favorite sounds. Asthmatic and hollow. Though it was pure prejudice that I should feel that way. I hated golf.

Makimura set down his club and wiped his forehead with a towel. "Good to see you," he said to Yuki, who pretended not to have heard. Averting her eyes, she fished a stick of gum from the pocket of her jacket and began to chew with loud *crack*s. Then she wadded up the wrapper and tossed it into a potted plant.

"How about a hello at least?" Makimura tried again.

"Hello," Yuki sneered, plunging her hands into her pockets and wandering off.

"Boy, bring us some beer," Makimura called out rather curtly.

"Yes sir," the manservant answered in a clear voice and hurried into the house. Makimura coughed and spat, wiped his forehead again. Then ignoring my presence for the time being, he squinted at the target on the green net and concentrated. I concerned myself idly with the moss-covered rocks.

The whole scene seemed artificial—and more than a little absurd. There wasn't anything specific that seemed odd. It was more the sense that I had happened upon the stage of an elaborate parody. The author and his valet—except that Gotanda could have played either role better and with more sophistication and appeal.

"Yuki tells me you've been looking after her," said the famous man.

"It wasn't anything special," I said. "I merely got her onto a flight coming back from Hokkaido. More important, though, let me thank you for the help with the police."

"Uh, oh that? No, not at all. Glad to be able to return a

favor. It's so rare that my daughter asks me for anything. I
was very happy to help. I hate the police. I had a run-in with
them at the Diet way back in the sixties when Michiko
Kanba was killed. Back in those times—"

At that he bent over from the waist and gripped his golf
club, tapping its head on his foot. He turned to look me in
the face, then glanced down at my feet and up at my face
again.

"—when a man knew what was right and what wasn't
right," said Hiraku Makimura.

I nodded without much conviction.

"You play golf?"

"I'm afraid not," I said.

"You dislike golf?"

"I don't like it or dislike it. I've never played."

He laughed. "There's no such thing as not liking or dislik-
ing golf. People who've never played golf hate golf. That's
the way it is. So be honest with me."

"Okay, I don't like golf," I said.

"Why not?"

"I guess it strikes me as silly. The overblown gear, the cute
carts, the flags and the pompous clothes and shoes. The look
in the eyes, the way ears prick up when you crouch down to
read the turf. Little things like that bother me."

"The way ears prick up?"

"Just something I've observed. It doesn't mean anything.
But there's something about golf that doesn't sit well with
me," I answered, summing up.

Makimura stared at me blankly.

"Is there something wrong with you, son?"

"Not at all," I said. "I'm perfectly normal. I guess my
jokes aren't very funny."

Before long, the manservant brought out beer on a tray
with two glasses. He set the tray down, poured for us, then
quickly disappeared.

"Cheers," said Makimura, raising his glass.

"Cheers," I said, doing the same.

I couldn't quite place Makimura's age, but he had to be at least in his mid-forties. He wasn't tall, but his solid frame made him seem like a large man. Broad-chested, thick arms and neck. His neck was thick. If it were trimmer, he could have passed for a sportsman, as opposed to someone with years of dissipated living. I remembered photos of a young, slender Makimura with a piercing gaze. He hadn't been particularly handsome, but he had presence, which he still had. How many years ago had it been? Fifteen? Sixteen? Today, his hair was short, peppered with gray. He was well-tanned and wore a wine-red Lacoste shirt, which couldn't be buttoned around the neck.

"I hear you are a writer," said Makimura.

"Not a real writer," I said. "I produce fill on demand. Negligible stuff, based on how many words they need. Somebody's got to do it, and I figure it might as well be me. I'll spare you my spiel about shoveling snow."

"Shoveling snow, huh?" repeated Makimura, glancing over at the golf clubs he'd set aside. "Clever notion."

"Pleased you think so," I said.

"Well, you like writing?"

"I can't say I like or dislike it. I'm proficient at it, or should I say efficient? I've got the knack, the know-how, the stance, the punch, all that. I don't mind that aspect."

"Uh-huh."

"If the level of the job is low enough, it's very simple anyway."

"Hmm," he mused, pausing several seconds. "You think up that phrase, 'shoveling snow'?"

"I did," I said.

"Mind if I use it somewhere? It's an interesting expression."

"Go right ahead. I didn't take out a copyright on it."

"It's exactly the way I feel sometimes," said Makimura, fingering his earlobe. "That it doesn't amount to a hill of beans. It didn't used to be that way. The world was smaller, you could get a handle on things, you knew—or thought you knew—what you were doing. You knew what people wanted. The media wasn't this huge, vast thing."

He drained his glass, then poured us two more glasses. I declined, said I was driving, but he ignored me.

"But not now. There's no justice. No one cares. People do whatever they have to do to survive. Shoveling snow. Just like you say," he said, eyeing the green net stretched between the tree trunks. Thirty or forty white golf balls lay on the grass.

Makimura seemed to be thinking of what to say next. That took time. Not that it concerned him, he was used to people waiting on his every word. I decided to do the same. He kept pulling at his earlobe.

"My daughter's taken to you," Makimura began again, finally. "And she doesn't take to just anyone. Or rather, she doesn't take to almost everyone. She hardly says a word to me. She doesn't say much to her mother either, but at least she respects her. She's got no respect for me. None whatsoever. She thinks I'm a fool. She hasn't got any friends. She doesn't go to school, she just stays in her room alone, listening to that noise she calls music. She's got problems with people. But for some reason, you, she takes to you. I don't know why."

"Me either."

"Maybe you're a kindred spirit?"

"Maybe."

"Tell me, what do you think of Yuki?"

This was starting to feel like a job interview. "Yuki's thirteen, a terrible age," I answered straightforwardly. "And from what I can see, her home environment's a disaster. No one looks after her. No one takes responsibility for her. No one talks to her. She's lonely and she's hurt. She's got two famous parents. She's too beautiful for her own good. And she's acutely sensitive to everything around her. That's a pretty heavy burden for a thirteen-year-old girl to bear."

"And no one's giving her proper attention."

"That's what I think."

He heaved a long sigh. He let go of his ear and stared at his fingers. "I think you're right, absolutely right. But *I* can't do a thing about it. When her mother and I divorced, I signed papers that said I would lay off Yuki. I can't get around that. I wasn't the most faithful husband at the time, so I wasn't in any position to contest it. In fact, I'm supposed to get Amé's permission even before seeing Yuki like this. And the other thing is, like I said before, Yuki doesn't have a whole lot of respect for me. So I'm in a double bind. But I'd do anything for her if I could."

He turned his gaze back toward the green net. Evening was gathering, darker and deeper.

"Still, things can't continue the way they've been going," I said. "You know that her mother flew off to Kathmandu and it was three days before she remembered that Yuki was still in that hotel in Hokkaido? Three days! And after I brought Yuki back to Tokyo, she stayed in that apartment and didn't go anywhere for days. As far as I know, all she did was listen to rock and eat junk food. I hate to sound wholesome and middle-class, but this isn't healthy."

"I'm not arguing. What you say is one hundred percent correct," said Makimura. "No, make that two hundred percent. That's why I wanted to talk to you. Why I had you come all the way down here."

I had an ominous feeling. The horses were dead. The Indians had stopped beating their drums. It was too quiet. I scratched my temple.

"I was wondering," he began cautiously, "if you wouldn't like to look after Yuki. Nothing formal or anything like that. Just two or three hours a day. Spend time with her, make sure she's all right and eating reasonable meals. That's all. I'll pay you for your time. You can think of it as tutoring without having to teach. I don't know how much you make, but I can guarantee you something close to that. The rest of the time you can do as you like. That's not such a bad deal, is it? I've already talked to her mother about it. She's in Hawaii now, and she agreed that it was a good idea. Even if it doesn't look that way, she has Yuki's best interests at heart, really. She's just . . . different. She's brilliant, but sometimes her head's off in the stratosphere. She forgets about people and things around her. She even has trouble with arithmetic."

"Right," I said, smiling without much conviction, "but what Yuki needs more than anything else is a parent's love—you know, completely unconditional love. I'm not her parent and I can't give her that. She also needs friends her own age. Which leads me to another thing: I'm a man, and I'm too old. A thirteen-year-old girl is already a woman in some ways. Yuki's very pretty and emotionally unstable. Are you going to put a girl like that in the care of some guy out of nowhere? What do you know about me? I was just hauled in by the cops in connection with a homicide. What if I was the murderer?"

"Are you the killer?"

"Of course not."

"Well, then what's the problem? I trust you. If you say you're not the killer, then you're not the killer."

"But why trust me?"

"You don't seem the killer type. You don't seem the statutory rapist type either. Those things are pretty clear," said Makimura. "Plus Yuki's the key here, and I trust Yuki's instincts. Sometimes, as a matter of fact, her instincts are too acute for comfort. She's like a medium. There've been times when I could tell she was seeing something I couldn't. Know what I mean?"

"Kind of," I said.

"She gets it from her mother. It's her eccentric side. Her mother focused all of it on her art. That way, people call it talent. But Yuki hasn't got any place to direct that side of her, not yet anyway. It's just overflowing, with no place to go. Like water spilling out of a bucket. I'm not like either of them. I'm not eccentric. Which is why neither of them gives

me the time of day. When we were living together, it got so I
didn't want to see another woman's face. I don't know if you
can imagine what it was like, living with Amé and Yuki.
Rain and snow. Amé's private joke! Frigging weather report.
They wore me out completely. Of course I love them both. I
still talk to Amé now and then. But I don't ever want to live
with her again. That was hell. I may have had talent once,
but living like that sapped me dry. That's the truth. But even
so, I haven't done badly, I must say. Shoveling snow, huh? I
like that. But we're getting off track—what were we talking
about?"

"About whether you should trust me."

"That's right. I trust Yuki's intuition. Yuki trusts you.
Therefore I trust you. And you can trust me. I'm not such a
bad person. I may write crap, but I can be trusted," he said,
spitting again. "Well, how about it? Will you look after
Yuki? What you've said about the role of the parent isn't lost
on me. I agree entirely. But the kid is, well, exceptional. And
as you can see, she'll barely talk to me. You're the only one I
can depend on."

I peered down into the foam of the beer in my glass.
What was I supposed to do? Strange family. Three misfits
and Boy Friday. Space Family Robinson.

"I don't mind seeing Yuki that often," I said, "but I can't,
I won't, do it every day. I have my own life to look after, and
I don't like seeing people out of obligation. I'll see her when
I feel like it. I don't need your money, I don't want your
money. I'm not hard up and the money I spend with Yuki
won't be any different than the money I spend with friends. I
like Yuki a lot and I enjoy seeing her, but I don't want the
responsibility. Do you read me? Because whatever happens
with Yuki, the responsibility ultimately comes back to you."

Makimura nodded several times. The rolls of flesh
beneath his ears quivered. Golf wasn't going to trim away
that fat. That called for a whole change of life. But that was
beyond him. If he'd been capable, he'd have changed long
ago.

"I understand what you're saying, son, and it makes a lot of sense," he said. "I'm not trying to push any responsibility onto you. No need to assume responsibility at all. I just don't have any other options, so I bow to your judgment. This isn't about responsibility. And the money we can think about when the time comes. I'm a man who always pays his debts. Just remember that. I leave it to you. You do as you like. If you need money, you get in touch with me or Amé. Neither of us is short in that department. So don't be a stranger."

I didn't say a word.

"I'd say you're one stubborn young man," Makimura added.

"I'm not stubborn. I just work according to my system."

"Your system," he said. Then he fingered his earlobe again. "Your system may be beside the point these days. It went out with handmade vacuum tube amplifiers. Instead of wasting all your time trying to build your own, you ought to buy a brand-new transistor job. It's cheaper and it sounds better. And if it breaks down they come fix it in no time. When it gets old, you can trade it in. Your system may not be so watertight anymore, son. It might've been worth something once upon a time. But not now. Nowadays money talks. It's whatever money will buy. You can buy off the rack and piece it all together. It's simple. It's not so bad. Get stuck on your system and you'll be left behind. You can't cut tight turns and you get in everybody's way."

"Advanced capitalist society."

"You got it," said Makimura. Then he fell silent.

Nearby a dog was baying neurotically. Someone was fumbling through a Mozart piano sonata. Makimura sat down on the back porch with his beer, thinking.

Darkness was swallowing the whole scene. Things were losing their shapes and melting together. Suddenly there was Gotanda, his graceful fingers stroking Kiki's bare back; there were the snow-swept streets of Sapporo, *Cuck–koo* from Mei the Goat Girl, the flatfoot rapping the plastic ruler in the palm of his hand, the Sheep Man at the end of a dark corridor, . . . all fusing and blending. I must be tired, I thought. But I wasn't. It was only the essence of things leaching away, then swirling into chaos. And I was looking down on it as if it were some cosmic sphere. A piano played, a dog barked, someone was saying something. Someone was speaking to me.

"Say, son—." It was Makimura.

I glanced up at him.

"You know something about that murdered woman, don't you?" he was saying. "The newspapers say they still don't know who she is, and the only lead is a business card in her wallet. They were supposed to be questioning that party, but your name didn't come out. According to my lawyer, you pulled one over on them. You said you didn't know anything, but that's not to say you don't, am I right?"

"What makes you think that?"

"I just do," he said, picking up a golf club and holding it straight out like a sword. "The more I listened to you talk, the more it kind of grew on me. You fuss over tiny details, but you're awful generous with big things. There's a pattern that builds up. I figure you know more than you say, maybe you're covering for somebody. You're an interesting character. Almost like Yuki that way. You have a hard time just surviving. This time you came through okay, but the next time you may not be so lucky. Remember, the police aren't so nice. I've got no beef with your system—I actually have respect for it—but you could get hurt, sticking to your guns like that. Times have changed. You got to adapt."

"I'm not sticking to my guns," I said. "It's more like just a dance. Something the body remembers. It's a habit. The music plays, the body moves. It almost doesn't matter what else is happening. If too many things get in my head, I might end up blowing my steps. I'm clumsy, not trendy."

Hiraku Makimura glared at his golf club in silence.

"You're odd, you know?" he said. "You remind me of something."

"Same here." Picasso's *Dutch Vase and Three Bearded Knights*?

"I like you, son. I trust you as a person. I'm sorry that I have to ask you to look out for Yuki. But I'll make it up to you someday. I always repay favors. Like I said before."

"I heard."

25

At seven o'clock, Yuki came sauntering back. She'd
been walking on the beach. Would she like dinner,
then? Not hungry, she said. She wanted to go home.

"Well, drop by whenever you feel in the mood," said her
father. "This month I'll be in Japan straight through." Then
he turned to me and thanked me for making the long trip,
apologizing for not being able to be more hospitable.

Boy Friday saw us out. As we turned the corner from the
backyard, I spied a four-wheel-drive Jeep Cherokee, a
Honda 750cc, and an off-road mountain bike parked in a
corner of the grounds.

"Heavy-duty living, eh?" I commented to Friday.

"Well, it's not namby-pamby," Friday responded after a
moment. "Mr. Makimura doesn't live in an ivory tower. He's
into action, he lives for adventure."

"A bozo," Yuki mumbled.

Both Friday and I pretended not to have heard her.

No sooner had we gotten into the Subaru than Yuki said
she was famished. I pulled into a Hungry Tiger along the
coast road and we ordered steaks.

"What did you talk about?" she asked me over dessert.

There was no reason to hide anything, so I gave her a
general recap.

"Figures," she sneered. "Just the sort of thing he'd dream up. What'd you tell him?"

"I said I wasn't cut out for an arrangement like that. It wouldn't be bad, us getting together and hanging out, whenever we wanted to. That could be fun, but no formal arrangement. You know, I may be an old man next to you, but we still have plenty to talk about, don't you think?"

She shrugged.

"If you didn't feel like seeing me, you could just say so. People shouldn't feel obligated to see each other. See me when you feel like it. We could tell each other things we can't say to anyone else, share secrets. Or no?"

She seemed to hesitate, then nodded, "Umm."

"You shouldn't let the stuff build up inside. It gets to a point where you can't keep it under control. You got to let off the pressure or it'll explode. *Bang!* Know what I mean? Life is hard enough. Holding down the fort all by your lonesome is tough. And it's tough for me too. But the two of us, I think maybe we can understand each other. We can talk pretty honestly."

She nodded.

"I can't force you. But if you want to talk, just call up. This has nothing to do with what your father and I discussed. And try not to think of me as a big brother or something. We're friends. I think we can be good for each other."

Yuki didn't respond. She finished off her dessert and gulped down a glass of water. Then she peered over at the heavyset family stuffing their jowls at the next table. Mother and father and daughter and baby brother. All wonderfully rotund.

I planted my elbows on the table and drank my coffee, watching Yuki watch them. She was truly a beautiful girl. I could feel a small polished stone sinking through the darkest waters of my heart. All those deep convoluted channels and passageways, and yet she managed to toss her pebble right down to the bottom of it all. If I were fifteen, I'd have been a goner for sure, I thought for the twentieth time.

How could her classmates be so rotten? Was her beauty too much to be around everyday? Too pointed? Too intense? Too aloof? Did she make them afraid of her?

Well, she certainly wasn't cool like Gotanda. Gotanda had this remarkable awareness of the effect he had on others, and he held it in reserve. He controlled it. He never lorded it over people, never scared them off. And even when his presence had inflated to star proportions, he could smile and joke about it. It was his nature. That way everyone around him could smile along and think, *Now there's one nice guy*. And Gotanda really was a nice guy. But Yuki was different. Yuki was not nice.

She didn't have it in her to keep tabs on everyone else's emotions and then to fit her own emotions in without stomping on people. It was all she could do to keep on top of herself. As a result, she hurt others, which only hurt herself. A hard life. A little too hard for a thirteen-year-old. Hard even for an adult.

I couldn't begin to predict what the girl would do from here on. Maybe she'd find a way to express herself, like her mother did, and make her way in art. Maybe she'd channel her powers into something positive. I couldn't swear to it, but like her father, I could sense an aura, a talent, in her. She was extraordinary.

Then again, she might become a perfectly normal eighteen-year-old. It wouldn't be the first time.

Humans achieve their peak in different ways. But whoever you are, once you're over the summit, it's downhill all the way. Nothing anyone can do about it. And the worst of it is, you never know where that peak is. You think you're still going strong, when suddenly you've crossed the great divide. No one can tell. Some people peak at twelve, then lead rather uneventful lives from then on. Some carry on until they die; some die at their peak. Poets and composers have lived like furies, pushing themselves to such a pitch they're gone by thirty. Then there are those like Picasso, who kept breaking ground until well past eighty.

And what about me?

My peak? Would I even have one? I hardly had had anything you could call a life. A few ripples. Some rises and falls. But that's it. Almost nothing. Nothing born of nothing. I'd loved and been loved, but I had nothing to show. It was a singularly plain, featureless landscape. I felt like I was in a video game. A surrogate Pacman, crunching blindly through a labyrinth of dotted lines. The only certainty was my death.

No promises you're gonna be happy, the Sheep Man had said. *So you gotta dance. Dance so it all keeps spinning.*

I gave up and closed my eyes.

When I opened them again, Yuki was sitting across the table from me.

"You okay?" she said, concerned. "You looked like you blew a fuse. Did I say something wrong?"

I smiled. "No, it wasn't anything you said."

"You just thought of something unpleasant?"

"No, I just thought that you're too beautiful."

Yuki looked at me with her father's blank stare. Then silently she shook her head.

Yuki paid for dinner. Her father had given her lots of money, she informed me. She took the check over to the register, peeled a ten-thousand-yen note from a wad of five or six, handed it over to the cashier, then scooped up the change without even looking at it.

"Papa thinks that all he has to do is fork over money and everything's cool," she said, piqued. "He's real dim. But that's why I can treat you today. Makes us even, kind of, right? You're always treating me, so fair's fair."

"Thank you," I said. "But you know, all this goes against classic date etiquette."

"Huh?"

"On a dinner date, even if the girl is paying for it, she doesn't run up to the register with the bill. She lets the guy do it, then pays him back, or she gives him the money ahead of time. That's the way to do it. Males are very sensitive creatures. Of course, I'm not such a macho guy, so I don't care. But you ought to know that there are lots of sensitive fellows out there who really do care."

"Gross!" she said. "I'll never go out with guys like that."

"It's, well, just an angle on things," I said, easing the Subaru out of the parking space. "People fall in love without reason, without even wanting to. You can't predict it. That's love. When you get to the age that you wear a brassiere, you'll understand."

"I told you, dummy. I already have one!" she screamed and pounded me on the shoulder.

I almost plowed the car into a dumpster, and had to stop. "I was only kidding," I said. "It was a stupid joke, but you ought to give your laugh muscles some practice anyway."

"Hmmph," she pouted.

"Hmmph," I echoed.

"It was stupid, that's for sure," she said.

"It was stupid, that's for sure," I said.

"Stop it!" she cried.

I was tempted not to, but didn't, and pulled the car out of the lot.

"One thing, Yuki, and this is not a joke. Don't hit people while they're driving," I said. "You could get us killed. So date etiquette lesson number two: *Don't die. Go on living.*"

On the way back, Yuki hardly said a word to me. She melted into her seat, and appeared to be thinking. Though it was hard to tell if she was asleep or awake. She wasn't listening to her tapes. So I put on Coltrane's *Ballads* that I'd brought along. She didn't utter a word, barely noticed anything was on. I hummed along with the solos.

The road was a bore. I concentrated on the taillights of the cars ahead. When we got onto the expressway, Yuki sat up and started chewing gum. Then she lit a cigarette. Three, four puffs and out the window it went. I was going to say something if she lit up a second, but she didn't. She could tell what was on my mind.

As I pulled up in front of the Akasaka condo, I announced, "Here we are, Princess."

Whereupon she balled up her wad of gum in its wrapper and placed it on the dashboard. Then she sluggishly opened the car door, got out, and started walking. Didn't say good-bye, didn't shut the door, didn't look back. Okay, a difficult age, I thought. She seemed like a character out of Gotanda's movies. The sensitive, complex girl. No doubt, Gotanda could have played my part loads better than I did. And probably Yuki would be head over heels in love with him. It wouldn't make a movie otherwise. Good grief, I can't stop thinking about Gotanda! I reached across her seat and pulled the door shut. *Slam!* Then I listened to Freddie Hubbard's "Red Clay" on the way home.

After waking the next morning, I went to the train station. Before nine and Shibuya was swarming with commuters. Yet despite the spring air, you could count the number of smiles on one hand. I bought two papers at the kiosk, went to Dunkin' Donuts, and read the news over coffee. Opening ceremonies for Tokyo Disneyland, fighting between Vietnam and Cambodia, Tokyo mayoral election, violence in the schools. Not one line about a beautiful young woman strangled in an Akasaka hotel. What's one homicide compared to the opening of a Disney theme park anyway? It's just one more thing to forget.

I checked the movie listings and saw that *Unrequited Love* had finished its run. Which brought Gotanda to mind again. I had to let him know about Mei.

I tried calling him from the pink phone in Dunkin' Donuts. Naturally he was out, so I left a message on his machine: urgent. Then I tossed the newspapers in the trash and headed home. Walking back, I tried to imagine why on earth Vietnam and Cambodia, two communist countries, should be fighting. Complicated world.

It was my day for catching up on things.

There were tons of things I had to do. Very practical matters. I put on my practical-minded best and attacked things head-on.

I took shirts to the cleaners and picked some up. I stopped by the bank, got some cash from the ATM, paid my phone and gas bills, paid my rent. I had new heels put on my shoes. I bought batteries for the alarm clock. I returned home and straightened up the place while listening to FEN. I scrubbed the bathtub. I cleaned the refrigerator, the stove, the fan, the floors, the windows. I bagged the garbage. I changed the sheets. I ran the vacuum cleaner. I was wiping the blinds, singing along to Styx's "Mister Roboto," when the phone rang at two.

It was Gotanda.

"Can you meet me? I can't talk over the phone," I said.

"Sure. But how urgent is it? I'm right in the middle of a shoot right now. Can it wait two or three days?"

"I don't think it can. Someone's been killed," I said. "Someone we both know and the cops are on the move."

Silence came over the line. An eloquent silence as only Gotanda could deliver. Smart, cool, and intelligent. I could almost hear his mental gears whirring at high speed. "Okay, how about tonight? It'll have to be pretty late. That okay?"

"Fine."

"I'll call you around one or two. Sorry, but I won't have one free minute before that."

"No problem. I'll be up."

We hung up and I replayed the entire conversation in my mind.

Someone's been killed. Someone we both know and the cops are on the move.

A regular mob flick. Involve Gotanda and everything becomes a scene from the movies. Little by little reality retreated from view. Made me feel like I was playing a scripted role. Gotanda in dark glasses, trench coat collar turned up, leaning against his Maserati. Charming. A radial tire commercial. I shook the image off and returned to my blinds.

At five, I walked to Harajuku and wandered through the teenybopper stalls along Takeshita Street. There was plenty of stuff inscribed with Kiss and Iron Maiden and AC/DC and Motorhead and Michael Jackson and Prince, but Elvis? No. Finally, after visiting several stores, I found what I was looking for: a badge that read ELVIS THE KING.

Then to Tsuruoka's for tempura and beer. The sun went down, the hours passed. My Pacman kept crunching away at the dotted lines. I was making no progress. Getting closer to nothing. Even as the lines seemed to be multiplying. But lines to Kiki were nowhere to be seen. I'd been sent off on detours. Energies expended on sideshows, never on the main event. Where the hell was the main event? *Was* there a main event?

Free until after midnight, I went to see Paul Newman in *The Verdict*. Not a bad movie, but I kept losing myself in thought and losing track of the story. I was expecting Kiki's naked back to appear on screen at any moment. Kiki, Kiki, what did you want from me?

The end credits came on and I left the theater, hardly having any grasp of the plot. I walked, stepped into a bar, and had a couple vodka gimlets. I got back home at ten and read, waiting for Gotanda to call.

I eventually tossed my book aside and lay back in bed. I thought about Kipper. Dead and buried, quiet in the quiet ground.

The next thing I knew the room was flooded with silence.

Waves of helplessness washed over me. I needed to rouse myself. I closed my eyes and counted from one to ten in Spanish, ending in a loud *finito* and a clap of the hands. My own spell to conquer helplessness. One of the many skills I'd acquired living alone. Without these tricks I may not have survived.

26

I t was twelve-thirty when Gotanda called.

"Things have been crazy. Sorry about the late hour, but could I ask you to drive to my place this time?"

No problem, I told him, and I was on my way.

He came down immediately after I rang the doorbell. To my surprise, he *really* had a trench coat on. Which did suit him. No dark glasses though, just a pair of normal glasses, which gave him the look of an intellectual.

"Again, sorry this had to be so late," Gotanda said as we greeted each other. "What a day it's been. Incredibly busy. And I have to go to Yokohama after this. A shoot first thing in the morning, so they booked me a room."

"Why don't I drive you there?" I offered. "We'd have more time to talk, and it'd save you some time too."

"Great, if you're sure you don't mind."

Not at all, I assured him, and he quickly got his things together.

"Nice car," he said as we settled into the Subaru. "Honest, it's got a nice feel to it."

"We have an understanding."

"Uh-huh," he said, nodding as if he understood.

I slid a Beach Boys tape into the stereo and we were on our way. As soon as we got on the expressway to Yokohama, it began to drizzle. I turned on the wipers, then stopped them, then turned them on again. It was a very fine spring rain.

"What do you remember about junior high?" Gotanda asked out of nowhere.

"That I was a hopeless nobody," I answered.

"Anything else?"

I thought a second. "You're going to think I'm nuts, but I remember you lighting Bunsen burners in science class.

"What?"

"It was just, I don't know, so perfect. You made lighting the flame seem like a great moment in the history of mankind."

"Well of course it was," he laughed. "But, okay, I get what you mean. Believe me, it was never my intention to show anybody up. Even though I guess I did look like a prima donna. Ever since I was a kid, people were always watching me. Why? I don't know. Naturally I knew it was happening, and it made me into a little performer. It just stuck with me. I was always acting. So when I actually became an actor, it was a relief. I didn't have to be embarrassed about it," he said, placing one palm atop the other on his lap and gazing down at them. "I hope I wasn't a total shit, or was I?"

"Nah," I said. "But that's not what I meant at all. I only wanted to say you lighted that burner with style. I'd almost like to see you do it again sometime."

He laughed and wiped his glasses. With style, of course. "Anytime," he said. "I'll be waiting with the burner and matches."

"I'll bring a pillow in case I swoon," I added.

We laughed some more. Then Gotanda put his glasses back on and turned the stereo down slightly. "Shall we get on with our talk, about that dead person?"

"It was Mei," I said flat out, peering out beyond the wipers. "She's been murdered. Her body was found in a hotel in Akasaka, strangled with a stocking. Killer unknown.'"

Gotanda faced me abruptly. It took him three or four seconds to grasp what I had said, then his face wrenched in
realization. Like a window frame twisting in a big quake. I
glanced over at him out of the corner of my eye. He seemed
to be in shock.

"When was she killed?" he asked finally.

I gave him the details, and he was quiet again, as if to set
his feelings in order.

"That's horrible," he finally said, shaking his head. "Horrible. Why? Why would anyone kill Mei? She was such a
good kid. It's just—" He shook his head again.

"A good kid, yes," I said. "Right out of a fairy tale."

He sighed deeply, his face suddenly aged with fatigue.
Until this moment he had managed to contain an unbearable
strain within himself. Yet, even fatigue was becoming to
him, serving as a rather distinguished accent on his life.
Unfair to say, I suppose, hurt and tired as he was. Whatever
he touched, even pain, seemed to turn to refinement.

"The three of us used to talk until dawn," Gotanda spoke,
his voice barely a whisper. "Me and Mei and Kiki. Maybe it
was right out of a fairy tale, but where do you even find a
fairy tale these days? Man, those times were wonderful."

I stared at the road ahead, Gotanda stared at the dashboard. I turned the wipers on and off. The stereo played on,
low, the Beach Boys and sun and surf and dune buggies.

"How did you know she'd been killed?" Gotanda asked.

"The police hauled me in," I explained. "I'd given Mei
my business card, and she had it deep in her wallet. Matter
of fact, it was the only thing on her with any kind of name.
So they picked me up for questioning. Wanted to know how
I knew her. A couple of tough, dumb flatfoots. But I lied. I
told them I'd never seen her before."

"Why'd you lie?"

"Why? You were the one introduced us, buying those two
girls that night, right? What do you think would've happened if I'd blabbed? Have you lost your thinking gear?"

"Forgive me," he said. "I'm a little confused. Stupid."

"The cops didn't believe me at all. They could smell the lies. They put me through the wringer for three days. A thorough job, careful not to infringe on the law. They never touched me, bodily, that is. But it was hard. I'm getting old, I'm not what I used to be. They pretended they didn't have a place for me to sleep and threw me in the tank. Technically, I wasn't in the tank because they didn't lock the door. It was no picnic, let me tell you. You think you're losing your mind."

"Know what you mean. I was held for two weeks once. Not pleasant. I didn't get to see the sun the whole time. I thought I'd never get out. It gets to you, how they ride you. They know how to break you," he said, staring at his fingernails. "But three days and you didn't talk?"

"What do you think? Of course not. If I started in midway with 'Well, actually—,' it'd be all over. Once you take a line, you've got to stick by it to the end."

Gotanda's face twisted again. "Forgive me. Introducing you to Mei and getting you caught up in this mess."

"No reason for you to apologize," I said. "I thoroughly enjoyed myself with her. That was then. This is something else. It's not your fault she's dead."

"No, it's not, but still you had to lie to the cops for me. You got dragged into the middle of it. *That* was my fault. Because I was involved."

I turned to give him a good hard look and then went straight to the heart of the matter. "*That* isn't a problem. Don't worry about it. No need to apologize. You got your stake and I respect it, fully. The bigger problem is, they weren't able to identify her. She's got relatives, hasn't she? We want to catch the psycho who killed her, don't we? I would have told them everything if I could. That's what's eating me. Mei didn't deserve to die that way. At the least, she should have a name."

Gotanda closed his eyes for so long I almost thought he'd gone to sleep. The Beach Boys had finished their serenade. I pushed the EJECT button. Everything went dead silent. There was only the drone of the tires on the wet asphalt.

"I'll call the police," Gotanda intoned as he opened his
eyes. "An anonymous phone call. And I'll name the club she
was working for. That way they can get on with their investigation."

"Genius," I said. "You've got a good head on your shoulders. Why didn't I think of it? But suppose the police put the
screws to the club. They'll find out that a few days before
she was killed, you had Mei sent to your place. Bingo,
they've got you downtown. What's the point of me keeping
my mouth shut for three days?"

"You're right. You got me. I *am* confused."

"When you're confused," I said, "the best thing to do is
sit tight and wait for the coast to clear. It's only a matter of
time. A woman got strangled to death in a hotel. It happens.
People forget about it. No reason to feel guilty. Just lie low
and keep quiet. You start acting smart now, you'll only make
things worse."

Maybe I was being hard on him. My tone a little too cold,
my words too harsh, but hell, I was in this pretty deep too. I
apologized. "Sorry," I said. "I didn't mean to light into you
like that. I couldn't lift a finger to help the girl. That's all, it's
not your fault."

"But it is my fault," he insisted.

Silence was growing oppressive, so I put on another tape.
Ben E. King's "Spanish Harlem." We said nothing more until
we reached Yokohama, an unspoken bond between us. I
wanted to pat him on the back and say it's okay, it's all over
and done with. But a person had died. She was cold, alone,
and nameless. That fact weighed more heavily than I could
bear.

"Who do you think killed her?" asked Gotanda much
later.

"Who knows?" I said. "In that line of work, you get all
types. Anything can happen."

"But the club is real careful about screening the clients. It's so organized, they should be able to find the guy easily."

"You'd think so, but it could be anybody else too. Whatever, she made a mistake, and it turned out to be fatal. It happens, I guess," I said. "She lived in this world of images that was safe and pure. But there are rules even in that world. Somebody breaks the rules and the fantasy's kaput."

"It doesn't make sense," said Gotanda. "Why would such a beautiful, intelligent girl want to become a hooker? Why? She could've had a good life, a decent job. She could've modeled, she could've married a rich guy. How come a hooker? Okay, the money's good, but she didn't seem all that interested in money. You think she really wanted this fairy tale?"

"Maybe," I answered. "Like me, like you. Like everybody. Only everybody goes about it different. That's why you never know what's going to happen."

When we pulled up to the New Grand Hotel in Yokohama, Gotanda suggested I stay over too. "I'm sure we can get you a room. We'll call up room service and knock back some drinks. I don't think I can sleep right away."

I shook my head, no. "I'll take a rain check on those drinks. I'm pretty worn out. I'll just go home and collapse."

"You sure?" he said. "Well, thanks for driving me down here. I feel like I haven't said a responsible thing all day."

"You're tired too," I said. "But listen, with someone who's dead, there's no rush to make amends. She'll be dead for a long time. Let's think things over when we're in better spirits. You hear what I'm saying? She's dead. Extremely, irrevocably dead. Feel guilt, feel whatever you like, she's not coming back."

Gotanda nodded. "I hear you."

"Good night," I said.

"Thanks again," he said.

"Light a Bunsen burner for me next time, and we'll call it even."

He smiled as he got out of the car. "Strange to say, but you're the only friend I have who'd say that. Not another soul. We meet after twenty years, and the thing you chose to remember!"

At that he was off. He turned up the collar of his trench coat and headed through the spring drizzle into the New Grand. Almost like *Casablanca*. The beginning of a beautiful friendship . . .

The rain kept coming down, steadily, evenly. Soft and gentle, drawing new green shoots up into the spring night. *Extremely, irrevocably dead,* I said aloud.

I should have stayed overnight and drunk with Gotanda, it occurred to me. Gotanda and I had four things in common. One, we'd been in the same science lab unit. Two, we were both divorced. Three, we'd both slept with Kiki. And four, we'd both slept with Mei. Now Mei was dead. *Extremely, irrevocably.* Worth a drink together. Why didn't I stay and keep him company? I had time on my hands, I had nothing planned for tomorrow. What prevented me? Maybe, somehow, I didn't want it to seem like a scene from a movie. Poor guy. He was just so unbearably charming. And it wasn't his fault. Probably.

When I got back to my Shibuya apartment, I poured myself a whiskey and watched the cars on the expressway through the blinds.

27

A week passed. Spring made solid advances, never once retreated. A world away from March. The cherries bloomed and the blossoms scattered in the evening showers. Elections came and went, a new school year started. Bjorn Borg retired. Michael Jackson was number one in the charts the whole time. The dead stayed dead.

It was a succession of aimless days. I went swimming twice. I went to the barber. I bought newspapers, never saw an article about Mei. Maybe they couldn't identify her.

On Tuesday and Thursday Yuki and I went out to eat. On Monday we went for a drive with the music playing. I enjoyed these times. We shared one thing. We had time to waste.

When I didn't see her, Yuki stayed indoors during the day, afraid that truant officers might nab her. Her mother had yet to return.

"Why don't we go to Disneyland then?" I asked.

"I don't want to go," she sneered. "I hate those places."

"You hate all that gooey Mickey Mouse kid stuff, I take it?"

"Of course I hate it," she said.

"But it's not good for you to stay indoors all the time," I said.

"So why don't we go to Hawaii?" she said.

"What? Hawaii?"

"Mama phoned up and asked if I wanted to come to Hawaii. That's where she is right now, taking pictures. She leaves me alone all this time and then suddenly she gets worried about me. She can't come home yet, and since I'm not going to school anyway, she said to get on a plane and come see her. Hawaii's not such a bad idea, yeah? Mama said she'd pay your way. I mean, I can't go alone, right? Let's go, please. Just for one week. It'll be fun."

I laughed. "What exactly is the difference between Disneyland and Hawaii?"

"No truant officers in Hawaii."

"Well, you got a point there."

"Then you'll go?"

I thought it over, and the more I thought about it the more I liked it. Getting out of Tokyo *had* to be a good idea. I'd reached a dead end here. My head was stuck. I was in a funk. And Mei was extremely, irrevocably dead.

I'd been to Hawaii once. For one day only. I was going to Los Angeles on business and the plane had engine trouble, so we set down in Hawaii overnight. I bought a pair of sunglasses and swim trunks in the hotel and spent the day on the beach. A great day. No, Hawaii was not such a bad idea.

Swim, drink fruit drinks, get a tan, and relax. I might even have a good time. Then I could reset my sights and get on with whatever I had to do.

"Okay, let's go," I said.

"Goody!" Yuki squealed. "Let's go buy the tickets."

But before doing that, I made a call to Hiraku Makimura and explained the offer that was on the table.

He was immediately positive. "Might do you some good too, son. You need to stretch your legs," he said, "take a break from all that shoveling you do. It'd also put you out of harm's way with the police. That mess isn't cleared up yet, is it? They're bound to knock on your door again."

"Maybe so," I said.

"Go. And don't worry about money," he said. Any discussions you had with this guy always turned to money. "Go for as long as you like."

"I figure on a week at the most. I still have a pile of things to get back to."

"As you like," Makimura said. "When are you going? Probably the sooner the better. That's how it is with vacations. Go when the mood strikes. That's the trick. You hardly need to take anything with you anyway. I tell you what—we'll get you tickets for the day after tomorrow. How's that?"

"Fine, but I can buy my own ticket."

"Details, details, always fussing. This is in my line of work. I know how to get the best seats for the cheapest price. Let me do this. Each to his own abilities. Don't say anything. I don't want to hear your-system-this your-system-that. I'll take care of the hotel too. Two rooms. What do you think—you want something with a kitchenette?"

"Well, I like to be able to cook my own sometimes, but it's—"

"I know just the place. I stayed there once myself. Near the beach, quiet, clean."

"But I—"

"Just leave it all to me, okay? I'll get the word to Amé. You just go to Honolulu with Yuki, lie on the beach and have a good time. Her mother's going to be busy anyway. When she's working, daughter or whoever doesn't exist. So don't worry. Just make sure Yuki eats well. And, oh yes, you got a visa?"

"Yes, but—"

"Good. Day after tomorrow, son. Don't forget your passport. Whatever you need, get it there. You're not going to Siberia. Siberia was rough, let me tell you. Horrible place. Afghanistan wasn't much better either. Compared to them, Hawaii's like Disneyland. And you're there in no time. Fall asleep with your mouth open and you're there. By the way, son, you speak English?"

"In normal conversation I—"

"Good," he said. "Perfect in fact. There's nothing more to say. Nakamura will meet you with the tickets tomorrow. He'll also bring the money I owe you for Yuki's flight down from Hokkaido."

"Who's Nakamura?"

"My assistant. The young man who lives with me."

Boy Friday.

"Any other questions?" asked Makimura. "You know, I like you, son. Hawaii. Wonderful place. Wonderful smells. A playground. Relax. No snow to shovel over there. I'll see you whenever you get back."

Then he hung up.

The famous writer.

When I reported to Yuki that all systems were go, she squealed again.

"Can you get ready by yourself? Pack your swimsuit and whatever you need?"

"It's only Hawaii," she said patronizingly. "It's like going to the beach at Oiso. We're not going to Kathmandu, you know."

The next day I ran errands: to the bank for cash, to the bookstore for a few paperbacks, to the cleaners for my shirts. At three o'clock, I met Boy Friday at a coffee shop in Shibuya, where he handed me a thick envelope of cash, two first-class open tickets to Hawaii, two packets of American Express travelers cheques, and a map to the hotel in Honolulu.

"It's all been arranged. Just give them your name when you get there," Nakamura said. "The reservation's for two weeks, but it can be changed for shorter or longer. Don't forget to sign the travelers cheques when you get home. Use them as you please. It's all on expense account. That's the word from Mr. Makimura."

"Everything's on expense account?" I couldn't believe it.

"Maybe not everything, but as long as you get receipts, it should be fine. That's my job. Please get receipts for whatever you spend," he laughed good-naturedly.

I promised I would.

"Take care of yourselves and have a good trip," he said.

"Thanks," I said.

At nightfall I rummaged through the refrigerator and made dinner.

Then I quickly threw together some things for the trip. Was I forgetting anything?

Nothing I could think of.

Going to Hawaii's no big deal. You need to take a lot more stuff going to Hokkaido.

I parked my travel bag on the floor and laid out what I'd wear the next day. Nothing more to do, I took a bath, then drank a beer while watching the news. No news to speak of, except for a not-too-promising weather forecast. Great, we'll be in Hawaii. I lay in bed and had another beer. And I thought of Mei. Extremely, irrevocably dead Mei. She was in a very cold place now. Unidentified. Without customers. Without Dire Straits or Bob Dylan. Tomorrow Yuki and I were going to Hawaii, on someone else's expense account. Was this any way to run a world?

I tried to shake Mei's image from my head.

I tried to think about my receptionist friend at the Dolphin Hotel. The one with the glasses, the one whose name I didn't know. For some reason the last couple of days I'd been wishing I could talk to her. I'd even dreamed about her. But how could I even ring her up? What was I supposed to say— "Hello, I'd like to talk to the receptionist with glasses at the front desk"? They'd probably think I was some joker. A hotel is serious business.

There had to be a way. Where there's a will, et cetera.

I rang up Yuki and set a time to meet the next day. Then asked if by chance she knew the name of the receptionist in

Sapporo, the one who'd entrusted her to me, the very one with the glasses.

"I think so," she said, "because it was an odd name. I'm sure I wrote it in my diary. I don't remember it, but I could check."

"Would you, right now?" I asked.

"I'm watching TV."

"Forgive me, but it's urgent. Very urgent."

She grumbled, but fetched her diary. "It's Miss Yumiyoshi," she said.

"Yumiyoshi?" I repeated.

"I told you it was an odd name. Sounds Okinawan, doesn't it?"

"No, they don't have names like that in Okinawa."

"Well, anyway, that's her name. Yu-mi-yo-shi," Yuki pronounced. "Okay? Can I watch TV now?"

"What are you watching?"

She hung up without responding.

Next I rang up the Dolphin Hotel and asked to speak to my receptionist friend by name. I didn't know how far this would go, but the operator connected us and Miss Yumiyoshi even remembered me. I hadn't been written off entirely.

"I'm working," she spoke in a low voice, cool and clean. "I'll call you later."

"Fine then, later," I said.

While waiting for her call back, I rang up Gotanda and was just leaving a message that I was going to Hawaii when he came on the line.

"Sounds great. I'm envious," he said. "Wish I could go too."

"Why not? What's stopping you?" I asked.

"Not as easy as you think. It looks like I'm loaded, but I'm so deep in debt you wouldn't believe."

"Oh?"

"The divorce, the loans. You think I do all these ridiculous commercials for fun? I can write off expenses, but I can't pay off my debts. Tell me you don't think that's odd."

"You owe that much?"

"I owe a lot," he said. "I'm not even sure how much. Not as smart as I look, am I? Money gives me the creeps. The way I was brought up. Vulgar to think about it, you know. Didn't your mother ever tell you that? All I had to do was work hard, live modestly, look at the big picture. Good advice—for then maybe. Whoever heard of living modestly these days? Whoever heard of the big picture? What my mother never told me was where the tax accountant fit in. Maybe my mother never heard about debts and deductions. Well, I got plenty of both. Which means I gotta work and I can't go to Hawaii with you. Sorry, once you get me going I can't stop."

"That's okay, I don't mind," I said.

"Anyway, it's my problem, not yours. We'll go together the next time, okay? I'm going to miss you. Take care of yourself."

"It's just Hawaii," I laughed. "I'll be back in a week."

"Still. Give me a call when you get back, will you?"

"Sure thing," I said.

"And while you're lying on the beach at Waikiki, think of me. Playing dentist to pay my debts."

Miss Yumiyoshi called a little before ten. She was back at her apartment. Ah yes—simple building, simple stairs, simple door. Her nervous smile. It all came back so poignantly. I closed my eyes, and the snowflakes danced silently in the depths of the night. I almost felt like I was in love.

"How did you know my name?" was the first thing she asked.

"Don't worry. I didn't do anything I shouldn't have. Didn't pay anyone off. Didn't tap your phone. Didn't work anybody over until they talked." I explained that Yuki had told me.

"I see," she said. "How did it go with her, by the way? Did you get her to Tokyo safe and sound?"

"Safe and sound," I said. "I got her to her front door. In fact I still see her now and then. She's fine. Odd, but fine."

"Kind of like you," said Yumiyoshi matter-of-factly. She spoke as if she were relating the most commonly known fact in the world. Monkeys like bananas, it doesn't rain much in the Sahara. "Tell me, why did you want to keep me in the dark about your name?" I asked.

"I didn't mean to, honest. I meant to tell you the next time we met," she said. "If you have an unusual name, you tend to be careful about it."

"I checked the telephone directory. Did you know that there are only two Yumiyoshis in all of Tokyo?"

"I know," she said. "I used to live in Tokyo, remember? I used to check the telephone book all the time. Wherever I went, I checked the phone book. There's one Yumiyoshi in Kyoto. Anyway, what did you want?"

"Nothing special," I said. "I'm going on a trip from tomorrow. And I wanted to hear your voice before I left. That's all. Sometimes I miss your voice."

She didn't respond, and in her silence I could hear the slight cross talk of a woman speaking, as if at the end of a long corridor. Quiet yet crisp, strangely charged electricity, with what I took to be a tone of bitterness. There were pained breaks and jags in her voice.

"You know how I told you about the sixteenth floor in total darkness?" Yumiyoshi spoke up.

"Uh-huh," I said.

"Actually, it happened again," she said.

It was my turn not to respond.

"Are you still there?" she asked.

"I'm here," I said. "Go on."

"First, you have to tell me the truth. Did you *honestly* believe what I told you that time? Or were you just humoring me?"

"I *honestly* believed you," I said. "I didn't have the

chance to tell you, but the very same thing happened to me. I took the elevator, stepped out into total darkness. I experienced the very same thing. So I believe you, I believe you."

"You went there?"

"I'll give you the whole story next time. I still don't know how to put it into words. Lots of things I don't understand. So you see, I really do need to talk to you again. But never mind that, tell me what happened to you. That's much more important."

Silence. The cross talk had died.

"Well, about ten days ago," Yumiyoshi began, "I was riding in the elevator down to the parking garage. It was around eight at night. The elevator went down, the door opened, and suddenly I was in that place again. Exactly like before. It wasn't in the middle of the night, and it wasn't on the sixteenth floor. But it was the same thing. Totally dark, moldy, kind of dank. The smell and the air were exactly the same. This time, I didn't go looking around. I stood still and waited for the elevator to come back. I ended up waiting a long time, I don't know how long. When the elevator finally got there, I got in and left. That was it."

"Did you tell anyone about it?" I asked.

"You think I'm crazy?" she said. "After the way they reacted the last time? Not on your life."

"Yeah, better not tell a soul."

"But what am I supposed to do? Whenever I get into an elevator now, I'm scared that I'm going to end up in darkness. And in a hotel like this, you have to ride the elevators a lot. What am I going to do? I can't talk to anybody but you about this."

"So why didn't you call sooner?" I asked.

"I did, several times," her voice hushed to a whisper. "But you were never in."

"But my machine was on, wasn't it?"

"I hate those things. They make me nervous."

"Fair enough. Well, let me tell you what I know about what's going on. There's nothing evil about that darkness. It doesn't harbor any ill will, so there's no need to feel threatened. But there *is* someone who lives there. This guy heard your footsteps, but he's someone who'd never do you any harm. He'd never hurt a fly. So I think that if you find yourself in that darkness again, you should just shut your eyes, get back in the elevator, and leave. Okay?"

Yumiyoshi chewed silently on my words. "May I say what I honestly think?"

"Of course."

"I don't understand you," she said. "I don't understand you at all. When I think about you, I realize I don't know a thing about you, really."

"Hmm. I've told you already how old I am. But I guess for someone my age, I've got a lot of undefined territory. I've left too many loose ends hanging. So now, I'm trying to tie up as many of those loose ends as I can. If I manage to do that, maybe then I can explain things a little more clearly. Maybe then we can understand each other better."

"We can only hope," she said with third-person detachment. She sounded like a TV anchorwoman. *We can only hope. Next on the news . . .*

I told her I was going to Hawaii.

"Oh," she remarked, unmoved. End of conversation. We said good-bye and hung up. I drank a shot of whiskey, turned out the light, and went to sleep.

28

ext on the news. I lay on the beach at Fort DeRussy looking up at the high blue sky and palm fronds and sea gulls and did my newscaster spiel. Yuki was next to me. I lay face up on my beach mat, she lay on her belly with her eyes shut. Next to her a huge Sanyo radio-cassette deck was playing Eric Clapton's latest. Yuki wore an olive-green bikini and was covered head-to-toe with coconut oil. She looked sleek and shiny as a slim, young dolphin. A burly Samoan trudged by carrying a surfboard, while a deep-brown lifeguard surveyed the goings-on from his watchtower, his gold chain flashing. The whole town smelled of flowers and fruit and suntan oil.

Next on the news.

Stuff happened, people appeared, scenes changed. Not very long ago I was wandering around, nearly blind, in a Sapporo blizzard. Now I was lolling on the beach at Waikiki, gazing up at the blue. One thing led to another. Connect the dots. Dance to the music and here's where it gets you. *Was I dancing my best?* I checked back over my steps in order. Not so bad. Not sublime, but not so bad. Put me back in the same position and I'd make the same moves. That's what you call a system. Or tendencies. Anyway my feet were in motion. I was keeping in step.

And now I was in Honolulu. Break time.

Break time. I hadn't meant to say it aloud, but apparently I did. Yuki rolled over and squinted at me suspiciously.

"What've you been thinking about?" she said hoarsely.

"Nothing much," I said.

"Not that I care, but would you mind not talking to yourself so loud that I can hear? Couldn't you do it when you're alone?"

"Sorry, I'll keep quiet."

Yuki gave me a restive look.

"You act like an old geezer who's not used to being around people," said Yuki, then rolled over away from me.

We'd taken a taxi from the airport to the hotel, changed into T-shirts and shorts, and the first thing we did was to go buy that big portable radio-cassette deck. It was what Yuki wanted.

"A real blaster," as she said to the clerk.

Other than a few tapes, she needed nothing else. Just the blaster, which she took with her whenever we went to the beach. Or rather, that was my role. Native porter. B'wana memsahib with blaster in tow.

The hotel, courtesy of Makimura, was just fine. A certain unstylishness of furniture and decor notwithstanding (though who went to Hawaii in search of chic?), the accommodations were exceedingly comfortable. Convenient to the beach. Tenth-floor tranquillity, with view of the horizon. Sea-view terrace for sunbathing. Kitchenette spacious, clean, outfitted with every appliance from microwave to dishwasher. Yuki had the room next door, a little smaller than mine.

We stocked up on beer and California wine and fruit and juice, plus sandwich fixings. Things we could take to the beach.

And then we spent whole days on the beach, hardly talking. Turning our bodies over, now front, now back, soaking up the rays. Sea breezes rustled the palms. I'd doze off, only to be roused by the voices of passersby, which made me wonder where I was. Hawaii, it'd take me a few moments to realize. Hawaii. Sweat and suntan oil ran down my cheek. A range of sounds ebbed and flowed with the waves, mingling with my heartbeat. My heart had taken its place in the grand workings of the world.

My springs loosened. I relaxed. *Break time.*

Yuki's features underwent a remarkable change from the moment we touched down and that sweet, warm Hawaiian air hit her. She closed her eyes, took a deep breath, then looked at me. Tension seemed to fall off her. No more defensiveness, no irritation. Her gestures, the way she ran her hands through her hair, the way she wadded up her chewing gum, the way she shrugged, . . . She eased up, she slowed down.

With her tiny bikini, dark sunglasses, and hair tied tight atop her head, it was hard to tell Yuki's age. Her body was still a child's body, but she had a kind of poise far more grown-up than her years. Her slender limbs showed strength. She seemed to have entered her most dynamic phase of growth. She was becoming an adult.

We rubbed oil on each other. It was the first time anyone ever told me I had a "big back." Yuki, though, was so ticklish she couldn't stay still. It made me smile. Her small white ears and the nape of her neck, how like a *girl's* neck it was. How different from a mature woman's neck. Though don't ask me what I mean by that.

"It's better to tan slow at first," Yuki told me with authority. "First you tan in the shade, then out in direct sun, then back in the shade. That way you don't get burned. If you blister, it leaves ugly scars."

"Shade, sun, shade," I intoned dutifully as I oiled her back.

And so I spent our first afternoon in Hawaii lying in the shade of a palm tree listening to an FM station. From time to time I'd go in the water or go to a bar at the beach for an ice-cold piña colada. Yuki didn't swim a single stroke. She aimed to relax, she said. She had a hot dog and pineapple juice.

The sun, which seemed huge, sank into the ocean, and the sky turned brilliant shades of red and yellow and orange. We lay and watched the sky tint the sails of the sunset-cruise catamarans. Yuki could hardly be budged.

"Let's go," I urged. "The sun's gone down and I'm hungry. Let's go get a fat, juicy, charcoal-broiled hamburger."

Yuki nodded, sort of, but didn't get up. As if she were loath to forfeit what little time that remained. I rolled up the beach mats and picked up the blaster.

"Don't worry. There's still tomorrow. And after tomorrow, there's the day after tomorrow," I said.

She looked up at me with a hint of a smile. And when I held out my hand, she grabbed it and pulled herself up.

29␣␣␣␣␣

The following morning, Yuki said she wanted to go see
her mother. She didn't know where she was, but she
had her phone number. So I rang up, exchanged greetings, and got directions. Amé had rented a small cottage
near Makaha, about forty-five minutes out of Honolulu.

We rented a Mitsubishi Lancer, turned the radio up loud,
rolled down the windows, and were on our way. Everywhere
we passed was filled with light and surf and the scent of
flowers.

"Does your mother live alone?" I asked Yuki.

"Are you kidding?" Yuki curled her lip. "No way the old
lady could get by in a foreign country on her own. She's the
most impractical person you ever met. If she didn't have
someone looking after her, she'd get lost. How much you
want to bet she's got a boyfriend out there? Probably young
and handsome. Just like Papa's."

"Huh?"

"Remember, at Papa's place, that pretty gay boy who lives
with him? He's so–o clean."

"Gay?"

"Didn't you think so?"

"No, I didn't think anything."

"You're dense, you know that! You could tell just by
looking at him," said Yuki. "I don't know if Papa's gay too,

but that boy sure is. Absolutely, two hundred percent gay."

Roxy Music came on the radio and Yuki turned the volume up full blast.

"Anyway, Mama's weakness is for poets. Young poets, failed poets, any kind of poets. She makes them recite to her while she's developing film. That's her idea of a good time. Kind of nerdy if you ask me. Papa should've been a poet, but he couldn't write a poem if he got showered with flowers out of the clear blue sky."

What a family! Rough-and-tumble writer father with gay Boy Friday, genius photographer mother with poet boyfriends, and spiritual medium daughter with . . . Wait a minute. Was I supposed to be fitting into this psychedelic extended family? I remembered Boy Friday's friendly, attractive smile. Maybe, just maybe, he was saying, *Welcome to the club*. Hold it right there. This gig with the family is strictly temporary. Understand? A short R&R before I go back to shoveling. At which point I won't have time for the likes of this craziness. At which point I go my own way. I like things less involved.

Following Amé's instructions, I turned right off the highway before Makaha and headed toward the hills. Houses with roofs half-ready to blow off in the next hurricane lined either side of the road, growing fewer and fewer until we reached the gate of a private resort community. The gatekeeper let us in at the mention of Amé's name.

Inside the grounds spread a vast, well-kept lawn. Gardeners transported themselves in golf carts, as they diligently attended to turf and trees. Yellow-billed birds fluttered about. Yuki's mother's place was beyond a swimming pool, trees, a further expanse of hill and lawn.

The cottage was tropical modern, surrounded by a mix of trees in fruit. We rang the doorbell. The drowsy, dry ring of the wind chime mingled pleasantly with strains of Vivaldi coming from the wide-open windows. After a few seconds the door opened, and we were met by a tall, well-tanned white man. He was solidly built, mustachioed, and wore a faded aloha shirt, jogging pants, and rubber thongs. He seemed to be about my age, decent-looking, if not exactly handsome, and a bit too tough to be a poet, though surely the world's got to have tough poets too. His most distinguished feature was the entire lack of a left arm from the shoulder down.

He looked at me, he looked at Yuki, he looked back at me, he cocked his jaw ever so slightly and smiled. "Hello," he greeted us quietly, then switched to Japanese, "*Konnichiwa.*" He shook our hands, and said come on in. His Japanese was flawless.

"Amé's developing pictures right now. She'll be another ten minutes," he said. "Sorry for the wait. Let me introduce myself. I'm Dick. Dick North. I live here with Amé."

Dick showed us into the spacious living room. The room had large windows and a ceiling fan, like something out of a Somerset Maugham novel. Polynesian folkcrafts decorated the walls. He sat us on the sizable sofa, then he brought out two Primos and a coke. Dick and I drank our beers, but Yuki didn't touch her drink.

She stared out the window and said nothing. Between the fruit trees you could see the shimmering sea. Out on the horizon floated one lone cloud, the shape of a pithecanthropus skull. Stubbornly unmoving, a permanent fixture of the seascape. Bleached perfectly white, outlined sharp against the sky. Birds warbled as they darted past. Vivaldi crescendoed to a finish, whereupon Dick got up to slip the record back in its jacket and onto a rack. He was amazingly dexterous with his one arm.

"Where did you pick up such excellent Japanese?" I asked him for lack of anything else to say.

Dick raised an eyebrow and smiled. "I lived in Japan for ten years," he said, very slowly. "I first went there during the War—the Vietnam War. I liked it, and when I got out, I went to Sophia University. I studied Japanese poetry, haiku and tanka, which I translate now. It's not easy, but since I'm a poet myself, it's all for a good cause."

"I would imagine so," I said politely. Not young, not especially handsome, but a poet. One out of three.

"Strange, you know," he spoke as if resuming his train of thought, "you never hear of any one-armed poets. You hear of one-armed painters, one-armed pianists. Even one-armed pitchers. Why no one-armed poets?"

True enough.

"Let me know if you think of one," said Dick.

I shook my head. I wasn't versed in poets in general, even the two-armed variety.

"There are a number of one-armed surfers," he continued. "They paddle with their feet. And they do all right too. I surf a little."

Yuki stood up and knocked about the room. She pulled down records from the rack, but apparently finding nothing to her liking, she frowned. With no music, the surroundings were so quiet they could lull you into drowsiness. In the distance there was the occasional rumble of a lawn mower, someone's voice, the ring of a wind chime, birds singing.

"Quiet here," I remarked.

Dick North peered down thoughtfully into the palm of his one hand.

"Yes. Silence. That's the most important thing. Especially for people in Amé's line of work. In my work too, silence is essential. I can't handle hustle and bustle. Noise, didn't you find Honolulu noisy?"

I didn't especially, but I agreed so as to move the conversation along. Yuki was again looking out the window with her *what-a-drag* sneer in place.

"I'd rather live on Kauai. Really, a wonderful place. Quieter, fewer people. Oahu's not the kind of place I like to live in. Too touristy, too many cars, too much crime. But Amé has to stay here for her work. She goes into Honolulu two or three times a week for equipment and supplies. Also, of course, it's easier to do business and to meet people here.

She's been taking photos of fishermen and gardeners and farmers and cooks and road workers, you name it. She's a fantastic photographer."

I'd never looked that carefully at Amé's photographic works, but again, for convenience sake, I agreed. Yuki made an indistinct toot through her nose.

He asked me what sort of work I did.

A free-lance writer, I told him. He seemed to show interest, thinking probably I was a kindred spirit. He asked me what sort of things I wrote.

Whatever, I write to order. Like shoveling snow, I said, trying the line now on him.

Shoveling snow, he repeated gravely. He didn't seem to understand. I was about to explain when Amé came into the room.

Amé was dressed in a denim shirt and white shorts. She wore no makeup and her hair was unkempt, as if she'd just woken up. Even so, she was exceedingly attractive, exuding the dignity and presence that impressed me about her at the Dolphin Hotel. The moment she walked into the room, she drew everyone's attention to her. Instantaneously, without explanation, without show.

And without a word of greeting, she walked over to Yuki, mussed her hair lovingly, then pressed the tip of her nose to the girl's temple. Yuki clearly didn't enjoy this, but she put up with it. She shook her head briskly, which got her hair more or less back into place, then cast a cool eye at a vase on a shelf. This was not the utter contempt she showed her father, however. Here, she was displaying her awkwardness, composing herself.

There was some unspoken communication going on between mother and daughter. There was no "How are you?" or "You doing okay?" Just the mussing of hair and the touch of the nose. Then Amé came over and sat down next to me, pulled out a pack of Salems and lit up. The poet ferreted out an ashtray and placed it ceremoniously on the table. Amé deposited the matchstick in it, exhaled a puff of smoke, wrinkled up her nose, then put her cigarette to rest.

"Sorry. I couldn't get away from my work," she began. "You know how it is with pictures. Impossible to stop midway."

The poet brought Amé a beer and a glass, and poured for her.

"How long are you going to be in Hawaii?" Amé turned to me and asked.

"About a week," I said. "We don't have a fixed schedule. I'm on a break right now, but I'm going to have to get back to work one of these days."

"You should stay as long as you can. It's nice here."

"Yes, I'm sure it's nice here," I responded, but her mind was already somewhere else.

"Have you eaten?" she then asked.

"I had a sandwich along the way," I answered, "but not Yuki."

"What are we doing for lunch?" she directed her question toward the poet.

"I seem to remember us fixing spaghetti an hour ago," he spoke slowly and deliberately. "An hour ago would have been twelve-fifteen, so that probably would qualify as what we did for lunch."

"Is that right?" she commented vaguely.

"Yes, indeed," said the poet, smiling in my direction. "When Amé gets wrapped up in her work, she loses all track of everything. She forgets whether she's eaten or not, what she'd been doing where. Her mind goes blank from concentrating so intensely."

I smiled politely. But intense concentration? This seemed more in the realm of psychopathology.

Amé eyed her beer glass absently for a while before picking it up. "That may be so, but I'm still hungry. After all, we didn't eat any breakfast," she said. "Or did we?"

"Let me relate the facts as I remember them. At seven-thirty this morning you had a fairly large breakfast of grapefruit and toast and yogurt," Dick recounted. "In fact, you were rather enthusiastic about it, saying how a good breakfast is one of the pleasures in life."

"Did I?" said Amé, scratching the side of her nose. She stared off into space thinking it over, like a scene out of Hitchcock. Reality recedes until you can't tell who's sane and who's not.

"Well, it doesn't matter. I'm incredibly hungry," she said. "You don't mind if I've already eaten, do you?"

"No, I don't mind," laughed her poet lover. "It's your stomach, not mine. And if you want to eat, I say you should eat as much as you want. Appetite's a good thing. It's always that way with you. When your work's going well, you get an appetite. Shall I fix you a sandwich?"

"Thanks. And could you get me another beer?"

"Certainly," he said, disappearing into the kitchen.

"And you, have you had lunch?" Amé asked me.

"I had a sandwich en route," I repeated.

"Yuki?"

No, was Yuki's terse reply.

"Dick and I met in Tokyo," Amé spoke to me as she crossed her legs. But she could have as well been explaining things to Yuki. "He's the one who suggested I go to Kathmandu. He said it would inspire me. Kathmandu was wonderful, really. Dick lost his arm in Vietnam. It was a land mine. A 'Bouncing Betty,' the ones that fly up into the air and explode. *Boom!* The guy next to him stepped on it and Dick lost his arm. Dick's a poet. He speaks good Japanese too, don't you think? We stayed in Kathmandu a while, then we came here to Hawaii. After Kathmandu, we wanted somewhere warm. That's when Dick found this place. The cottage belongs to a friend of his. I use the guest bathroom as a darkroom. Nice place, don't you think?"

Then she exhaled deeply, as if she'd said all there was to say. She stretched and was quiet. The afternoon silence deepened, particles of light flickered like dust, drifting freely in all directions. The white pithecanthropus skull cloud still floated above the horizon. Obstinate as ever. Amé's Salem lay burning in the ashtray, hardly touched.

How did Dick manage to make sandwiches with just one arm? I found myself wondering. How did he slice the bread? How did he keep the bread in place? Was it a matter of meter and rhyme?

When the poet emerged bearing a tray of beautiful ham sandwiches, well-made, well-cut, there was no end to my admiration. Then he opened a beer and poured it for Amé.

"Thanks, Dick," she said, then turned to me. "Dick's a great cook."

"If there were a cooking competition for one-armed poets, I'd win hands down," he said with a wink. And then he was back in the kitchen, making coffee. Despite his lack of an arm, Dick was far from helpless.

Amé offered me a sandwich. It was delicious, and somehow lyrical in composition. Dick's coffee was good too.

"It's no problem, you with Yuki, just the two of you?" Amé picked up the conversation again.

"Excuse me?"

"I'm talking about the music, of course. That rock stuff. It doesn't give you a headache?"

"No, not especially," I said.

"I can't listen to that stuff for more than thirty seconds before I get a splitting headache. Being with Yuki is fine, but the music is intolerable," she said, screwing her index finger into her temple. "The kinds of music I can put up with are very limited. Some baroque, certain kinds of jazz. Ethnic music. Sounds that put you at ease. That's what I like. I also like poetry. Harmony and peace."

She lit up another cigarette, took one puff, then set it down in the ashtray. I was sure she would forget about it too, and she did. Amazing that she hadn't set the house on fire. I was beginning to understand what Hiraku Makimura meant about Amé's wearing him down. Amé didn't give anything. She only took. She consumed those around her to sustain herself. And those around her always gave. Her talent was manifested in a powerful gravitational pull. She believed it was her privilege, her right. *Harmony and peace.* In order for her to have that, she had everyone waiting on her hand and foot.

Not that it made any difference to me, I wanted to shout. I was here on vacation. I had my own life, even if it was doing you-know-what. Let all this weirdness reach its natural level. But maybe it didn't matter what I thought? I was a member of the supporting cast.

Amé finished her sandwich and walked over to Yuki, slowly running her fingers through the girl's hair again. Yuki stared at the coffee cups on the table, expressionless. "Beautiful hair," said Amé. "The hair I always wanted. So shiny and silky straight. My hair's so unmanageable. Isn't that right, Princess?" Again she touched the tip of her nose to Yuki's temple.

Dick cleared away the dishes. Then he put on some Mozart chamber music. He asked me if I wanted another beer, but I told him I'd already had enough.

"Dick, I'd like to discuss some family matters with Yuki," Amé spoke with a snap in her voice. "Mother and daughter talk. Why don't you show this gentleman the beach? We should be about an hour."

"Sure," the poet answered, rising to his feet. He gave Amé a loving peck on the forehead, donned a white canvas hat and green Ray-Bans. "See you in an hour. Have a nice chat." Then he took me by the arm and led me out. "We've got a great beach here," he said.

Yuki shrugged and gave me a blank look. Amé was about to light up another Salem. Leaving the women on their own, we stepped out into the afternoon sun.

As I drove the Lancer down to the beach, Dick mentioned that with a prosthetic arm, driving would be no problem.

Still, he preferred not to wear one. "It's unnatural," he
explained. "I wouldn't feel at ease. It might be more convenient having one, but I'd be so self-conscious with it. It
wouldn't be me. I'm trying to train myself to live one-armed.
I'm limited in what I can do, but I do okay."

"How do you slice bread?"

"Bread?" He thought it over a second, as if he didn't
know what I was talking about. Then it dawned on him.
"Oh, slicing bread? Why sure, that's a reasonable question.
It's not so hard. I use one hand, of course, but I don't hold
the knife the usual way. I'd be useless if I did that. The trick
is to keep the bread in place with your fingers while you
move the blade. Like this."

Dick demonstrated with his hand, but for the life of me I
couldn't imagine how it would actually work. Yet I'd seen
his handiwork. His slices were cleaner than most people
with two hands could cut.

"Works perfectly well," he declared with a smile. "Most
things I can manage with one hand. I can't clap, but I can do
push-ups. Chin-ups too. It takes practice, but it's not impossible. How did you think I sliced bread?"

"I don't know, maybe with your feet?"

That drew a laugh from him. "Clever," he said. "I'll have
to write a poem about that. The one-armed poet making
sandwiches with his feet. Very clever."

I didn't know whether to agree or not.

A little ways down the coast highway, we pulled over and
bought a six-pack, then walked to a deserted area of the
beach. We lay down and drank beer after beer, but it was so
hot the beer didn't seem to go to my head.

The beach was very un-Hawaiian. Unsightly scrub
bushes, uneven sands, somehow rocky, but at least it was off
the tourist track. A few pickup trucks were parked nearby,
local families hanging out, veteran surfers doing their stuff.
The pithecanthropus cloud was still pinned in place, sea

gulls going around like washing-machine suds.

We talked in spurts. Dick had nothing but awe and respect for Amé. She was a true artist, he repeated several times. When he spoke about her, his Japanese trailed off into English. He said he couldn't express his feelings in Japanese.

"Since meeting her, my own thinking about poetry has changed. Her photographs—how can I put it?—strip poetry bare. I mean, here we are, choosing our words, braiding strands to cut a figure. But with her photos it's immediate, the embodiment. Out of thin air, out of light, in the gap between moments, she grabs things just like that. She gives physical presence to the depths of the human psyche. Do you know what I mean?"

Kind of, I allowed.

"Sometimes it frightens me, looking at her photos. My whole being is thrown into question. It's that overwhelming. She's a genius. Not like me and not like you . . . Forgive me, that's awfully presumptuous of me. I don't even know a thing about you."

I shook my head. "That's okay, I understand what you're saying."

"Genius is rare. I'm not talking about talent, or even first-rate talent. With genius, you're lucky just to encounter it, to see it right there before your eyes. And yet—," he paused, opening his hand up in a gesture of helplessness. "And yet, in some sense, the experience can be pretty upsetting. Sometimes it's like a needle piercing straight through my ego."

I gazed out at the ocean as I listened. The surf was rough, the waves breaking hard. I buried my fingers in the hot sand, scooped some up and let it drizzle down. Over and over again. Meanwhile, the surfers caught the waves they'd been waiting for and paddled back out.

"But you know," Dick went on, "even with my ego sacrificed, her talent attracts me. It makes me love her even more. Sometimes I think I've been drawn into a whirlpool. I already have a wife—she's Japanese too—and we have a child. I love them, I love them very much. Even now I love

them. But from the first time I met Amé, I was drawn right
in to her. I couldn't resist her. And I knew it was happening.
I knew it wasn't going to come my way again, not in this
life. That's when I decided—if I go with her, there'll come a
time that I'll regret it. But if I don't go with her, I'll be losing
the key to my existence. Have you ever felt that way about
something?"

Never, I told him.

"Odd," Dick continued. "I'd struggled so hard to have a
quiet, stable life. A wife and kid, a small house, my own
work. I didn't make a lot of money, but the work was worth
doing. I was writing and translating, and it was a good life, I
thought. I'd lost my arm in the war, and that was pretty
traumatic, but I worked hard at getting my head together
and I found some peace and I was doing all right. Life was
all right. And then—" He lifted his palm in a broad flat
sweep. "In an instant it was lost. Just like that. I have no
place to go. I have no home in Japan anymore, I have no
home in America. I've been away too long."

I wanted to offer him some words of comfort, but didn't
know what to say. I continued scooping up sand and letting
it fall. Dick stood up, walked over to a bush and took a leak,
then walked slowly back.

"Confession time," he said, then smiled. "I wanted to tell
someone. What do you think?"

What was I supposed to think? We weren't kids. You
choose who you sleep with, and whirlpool or tornado or
sandstorm, you make a go of what you choose. This Dick
made a good impression on me. I respected him for all the
difficulties he overcame with only one arm. But this diffi-
culty probably cut deeper.

"I'm afraid I'm not an artist," I said. "So I can't really
understand what it means to have an artistically inspiring
relationship. It's beyond me. I'm sorry."

Dick seemed saddened by my response and looked out to
sea. I shut my eyes. And the next thing I knew, I was waking
up. I'd dozed off. Maybe the beer after all. The heat made

my head feel light. My watch read half past two. I shook my head from side to side and sat up. Dick was playing with a dog at the edge of the surf. I felt bad. I hoped I hadn't offended him.

But what was I supposed to have said?

Was I cold? Of course I could appreciate his feelings. One arm or two, poet or not, it's a tough world. We all have to live with our problems. But weren't we adults? Hadn't we come this far already? At the very least, you don't go asking impossible questions of someone you've just met. That wasn't courteous.

Cold.

Dick rang the doorbell when we got back, and Yuki opened the door with a totally unamused look on her face. Amé was seated on the sofa, cigarette at her lips, eyes peering off into space as if she were in Zen meditation. Dick walked over and planted a kiss on her forehead.

"Finished talking?" he asked.

"Mmm," she said, cigarette still in her mouth. Affirmative, I assumed.

"We had a nice relaxing time on the beach, looked off the edge of the earth, and caught some rays," Dick reported.

"We have to be going," said Yuki flatly.

My thoughts exactly. Time we were getting back to the real world of tourist-town Honolulu.

Amé stood up. "Well, come visit again. I'd like to see you," she said, giving her daughter a tweak on the cheek.

I thanked Dick for his hospitality and had just helped Yuki into the car when Amé hooked me by the elbow. "I have something to tell you," she said. She led me to a small playground a bit up the road. Leaning against the jungle gym, she put a cigarette to her mouth and seemed almost bothered that she'd have to strike a match to light it.

"You're a decent fellow, I can tell," she began earnestly. "So I know I can ask a favor of you. I want you to bring the

child here as often as you can. I don't have to tell you that I
love her. She's my child. I want to see more of her. Understand? I want to talk with her. I want to become friends with
her. I think we can become friends, good friends, even before
being parent and child. So while she's here, I want to talk
with her a lot."

Amé gave me a meaningful look.

I couldn't think of an appropriate reply. But I had to say
something. "That's between you and her."

"Of course," she said.

"So if she wants to see you, certainly, I'll be happy to
bring her around," I said. "Or if you, as her parent, tell me
to bring her here, I'll do that. One way or the other. But
other than that, I have no say in this. Friends don't need the
intervention of a third party. Friendship's a voluntary thing.
At least that's the way I know it."

Amé pondered over what I'd said.

I got started again: "You say you want to be her friend.
That's very good. But before being Yuki's friend, you're her
mother, whether you like it or not. Yuki's thirteen. She *needs*
a mother. She needs someone who will love her and hold her
and be with her. I know I'm way out of line shooting my
mouth off like this. But Yuki doesn't need a part-time friend;
she needs a situation that accepts her one hundred percent.
That's what she needs first."

"You don't understand," said Amé.

"Exactly. I don't understand," I said. "But let's get this
straight. Yuki's still a child and she's been hurt. Someone
needs to protect her. It's a lot of trouble, but somebody's got
to do it. That's responsibility. Can't you understand that?"

"I'm not asking you to bring her here every day," she
said. "Just when she wants to come. I'll be calling regularly
too. Because I don't want to lose that child. The way things
are going, she's going to move away from me as she grows
up. I understand that, so what I want are psychological ties.
I want a bond. I know I probably haven't been a great
mother. But I have so much to do before being a mother.

There's nothing I can do about it. The child knows that. That's why what I want is a relationship beyond mother and daughter. Maybe you could call it blood friends."

On the drive back, we listened to the radio. We didn't talk. Occasionally I'd whistle, but otherwise silence prevailed. Yuki gazed out the window, face turned away from me. For fifteen minutes. But I knew something was coming. I told myself, very plainly: You'd better stop the car somewhere.

So that's what I did. I pulled over into a beach parking lot. I asked Yuki how she was feeling. I asked her if she wanted something to drink. Yuki said nothing.

Two girls wearing identical swimsuits walked slowly under the palms, across my field of vision, stepping like cats balancing on a fence. Their swimsuits were a skimpy patchwork of tiny handkerchiefs that any gust of wind might easily blow away. The whole scene had this wild, too-real unreality of a suppressed dream.

I looked up at the sky. A mother wants to make friends with her daughter. The daughter wants a mother more than a friend. Ships passing in broad daylight. Mother has a boyfriend. A homeless, one-armed poet. Father also has a boyfriend. A gay Boy Friday. What does the daughter have?

Ten minutes later it began. Soft sobs at first, but then the dam burst. Her hands neatly folded in her lap, her nose buried in my shoulder, her slim body trembling. *Cry, go ahead and cry. If I were in your position I'd cry too. You better believe I'd cry.*

I put my arm around her. And she cried. She cried until my shirt sleeve was sopping. She cried and cried and cried.

Two policemen in sunglasses crossed the parking lot flashing revolvers. A German shepherd wandered by, panting in the heat. Palm trees swayed. A huge Samoan climbed out of a pickup truck and walked his girlfriend to the beach. The radio was playing.

"Don't ever call me Princess again," she said, head still resting in my shoulder.

"Did I do that?" I asked.

"Yes, you did."

"I don't remember."

"Driving back from Tsujido, that night. Don't say it again."

"I won't. I promise I won't. I swear on Boy George and Duran Duran. Never, never, never again."

"That's what Mama always calls me. *Princess*."

"I won't call you that again."

"Mama, she's always hurting me. She's just got no idea. And yet she loves me. I know she does."

"Yes, she does."

"So what am I supposed to do?"

"The only thing you can. Grow up."

"I don't want to."

"No other way," I said. "Everyone does, like it or not. People get older. That's how they deal with it. They deal with it till the day they die. It's always been this way. Always will be. It's not just you."

She looked up at me, her face streaked with tears. "Don't you believe in comforting people?"

"I *was* comforting you."

She brushed my arm from her shoulder and took a tissue from her bag. "There's something really abnormal about you, you know," she said.

We went back to the hotel. We swam. We showered. We went to the supermarket and bought fixings for dinner. We grilled the steak with onions and soy sauce, we tossed a salad, we had miso soup with tofu and scallions. A pleasant supper. Yuki even had half a glass of California wine.

"You're not such a bad cook," Yuki said.

"No, not true. I just put my heart into it. That's the difference. It's a question of attitude. If you really work at something, you can do it, up to a point. If you really work at being happy, you can do it, up to a point."

"But anything more than that, you can't."

"Anything more than that is luck," I said.

"You really know how to depress people, don't you? Is that what you call being adult?"

We washed the dishes, then went out walking on Kalakaua Avenue as the lights were blinking on. We critiqued the merchandise of different offbeat shops, eyed the outfits of the passersby, took a rest stop at the crowded Royal Hawaiian Hotel garden bar. I got my requisite piña colada; Yuki asked for fruit punch. I thought of Dick North and how he would hate the noisy city night. I didn't mind it so much myself.

"What do you think of my mother?" Yuki asked when our drinks arrived.

"Honestly, I don't know what to think," I said after a moment. "It takes me a while to consider everything and pass judgment. Afraid I'm not very bright."

"But she did get you a little mad, right?"

"Oh yeah?"

"It was all over your face," said Yuki.

"Maybe so," I said, taking a sip and looking out on the night sea. "I guess I did get a little annoyed."

"At what?"

"At the total lack of responsibility of the people who should be looking after you. But what's the use? Who am I to get mad? As if it does any good."

Yuki nibbled at a pretzel from a dish on the table. "I guess nobody knows what to do. They want to do something, but they don't know how."

"Nobody seems to know how."

"And you do?"

"I'm waiting for hints to take shape, then I'll know what action to take."

Yuki fingered the neck of her T-shirt. "I don't get it," she said.

"All you have to do is wait," I explained. "Sit tight and wait for the right moment. Not try to change anything by force, just watch the drift of things. Make an effort to cast a fair eye on everything. If you do that, you just naturally know what to do. But everyone's always too busy. They're too talented, their schedules are too full. They're too interested in themselves to think about what's fair."

Yuki planted an elbow on the table, then swept the pretzel crumbs from the tablecloth. A retired couple in matching aloha shirt and muumuu at the next table sipped out of a big, brash tropical drink. They looked so happy. In the torch-lit courtyard, a woman was playing the electric piano. Her singing was less than wonderful, but two or three pairs of hands clapped when her vocal stylings were over. And then Yuki grabbed my piña colada and took a quick sip.

"Yum," she exclaimed.

"Two votes yum," I said. "Motion passed."

Yuki stared at me. "What is *with* you? I can't figure you out. One minute you're Mister Cool, the next you're bonkers from the toes up."

"If you're sane, that means you're off your rocker. So don't worry about it," I replied, then ordered another piña colada from a frighteningly cheerful waitress. She wiggled off, trotted back with the drink, then vanished leaving behind a mile-wide Cheshire grin.

"Okay, so what am I supposed to do?" said Yuki.

"Your mother wants to see more of you," I said. "I don't know any more than that. She's not my family, and she's as unusual as they come. As I understand her, she wants to get out of the rut of a mother-daughter relationship and become friends with you."

"Making friends isn't so easy."

"Agreed," I said. "Two votes not so easy."

With both elbows now on the table, Yuki gave me a dubious look.

"And what do you think? About Mama's way of thinking."

"What I think doesn't matter. The question is, what do you think? You could think it's wishful thinking on her part. Or you could think it's a constructive stance worth considering. It all depends on you. But don't make any rush decisions. You should take your time thinking it over."

Yuki propped her chin up on her hands. There was a loud guffaw from the counter. The pianist launched into "Blue Hawaii." Heavy breathing to a tinkling of high notes. *The night is young and so are we. . . .*

"We're not doing so well right now," said Yuki. "Before going to Sapporo was the worst. She was on my case about not going to school. It was real messy. We hardly spoke to each other. I never wanted to see her. That dragged on and on. But then Mama doesn't think like normal people do. She says whatever comes into her head and then she forgets it right after she's said it. She's serious when she says it, but after that she might as well have never said a thing. And then out of nowhere, she wants to play mother again. That's what really pisses me off."

"But—," I tried to interrupt.

"But she *is* interesting. She isn't like anybody else in the world. She may be the pits as a mother and she's really screwed me up, but she *is* interesting. Not like Papa. I don't really know what to think, though. Now she says she wants to be friends. She's so . . . overwhelming, so powerful, and I'm just a kid. Anyone can see that, right? But *no–o*, not her. Mama says she wants to be friends, but the harder she tries, the more it hurts me. That's how it was in Sapporo. She tried to get close to me, she actually tried. So I started to get closer to her. I tried, honest. But her head's always so full of stuff, she just spaces out. And the next thing I know, she's gone." Yuki sent her half-nibbled pretzel out over the sand. "Now if that's not loopy, what is? I like Mama. I guess I like her. And I guess I wouldn't mind if we were friends. I just don't want to have everything dumped back on me again like that. I hate that."

"Everything you say is right," I said. "Completely understandable."

"Not for Mama. She wouldn't understand if you spelled it all out for her."

"No, I don't think so either."

The next day dawned with another glorious Hawaiian sunrise. We ate breakfast, then went to the beach in front of the Sheraton. We rented boards and tried to surf. Yuki enjoyed herself so much that afterward we went to a surf shop near the Ala Moana Shopping Center and bought two used boards. The salesclerk asked if we were brother and sister. I said yes. I was glad we didn't look like father and daughter.

At two o'clock we were back on the beach, lazing. Sunbathing, swimming, napping, listening to the radio and tuning out, thumbing through paperbacks, people-watching, listening to the wind in the palms. The sun slowly traveled its prescribed path. When it went down, we returned to our rooms, showered, ate some spaghetti and salad, then we went to see a Spielberg movie. After the movie we took a walk and ended up at the Halekulani poolside bar, where I had a piña colada again and Yuki her usual fruit punch.

A dance band was playing "Frenesi." An elderly clarinetist took a long solo, reminiscent of Artie Shaw, while a dozen retired couples in silks and satins danced around the pool, faces illuminated by the rippling blue light from below. A hallucinatory vision. After how many years, these people had finally made it to Hawaii. They glided gracefully, their steps learned and true. The men moved with their backs straight, chins tucked in, the women with their evening dresses swirling, drawing cheek-to-cheek as the band played "Moon Glow."

"I'm getting sleepy again," said Yuki. But this time, she walked back alone. Progress.

Returning to my room, I opened a bottle of wine and watched Clint Eastwood's *Hang 'Em High* on the tube. By the time I was on my third glass, I was so sleepy I gave up on the whole thing and got ready to knock off. It'd been another perfect Hawaiian day.

And it wasn't over yet.

Five minutes after I'd crawled into bed, the doorbell rang. A little before midnight. Terrific. What did Yuki want now? I got myself decent and got to the door as the bell sounded another time. I flung the door open—only to find that it wasn't Yuki at all. It was an attractive young woman.

"Hi," said the attractive young woman.

"Hi," I said back.

"My name is June," she said with a slight accent. She seemed to be Southeast Asian, maybe Thai or Filipino or Vietnamese. Petite and dark, big eyes. Wearing a sleek dress of some lustrous pink material. Her purse and shoes were pink too. Tied on her left wrist was a large pink ribbon. Gift-wrapped. She placed a hand on the door and smiled.

"Hi, June," I said.

"I come in?" she asked, pointing behind me.

"Just a minute. You must have the wrong party. Which room do you want?"

"Umm, wait second," she said and pulled a piece of paper from her purse. "Mmm, Mistah . . ." She showed me the note.

"That's me."

"No mistake?"

"No mistake. But not so fast," I said. "I'm the fellow you want, but I don't know who you are. What's going on?"

"I come in first? Here people listen. People think strange things. Everything relax, no problem. No gun, no holdup. Okay?"

True, we'd wake Yuki up if we continued talking in the corridor. I let June in.

I asked her if she wanted something to drink. She'd have what I'd have. I mixed two gin-and-tonics, which I placed on the low table between us. She boldly crossed her legs as she brought the drink to her lips. Beautiful legs.

"Okay, June, why are you here and what do you want?"

"I come make you happy," she said naturally.

"Who told you to come?"

She shrugged. "Gentleman friend who not want say. He already pay. He pay from Japan. He pay for you. Understand?"

Makimura. It had to be Makimura. The way that man's mind worked! What a world! Everyone wanting to buy me women.

"He pay for all night. So we can enjoy. I very good," June said, lifting her legs to remove her pink high heels. She then lay down on the floor, very provocatively.

"I'm sorry, but I can't go through with this," I interrupted her.

"Why? You gay?"

"No, I'm not gay. It's a difference of opinion between me and the gentleman who paid for you. I'm afraid I can't accept, June."

"But I get money. I cannot pay back. He care whether we fuck or not fuck? I don't call overseas and say, 'Yessir, we fuck three times.'"

I sighed.

"Let's do it," she said simply. "It feel good."

I didn't know what to think. One foot in dreamland after a long day, then someone you don't know shows up and says "Let's fuck." Good grief.

"We drink one more gin tonic, okay?"

I agreed somehow. June fixed our drinks, then switched the radio on. "*Saiko!*" June said, throwing in some Japanese for effect, relaxing as if she were at home. "Great." Then sipping her drink, she leaned against me. "Don't think too much," she said, reading my mind. "I very good. I know very much. Don't try do nothing, I do everything. Gentleman in Japan out of picture. Now just you and me."

June ran her fingers across my chest. My resolve was weakening steadily. This was beginning to seem quite easy. If I could just live with the fact that Makimura had bought me a prostitute. But it was only sex. Erection, insertion, ejaculation, that's all folks.

"Okay," I said, "Let's do it."

"Thatta boy!" exclaimed June, downing her gin-and-tonic.

"But tonight I'm very tired. So no special stunts."

"I do everything. But you do two things."

"Which are?"

"Turn off light, untie ribbon."

Done. We headed into the bedroom. June had her dress off in a flash, then set about undressing me. She may not have been Mei, but she was skilled at her job and she took pride in her skills. She was fingers and tongue all over me. She got me hard and then she made me come to the beat of Foreigner on the radio. The night had just begun.

"Was that good?"

"V—very," I panted.

We treated ourselves to another round of drinks.

Suddenly I had a thought. "June, last month you wouldn't have had a 'Mei' here, would you?"

"Funny man!" June burst out laughing. "I like jokes. And next month she is July, right?"

I tried to tell her that it wasn't a joke, but it didn't do any good. So I shut up. And when I did, June did another professional job on me. I didn't have to do a thing, exactly like she said. I just lay there.

She was as fast and efficient as a service station attendant. You pull up and hand over the keys. She takes care of everything else: fill up the tank, wash and wax, check the oil, empty the ashes. Could you call it sex? Well, whatever it was, we kept at it until past two when we finally ran out of gas and conked out. It was already light out when we awoke. We'd left the radio on. June was curled up naked next to me, her pink dress and pink shoes and pink ribbon lying on the floor.

"Hey, get up," I said, trying to rouse her. "You've got to get out of here. There's a little girl coming over for break-.fast."

"Okay, okay," she muttered, grabbing up her bag and walking naked into the bathroom to brush her teeth and comb her hair.

When she was ready to leave, she tossed her lipstick into her bag and closed it with a snap. "So when I come next?"

"Next?"

"I get money for three nights. We fuck last night, we fuck two more nights. Maybe you want different girl? I no mind. Men like sleep with lots girls."

"No, you're who I want, of course," I said, at a loss for what else to say. Three nights? Did Makimura want me milked dry?

"You very nice. You no regret. I do wild next time. Okay? You count on me. Night after tomorrow, okay? I have free night. I do whole works."

"Okay," I told her, handing her ten dollars for carfare.

"Thank you, you very nice. Bye-bye."

I cleaned the place up before Yuki arrived, got rid of all the telltale signs, including the pink ribbon. But the moment Yuki stepped into the room a stern expression came over her face. She knew right away. I pretended not to notice her demeanor, whistling as I prepared the coffee and toast and brought them to the table.

She didn't say a word through breakfast, refused to respond to my attempts at conversation.

Finally she placed both hands on the table and glared at me. "You had a woman here last night, didn't you?" she said.

"You really pick up on things, don't you?" I tried to make light of the situation.

"Who was she? Some girl you picked up somewhere?"

"Oh c'mon. I'm not that good. She came here of her own doing."

"Don't lie to me! Nothing happens like that."

"I'm not lying, I promise. The woman really did come here on her own," I said. I tried to explain: The woman suddenly showed up and turned out to be a gift from her father. Maybe it was his idea of giving me a good time, or maybe he was worried and figured if I was sexually sated, I'd stay out of his daughter's bed.

"That's exactly the kind of garbage he'd pull," said Yuki, resigned but angry. "Why does he always operate on the lowest level? He never understands anything, anything important. Mama's screwy, but Papa's head is on ass backwards."

"Yeah, he's totally off the mark."

"So then why'd you let her in? That woman."

"I didn't know what was coming off. I had to talk with her."

"But don't tell me you . . ."

"It wasn't so simple, I—"

"You didn't!" Yuki flew into a huff. Then, at a loss for what to say, she blushed.

"Well, yes. It's a long story. But the truth of the matter is, I couldn't say no."

She closed her eyes and pressed her hands to her cheeks. "I don't believe this!" Yuki screamed, her voice breaking. "I can't believe you'd do such a thing!"

"Of course, I refused at first," I tried to defend myself. "But in the end—what can I say?—I gave in. It wasn't just the woman, though of course it was the woman. It was your father and your mother and the way they have this influence on everybody they meet. So I figured what the hell. Also, the woman didn't seem like such a bad deal."

"I can't believe you're saying this!" Yuki cried. "You let Papa buy a woman for you? And you think nothing of it? That's so shameless, that's wrong. How could you?"

She had a point.

"You have a point," I said.

"That's really, really shameless."

"I admit it. It's really, really shameless."

We repaired to the beach and surfed until noon. During which time Yuki didn't speak a single word to me. When I asked if she wanted to have lunch, she nodded. Did she want to eat back at the hotel? She shook her head. Did she want to eat out? She nodded. After a bit more nonverbal conversation, we settled for hot dogs, sitting out on the grass by Fort DeRussy. Three hours and still not a peep out of her.

So I said, "Next time I'll just say no."

She removed her sunglasses and stared at me as if I were a rip in the sky. For a full thirty seconds. Then she brushed back her bangs. "Next time?!" she enunciated, incredulous. "What do you mean, *next time?*"

So I did my best to explain how her father had prepaid for two more nights. Yuki pounded the ground with her fist. "I don't *believe* this. This is really barfbag."

"I don't mean to upset you, Yuki, but think of it this way. Your father is at least showing concern. I mean, I am a male of the species and you are a young, very pretty female."

"Really and truly barfbag," Yuki screamed, holding back tears. She stormed off back to the hotel and I didn't see her until evening.

30

Hawaii.

The next few days were bliss. A respite of peace. When June showed up for my next installment, I begged a fever and turned her down politely. She was very gracious. She got a mechanical pencil from her bag and jotted down her number on a notepad. I could call when I felt up to it. Then she said good-bye and left, swinging her hips off into the sunset.

I took Yuki to her mother's a few more times. I took walks with Dick North on the beach, I swam in their pool. Dick could swim amazingly well. Having just one arm hardly seemed to make a difference. Yuki and her mother talked by themselves, about what I had no idea. Yuki never told me and I never asked.

On one occasion Dick recited some Robert Frost to me. My understanding of English wasn't good enough, but Dick's delivery alone conveyed the poetry, which flowed with rhythm and feeling. I also got to see some of Amé's photos, still wet from the developing. Pictures of Hawaiian faces. Ordinary portraits, but in her hands the subjects came alive with honest island vitality and grace. There was an earthiness, a chilling brutality, a sexiness. Powerful, yet unassuming. Yes, Amé had talent. *Not like me and not like you*, as Dick had said.

Dick looked after Amé in much the same way I looked after Yuki. Though he, of course, was far more thorough. He cleaned house, washed clothes, cooked meals, did the shopping. He recited poetry, told jokes, put out her cigarettes, kept her supplied with Tampax (I once accompanied him shopping), made sure she brushed her teeth, filed her photos, prepared a typewritten catalogue of all her works. All single-handedly. I didn't know where the poor guy found the time to do his own creative work. Though who was I to talk? I was having my trip paid by Yuki's father, with a call girl thrown in on top.

On days when we didn't visit Yuki's mother, we surfed, swam, lolled about on the beach, went shopping, drove around the island. Evenings, we went for strolls, saw movies, had piña coladas and fruit drinks. I had plenty of time to cook meals if I felt like it. We relaxed and got beautifully tanned, down to our fingertips. Yuki bought a new Hawaiian-print bikini at a boutique in the Hilton, and in it she looked like a real local girl. She got quite good at surfing and could catch waves that were beyond me. She listened to the Rolling Stones. Whenever I left her side on the beach, guys moved in, trying to strike up a conversation with her. But Yuki didn't speak a word of English, so she had no trouble ignoring them. They'd be shuffling off, disgruntled, when I got back.

"Do guys really desire girls so much?" Yuki asked.

"Yeah. Depends on the individual of course, but generally I guess you could say that men desire women. You know about sex, don't you?"

"I know enough," said Yuki dryly.

"Well, men have this physical desire to sleep with women," I explained. "It's a natural thing. The preservation of the species—"

"I don't care about the preservation of the species. I don't want to know about science and hygiene. I want to know about *sex drive*. How does that work?"

"Okay, suppose you were a bird," I said, "and flying was something you really enjoyed and made you feel good. But there were certain circumstances that, except on rare occasions, kept you from flying. I don't know, let's say, lousy weather conditions, the direction of the wind, the season, things like that. But the more you couldn't fly, the more you wanted to fly and your energy built up inside you and made you irritable. You felt bottled up or something like that. You got annoyed, maybe even angry. You get me?"

"I get you," she said. "I always feel that way."

"Well, that's your sex drive."

"So when was the last time you flew? That is, before Papa bought that prostitute for you?"

"The end of last month."

"Was it good?"

I nodded.

"Is it always good?"

"No, not always," I said. "Bring two imperfect beings together and things don't always go right. You're flying along nice and easy, and suddenly there's this enormous tree in front of you that you didn't see before, and *cr–rash*."

Yuki mulled this over. Imagining, perhaps, a bird flying high, its peripheral vision completely missing the danger straight ahead. Was this a bad explanation or what? Was she going to take things the wrong way? Aww, what the hell, she'd find out for herself soon enough.

"The chance of things going right gradually improves with age," I continued my explanation. "You get the knack of things, and you learn to read the weather and wind. On the other side of the coin, sex drive decreases with age. That's just how it goes."

"Pathetic," said Yuki.

"Yes, pathetic."

Hawaii.

Just how many days had I been in the Islands? The concept of time had vanished from my head. Today comes after yesterday, tomorrow comes after today. The sun comes up, the sun goes down; the moon rises, the moon sets; tide comes in, tide goes out.

I pulled out my appointment book and checked the calendar. We'd been in Hawaii for ten days! It was approaching the end of April. Wasn't I going to stay for one week? Or was it one month? Days of surfing and piña coladas. Not bad as far as that went.

But how did I get to this spot? It started with me looking for Kiki, except that I didn't know that was her name at the time. I'd retraced my steps to Sapporo, and ever since, there'd been one weird character after another. And now, look at me, lying in the shade of a coconut palm, tropical drink in hand, listening to Kalapana.

What happened along the way? Mei was murdered. The police hauled me in. Whatever happened with Mei's case? Did the cops find out who she was? What about Gotanda? How was he doing? The last time I saw him he looked awful, tired and run-down. And then we left everything half-assed up in the air.

Pretty soon I had to be getting back to Japan. But it was so hard to take the first step in that direction. Hawaii had been the first real release from tension in ages—for both Yuki and me—and boy, had we needed it. Day after day I was thinking about almost nothing. Just swimming and lying in the sun getting tan, driving around the island listening to the Stones and Bruce Springsteen, walking moonlit beaches, drinking in hotel bars.

I knew this couldn't go on forever. But I couldn't get myself moving. And I couldn't bear to see Yuki get all uptight again. It was a perfect excuse.

Two weeks passed.

One day toward dusk, Yuki and I motored our way through downtown Honolulu. Traffic was bad, but we were in no hurry, content to drive around and take in all the roadside attractions. Porno theaters, thrift shops, Chinese grocers, Vietnamese clothing stores, used book and record shops, old men playing go, guys with blurry eyes standing on street corners. Funny town, Honolulu. Full of cheap, good, interesting places to eat. But not a place for a girl to walk alone.

Right outside the downtown area, toward the harbor, the city blocks became sparser, less inviting. There were office buildings and warehouses and coffee shops missing letters from their signs, and the buses were full of people going home from work.

That's when Yuki said she wanted to see *E.T.* again.

Okay, after dinner, I said.

Then she said what a great movie it was and how she wished I was more like E.T. and then she touched my forehead with her index finger.

"Don't do that," I said. "It'll never heal."

That drew a chuckle from her.

And that's when it happened.

When something connected up inside my head with a loud *clink*. Something happened, though I didn't know then what it was.

It was enough to make me slam on the brakes, though. The Camaro behind us honked bitterly and showered me with abuses as it pulled around us. I had seen something, and something connected. Just there now, something very important.

"What's the matter?" Yuki said, or so I thought she said.

I may not have heard a thing. Because I was deep in thought at that moment. I was deep in thought thinking that I'd just seen *her*. *Kiki*. I'd just seen Kiki—in downtown Honolulu! She was here! Why? It was definitely her. I'd driven past, close enough to have reached out and touched her. She was walking in the opposite direction, right beside the car.

"Listen, close all the windows and lock all the doors. Don't set a foot outside. And don't open up for anyone. I'll be right back," I said, leaping out of the car.

"Hey, wait! Don't leave me here!"

But I was already running down the sidewalk, bumping into people, pushing them out of my way. I didn't have time to be polite. I had to catch up with her. I had to stop her, I had to talk to her, I had found her! I ran for two blocks, I ran for three blocks. And then, way up ahead, I spotted her, in a blue dress with a white bag swinging at her side in the early evening light. She was heading back toward the hustle and bustle of town. I followed, reaching the main drag, where the sidewalk traffic got thicker. A woman three times the size of Yuki couldn't seem to get out of my way. But I kept going, trying to catch up. As Kiki kept walking. Not fast, not slow, at normal speed. But not turning around to look behind her, not glancing to the side, not stopping to board a bus, just walking straight ahead. You'd think I'd be right up with her any second now, but the distance between us never seemed to close.

The next thing I knew she turned a corner to the left. Naturally I followed suit. It was a narrow street, lined on both sides with nondescript, old office buildings. There was no sign of her anywhere. Out of breath, I came to a standstill. What is this? How could she disappear on me again? But Kiki hadn't disappeared. She'd just been hidden from view by a large delivery truck, because there she was again, walking at the same clip on the far sidewalk.

"Kiki!" I yelled.

She heard me, apparently. She shot a glance back in my direction. There was still some distance between us, it was dusk, and the streetlights weren't on yet, but it was Kiki all right. I was sure of it. I *knew* it was her. And she knew who was calling her. She even smiled.

But she didn't stop. She'd simply glanced over her shoulder at me. She didn't slacken her pace. She kept on walking and then entered a building. By the time I got there, it was too late. No one was in the foyer, and the elevator door was just shutting. It was an old elevator, the kind with a clock-like dial that told you what floor it was on. I took the time to breathe, eyes glued to the dial. Eight. She'd gotten off on eight. I pressed the button, then impulsively decided to take the stairs instead.

The whole building seemed to be empty, dead quiet. The gummy slap of my rubber soles on the linoleum steps resounded hollow through the dusty stairwell.

The eighth floor wasn't any different. Not a soul in sight. I looked left and right and saw nothing to suggest life. I walked down the hall and read the signs on each of the seven or eight doors. A trading company, a law office, a dentist, . . . None in business, the signs old and smudged. Nondescript offices on a nondescript floor of a nondescript building on a nondescript street. I went back and reexamined the signs on the doors. Nothing seemed to connect to Kiki; nothing made sense. I strained my ears, but the building was as quiet as a ruins.

Then came the sound. A clicking of heels, high heels. Echoing eerily off the ceilings, bearing a weight . . . the dry weight of old memories. All of a sudden, I was wandering through the labyrinthine viscera of a large organism. Long-dead, cracked, eroded. By something beyond reality, beyond human rationality, I had slipped through a fault in time and entered this . . . thing.

The clicking heels continued to echo, so loudly, so deeply, that it was difficult to determine which direction they were coming from. But listening carefully, I traced the steps to the distant end of a corridor that turned to the right. I moved quickly, quietly, to the door farthest. Those steps, the clicking of the heels, grew murky, remote, but they were there, beyond the door. An unmarked door. Which was unnerving. When I'd checked a minute before, each door had a sign.

Was this a dream? No, not with such continuity. All the details followed in perfect order. I'm in downtown Honolulu, I chased Kiki here. Something's gone whacky, but it's real.

I knocked.

The footsteps stopped, the last echo sucked up midair. Silence filled the vacuum.

For thirty seconds I waited. Nothing. I tried the doorknob. And with a low, grating grumble, the door opened inward. Into a room that was dark, tinged with the somber blue of the waning of the day. There was a faint smell of floor wax. The room was empty, with the exception of old newspapers scattered on the floor.

Footsteps again. Exactly four footsteps, then silence.

The sound seemed to emerge from somewhere even farther. I walked toward the window and discovered another door set off to the side. It opened onto a stairwell that went up. I gripped the cold metal handrail, tested my footing, then slowly climbed into what became total black darkness. The stairs rose at a steep pitch. I imagined I could hear sounds above. The stairs ended. I groped for a light switch; there wasn't any. Instead, my hand found another door.

It opened into what I sensed to be a sizable space, perhaps an attic. There was not the total darkness of the stairwell, but it was still not light enough to see. Faint refractions from the glow of the streetlights below stole in through a skylight. I held on to the doorknob.

"Kiki!" I shouted.

There was no response.

I stood still, waiting, not knowing what to do. Time evaporated. I peered into the darkness, ears alert. Slowly, uncertainly, the light filtering into the room seemed to increase. The moon? The lights of the city? I proceeded cautiously into the center of the space.

"Kiki!" I called out again.

No response.

I turned slowly around, straining to see what I could. Odd pieces of furniture were arranged in the corners of the room. Gray silhouettes that might be a sofa, chairs, a table, a chest. Peculiar, very peculiar. The stage had been set as if by centrifuge, surreal, but real. I mean, the furniture looked *real*.

On the sofa was a white object. A sheet? Or the white bag Kiki'd been carrying? I walked closer and discovered that it was something quite different.

The something was bones.

Two human skeletons were seated side by side on the sofa. Two complete skeletons, one larger, one smaller, sitting exactly as they might have when they were alive. The larger skeleton rested one arm on the back of the sofa. The smaller one had both hands placed neatly on its lap. It was as if they'd died instantly, before they knew what hit them, their flesh having fallen away, their position intact. They almost seemed to be smiling. Smiling, and incredibly white.

I felt no fear. Why, I don't have the slightest idea, but I was quite calm. Everything in this room was so still, the bones clean and quiet. These two skeletons were extremely, irrevocably dead. There was nothing to fear.

I walked slowly around the room. There were six skeletons in all. Except for one, all were whole. All sat in natural positions. One man (at least from the size, I imagined it was a man) had his line of vision fixed on a television. Another was bent over a table still set with dishes, the food now dust. Yet another, the only skeleton in an imperfect state, lay in bed. Its left arm was missing from the shoulder.

I squeezed my eyes shut.

What on earth was this? Kiki, what are you trying to show me?

Again, I heard footsteps. Coming from another room, but in which direction? It seemed to have no location at all. As far as I could see, this room was a dead end. There was no other way out. The footsteps persisted, then vanished. The silence that lingered then was so dense it was suffocating. I wiped the sweat from my face with the palm of my hand. Kiki had disappeared again.

I exited through the door I'd entered from. One last glance: the six skeletons glowing faintly in the deep blue gloom. They almost seemed ready to get up and move about once I was gone. They'd switch on the TV, help themselves to hot food. I closed the door quietly, so as not to disturb them, then went back downstairs to the empty office. It was as before, not a soul around, old newspapers scattered on the floor.

I went over to the window and looked down. The street-lights glowed brightly; the same trucks and vans were parked in the narrow thoroughfare. The sun had completely set. Nobody in sight.

But lying on the dust-covered windowsill, I noticed a scrap of paper, the size of a business card. I picked it up and studied it carefully. There was a phone number on it. The paper was fresh, the ink unfaded. Curious. I slipped it in my pocket and went out into the corridor.

I was trying to find the building superintendent to ask about the office, when I remembered Yuki, stranded in the car, in a seedy section of town. How long had I left her there? Twenty minutes? An hour? The sky was sliding into night.

Yuki was dazed, her face buried into the seat, the radio on, when I got back to the car. I tapped on the window, and she unlocked the door.

"Sorry," I said solemnly.

"All kinds of weird people came. They yelled and they banged on the windshield and rocked the car," she said, almost numb. "I was scared out of my mind."

"I'm very sorry."

She looked me in the face. Then her eyes turned to ice. The pupils lost their color, the slightest tremor raced over her features like the surface of a lake rippled by a fallen leaf. Her lips formed unspoken words. *Where on earth did you go?*

"I don't know," my voice issued from somewhere and blurred out into the distance like those echoing footsteps. I pulled a handkerchief from my pocket and slowly wiped the sweat from my brow. "I don't know."

Yuki squinted and reached out to touch my cheek. Her

fingertips were soft and smooth. She sniffed the air around me, her tiny nostrils swelling slightly. She gave me another long look. "You *saw* something, didn't you?"

I nodded.

"But you can't say what. You can't put it into words. Can't explain, not to anyone. But I can see it." She leaned over and grazed her cheek against mine. "Poor thing," she said.

"How come?" I asked, laughing. There was no reason to laugh, but I couldn't not laugh. "All things considered, I'm the most ordinary guy you could hope to find. So why do these weird things keep happening to me?"

"Yeah, why?" said Yuki. "Don't look at me. I'm just a kid. You're the adult here."

"True enough."

"But I understand how you feel."

"I don't."

"At times like this, adults need a drink."

We went to the Halekulani bar. The one indoors, not the one by the pool. I ordered a martini this time, and Yuki got a lemon soda. We were the only customers in the place. The balding pianist, with a Rachmaninoff scowl, was at the concert grand running through old standards—"Stardust," "But Not for Me," "Moonlight in Vermont." Flawlessly, with lackluster. Then he finished off with a very serious Chopin prelude. Yuki clapped for this, and the pianist forced a smile.

On my third martini, I shut my eyes and that room came to mind again. The sort of scene where you wake up drenched in sweat, relieved that it was just a dream. But it hadn't been a dream. I knew it and so did Yuki. She knew I'd *seen* something. Those six skeletons. What did they mean? Who were they? Was that one-armed skeleton supposed to be Dick North?

What was Kiki trying to tell me?

I remembered the scrap of paper in my pocket, the scrap

of paper I'd found on the windowsill. I went to the phone
and dialed the number. No answer. Only endless ringing, like
plumb bobs hanging in bottomless oblivion. I returned to my
bar stool and sighed. "I'm thinking about going back to
Japan tomorrow. If I can get a seat, that is," I said. "I've
been here a little too long. It's been great, but time to go
back. I've got things I got to clear up back home."

Yuki nodded, as if she'd known this all along. "It's okay,
don't worry about me. Go back if you think you should."

"What are you going to do? Stay here? Or do you want
to go back with me?"

Yuki shrugged her shoulders. "I think I'll go stay with
Mama for a while. I don't think she'd mind. I'm not in the
mood to go back yet."

I finished up the last of my martini.

"We'll do this then: I'll drive you out to Makaha tomorrow. That way I get to see your mother one more time. And
then I'll head off to the airport."

That night we had our last dinner together at a seafood
restaurant near Aloha Tower. Yuki didn't talk much, and neither did I. I was sure I would drift off at any moment, mouth
full of fried oysters, to join those skeletons in the attic.

Yuki gave me meaningful glances throughout the meal.
After we were done, she said, "You better go home to bed.
You look terrible."

Back in my room I poured myself some wine and turned
on the television. The Yankees vs. the Orioles. I had no
desire to watch baseball, but I left the game on anyway. It
was a link to reality.

The wine had its effect. I got sleepy. And then I remembered the slip of paper in my pocket and tried the number
again. No answer again. I let the telephone ring fifteen times.
I glared at the tube to see Winfield step into the batter's box,
when something occurred to me.

What was it? My eyes were fixed on the screen.

Something resembled something. Something was connected to something.

Nah, unlikely. But what the hell, check it out. I took the slip of paper and went to get the notepad where June had written her phone number. I compared the two numbers.

Good grief. They were the same.

Everything, everything, was linking up. Except I didn't have a clue what it meant.

The next morning I rang up JAL and booked a flight for the afternoon. I paid our bills, and Yuki and I were on our way to Makaha. For once, the sky was overcast. A squall was brewing on the horizon.

"Sounds like there's a Pacman crunching away at your heart," said Yuki. "*Bip-bip-bip-bip-bip-bip-bip-bip.*"

"I don't understand."

"Something's eating you."

I thought about that as I drove on. "Every so often I glimpse this shadow of death," I began. "It's a very dense shadow. As if death was very close, enveloping me, holding me down by the ankles. Any minute now it could happen. But it doesn't scare me. Because it's never my death. It's always someone else's. Still, each time someone dies it wears *me* down. How come?"

Yuki shrugged.

"Death is always beside me, I don't know why. And given the slightest opening, it shows itself."

"Maybe that's your key. Maybe death's your connection to the world," Yuki said.

"What a depressing thought," I said.

Dick North seemed sincerely sad to see me leave. Not that we had a great deal in common, but we did enjoy a certain ease with each other. And I respected him for the poetry he brought to practical concerns. We shook hands. As we did, the one-armed skeleton came to mind. Could that really be this man?

"Dick, do you ever think about death? How you might die?" I asked him, as we sat around one last time.

He smiled. "I thought about death a lot during the War. There was death all around, so many ways you could get killed. But lately, no, I don't have time to worry about what I don't have control over. I'm busier in peace than in war," he laughed. "What makes you ask?"

No reason, I told him.

"I'll think about it. We'll talk about it next time we meet," he said.

Then Amé asked me to take a walk with her, and we strolled along a jogging path.

"Thanks for everything," said Amé. "Really, I mean it. I'm not very good at saying these things. But—umm—well, I mean it. You've really helped smooth things out. Yuki and I have been able to talk. We've gotten closer. And now she's come to stay with me."

"Isn't that nice," I said. I couldn't think of anything less banal to say. Of course Amé barely heard me.

"The child seems to have calmed down considerably since she met you. She's not so irritable and nervous. I don't know what it is, but you certainly have a way with her. What do you have in common with her?"

I assured her I didn't know.

What did I think ought to be done about Yuki's schooling?

"If she doesn't want to go to school, then maybe you should think of an alternative," I said. "Sometimes it's bad to force school on a kid, especially a kid like Yuki who's extra sensitive and attracts more attention than she likes. A tutor might be a good idea. I think it's pretty clear Yuki isn't cut out for all this cramming for entrance exams and all the silly competition and peer pressure and rules and extracurricular activities. Some people can do pretty well without it. I'm being idealistic, I know, but the important thing is that Yuki finds her talent and has a chance to cultivate it. Maybe she'll decide to go back to school. That would be okay too, if that's her decision."

"You're right, I suppose," Amé said after a moment's thought. "I'm not much of a group person, never kept up with school either, so I guess I understand what you're saying."

"If you understand, then there shouldn't be anything to think about. Where's the problem?"

She swiveled her head, going from side to side, popping her neck bones.

"There is no problem. I mean, the only problem is, I don't have unshakable confidence in myself as a mother. So I don't have it in me to stand up for her like that. If you lack confidence, you give in. Deep down, you worry that the idea of not going to school is socially wrong."

Socially wrong? "I can't make any reassurances, but who knows what's going to be right or what's going to be wrong? No one can read the future. The results could be devastating. But that could happen either way. I think if you showed the girl that you're really trying—as a mother or as a friend—to make things work with her, and if you showed her some respect, then she'd be sharp enough to pick up on it and do the rest for herself."

Amé stood there, hands in the pockets of her shorts, and was quiet. Then she said, "You really understand how the child feels, don't you? How come?"

Because I wasn't always on another planet, I felt like telling her. But I didn't.

Amé then said she wanted to give me something as an expression of her appreciation. I told her I'd already received more than enough from her former husband.

"But *I* want to. He's him and I'm me. And *I* want to thank you. And if I don't now, I'll forget to."

"I'd be quite happy if you forgot," I joked.

We sat down on a bench, and Amé pulled out a pack of Salems from her shirt pocket. She lit up, inhaled, exhaled. Then she let the thing turn to ash between her fingers.

Meanwhile, I listened to the birds singing and watched the gardeners whirring about in their carts. The sky was beginning to clear, though I did hear the faint report of thunder in the distance. Strong sunlight was breaking through thick gray cloud cover. In her sunglasses and short sleeves, Amé seemed oblivious to the glare and heat, although several trails of sweat had stained the neck of her shirt. Maybe it wasn't the sun. Maybe it was concentration, or mental diffusion. Ten minutes went by, apparently not registering with her. The passage of time was not a practical component in her life. Or if it was, it wasn't high on her list of priorities. It was different for me. I had a plane to catch.

"I have to be going," I said, glancing at my watch. "I've got to return the car before I check in."

She made a vague effort to refocus her eyes on me. A look I occasionally noted in Yuki. Like mother, like daughter, after all. "Ah, yes, the time. I hadn't noticed," said Amé. "Sorry."

We got up from the bench and walked back to the cottage.

They all came outside to see me off. I told Yuki to cut out the junk food, but figured Dick North would see to that. Lined up in the rearview mirror as I pulled away, the three of them made a curious sight. Dick waving his one arm on high; Amé staring ahead blankly, arms folded across her chest; Yuki looking off to the side and kicking a pebble. The remnant of a family in a makeshift corner of an imperfect universe. How had I ever gotten involved with them? A left-hand turn of the wheel and they were gone from sight. For the first time in ages I was alone.

31

Back at the Shibuya apartment, I went through my mail and messages. Nothing, of course, but petty work-related matters. How's that piece for the next issue coming along? Where the hell did you disappear to? Can you take on this new project? I returned nobody's call. Faster, simpler to get on with the work at hand.

But first, a phone call to Makimura. Friday picked up and promptly turned me over to the big man. I gave him a brief rundown of the trip, saying that Hawaii seemed to be a good breather for Yuki.

"Good," he said. "Many thanks for everything. I'll give Amé a call tomorrow. Did the money hold out, by the way?"

"With lots to spare."

"Well, go ahead and use it up. It's yours."

"I can't do that," I said. "Oh yes, I've been meaning to ask you about your little present."

"Oh, that," he said, making light of it.

"How did you arrange that?"

"Through channels. I trust you didn't stay up all night playing cards, eh?"

"No, I don't mean that. I want to know how you could buy me a woman in Honolulu all the way from Tokyo. I'm just curious how something like that is done."

Makimura was quiet, sizing up the extent of my curiosity.

"Well," he began, "it's like international flower delivery. I call the organization in Tokyo and tell them I want a girl sent to you, at such-and-such a place, at such-and-such a time. Then Tokyo contacts its affiliated Honolulu organization and they send the girl. I pay Tokyo. Tokyo takes a commission and wires the rest to Honolulu. Honolulu takes its commission and what's left goes to the girl. Convenient, eh? All kinds of systems in the modern world."

"Sure seems that way," I said. International flower delivery.

"Very convenient. It costs you, but you save on time and energy. I think they call it worldwide sex-o-grams. They're safe, too. No run-ins with violent pimps. Plus you can write it off as expenses."

"That so?" I said, nodding to myself. "I guess you couldn't give me the number to this organization?"

"Sorry, no go. It's absolutely confidential. Members only, very exclusive. You need glamour and money and social standing. You'd never pass. I mean, forget it. Listen, I'm already talking too much. I told you this much out of the kindness of my heart."

I thanked him for it.

"Well, was she good?" he asked

"Yes, quite good," I admitted.

"Glad to hear it. I asked them to send you the best. What was her name?"

"June."

"June, eh? Was she white?"

"No, Southeast Asian."

"I'll have to check her out next time," he said.

There wasn't much more to say, so I thanked him again and hung up.

Next, I rang Gotanda and got his answering machine. I left a message saying I was back and would appreciate a call. By then it was already getting late in the day, so I hopped in the Subaru and drove to Aoyama to do some shopping before the stores closed. More pedigreed vegetables, the latest shipment fresh from Kinokuniya's own pedigreed vegetable farms. Somewhere in the remote mountains of Nagano, pristine acres surrounded by barbed wire. Watchtower, guards with machine guns. A prison camp like in *The Great Escape*. Rows of lettuce and celery whipped into shape through unimaginably grueling supravegetable training. What a way to get your fiber.

No message from Gotanda when I got back.

The following morning, after a quick breakfast at Dunkin' Donuts, I headed to the library and combed through the last' month's newspapers. Checking if there'd been a breakthrough in the investigation of Mei's death. I read the *Asahi* and *Mainichi* and *Yomiuri* with extreme care, but found only election results and a statement by Revchenko and a big piece on delinquency in the schools and how for reasons of "musical impropriety" the White House had canceled a command performance by the Beach Boys. Anyway, not one line about the case.

I then read through back issues of various weekly magazines. And there it was: "Naked Beauty Found Strangled in Akasaka Hotel." A sensationalized, one-page article on Mei. Instead of a photograph, there was a sketch of the corpse by a specialist in criminal art. Next best thing if you didn't have the bloody photo itself. True, the sketch did look like Mei, but then I knew who it was supposed to be. Could anyone else have recognized her? No, Mei had been warm and animated. Full of hopes, full of illusions. She'd been gentle and smooth, fantastic, shoveling her sensual snow. It was the reason we could connect so well, could share those illusions. *Cuck–koo.* She was all innocence.

This lousy sketch made it cheap and dirty. I shook my head. I shut my eyes and sighed slowly. Yet that line drawing, better than any morgue photograph, hammered home the fact that Mei was dead. Extremely, irrevocably dead. She was gone. Her life had been sucked away into black nothingness.

The article fit the drawing. A young woman believed to

be in her early twenties was discovered strangled to death
with a stocking in a luxury Akasaka hotel. Completely
naked, without identification, an assumed name, et cetera, et
cetera. Nothing new to me, except for a one detail: Police
were running down probable links to a prostitution ring, an
organization that dispatched call girls to first-class hotels.

I returned the magazines to the racks and sat thinking.
How had the police been able to narrow their leads to the
prostitution ring? Had some hard evidence turned up? Not
that I was about to call those two cops to find out.

I left the library and ate a quick lunch nearby, then went
for a walk, waiting for a brilliant notion to pop into my
head. No such luck. I walked to Meiji Shrine, stretched out
on the grass and looked up at the sky.

I thought about the call girl organization. Worldwide sex-
o-grams. Place your order in Tokyo and your girl is waiting
in Honolulu. Systematic, efficient, sophisticated. No muss,
no fuss. Very businesslike. Just went to prove, once you've
got an illusion going, it can function on the market like any
other product. Advanced capitalism churning out goods for
every conceivable niche. Illusion, that was the key word
here. Whether prostitution or discrimination or personal
attacks or displaced sex drive, give it a pretty name, a pretty
package, and you could sell it. Before too long they'll have a
call girl catalog order service at the Seibu department store.
You can rely on us.

I looked up at the sky and thought about sex.

I wanted to sleep with Yumiyoshi. It wasn't out of the
question. Just get one foot in her door, so to speak, and tell
her, "You have to sleep with me. You *should* sleep with me."
Then I undress her, gently, like untying the ribbon on a present. First her coat, then her glasses, then her sweater. Her
clothes off, she'd turn into Mei. *Cuck–koo*, she says. "Like
my body?"

But before I can answer, the night is gone. Kiki is beside
me, Gotanda's graceful fingers playing over her back. The
door opens. Enter Yuki. She sees me making love with Kiki.

It's me this time, not Gotanda. Only the fingers are his.

"I can't believe this," says Yuki. "I really can't believe this."

"It's not like that," I say.

"What was *that* all about?" says Kiki for the umpteenth time.

It's not like that, I insist. *The one I want to sleep with is Yumiyoshi*. I just got my signals crossed.

First thing, I have to untangle the connections. Otherwise, I come away empty-handed. Or with someone else's hands. Or even a missing hand.

Leaving the grounds of Meiji Shrine, I went into a back-street café in Harajuku and had a good strong cup of coffee. Then I walked leisurely home.

In the evening Gotanda rang.

"Sorry, I don't have much time now," he spoke on the fly. "Can I see you tonight around eight or nine?"

"Don't see why not."

"Good, let's have dinner. I'll come pick you up."

While I waited, I put away my suitcase, then went over the receipts from the trip, methodically separating Maki-mura's charges from my own. Half the meals and the car rental go to him, along with Yuki's personal purchases—surfboard, blaster, swimsuit, . . . I itemized our expenses and slipped the calculations into an envelope together with the leftover travelers cheques, ready to be cashed at the bank and returned to Makimura. I always keep on top of these business details. But not because I like them. I just hate slop-piness in money matters.

After finishing with the accounting, I mixed up some baby whitefish with boiled spinach to go with a bottle of Kirin black label. Then I reread a Haruo Sato short story from years ago. It was a lovely uneventful spring evening. The sky grew darker, painted blue on blue, one stroke at a time, into deeper and deeper shades of night.

When I tired of reading, I put on the Stern-Rose-Istomin Trio playing Schubert's Opus 100, a piece I always reserve for spring. It breathed with the lush sadness of the night. Where off in the depths of gloom drifted six white skeletons. Life was sinking into an abyss, bones hard as memories positioned before me.

32

Gotanda swung by at eight-forty. He was wearing a perfectly ordinary gray V-neck sweater over a perfectly ordinary blue button-down shirt with—you got it—perfectly ordinary cotton slacks. And still he looked striking. Extraordinarily so.

He was curious about my digs, so I invited him in.

"Nice," he said with a shy smile. Such a sweet smile, it made you feel like offering to let him stay for a week.

"Takes me back," he said, as if to himself. "Reminds me of the place I used to have—before I hit it big." From anyone else, the comment would have been an unbearable snub, but from him it was a compliment, straightforward and pure.

I offered Gotanda a big cushion and got out my foldaway low table from the closet. Then I brought us black beer with my spinach-and-whitefish concoction and put on the Schubert again.

"Fantastic!"

"Really? How about something else?"

"I'd love it, but I don't want you to have to go to the trouble."

"No trouble at all. I can whip something up quick and easy. Nothing too fancy, though."

"Can I watch?"

"Sure," I said.

Scallions tossed with salt-plum. *Wakame* seaweed and shrimp vinaigrette. *Wasabi* preserves and grated daikon with sliced fish mousse. Slivered potatoes in olive oil and garlic with minced salami. Homemade cucumber pickles. Yesterday's *hijiki* seaweed plus tofu garnished with heaps of ginger.

"Amazing," sighed Gotanda. "You're a genius."

"Very kind of you to say so, but I assure you, it's real simple. Just throwing together stuff I have around."

"Sheer genius. I could never do it."

"Well, thank you, but I could never imitate a dentist."

"Aaa—," he said, dismissing my return of compliment. "You know, would you mind if we didn't go out tonight? This stuff is great."

"Fine by me."

So we drank and ate. When the beer ran out, we switched to Cutty Sark. We listened to Sly and the Family Stone, the Doors and Stones, Pink Floyd. We listened to the Beach Boys' *Surf's Up*. It was a sixties kind of night. The Loving Spoonful, Three Dog Night. Any self-respecting alien transponding in from Sirius would have thought himself caught in a time warp.

No alien showed, but from ten o'clock it did start to rain. Softly, quietly, barely audible on the eaves. Almost silent as the dead.

As the night wore on, we stopped putting on music. My apartment didn't have the thick walls of Gotanda's condominium, and loud noise after eleven asked for complaints. With the music off, the whisper of the rain underscored the tone of our conversation. The police hadn't made much headway on Mei's case, I lamented. No, they haven't, Gotanda sighed. He'd been checking the newspapers and magazines too.

I opened a second bottle of Cutty Sark, and for the first round we toasted Mei.

"The cops have narrowed their investigations down to prostitution rings," I went on, "so they must have gotten a hold somewhere. I'm worried that'll lead them to you."

"There's a chance," said Gotanda, knitting his eyebrows slightly. "But it's probably okay. I was a little nervous, so I asked the folks at my agency about it. Whether that club's as tight-lipped as they claim. And you know what? Seems the club has a lot of political connections, some pretty big names apparently. So even if the club did spill to the police, they wouldn't be able to go sniffing too far. They couldn't lay a hand on anybody. And for that matter, my agency has a bit of clout too. Some of the bigger stars have very close friends in high places. Sometimes in not-so-nice places. So either way, the cops don't have a lot of room to maneuver. And because I'm a money tree for the agency, they don't want anything to happen to me. I'm a major investment. They don't want to see my value plummet. True, if you'd mentioned my name to the cops, my ass would've been hauled in for sure. All the political connections in Ginza couldn't have kept that from happening. But no fear of that now. The rest is a power play, one system against another."

"It's a dirty world," I said.

"Isn't it, though," said Gotanda. "Dirty to the core."

"Two votes, dirty."

"Say what?"

"Two votes for dirty, motion adopted."

He nodded, then smiled sadly. "Two votes for dirty. No one can be bothered to think about a murder victim. Everyone's busy looking out for Number One," he said. "Myself included."

I went into the kitchen to replenish the ice, bringing out crackers and cheese.

"I want to ask you a favor," I said, sitting down. "Could you call up the organization and ask them something for me?"

He pinched his earlobe. "What do you want to know? Anything to do with this case is out of the question. They'd never crack."

"Completely unrelated. I want to know about a call girl I

met in Honolulu. I've heard a girl overseas could be arranged through the club."

"Who told you that?"

"Someone with no name. I'm willing to bet that the organization this guy was talking about is the same club we're talking about. Because you got to be rich and famous to join. Neither of which I begin to approach, or so I was told."

Gotanda smiled. "Yeah, I think I may have heard about a service like that. One phone call does the trick. I haven't had the pleasure, but it's probably the same setup. So, what about that hooker in Honolulu?"

"I just want to know if the club has a Southeast Asian woman named June working for them."

Gotanda thought about this, but didn't ask anything more. He jotted down the name in his datebook.

"June what?"

"Gimme a break. She's a call girl," I said. "It's just June."

"Got it. I'll ring the place up tomorrow."

"Thanks. I owe you," I said.

"Forget it. After what you've done for me, this is a pittance." He winked and gave me a thumbs-up. "You go to Hawaii alone, by the way?"

"Who goes to Hawaii alone? I went with a girl. She's only thirteen, though."

"You slept with a thirteen-year-old girl?"

"What do you think I am? The kid doesn't even wear a bra yet."

"Then why'd you go with her?"

"To teach her table manners, interpret the mysteries of the sex drive, bad-mouth Boy George, go see *E.T.* You know, the usual."

Gotanda gave me a long look. Then he skewed his lips into a smile. "You really are a little odd, you know?"

Now everyone seemed to think so. Motion passed by unanimous vote.

Gotanda drank some whiskey and nibbled on a cracker.

"I saw my ex-wife a couple of times while you were away," he said. "We're getting along pretty well. Strange to say, but sleeping with your ex-wife can be fun."

"I guess."

"Why don't you try seeing your ex-wife?"

"No way. She's about to get married. Didn't I tell you?"

He shook his head. "Didn't know. Well, too bad."

"No, it's better this way," I said and I meant it. "But what about your ex?"

He shook his head again. "It's hopeless. No other way to put it. Hopeless. A dead end. You know, we make better love than we ever have. We don't have to say a word. We understand each other. It's better than when we were married. *We love each other*, if you want to know. But it can't go on forever like this, meeting in love hotels. I wish we didn't have to hide, but if her family finds out, they'll make my life miserable. As if they haven't already. If it's between me or them, she'll pick them every time. I lose whichever way I turn. . . . God, the things I would give for a normal life with her." Gotanda swirled the ice in his glass, around and around. "Funny isn't it? I can get almost anything I want. Except the one thing I want the most."

"That's how it is," I said. "But I never could get everything I wanted, so I can't really talk."

"No, you've got it wrong," said Gotanda. "You never wanted things to begin with. For instance, would you ever want a Maserati or a condo in Azabu?"

"Well, if somebody forced them on me, . . . But I guess I *can* live without them. My little apartment and my trusty Subaru satisfy me all right. Well, maybe satisfy is an overstatement. But they suit me all right, they're easy to manage, they're not *dis*satisfying anyway. But who knows? Maybe there'll come a time when I need those things."

"No, you're wrong again. That's not what need is. This stuff isn't natural. It's manufactured. Take that place where I live. A roof over your head is the point, not what fancy part of town it's in. But the idiots at the agency say—Itabashi or

Kameido or Nakano Toritsukasei? No status. You big star, you live Azabu. The next thing I know, they've stuck me in that ridiculous condo. What bullshit! What the hell is so great about Azabu? A bunch of rip-off restaurants run by fashion designers and that eyesore called Tokyo Tower and all those crazed women wandering around all night. The same thing with the goddamn Maserati. Who the hell drives a Maserati in Tokyo? It's such bullshit! Subaru or Bluebird or Corona? Nope. Big star no get caught dead in anything but Maserati. The only saving grace of that car is that it's not new; they got it off some *enka* singer."

He poured some whiskey over melted ice, took a sip, frowned.

"That's my world. Azabu, European sports car, first-class. Stupid, meaningless, idiotic bullshit. How did all this . . . this . . . this total nonsense get started? Well, it's very, very simple. You just repeat the message and repeat the message and repeat the message. You pound that baby in. Until everybody believes it. Like a mantra. Azabu, BMW, Rolex, Azabu, BMW, Rolex, Azabu, BMW, Rolex, Azabu, . . .

"That's how you get those poor suckers who actually believe the bullshit. But if they believe that, they're exactly like everybody else. They're blind; they got zero imagination. I'm fed up with it. I'm fed up with this life they have me living. I'm their life-size dress-up doll. Sewed together with loans and mortgages. But who wants to hear this grief? After all, I live in a jet-stream condo in Azabu, I drive a Maserati, I have this Patek Philippe watch—a step up from Rolex, don't you know? And I can sleep with a high-class call girl anytime I feel like it. I'm the envy of the whole goddamn town. I want you to know I didn't ask for any of it. But the worst thing is—boy, this must be getting boring—as long as I keep living like this, I can't get what I really want."

"Like, for instance, love?" I said.

"Yeah, like, for instance, love. And tranquillity. And a healthy family. And a simple life," he ran down the list. Then he placed both hands together before his face. "Look at me, I had a world of possibilities, I had opportunities. But now I'm a puppet. I can get almost any woman I want. Yet the one woman I really want . . ."

Gotanda was getting good and drunk. It didn't show on him, but he sure was letting it all hang out. Which I could appreciate, absolutely, this urge to drink himself silly. We'd been going for almost four hours like this. Gotanda asked if he should get out of here, but I told him I wasn't doing anything special, same as always.

"Sorry to force myself on you," he said. "I don't have anyone else to talk to, to tell you the truth. If I told someone that deep down I'm a Subaru man, they'd think I was stark raving mad, they'd cart me off to a shrink. Of course, it's in fashion, you know, going to a shrink. Amazing bullshit. A show-business shrink is like a vomit clean-up specialist." He closed his eyes. "Seems like I came here just to bitch."

"You've said 'bullshit' at least twenty times."

"Have I?"

"Go ahead, blow it off, if that's what you want."

"No, enough of this. I'm sorry to make you listen to this garbage. It's just that I'm surrounded by all this steaming shit. Makes me want to puke."

"Then go ahead and puke."

"Idiots all around me," Gotanda practically spat out the words. "Bloodsuckers, fat, ugly bloodsuckers, slopping their fat asses around, feeding off the hopes and dreams of decent people. I tell myself it'd be a waste of good energy strangling them."

"Yeah, using a baseball bat would be better. Strangling takes too long."

"You're right," said Gotanda. "But strangling makes the point clearer. Instant death is too good. Why waste kindness on them."

"Ah, the voice of reason."

"Honestly—," he went on, ignoring my irony, then broke off with a sigh and brought his hands together in front of his face again. "I feel so much better."

"Well, now that we've settled that, how about some o-chazuke?"

"O-chazuke? You're kidding. I'd love some o-chazuke."

I boiled water for tea, tossed together some crumbled nori and salt-plum and wasabi horseradish, topped two bowls of rice with the mixture, and poured tea over each. O-chazuke. Yum.

"From where I sit, seems to me you don't have a bad life," Gotanda said.

I lay back against the wall and listened to the rain. "Some parts, sure. I'm not unhappy. But I'm like you. I feel like something's missing. I'm living a normal life, I suppose. I'm dancing. I know the steps, and I'm dancing. It's all right. But socially speaking, I've got nothing. I'm thirty-four, I'm not married, I don't have a regular job, I live from day to day. I can't get a public housing loan. I'm not sleeping with anybody. What am I going to be like in thirty years?"

"You'll get by."

"Or else I won't," I said. "Who knows? Same as everyone."

"But with my life, I don't even have parts I enjoy."

"Maybe not, but you look like you're doing pretty well for yourself."

Gotanda shook his head. "Do people who're doing pretty well for themselves pour out such endless streams of grief? Do they come bother you and slosh all over you?"

"Sometimes they do," I said. "We're talking about people, not common denominators."

At one-thirty, Gotanda announced he was leaving.

"You can stay if you like. I've got an extra futon. I'll even make you breakfast," I said.

"No, really, but thanks for the offer. I'm sober now, so I might as well go home," he said. "But I've got a favor to ask first. I'm afraid you're going to think it's a little strange."

"Fire away."

"Would you be willing to let me borrow the Subaru for a bit? I'll trade you the Maserati for it. The Maserati is so flashy, I can't go anywhere in peace, especially when I'm trying to see my ex-wife."

"Borrow the Subaru for as long as you like," I said. "But to be honest, I don't know about taking on the Maserati. I keep my heap in a parking lot, so it could easily get banged up at night. And if I dent it or something, I'll never be able to pay for it."

"Don't worry about it. I don't. If anything happens, the agency will take care of it. That baby's insured up the tail pipe. Drive the thing into the sea if you feel like. Honest. They'll only buy me a Ferrari next. There's a porno writer who's got one he wants to sell."

"A Ferrari?" I said limply.

"I know what you're thinking," he laughed. "But you can just shelve it. It's hard for you to understand, but in this debauched world of mine, you can't survive with good taste. Because a person with good taste is a twisted, poor person, a sap without money. You get sympathy, but no one thinks better of you."

So Gotanda drove off in my Subaru, and I pulled his Maserati into the lot. A superaggressive machine. All response and power. The slightest pressure on the accelerator and it practically left the ground.

"Easy baby, you don't have to try so hard," I said with an affectionate pat on the dashboard. But the Maserati wasn't listening to the likes of me. Cars know their class too.

33

The following morning, I went to check on the Maserati. It was still there, untouched. A curious picture, seeing it parked where the Subaru usually was. I climbed inside and sank into the seat, but just couldn't get comfortable. Like waking up and finding a beautiful woman you don't know sleeping next to you. She might be great to look at, but having her there doesn't feel right. Makes you a little tense. You need time to get used to things.

In the end, I left the car alone that day. Instead, I walked, saw a movie, bought some books.

Toward evening Gotanda rang. Thanks for yesterday. Don't mention it.

"About the Honolulu connection," he said. "I made a call to the club. And, well, yes, it is possible to reserve a woman in Hawaii from here. Modern conveniences, you know."

"Uh-huh."

"I also asked about this June of yours. I mentioned someone recommending this Southeast Asian girl to me. They went and checked their files. They made a big deal about their information being confidential, but seeing as how I was such a favored customer, blah blah blah. Not something to be so proud of, let me tell you. Anyway, they did have a listing for a June in Honolulu. A Filipino girl. But she quit three months ago."

"Three months ago?"

"That's what they said."

I thanked him and hung up. This was going to take some hard figuring.

I went out walking again.

June quit three months ago, but I slept with her not two weeks before. She gave me her telephone number, but when I called it, nobody answered. This made my third call girl— first Kiki, then Mei, now June—who'd disappeared. All of them somehow connected to Gotanda and Makimura and me.

I stepped into a coffee shop and drew a diagram in my notebook of these personal relations of mine. It looked like a chart of the European powers before the start of World War I.

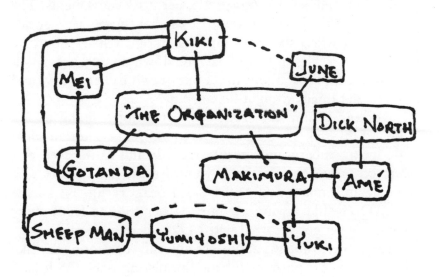

I pored over the diagram, half in admiration, half in despair. Three call girls, one too-charming-for-his-own-good actor, three artists, one budding teenage girl, and a very uptight hotel receptionist. If this was anything more than a network of casual relationships, I sure didn't see it. But it might make a good Agatha Christie novel. *By George, that's it! The Secretary did it!* Only who was laughing?

And who was I kidding? I didn't have a clue. The ball of yarn tangled wherever you tried to unravel it. First there were the Kiki and Mei and Gotanda threads. Add Makimura and June. Then Kiki and June were somehow connected by the same phone number. And around and around you go.

"Hard nut to crack, eh, Watson?" I addressed the ashtray before me. The ashtray, of course, did not respond. Smart ashtray. Same went for the coffee cup and sugar bowl and the bill. They all pretended not to hear. Stupid me. I was the one running amok in these weird goings-on. I was the worn-out one. Such a wonderful spring night, and no prospect for a date.

I went home and tried calling Yumiyoshi. No luck. The early shift? Or her swim club night? I wanted to see her badly. I missed her nervous patter, her brisk movements. The way she pushed her glasses up on her nose, her serious expression when she stole into the room. I liked how she took off her blazer before sitting down beside me. I felt warm just thinking about her. I felt drawn to her. But would we ever get things straight between us?

Working behind the front desk of a hotel, going to her swim club—that gave her satisfaction. While I found pleasure in my Subaru and my old records and eating well as I went on shoveling. That's the two of us. It might work and then again it might not. INSUFFICIENT DATA, PROGNOSIS IMPOSSIBLE. Or would I wind up hurting her too, as I did every woman I ever got involved with? Like my ex-wife said.

The more I thought about Yumiyoshi, the more I felt like flying up to Sapporo to fill in the missing data. At least I could tell her how I felt. But, no, first I had to untie some critical knots. Things were half-done. I didn't want to keep dragging them around with me. A half-gray shadow would cloud my path for the rest of my days. Not entirely ideal.

The problem was Kiki. I couldn't get over the feeling that she was at the heart of it. She was trying to reach me. In my dreams, in a movie in Sapporo, in downtown Honolulu. She kept crossing my path, trying to lead me somewhere, leave me a message. That much was clear. But nothing else. Kiki, what did you want from me?

What was I supposed to do?

I could only wait, until something showed. Same as ever. There was no point in rushing. Something was bound to happen. Something was bound to show. You had merely to wait for it to stir, up from the haze. Call it a lesson from experience.

Very well, then, I would wait.

I got together with Gotanda every few days after that. After a while, it became a habit. And each time we met, he'd apologize for keeping the Subaru so long.

"Haven't plowed the Maserati into the sea yet, have you?" he joked.

"Sorry to say, but I haven't had time to go to the sea," I parried.

Gotanda and I sat at a bar drinking vodka tonics. His pace a little faster than mine.

"I bet it would feel great, though. Plowing it into the sea," he said, raising his glass to his lips.

"Like a cool breeze," I said. "But then you'd only get yourself a Ferrari."

"I'd ditch that too."

"And after the Ferrari?"

"Hmm, who knows? But sooner or later, the insurance company's going to want a word with me."

"Insurance company? Who gives a damn about your insurance company? You got to think big. Go for the grand sweep. This is fantasy, not one of your low-budget movies. Fantasies don't have budgets, so why be middle class about it? Go wild! Lamborghini, Porsche, Jaguar! The sky's the limit! And the ocean's big enough to swallow cars by the thousands. Let your imagination do its stuff, man."

He laughed. "Well, it certainly lightens me up."

"Me too, especially since it's not my car and not my imagination," I said, then asked how things were going with his ex-wife.

He took a sip of his drink and looked out at the rain. The bar had emptied out except for us. The bartender had nothing to do but dust the bottles.

"Things're going okay," he said meekly, under a whisper of a smile. "We're in love. A love affirmed and consummated by divorce. Romantic, isn't it?"

"Isn't it, though. I might faint."

He chuckled.

"But it's true," he said.

"I know," I said.

That was the general drift of conversation each time I saw Gotanda. What we talked about was too serious to treat anything but lightly. Most of the jokes weren't terribly good, but it didn't matter. It was enough that we *could* joke, that there were jokes between us. We ourselves didn't know how serious we were.

Thirty-four is a difficult age. A different kind of difficult than age thirteen, but plenty difficult. Gotanda and I were both thirty-four, both beginning to acknowledge middle age. It was time we did. Readying things to keep us warm during the colder days ahead.

Gotanda put it succinctly. "Love. That's what I need."

"I'm so touched," I said. But the fact was, that's what I needed too.

Gotanda paused to consider what he'd said. I thought about it as well. I also thought about Yumiyoshi. How she drank all those Bloody Marys that snowy night.

"I've slept with so many women, I can't count them. You sleep with one, you've slept with them all. Hell, you go through the same motions," said Gotanda after a while. "Love's what I want. Here I am, baring my sentimental soul to you again. But I swear, the only woman I want to sleep with is my ex-wife."

I snapped my fingers. "Incredible. The Word from Above. O Light Resplendent. You've got to hold a press conference. Make your I-only-want-to-sleep-with-my-wife proclamation. Everyone will be moved beyond tears. You might even receive a citation from the Prime Minister."

"No, this is Nobel Prize material. Not something the common man can do."

"You'll need a frock coat for the ceremony."

"I'll buy it. Put it on my expense account."

"Sanctus tax deductum."

"I'll be on stage with the King of Sweden," Gotanda went on. "I'll declare it for all the world to hear. Ladies and gentlemen, the only woman I want to sleep with is my wife! Waves of emotion. Storm clouds part; sun breaks through."

"The ice cap melts, the Vikings are vanquished, the mermaids sing."

Ah, love. We both lapsed silent, meditating on its grandeur. I had a lot to think about. I had to make sure I picked up some vodka and tomato juice and Lea & Perrins and lemons.

"Or then again, maybe you won't receive an award," I piped up. "Maybe they'll just take you for a pervert."

Gotanda considered that. "Maybe. We're talking neo-sexual revolution here. The masses might rise up and trample me to death," he said. "I'd be a sexual martyr."

"The first actor martyred to the neo-sexual revolution."

"Martyred and never to sleep with his ex-wife again."

Time for another drink.

If he had a spare moment, Gotanda would call and we'd go out or he'd come over to my place or I'd go over to his. The days passed. I'd resolved not to work at all. I couldn't be bothered. The world was doing very well without me. Meanwhile I was waiting.

I mailed Hiraku Makimura the balance of his money and receipts from the trip.

The next day I got a call from Boy Friday, begging me to take it all.

It was too much trouble to go through the whole back-and-forth bow-and-scrape routine, so I gave in. If it made the Master happy, who was I to argue? And before you could say "money in the bank," Makimura had sent me a check for three hundred thousand yen. Also in the envelope was a receipt marked FOR SERVICES RENDERED—FIELD RESEARCH. I signed it, stamped it with my seal, and posted it. Back to the wonderful world of expense accounts.

I placed the check for three hundred thousand yen on my desk to appreciate $8^3/_4\%$ dust.

The Golden Week holidays came and went.

I called Yumiyoshi a number of times. She was always the one who determined the length of the conversation. Sometimes we talked for a long time, other times she'd simply say, "Busy, got to go now," and hang up. Or if a silence hung on the line too long, she'd cut me off without warning. But at least we talked. Exchanged data, a little at a time. And one day, she gave me her home phone number. Progress.

She went to her swim club twice a week. Which I found, to my dismay, still brought on moments of jealousy. Handsome instructors and all. I was as bad as a high school boy and I knew it. And what was worse, I was afraid she knew it. *Jealous of a swim club? That's ridiculous. You're so immature.* I was afraid she'd never want to see me again.

So whenever the subject came up, I held my tongue. Though not talking about it only inflated my paranoia. Visions of the instructor—Gotanda, of course—keeping Yumiyoshi after class for intensive one-on-one sessions. His hands supporting her chest and abdomen as she practiced the crawl. His hands caressing her breasts, easing between her thighs. But it's all right, he says.

It's all right. Don't you know? The only woman I want to sleep with is my wife.

Then he takes Yumiyoshi's hand and puts it on his crotch. She begins to massage it. An underwater erection, like coral. Yumiyoshi is in rapture.

It's all right. Don't you know? The only woman I want to sleep with is my wife.

Idiotic, yet that's what came to mind whenever I called Yumiyoshi. As time went on, the vision got more and more complex, with a whole cast of characters. Kiki and Mei and Yuki put in guest appearances. As Gotanda's fingers stroked her body, Yumiyoshi became Kiki.

"Listen, I'm just a plain, run-of-the-mill person," Yumiyoshi said one night. She seemed particularly drained after a long day's drudgery. "The only difference between me and anyone else is my name. Otherwise I'm the same. I'm just working behind the counter of a hotel day after day, pointlessly wearing down my life. Don't call me any more. I'm not worth the phone charges."

"But I thought you liked hotel work."

"I do."

"But?"

"The work is fine. But sometimes, I think the hotel's going to eat me up. Just sometimes. I ask myself, if I'm here or not, what's the difference? The hotel would still be there. But not me. I'm out of the picture. That's the difference."

"Aren't you taking this hotel business a little too seriously?" I asked. "The hotel's the hotel, you're you. I think about you a lot, and sometimes I think about the hotel. But never together. You're you, the hotel's the hotel."

"You think I don't know that? I know that, but people get confused. My private life and my identity get dragged into this hotel world, and then they get swallowed up."

"It happens to everyone. You get dragged into something and you lose track of where one thing ends and the other

begins. You're not the only one. It happens to me too," I
said.

"It's not the same thing, not at all," she declared.

"No, maybe not. But I can still sympathize, can't I? Because,
I mean, there's something about you that's very attractive."

Yumiyoshi went silent, out there in the telephone void.

"I . . . I'm frightened," said Yumiyoshi, verging into sobs.
"I'm frightened of that darkness. I'm frightened that it's
going to come again, soon."

"Hey, what's going on with you? Are you all right?"

"Of course I'm all right. What did you think?" She was
clearly sobbing now. "So I'm crying. Anything wrong with
that?"

"No, nothing at all. I was merely concerned."

"Can't you just be quiet?"

I did as told and Yumiyoshi cried until she couldn't cry
anymore, then she hung up on me.

On May seventh, Yuki called.

"I'm back," she announced. "Why don't we go out for a
ride?"

I tooled the Maserati to the Akasaka condo. But when
Yuki saw the car, she wrinkled up her face unpleasantly.

"What's with this?"

"I didn't steal it, don't worry. My car fell into an
enchanted spring and what do you know? The fairy of the
spring appeared looking like Isabelle Adjani and asked, 'Was
that a gold Maserati or a silver BMW just now?' And I said,
'Neither, that was a copper Subaru,' and—"

"C'mon, bag the stupid jokes," said Yuki. "I'm asking a
serious question. Where the heck did you get this thing?"

"I traded temporarily with a friend. He needed to borrow
the Subaru, for personal reasons."

"A friend?"

"You may not believe it, but yes, I do have at least one
friend."

She climbed into the passenger seat, took a look around inside, then made a funny face. "Weird car," she said. "Dopey."

"Now that you mention it, the owner said the same thing. Although his words were slightly different."

That shut her up.

I pointed the Maserati south, toward Shonan. Yuki wouldn't speak. I played a Steely Dan tape on low and drove with care. The weather was clear and warm, so I was wearing an aloha shirt and sunglasses, and Yuki had on a pink Polo shirt. It was like being in Hawaii again. In front was a livestock truck full of pigs, their red eyes peering through the slats at us. Could pigs distinguish between a Maserati and a Subaru?

"How was it in Hawaii after I left?" I finally asked.

Yuki shrugged.

"Things go all right with your mother?"

Another shrug.

"Get your surfing down?"

Still another shrug.

"You look real healthy. Perfectly tanned. Like café au lait, all smooth and delicious."

Shrug.

You couldn't say I wasn't trying. I was trying everything.

"Is it your period or something?"

The same.

So I shrugged back.

"I want to go home," Yuki said. "Hang a U."

"This is an expressway. Even Niki Lauda couldn't manage a U-turn here."

"Then exit someplace."

I turned to her. She looked exhausted suddenly, her eyes lifeless and unfocused. Perhaps a bit pale too; it was hard to tell through the tan.

"Want to stop and take a rest?"

"I don't want a rest stop. I want to go back to Tokyo. Now!"

We got off at the expressway at Yokohama, then headed
back on going in the opposite direction. When we reached
Akasaka, Yuki asked if we could go sit somewhere. So I
parked the Maserati in the lot, and we walked to the
grounds of Nogi Shrine and found a bench.

"I'm sorry," said Yuki, trying to be reasonable. "I felt
sick. I didn't want to say anything, so I held it in."

"You don't have to hold it in. I know how girls get. I'm
used to it."

"It's not like that!" she shouted. "That has nothing to do
with it! What got to me was riding in that car. That *stupid*
car!"

"What's wrong with the Maserati? It's not such a bad car.
It handles real well, rides pretty nice too. True, a bit too
flashy for my simple tastes. Even if I could afford it, I guess
I'd never buy a car like that."

"I don't care what brand that car is. The problem's *that
car*. Couldn't you feel it? It was *icky*. I was suffocating. I
could feel a pressure in my chest, and in my stomach too.
You didn't feel it?"

"No," I said. "Although I got to admit, I don't feel one
hundred percent comfortable in it. I thought it was because I
was used to the Subaru. You know, you like what you're
used to, but that's not this pressure you're talking about."

She shook her head. "No, it's not that at all. This is something real *peculiar*."

"Is this more of your . . . ?" I cut myself short. I didn't
want to say anything that sounded condescending.

"Yeah, it's more of that. I *felt* something."

"Well, what was it? What did you sense in that car?"

Yuki shrugged yet again, but this time she was talking.
"It'd be easy if I could explain, but I can't. I can't picture it.
There's just this feeling—a heavy, dark, awful lump of pressure in me. And it's totally . . ." Yuki searched for the word,
hands on her lap. "It's *wrong*! I don't know *what's* wrong.

But *some*thing's wrong. I couldn't breathe in there. I tried to ignore it, I thought maybe it was jet lag or something, but then it got worse and worse. I don't want to ride in that car ever again, you hear me? Get your Subaru back."

"The Curse of the Maserati," I intoned.

"This is no joke. You shouldn't be driving that car," she said, very seriously.

"Okay, okay," I gave in with a smile. "I know you're not kidding. I'll try not to drive the Maserati too much. Or maybe I should go sink the thing in the sea?"

"If possible," said a grave Yuki.

It took Yuki about an hour to recover from this shock to her system. We sat on the bench, and she rested her chin on her hands and kept her eyes shut. People passed through the grounds. Old folks, mothers with children, foreign tourists with cameras strung around their necks. Occasionally, a salesman-type or salaryman would stop and take a breather on a bench near us. Dark suit, plastic briefcase, glassy stare. Ten minutes later, he'd be off beating the pavement again. By most standards, a normal adult should be working at this hour, and a normal kid should be in school.

"What about your mother?" I asked. "Did she come back with you?"

"Mmm." That was Yuki saying yes. "She's up in Hakone with that one-armed guy. Sorting out her photos of Kathmandu and Hawaii."

"And you didn't want to stay in Hakone?"

"I didn't feel like it. There's nothing for me to do there."

"Just thought I'd ask," I said. "Tell me, what exactly is there for you to do on your own in Tokyo?"

One of her patented shrugs. Then, "I can hang out with you."

"Well, I couldn't ask for more myself. However, trying to be realistic, pretty soon I ought to be getting back to work. I can't afford to keep running around with you forever. And I don't want handouts from your father either."

Yuki sneered. "I can understand your not wanting to take handouts from my parents, but why do you have to make such a big deal about it? How do you think it makes me feel, dragging you all around the place like this?"

"So you want me to take the money?"

"If you did, I wouldn't feel so guilty."

"You don't get it, Yuki," I said. "I don't want money for being your friend. I don't want to be introduced at your wedding reception as 'the professional male companion of the bride since she was thirteen.' Everyone would be tittering, 'professional male companion, professional male companion.' I want to be introduced as 'the boyfriend of the bride when she was thirteen.'"

Yuki blushed. "You turkey. I'm not going to have a wedding reception."

"Great. I don't like weddings. All those absurd speeches and the bricks of wedding cake you're supposed to take home. Strains the boundaries of propriety. But all I want to say is, you don't buy friends. Especially not with expense account money."

"That makes a good moral for a fairy tale."

"Wow! You're finally getting the proper gift of gab. With practice we could be a couple of stand-up comics."

Shrug.

"But seriously, folks, . . ." I cleared my throat. "If you want to hang out with me every day, Yuki, I'm all for it. Who needs to work? It's just pointless shoveling anyway. But we have to have one thing clear: I'm not going to accept money for doing things with you. Hawaii was different. I took money for that. I even took the woman thrown in. Of course, I thought you weren't ever going to talk to me again. I hated myself for allowing the whole business about payment for services to happen at all. From now on, I'm doing things my way. I don't want to answer to anybody, and I don't want to be on somebody's dole. I'm not Dick North and I'm not your father's manservant, whatever his name is.

You don't need to feel guilty."

"You mean you'll really go out with me?" Yuki chirped, then looked down at her polished toenails.

"You bet. You and me, we could be this pair of outcasts. We could be quite an item. So, let's just relax and have a good time."

"Why are you being so kind?"

"I'm not."

Yuki traced a design in the dirt with the tip of her sandal. A squared spiral.

"And I'm not a burden on you?"

"Maybe you are and maybe you aren't. Don't worry your pretty little head about it. I want to be with you because I like you. Sometimes when I'm with you, I remember things I lost when I was your age. Like I remember the sound of the rain and the smell of the wind. And it's really a gift, getting these things back. Even if you think I'm weird. Maybe you'll understand what I mean some day."

"I already know what you mean."

"You do?"

"I mean, I've lost plenty of things this far in my life too," said Yuki.

"Well, then, there you are," I said.

She said nothing. I returned to looking at the visitors to the shrine grounds.

"I don't have anybody I can really talk to but you," Yuki spoke up. "Honest."

"What about Dick North?"

Yuki stuck out her tongue. "He's a goon."

"Maybe he is and maybe he isn't. But I think you should know, he does good, and he's not pushy about it. That's pretty rare. He may not be up to your mother's level, and he may not be a brilliant poet. But he genuinely cares for your mother. He probably loves her. He's a good cook, he's dependable, he's considerate."

"He's still a goon."

Okay, okay. Yuki obviously had her feelings on the matter. So I changed the subject. We talked about the good times we had in Hawaii. Sun and surf and tropical breezes and piña coladas. Yuki said this made her hungry, so we went to eat pancakes and fruit parfaits. Then we took in a movie.

The following week, Dick North died.

34

Dick North had been doing the shopping on a Monday evening in Hakone and had just stepped out from the supermarket with a bag of groceries under his arm when a truck came barreling down the road and slammed into him. The truck driver confessed that he didn't know what possessed him to gun full-speed ahead in such poor road visibility. And Dick himself had made a telling slip. He'd looked to his left, but was one or two breaths behind in checking his right. A common mistake among people who have lived overseas for any length of time and have just returned to Japan. You haven't gotten used to cars driving on the left-hand side yet. In most cases, you come away with chills, but sometimes it's worse. The truck sent Dick sailing into the opposite lane, where he was battered again by an oncoming van. He died instantly.

When I heard the news, the first thing that came to mind was going shopping with Dick at a probably similar supermarket in Makaha. How knowledgeably he selected his purchases, how he examined the fruit and vegetables and unembarrassedly tossed a box of Tampax into the

shopping cart. Poor bastard. Unlucky to the last. Arm blown
off in Vietnam when the guy next to him stepped on a mine.
Running around morning to night putting out Amé's smol-
dering cigarettes. Now dead on the asphalt holding onto a
load of groceries.

His funeral saw him returned to his rightful family, his
wife and child. Neither Amé nor Yuki nor I attended.

I borrowed the Subaru back from Gotanda and drove
Yuki to Hakone that Tuesday afternoon. It was at Yuki's
urging. "Mama can't get by on her own. Sure, there's the
maid, but she's too old to do anything and she goes home at
night. We can't leave Mama alone up there."

"Yeah, it's probably good for you to spend some time
with your mother," I said.

Yuki was flipping through the road atlas. "Hey, you
remember I said bad things about him?"

"Who? Dick North?"

"Yeah."

"You called him a goon," I said.

Yuki stowed the book in the door pocket, rested her
elbow on the window, and turned her gaze to the scenery
ahead. "But you know," she said, "he wasn't so bad. He was
nice to me. He spent time telling me how to surf and all.
Even without that arm, he was a lot more alive than most
people with two arms. Plus, he took good care of Mama."

"I know."

"But I said nasty things about him."

"You couldn't help yourself," I said. "It's not your fault."

She looked straight ahead the whole way. She didn't turn
to look at me. The breeze blowing in through the window
ruffled her bangs.

"It's sad, but I think he was that sort of person," I said. "A
nice guy, maybe even worthy of respect. But he got treated like
some kind of fancy trash basket. People were always dumping
on him. Maybe he was born with that tendency. Mediocrity's
like a spot on a shirt—it never comes off."

"It's unfair."

"As a rule, life is unfair," I said.

"Yeah, but I think I did say some awful things."

"To Dick?"

"Yeah."

I pulled the car over to the shoulder of the road and turned off the ignition.

"That's just stupid, that kind of thinking," I said, nailing her with my eyes. "Instead of regretting what you did, you could have treated him decently from the beginning. You could've tried to be fair. But you didn't. You don't even have the right to be sorry."

Yuki looked at me, shocked and hurt.

"Maybe I'm being too hard on you. But listen, I don't care what other people do. I don't want to hear that sort of talk from you. You shouldn't say things like that lightly, as if saying them is going to solve anything. They don't stick. You think you feel sorry about Dick, but I don't believe you really do. If I were Dick, I wouldn't want your easy regret. I wouldn't want people saying, 'Oh, I acted horribly.' It's not a question of manners; it's a question of fairness. That's something you have to learn."

Yuki couldn't respond. She pressed her fingers to her temples and quietly closed her eyes. She almost seemed to have dozed off, but for the slight flutter of her eyelashes, the trembling of her lips. Crying inside, without sobs or tears. Was I expecting too much of a thirteen-year-old girl? Who was I to be so self-righteous? Still, whether or not she was thirteen, whether or not I was an exemplary human being, you can't let everything slide. Stupidity is stupidity. I won't put up with it.

Yuki didn't move. I reached out and touched her arm.

"It's okay," I said. "I'm very narrow-minded. No, to be fair, you've done the best that can be expected."

A single tear trailed down her cheek and fell on her lap. That was all. Beautiful and noble.

"So what can I do now?" she spoke up a minute later.

"Nothing," I said. "Just think about what comes before

words. You owe that to the dead. As time goes on, you'll understand. What lasts, lasts; what doesn't, doesn't. Time solves most things. And what time can't solve, you have to solve yourself. Is that too much to ask?"

"A little," she said, trying to smile.

"Well, of course it is," I said, trying to smile too. "I doubt that this makes sense to most people. But I think I'm right. People die all the time. Life is a lot more fragile than we think. So you should treat others in a way that leaves no regrets. Fairly, and if possible, sincerely. It's too easy not to make the effort, then weep and wring your hands after the person dies. Personally, I don't buy it."

Yuki leaned against the car door.

"But that's real hard, isn't it?" she said.

"Real hard," I said. "But it's worth trying for. Look at Boy George: Even a fat gay kid who can't sing can become a star."

"Okay," she smiled, "but why are you always getting on Boy George's case? I bet you must really like him, deep down."

"Let me think about that one," I said.

Yuki's mother's house was in a large resort-housing tract. There was a big gate, with a pool and a coffee house adjacent. There was even a stop-and-shop minimart filled with junk food. No place someone like Dick North would have bought groceries at. Me either. As the road twisted and turned up the grade, my friendly Subaru began to gasp.

Halfway up the hill was Amé's house, too big for just a mother and daughter. I stopped the car and carried Yuki's bags up the steps to the side of the stone embankment. Down the slope, between the ranks of cedars, you could make out the ocean by Odawara. The air was hazy, the sea dull under the leaden glaze of spring.

Amé paced the large, sunny living room, lit cigarette in hand. A big crystal ashtray was overflowing with bent and

crushed Salem butts, the entire tabletop dusted with ashes.
She tossed her latest butt into the ashtray and came over to
greet Yuki, mussing her hair. She wore a chemical-spotted
oversized sweatshirt and faded jeans. Her hair was
uncombed, eyes bleary.

"It's been terrible," said Amé. "Why do these horrible
things always happen?"

I expressed my condolences and inquired about the details
of yesterday's accident. It was all so sudden, she told me, she
felt out of control, confused, uncertain. "And of course the
maid came down with a fever today and won't be in. Now
of all times, a fever! I'm going crazy. The police come, Dick's
wife calls, I don't know what they expect of me."

"What did Dick's wife have to say?"

"I couldn't make it out," she said. "She just cried. And
when she wasn't crying, she mumbled so I could barely understand what she was saying. And me, in this position, what was
I supposed to say? . . . What *was* I supposed to say?"

I shook my head.

"I told her I'd send along Dick's things as soon as I could,
but then the woman was crying even more. It was hopeless."

She let out a big sigh and collapsed into the sofa.

I asked her if she wanted anything to drink, and she
asked for coffee. For good measure, I also cleared away the
ashtray and cocoa-caked mugs, and wiped off the table.
While I waited for the water to boil, I tidied up the kitchen.
Dick North had kept a neat pantry, but already it was a
mess. Dirty dishes were piled in the sink, cocoa had been
dribbled across the stainless steel cooktop, knives lay here
and there smeared with cheese and who-knows-what, the lid
of the sugar container was nowhere in sight.

Poor bastard, I thought as I made a strong pot of coffee.
He tried so hard to bring order to this place. Now in the
space of one day, it was gone. Just like that. People leave
traces of themselves where they feel most comfortable, most
worthwhile. With Dick, that place was the kitchen. But even
that tenuous presence was on its way out.

Poor bastard.

I carried in the coffee and found Amé and Yuki sitting on the sofa. Amé's head rested on her daughter's shoulder. She looked drugged and drained. Yuki seemed ill at ease. How odd they appeared together—so different from when they were apart—how doubly unapproachable.

Amé accepted the coffee with both hands and drank it slowly, preciously. The slightest glow came to her eyes.

"You want anything to drink?" I asked Yuki.

She shook her head with no expression whatsoever.

"Has everything been taken care of?" I asked Amé. "The business about the accident, legal matters, and all that?"

"Done. The actual procedure wasn't so difficult. It was a perfectly common accident. A policeman came to the house to tell me the news, and that was it. I told them to contact Dick's wife, and she handled everything. I mean, I had no legal or even professional relationship with Dick. Then the wife called here. She hardly said a word, she just cried. She didn't even scream, nothing."

A perfectly common accident.

Another three weeks and Amé wouldn't remember there ever was someone in her life named Dick North. Amé was the forgetful type, and, unfortunately, Dick was forgettable.

"Is there anything I can do to help?" I asked.

"Well, yes. Dick's belongings," she muttered. "I told you I was going to return them to her, didn't I?"

"Yes."

"Well, last night I put his things in order. His manuscripts and typewriter and books and clothes—they all fit in one suitcase. There wasn't that much stuff. Just one suitcase full. I hate to ask, but could you deliver it to his wife?"

"Sure. Where does the family live?"

"I don't know exactly. Somewhere in Gotokuji, I know. Could you find out for me?"

Yuki showed me the study where Dick's things were. Upstairs, a long, narrow garret at the end of the hall, what had originally been the maid's room. It was pleasant enough, and naturally Dick had kept everything in immaculate order. On the desk were arranged five precision-sharpened pencils and an eraser, an unqualified still life. A calendar on the wall had been annotated with meticulous handwriting.

Yuki leaned in the doorway and scanned the interior in silence. All you could hear were the birds outside. I recalled the cottage in Makaha. It had been just as quiet, and there had been birds too.

The tag on the suitcase, also in Dick's hand, had his name and address. I lugged it downstairs. With his books and papers, it was much heavier than it looked. The weight yet another reminder of the fate of Dick North.

"There's not much here to eat," said Amé. "Dick went out to do the shopping and then all this happened."

"Don't worry. I'll go to the store," I said.

I checked the contents of the refrigerator to see what she did have. Then I drove down to town, to the supermarket where Dick had spent the last moments of his life, and purchased four or five days' worth of provisions.

I put away the groceries, and Amé thanked me. I felt like I was merely finishing up the task that Dick had left undone.

The two women saw me off from atop the stone embankment. The same as in Makaha, only this time nobody was waving. That had been Dick's role. The two stood there, not moving, gazing down on me. An almost mythological scene, like an icon. I heaved the gray suitcase into the backseat and slid behind the wheel. Mother and daughter were still standing there when I turned the curve and headed out of their sight. The sun was starting to sink into an orange sea. How would they spend the night? I wondered.

That one-armed skeleton in the eerie gloom of the room in Honolulu, it was now clear, *was* Dick North. So, who could the other five be?

Let's say my old friend, the Rat, for one. Dead several years now, in Hokkaido.

Then Mei, for another.

That left three. Three more.

What was Kiki doing there? Why did she want to show me these six deaths?

I made it down to Odawara and got on the Tokyo–Nagoya Expressway. Exiting at Sangenjaya, I navigated my way into the suburbs of Setagaya by map and found Dick North's house. An ordinary two-story suburban home, very small. The door and windows and mailbox and entry light—everything seemed to be in miniature. A mongrel on a chain patrolled the front door. There were lights on inside the house, the sound of voices. Dick's wake was in progress. At least he had somewhere to come home to.

I took the suitcase out of the car and hauled it to the front door. I rang the doorbell and a middle-aged man appeared. I explained that I'd brought Dick's things; my expression said I didn't know any more than that. The man looked at the name tag and grasped the situation immediately.

"Very much obliged," said the man, stiff but cordial.

And so, with no more resolve than before, I returned to my Shibuya apartment.

Three more, I thought.

In the scheme of things, what possible meaning was there to Dick North's death?

Alone in my room, I mulled it over a whiskey. It happened so suddenly, how could there have been meaning? All these blank spots in the puzzle and this piece didn't fit anywhere. Flip it over, turn it sideways, still no good. Did the piece belong somewhere else entirely?

Even if Dick's death had no meaning in itself, a major change of circumstances seemed inevitable. And not for the better either, my intuition told me. Dick North was a man of good intentions. In his own way, he had held things together.

But now that he was gone, things were going to change, things were going to get harder.

For instance?

For instance, I didn't care for Yuki's blank expression whenever she was with Amé. Nor did I like Amé's dull, spaced-out stare when she was with Yuki. There was something bad there. I liked Yuki. She was a good kid. Smart, maybe a little stubborn at times, but sensitive underneath it all. And I had nothing against Amé, really. She was attractive, full of vision, defenseless. But put the two of them together and the combination was devastating.

There was an energy that mounted with the two females together.

Dick North had been the buffer after Makimura. But now that he was gone, I was the only one left to deal with them.

For instance—

I rang up Yumiyoshi a few times. She was as cool as ever, although I may have detected a hint of pleasure in her voice. Apparently I wasn't too much of a nuisance. She was working every day, going to her swim club twice a week, dating occasionally. The previous Sunday, she told me, a guy had taken her for a drive to a lake.

"He's just a friend. An old classmate, now working in Sapporo. That's all."

I didn't mind, I said. Drive or hike or like, I didn't need to know. What really got to me was her swim club.

"But anyway, I just wanted to tell you," said Yumiyoshi. "I hate to hide things."

"I don't mind," I repeated. "All I care about is that I get up to Sapporo to see you again. You can go out with anybody you like. That's got nothing to do with us. You've been in my thoughts. Like I said before, I feel a bond between us."

Once again, she asked me what I meant. And again, my heart was in my words, but the explanation made no sense. Typical me.

A moderate silence ensued. A neutral-to-slightly-positive silence. True, silence is still silence, except when you think about it too much.

Gotanda looked tired whenever I saw him. He'd been squeezing trysts with his ex-wife into an already tight work schedule.

"All I know is, I can't keep this up forever," he said, sighing deeply. "I'm not cut out for this living on the fringes. I'm a homebody. That's why I'm so run-down. I'm over-extended, burned out."

"You ought to go to Hawaii for a break," I said. "Just the two of you."

"Wouldn't I love to," he said, smiling weakly. "Maybe for five days, lying on the beach, doing nothing. Even three days would be terrific."

That evening I'd gone to his condo in Azabu, sat on his chic sofa with a drink in my hand, and watched a compilation tape of the antacid commercials he'd appeared in. The first time I'd ever seen them.

Four office building elevators without walls or doors are rising and falling at high speeds like pistons. Gotanda is in a dark suit, briefcase in hand, every inch the elite businessman. He's hopping back and forth from elevator to elevator, conferring with his boss in one, making a date with a pretty young secretary in another, picking up papers here, rushing to dispatch them there. Two elevators away a telephone is ringing. All this jumping back and forth between speeding elevators is no easy trick, but Gotanda isn't losing his cool mask. He looks more and more serious.

VOICE OVER

Everyday stress builds up in your stomach. Give the busi-
ness to your busy-ness with a gentle remedy. . . .

I laughed. "That was fun."

"I think so too," he said. "Idiotic but fun. All commercials are nonsense, but this one is well shot. It's a damn sight better than most of my feature films, I'm sorry to say. Ad people have no qualms about spending on details, and the sets and those special effects cost a lot. It's not a bad concept either."

"And it's practically autobiographical."

"You said it," he laughed. "Boy, does my stomach get stressed out. But let me tell you, that stuff doesn't do a damn thing. They gave me a dozen packs to try, and it's a wonder how little it works."

"You really do move, though," I said, rewinding the tape by remote control to watch the commercial again. "You're a regular Buster Keaton. You might have found your calling."

A smile floated across Gotanda's lips. "I'd be interested. I like comedy. There's something to be said when a straight man like me can bring out the humor of a routine like that. You try to live straight in this crazy, crooked, mixed-up world—*that's* what's funny. You know what I mean?"

"I do, I do," I said.

"You don't even have to do anything especially funny. You just act normal. That alone looks strange and funny. Acting like that interests me. That type of actor simply doesn't exist in Japan today. People always overact when it comes to comedy. What I want to do is the reverse. Not act." He took a sip of his drink and looked up at the ceiling. "But no one brings me roles like that. The only roles they ever, ever bring into my agency are doctors or teachers or lawyers. You've heard me go on about this before, and let me tell you, I'm bored, bored, bored, *bored*. I'd like to turn them down, but I'm in no position to reject anything, and my stomach takes a beating."

Gotanda's first antacid commercial had been so well received, he'd made a number of sequels. The pattern was always the same. If he wasn't jumping back and forth between trains and buses and planes with split-second timing, he was scaling a skyscraper with papers under his arms

or tightrope-walking between offices. Through it all, Gotanda kept a perfect deadpan.

"At first the director told me to look tired. Like I was
about to keel over from exhaustion. But I told him, no, that
it'd come off better if I just played it straight. Of course,
they're all idiots, they didn't go for it at all. But I didn't give
in. I don't do these commercials for fun, but I was sure
about the right way to do it. I insisted. So they shot it two
ways and everyone liked mine much more. And then, of
course, the commercial was a success, so the director took
all the credit. He even won some kind of prize for it. Not
that I care. What eats me is how they all act so big, as if they
thought the whole thing up. The ones with no imagination
are always the quickest to justify themselves."

Gotanda switched off the video and put on a Bill Evans
record.

"All these idiots think they're so sharp, they got me dancing on their pinheads. Go here, go there. Do this, do that.
Drive this car, go out with that woman. It's a bad movie of a
bad life. How long can it last?"

"Maybe you ought to just toss it and start again from
scratch. If anyone could do it, you could. Leave your agency,
and take your time paying back what you owe."

"Don't think I haven't thought about it. If I was on my
own, that's what I'd do. Go back to square one, and join
some theater group. I wouldn't mind, believe me. But if I
did, my ex-wife would drop me, just like that. She grew up
under pressure—star-system pressure—and she needs people
around her who feel that pressure too. If the atmosphere
drops, she can't breathe. So if I want to be with her, I haven't
got a choice," said Gotanda, with a smile of resignation.
"Let's talk about something else. I could go on until morning
and still not get anywhere."

And so he brought up Kiki.

It was because of Kiki that Gotanda and I had become
friends, yet he'd hardly heard a word out of my mouth

about her. Did I find it hard to talk about her? If so, he wouldn't insist.

No, I told him, not at all.

I told him that Kiki and I got together entirely by chance and that we were living together soon after that. She burrowed into my life so unobtrusively, I could hardly believe she hadn't always been there. "I didn't notice how extraordinary it was at the time. But when I thought it over later, the whole scenario seemed completely unreal. And when I put it into words, it sounds silly. Which is why I haven't told anyone about it."

I took a drink, swirling the ice in my glass.

"In those days, Kiki was working as an ear model, and I'd seen these photos of her ears and, well, I got obsessed, to put it mildly. Her ear was going to appear in this ad—I forget what for—and my job was to write the copy. I was given these three photos, these three enormous close-ups of her ears, close enough to see the baby fuzz, and I tacked them up on my wall. I started gazing at these ears, day in and day out. At first I was fishing for some kind of inspiration, some kind of catchphrase, but then the ears became a part of my life. Even after I finished the job, I kept the photos up. They were incredible—they were perfectly formed, bewitching. The dream image of an ear. You'd have to see the real thing, though. They were . . ."

"Yeah, you did mention something about her ears."

"I had this total fixation. So I made these calls and found out who she was and I finally got ahold of her and she agreed to see me. The first day we met, we were at a restaurant and she personally *showed* me her ears. Personally, I mean, not professionally, and they were even more amazing than in the photograph. They were exquisite! Fantastic! When she exposed her ears professionally—that is, when she modeled them—she *blocked* them, she said. So they were gorgeous but they were different from her ears when she *showed* them. And when she did, it was like the entire world underwent a transformation. I know that sounds ludicrous, but I don't know how else to put it."

Gotanda considered seriously what I'd said. "What do you mean by her 'blocking' her ears?"

"Severing her ears from her consciousness."

"Oh."

"She pulled the plug on her ears."

"Uh-huh."

"Sounds crazy, but it's true."

"Oh, I believe you. I'm honestly trying to understand. Really, no kidding."

I eased back into the sofa and looked at a painting on the wall.

"Her ears had special power. They were like some great whirlpool of fate sucking me in. And they could lead people to the right place."

Gotanda pondered my words again. "And," he said, "did Kiki lead you anywhere? To some 'right place'?"

I nodded, but didn't say more about it. Too long and involved to explain.

"Now," I said, "she's trying to lead me somewhere again. I can sense it, very strongly. For the last few months, I've had this nagging feeling. And little by little I've been reeling in the line. It's a very fine line. It got snagged a couple of times, but it's gotten me this far. It's brought me in contact with a lot of different people. You, for instance. You're one of the central figures in this drama. Still, I can't get a grip on what's going on. Two people I knew have died recently. One was Mei. The other was a one-armed poet. I don't know what's going on, but I know *something* is."

The ice in the bucket had all but melted, so Gotanda fetched a new batch from the kitchen to freshen both our drinks.

"So you see, I'm stuck too," I picked up again. "Just like you."

"No, there you're wrong. You and I are not alike,"

Gotanda said. "I'm in love with one woman. And it's a dead-end kind of love. But not you. Maybe you're confused and wandering in a maze, but compared with this emotional morass I've gotten myself dragged into, you're much, much better off. You're being guided somewhere. You've got hope. There's possibility of a way out. But not for me, not at all. That's the big difference between us."

Well, maybe, maybe so. "Whatever. I've been clinging to this line from Kiki. That's all I can do for now. She's been sending these signals, these messages. So I spend my time trying to stay tuned in."

"Do you think," Gotanda started cautiously, "that there's a possibility Kiki's been killed?"

"Like Mei?"

"Uh-huh. I mean, she disappeared so suddenly. When I heard Mei was murdered, right away I thought about Kiki. Like maybe the same thing happened to her. I didn't want to say it before."

And yet I'd seen her, in downtown Honolulu, in the dim dusk light. I'd actually seen her. And Yuki knew it.

"Just something that crossed my mind. I didn't mean any-thing by it," Gotanda said.

"Sure, the possibility exists. But she's still sending me messages. Loud and clear."

Gotanda crossed his arms for a few minutes, pensive. He looked so exhausted, I thought he might nod off. Night was stealing into the room, enveloping his trim physique in fluid shadow.

I swirled the ice around in my glass again and took a sip.

That was when I noticed a third presence in the room. Someone else was here besides Gotanda and myself. I sensed body heat, breathing, odor. Yet it wasn't human. I froze. I glanced quickly around the room, but I saw nothing. There was only the feeling of *something*. Something solid, but invisible. I breathed deeply. I strained to hear.

It waited, crouching, holding its breath. Then it was gone.

I eased up and took another sip.

A minute or two later Gotanda opened his eyes and smiled at me. "Sorry. Seems we're making a depressing evening of it," he said.

"That's because, basically speaking, we're both depressing people," I said.

Gotanda laughed, but offered no further comment.

35

oward the end of May, by chance—as far as I know—I
ran into one of the cops who'd grilled me about Mei's
murder. Bookish. I was coming out of Tokyu Hands,
the department store with everything for the home you ever
wanted, and found myself squeezed up against him at the
exit. The day seemed like midsummer, yet here he was in a
heavy tweed jacket, entirely unaffected by the heat. Maybe
police stiffs are trained to be insensitive. He was holding a
Tokyu Hands bag like me. I pretended not to see him and
was moving past when the undaunted detective spoke
directly to me.

"You don't have to be so standoffish, you know," he
quipped. "As if we didn't know each other."

"I'm in a hurry," was all I said.

"Oh?" said he, not swallowing the line for a second.

"I have to be getting back to work," I stammered.

"I can imagine," said he. "But surely even a busy man
like yourself can spare ten minutes. Let me buy you a cup of
coffee. I've been wanting to talk to you, business aside.
Honest, just ten minutes of your time."

I followed him into a crowded coffee shop. Don't ask me
why. I could've politely said sorry and gone home. But I
didn't. We went in and sat down alongside young couples
and clusters of students. The coffee tasted horrible, the air

was bad. Bookish pulled out a cigarette and lit up.

"Been trying to quit," he said. "But there's something about the job. When I'm working, I gotta smoke."

I wasn't going to say anything.

"The job's rough on the nerves. Everybody hates you. The longer you're in homicide, the more they hate you. Your eyes go, your complexion starts to look like shit. You wouldn't know your own age. Even the way you talk changes. Not a healthy way to live."

He added three spoonfuls of sugar and creamer to his coffee, stirred well, and drank it like a connoisseur.

I looked at my watch.

"Ah, yes, the time," said Bookish. "We still have five minutes, right? Fine. I'll keep this short. So about that murdered girl. Mei."

"Mei?" I asked. I'm not snared that easily.

He twisted his lips, insinuating. "Oh, right, sure. The deceased young woman's name was Mei. Not her real name, of course. Her *nom d'amour*. She turned out to be a hooker, just like I thought. She may not have looked professional, but I could tell. Used to be you could spot the hookers in a second. The clothes, the makeup, the look on their faces. But nowadays you get girls you'd never believe in the trade. It's the money, or they're curious. I don't like it. And it's dangerous. Or don't you think so? Meeting unknown men behind closed doors. There's all types out there. Perverts and nut cases."

I forced a nod.

"But young girls, they don't know that. They think everything's cool. Can't be helped. When you're young, you think you can handle anything. By the time you find out otherwise, it's already too late. You got a stocking wrapped around your neck. Poor thing."

"So did you find the killer?"

Bookish shook his head and frowned. "Not yet, unfortunately. We did discover some interesting facts. Only we didn't publish them in the newspaper. Seeing as how the investigation is still going on. For example, we found out her professional name was Mei, but her real name was . . . Aww, what difference does it make what her real name was. The girl was born in Kumamoto. Father a public servant. Kumamoto's not such a big city, but he was next-to-top there. Family very well-off. Mother came to Tokyo once or twice a month to shop. No financial problems. The girl got a good allowance from them. She told them she was in the fashion business. She had one older sister, married to a doctor; one younger brother, studying law at Kyushu University. So what's a nice girl from a good home like that doing selling her tail? The family had a big shock coming. We spared them the call girl part, but their darling daughter strangled to death in a hotel room was pretty unsettling."

I said nothing and let him continue.

"We looked into the prostitute ring she was involved in. It wasn't easy, but we managed to track it down. How do you think we did it? We staked out the lobbies of some luxury hotels around town and hauled in a few women on suspicion of illegal commerce. We showed them the same photos we showed you and asked a few questions. One of them cracked. Not everyone's got a tough hide like you, heh heh. Anyway, turns out the deceased worked for this exclusive operation. Superexpensive membership. Nothing the likes of you or me can swing. I mean, can you pay seventy thousand yen a pop? I know *I* can't. At that price, I'd just as soon screw the wife and buy the kid a new bike," he laughed nervously. "But suppose I *could* swing the seventy grand, I still wouldn't be good enough. They run a background check, you see. Safety first. They can't afford weird shit from customers. But also they prefer a certain *class* of customer. No way a detective can get membership. Not that law enforcement is necessarily a strike against you. If you're top brass, real top brass, that's another story. You might come in handy someday. But a cop like me, no way."

He finished his coffee and lit up another cigarette.

"So we went to the captain for a search warrant. It took

three days to come through. By the time we set foot in the
place, the whole operation had been cleaned out. Spotless.
Not a speck of dust. There'd been a leak. And where do you
think that leak came from?"

I didn't know.

"C'mon, man, you're not dumb. The leak came from
inside. I'm talking *inside the police.* Somebody on top. No
proof, of course. But we grunts on the street know an inside
job when we see one. The word goes out to get scarce. Sorry
state of affairs. But predictable. And an operation like that
one is used to this sort of thing. They can move in the time it
takes us to use the toilet. They are *gone.* They find another
place to rent, buy new phone lines, and just like that they're
back in business. No sweat off their back. They still got their
subscriber list, they still got their girls lined up, they barely
been inconvenienced. And there's no way to trace them. The
thread's cut. With this dead girl, if we had some idea what
type of customer was her specialty, we could do something.
But as it is, we gotta throw up our hands."

"Don't look at me," I said.

"You sure you don't know anything?"

"Hey, if she was part of this exclusive call girl setup like
you say, they'd know in an instant who killed her, right?"

"Exactly," said Bookish. "So chances are the killer was
probably someone not on the list. The girl's own private
lover, or else she was turning tricks on the side. We searched
her apartment. Not a clue."

"Listen, I didn't kill her."

"I know *that*," said Bookish. "I already told you that.
You're not the killer type. I can tell by looking at you. Your
type never kills anybody. But you do know something, I
know that. You know more than you're letting on. So why
don't you come out with it? That's all I want. No hard-lin-
ing. I give you my word of honor."

"I don't know a thing," I said.

"Figures," Bookish mumbled, puffing his smoke. "This is
going nowhere. Fact is, the boys upstairs aren't crazy about

this investigation. After all, it's only a hooker killed in a hotel, no big deal. To them, that is. They probably think a hooker's better off dead anyway. The guys on top, they hardly ever set eyes on a stiff. They haven't got the vaguest idea what it's like to see a beautiful girl naked and strangled like that. They can't imagine how *pitiful* it is. And you can bet that it's not just police brass in on this prostitution racket. There's always a few upstanding public servants got their fingers in the pie too. You can see the gold lapel pins flashing in the dark. Cops develop an eye for this sort of business. We see the least little glint, and we pull in our necks, like turtles. Something you learn from your superiors. So that's how it goes. Somehow, the drift is, our Miss Mei's murder is just going to get buried. Poor thing."

The waitress cleared away Bookish's cup. I still had half of my coffee left.

"It's weird, but I feel close to this Mei girl," said Bookish. "Now why should that be? It doesn't figure, does it? But when I saw her strangled naked on that hotel bed, she did a number on me. And I decided, I made this pledge to her, I was going to get the fucker who did it. Now, I've seen more stiffs than I care to. So what's one more corpse, you say? This one was special. Strange and beautiful. The sunlight was pouring in through the window, the girl lying there, frozen. Eyes wide open, tongue hanging out of her mouth, stocking around her throat. Just like a necktie. Her legs were spread, and she'd pissed. When I saw that, I knew. The girl was asking me for help. Must seem remarkable to you, this soft touch I have. No?"

I couldn't say.

"You, you've been away a while. Got a tan I see," said the detective.

I mumbled something about Hawaii on business.

"Nice business. Wish I could switch saddles to your line of work, instead of looking at stiffs morning to night. Makes a fellow real fun company. You ever see a corpse?"

No, I hadn't.

He shook his head and looked at the clock. "Very well, then, hope you excuse me for wasting your time. But like they say, small world running into you at a place like this. What do you got in your bag?"

A soldering iron.

"Oh yeah? I got some drainpipe cleaner. Sink in the house backed up."

He paid the bill. I offered to pay my portion, but he insisted.

As we were walking out, I asked casually if prostitute murders happened a lot.

"Well, I guess you could say so," he said, eyes sharpening slightly. "Not every day, but not only on holidays either. Any reason you're so interested in prostitute murders?"

Just curious is all.

We went our separate ways, but the queasy feeling in the pit of my stomach still hadn't gone away the following morning.

36

May drifted past, slow as clouds.

It had been two and a half months since I'd worked. Fewer and fewer work calls came in. The trade was gradually forgetting about me. To be sure, no work, no money coming in, but I still had plenty in my account. I didn't lead an expensive life. I did my own cooking and washing, didn't spend a lot. No loans, no fancy tastes in clothes or cars. So for the time being, money was no problem. I calculated my monthly expenses, divided it into my bank balance, and figured I had another five months or so. Something would come of this wait-and-see. And if it didn't, well, I could think it over then. Besides, Makimura's check for three hundred thousand yen still graced my desktop. No, I wasn't going to starve.

All I had to do was keep things at a steady pace and be patient. I went to the pool several times a week, did the shopping, fixed meals. Evenings, I listened to records or read.

I began going to the library, leafing through the bound editions of newspapers, reading every murder case of the last few months. Female victims only. Shocking, the number of women murdered in the world. Stabbings, beatings, stranglings. No mention of anyone resembling Kiki. No body resembling Kiki, in any case. Sure, there were ways to

dispose of a body. Weight it down and throw it in the sea.
Haul it up into the hills and bury it. Just like I'd buried Kipper. Nobody would ever find him.

Maybe it was an accident? Maybe she'd gotten run over,
like Dick North. I checked the obituaries for accident victims. Women victims. Again, a *lot* of accidents that killed a
lot of women. Automobiles, fires, gas. Still no Kiki.

Suicides? Heart attacks? The papers didn't seem interested. The world was full of ways to die, too many to cover.
Newsworthy deaths had to be exceptional. Most people go
unobserved.

So anything was possible. I had no evidence that Kiki was
dead, no evidence that she was alive.

I called Yuki now and then. But always, when I asked
how she was, the answer was noncommittal.

"Not good, not bad. Nothing much."

"And your mother?"

"She's taking it easy, not working a lot. She sits around
all day, kind of out of it."

"Anything I can do? The shopping or something?"

"The maid does the shopping, so we're okay. The store
delivers. Mama and I are just spacing out. It's like . . . up
here, time's standing still. Is time really passing?"

"Unfortunately, the clock is ticking, the hours are going
by. The past increases, the future recedes. Possibilities
decreasing, regrets mounting."

Yuki let that pass.

"You don't sound like you have much vim and vigor," I
said.

"Oh really?"

"Oh really?"

"What's with you?"

"What's with you?"

"Stop mimicking me."

"Who's mimicking you? I'm just a mental echo, a figment

of your imagination. A rebound to demonstrate the fullness of our conversation."

"Dumb as usual," said Yuki. "You're acting like a child."

"Not so. I'm solid with deep inner reflection and pragmatic spirit. I'm echo as metaphor. The game is the message. This is of a different order than child's play."

"Hmph, nonsense."

"Hmph, nonsense."

"Quit it. I mean it!" yelled Yuki.

"Okay, quits," I said. "Let's take it again from the top. You don't sound like you have much vim and vigor, Yuki."

She let out a sigh. "Okay, maybe not. When I'm with Mama . . . I end up with one of her moods. It's like she has this power over how I feel. All she ever thinks about is herself. She never thinks about anyone else. That's what makes her so strong. You know what I mean. You've seen it. You just get all wrapped up in it. So when she's feeling down, I feel down. When she's up, I'm up."

I heard the flicking of a lighter.

"Maybe I could come up and visit you," I said.

"Could you?"

"Tomorrow all right?"

"Great," said Yuki. "I feel better already."

"I'm glad."

"I'm glad."

"Stop it."

"Stop it."

"Tomorrow then," I said and hung up before she could say it.

Amé was indeed "kind of out of it." She sat on the sofa, legs neatly crossed, gazing blankly at a photography magazine on her lap. She was a scene out of an impressionist painting. The window was open, but not a breeze stirred the curtains or pages. She looked up ever so slightly and smiled when I entered the room. The very air seemed to vibrate around her smile. Then she raised a slender finger a scant five centimeters and motioned for me to sit down on the chair opposite. The maid brought us tea.

"I delivered the suitcase to Dick's house," I said.

"Did you meet his wife?" Amé asked.

"No, I just handed it over to the man who came to the door."

"Thank you."

"Not at all."

She closed her eyes and put her hands together in front of her face. Then she opened her eyes again and looked around the room. There was only the two of us. I lifted my cup and sipped my tea.

Amé wasn't wearing her usual denim shirt. She had on a white lace blouse and a pale green skirt. Her hair was neatly brushed, her mouth freshened with lipstick. Her usual vitality had been replaced by a fragility that enveloped her like mist. A perfumed atmosphere that wavered on evaporation. Amé's beauty was wholly unlike Yuki's. It was the chromatic opposite, a beauty of experience. She had a firm grasp on it, knew how to use it, whereas Yuki's beauty was without purpose, undirected, unsure. Appreciating an attractive middle-aged woman is one of the great luxuries in life.

"Why is it . . . ?" Amé wondered aloud, her words trailing off. I waited for her to continue.

". . . why is it," she picked up again, "I'm so depressed?"

"Someone close to you has died. It's only natural that you feel this way," I said.

"I suppose," she said weakly.

"Still—"

Amé looked me in the face, then shook her head. "You're not stupid. You know what I want to say."

"That it shouldn't be such a shock to you? Is that it?"

"Yes, well, something like that."

That even if he wasn't such a great man. Even if he wasn't so talented. Still he was true. He fulfilled his duties nobly, excellently. He forfeited what he treasured and worked hard to attain, then he died. It was only after his death that his worth became apparent. I wanted to say that—but didn't. Some things I can't bring myself to utter.

"Why is it?" she addressed a point in space. "Why is it all my men end up like this? Why do they all go in strange ways? Why do they always leave me? Why can't I get things right?"

I stared at the lace collar of her blouse. It looked like pristinely scrubbed folds of tissue, the bleached entrails of a rare organism. A subtle shaft of smoke rose from her Salem in the ashtray, merging into a dust of silence.

Yuki reappeared, her clothes changed, and indicated that she wanted to leave. I got up and told Amé we were going out for a bit.

Amé wasn't listening. Yuki shouted, "Mother, we're going out now," but Amé scarcely nodded as she lit another cigarette.

We left Amé sitting on the sofa motionless. The house was still haunted by Dick North's presence. Dick North was still inside me as well. I remembered his smile, his surprised look when I asked if he used his feet to slice bread.

Interesting man. He'd come more alive since his death.

37

I went up to see Yuki a few more times. Three times, to be exact.

Staying in the mountains of Hakone with her mother didn't seem to hold any particular attraction for her. She wasn't happy there, but she didn't hate it either. Nor did she feel compelled to look after her mother. Yuki let herself be blown along by the prevailing winds. She simply existed, without enthusiasm for all aspects of living.

Taking her out seemed to bring back her spirits. My bad jokes slowly began to elicit responses, her voice regained its cool edge. Yet, no sooner would she return to the house than she became a wooden figure again. Her voice went slack, the light left her eyes. To conserve energy, her little planet stopped spinning.

"Wouldn't it be better for you to be back on your own in Tokyo for a while?" I asked her as we sat on the beach. "Just for a change of pace. Three or four days. A different environment can do wonders. Staying here in Hakone's only going to bring you down. You're not the same person you were in Hawaii."

"No way around it," said Yuki. "But it's like a phase I have to go through. Wouldn't matter where I was, I'd still be like this."

"Because Dick North died and your mother's like that?"

"Maybe. But it's not the whole thing. Just getting away from Mama isn't going to solve everything. I can't do anything on my own. I don't know, it's just the way I feel. Like my head and body aren't really together. My signs aren't so good right now."

I turned and looked out to sea. The sky was overcast. A warm breeze rustled through the clumps of grasses on the sand.

"Your signs?" I asked.

"My star signs," Yuki smiled. "It's true, you know. The signs are getting worse. Both for Mama and me. We're on the same wavelength. We're connected that way, even if I'm away from her."

"Connected?"

"Yeah, mentally connected," Yuki said. "Sometimes I can't stand it and I try to fight it. Sometimes I'm just too tired and I give in, and I don't care. It's like I'm not really in control of myself. Like I'm being moved around by some force. I can't stand it. I want to throw everything out the window. I want to scream 'I'm only a kid!' and go hide in a corner."

Before it got too late I drove Yuki home and headed back to Tokyo. Amé asked me to stay for dinner, as she invariably did, but I always declined. A very unappetizing prospect, the idea of sitting down to a meal with mother dreary and her disinterested daughter, both on the same wavelength, there in the lingering presence of the deceased. The dead-weighted air. The silence. The night so quiet you could hear any sound. The thought of it sank a stone in my stomach. The Mad Hatter's tea party might have been just as absurd, but at least it was more animated.

I played loud rock 'n' roll on the car stereo all the way home, had a beer while cooking supper, and ate alone in peace.

Yuki and I never did much. We listened to music as we drove, lolled around gazing at clouds, ate ice cream at the Fujiya Hotel, rented a boat on Lake Ashinoko. Mostly we just talked and spent the whole afternoon watching the day pass. The pensioners' life.

Once, upon Yuki's suggestion that we see a movie, we drove all the way down to Odawara. We checked the listings and found nothing of interest. Gotanda's *Unrequited Love* was playing at a second-run theater, and when I mentioned that Gotanda was a classmate from junior high school, whom I got together with occasionally, Yuki got curious.

"Did you see it?"

"Yeah," I admitted, "I saw it." I didn't say how many times.

"Was it good?" asked Yuki.

"No, it was dumb. A waste of film, to put it mildly."

"What does your friend say about the movie?"

"He said it was a dumb movie and a waste of film," I laughed. "And if the performer himself says so, you can be sure it's bad."

"But I want to see it anyway."

"As you wish."

"You don't mind?"

"It's okay. One more time's not going to hurt me," I said.

On a weekday afternoon, the theater was practically empty. The seats were hard and the place smelled like a closet. I bought Yuki a chocolate bar from the snack bar as we waited for the movie to start. She broke off a piece for me. When I told her it'd been a year since I'd last eaten chocolate, she couldn't believe it.

"Don't you like chocolate?"

"It's not a matter of like or dislike," I said. "I guess I'm just not interested in it."

"Interested? You are weird. Whoever heard of not *liking* chocolate? That's abnormal."

"No, it's not. Some things are like that. Do you like the Dalai Lama?"

"What's that?"

"It's not a 'what,' it's a 'who.' He's the top priest of Tibet."

"How would I know?"

"Well, then, do you like the Panama Canal?"

"Yes, no, I don't care."

"Okay, how about the International Date Line? Or *pi*? Or the Anti-Trust Act? Or the Jurassic Period? Or the Senegalese national anthem? Do you like or dislike November 8, 1987?"

"Shut up, will you? How can you churn out so much garbage so fast?" she struck back. "So you don't like or dislike chocolate, you're just not interested in it. Happy?"

Presently the movie began. I knew the whole story backwards, so I didn't bother paying a lot of attention. Yuki didn't think much of the picture either, if the way she muttered to herself was any indication.

On screen, the handsome teacher Gotanda was explaining to his class how mollusks breathe. Simply, patiently, with just the right touch of humor. The girl lead gazed at him.

"Is that guy your friend?" Yuki asked.

"Yeah."

"Seems like a real airhead," said Yuki.

"You said it," I said. "But only in the film. In real life, he's a good guy."

"Then maybe he should get into some good movies."

"That's what he wants to do. Not so easy, though. It's a long story."

The movie creaked along, obvious and mediocre plot. Mediocre script, mediocre music. They ought to have sealed the thing in a time capsule marked "Late 20th Century Mediocrity" and buried it somewhere.

Finally Kiki's scene came up. The most intense point in the movie. Gotanda and Kiki sleeping together. The Sunday morning scene.

I took a deep breath and concentrated on the screen. Sunday morning sunlight slanting through the blinds, the same

light, same exposure, same colors as always. I'd engraved
every detail of that room in my brain. I could almost breathe
the atmosphere of that room. Zoom in on Gotanda. His
hand moves down Kiki's spine. Sensuously, effortlessly,
caressing. The slightest tremor of response runs through her
body. Like a candle flame just flickering in a microcurrent of
air that the skin doesn't feel. I hold my breath. Close-up of
Gotanda's fingers. The camera starts to pan. Kiki's face
comes into view. Enter lead girl. She climbs the apartment
stairs, knocks on the door, opens it. Once again, I ask
myself, why isn't it locked? Makes no sense. But it doesn't
have to. It's just a film and a mediocre one at that. The girl
walks in, sees Gotanda and Kiki getting it on. Her eyes register shock. She drops her cookies and runs. Gotanda sits up
in bed, numbly observing what has transpired. Kiki has her
line, "What was *that* all about?"

The very same as always. Exactly the same.

I shut my eyes. The Sunday morning light, Gotanda's
hand, Kiki's back, everything floats up with singular clarity.
A discrete little world existing in a dimension all its own.

The next thing I know, Yuki was bent forward, head on
the backrest of the seat in front, with both arms wrapped
around herself as if to ward off the cold. Dead silent, not
moving a hair. Hardly a sign of breathing.

"Hey, are you all right?" I asked.

"No, I don't feel very well," Yuki barely squeezed out the
words.

"Let's get out of here. Do you think you can manage?"

Yuki half-nodded. I held her stiffened arms and helped
her out of the theater. As we walked up the aisle, Gotanda
was up on the screen behind us, lecturing the class in biology. Outside, the streets were hushed under a curtain of fine
rain. The scent of surf blew in from the sea. Supporting her
by the elbow, I walked her slowly to the car. Yuki was biting
her lip, not saying anything. I didn't say anything either. The
parking lot was scarcely two hundred meters from the theater, but it took forever.

38

I sat Yuki in the front seat and wound her window open. Soft rain fell, undetectable to the eye, though the asphalt was slowly staining black. There was the smell of rain. Some people had their umbrellas up, others walked along as if nothing was coming down. An outstretched hand would be retracted with only a hint of dampness. It was that fine a rain.

Yuki rested an arm on the door and her chin upon that, the tilt of her neck turning her face half out of the car. She held that pose for a good while, not moving except to breathe. Each tiny rise followed by a tiny fall, the slightest crest and trough of breath. How could anyone look so fragile, so defenseless? From where I sat, it seemed that the least impact would be enough to snap off her head and elbow. Was it merely that she was a child, not hardened to the ways of the world, while I was an adult, who, however inexpertly, had endured?

"Is there anything I can I do?" I asked.

"Not really," said Yuki, swallowing as she spoke face-down. The saliva clearing her throat sounded unnaturally loud. "Take me somewhere quiet where there's no people, but not too far."

"The beach?"

"Wherever. But don't drive fast. I might throw up if we bump too much."

I lifted her head inside onto the headrest, careful as if cradling an egg, and rolled up her window halfway. Then as slowly as the traffic would allow, we headed to the Kunifuzu seaside. We parked the car and walked to the beach, where Yuki vomited onto the sand. There'd been hardly anything in her stomach, only the chocolate and gastric juices. The most excruciating way to get sick. The body is in spasms, but nothing comes. You're wringing out your entire system, until your stomach is a knot the size of a fist. I massaged her back. The misting rain continued, but Yuki didn't notice.

Glyauughhh . . . Yuki's eyes welled up with tears as she retched.

I tried lamely to comfort her.

After ten minutes of this, I wiped her mouth with a handkerchief and kicked sand over the mess. Then holding her by the elbow, I walked her over to a nearby jetty. We sat down, leaning back against the seawall as the rain began to fall. We stared off into the waves, at the cars droning in the background on the West Shonan Causeway. The only people around were standing in the water before us, fishing. They wore slickers and rain hats, their eyes trained somewhere below the horizon, their rods unbending. They didn't turn around to see us. Yuki lay her head on my shoulder, but didn't say a word. We must have seemed like lovers.

Yuki closed her eyes. Breathing so lightly, she seemed to be asleep. Her wet bangs were plastered in a clump across her forehead, her skin still tan from last month. But beneath the overcast sky, Yuki looked sickly. I wiped the rain and tears from her face. Rain kept falling silently over the boundless sea. Self-Defense Force submarine-spotting planes groaned past overhead like dragonflies in heat.

Finally, her head still resting on my shoulder, she opened her eyes and looked at me in soft focus. She pulled a Virginia Slim from her hip pocket and lit up. Or tried to repeatedly—she barely had the strength to light a match. No lectures from me about smoking, not this time. Eventually she got it lit and flicked the match away. Then after two drags on the cigarette, she tossed it away too. It continued burning until the rain put it out.

"Your stomach still hurt?" I asked.

"A little."

"Let's just stay put a while though. You're not cold?"

"I'm fine. The rain feels good."

The fishermen were still transfixed on the Pacific. What was the attraction of fishing? It couldn't be merely catching fish. Was it just one of those acquired tastes? Like sitting out on a rainy beach with a high-strung thirteen-year-old?

"Your friend," Yuki ventured cautiously, her voice cracking.

"My friend?"

"Yeah, the one in the film."

"His real name's Gotanda," I said. "Like the station on the Yamanote Line. The one after Meguro and before Osaki."

"He killed that woman."

I squinted at Yuki, hard. She looked wan. Her breathing came irregularly, like a nearly drowned soul trawled up from the drink. What was the girl saying? It didn't register. "Killed what woman?" I asked.

"That woman. The one he was sleeping with on Sunday morning."

I didn't get it. I couldn't get it. What was she talking about? Half-consciously, I smiled and said, "But nobody dies in the movie. You must be mistaken."

"Not in the movie. In real life. He actually killed her. I saw it," said Yuki, clutching my arm. "It scared me so much I could hardly breathe. That *whatever-it-is* came over me again. I could see the whole murder, sharp and clear. Your friend killed that woman. I'm not making this up. Honest."

My spine turned to ice, I couldn't utter a word. Everything was falling out of place, tumbling down, out of my hands. I couldn't hold on to anything.

"I'm sorry. Maybe I shouldn't have said anything," said

Yuki. She sighed and let go of my arm. "The honest truth is, I don't know. I can *feel* that it's real, but I can't *really* be sure if it's real or not. And I know you'll probably hate me like everyone else for saying so. But I couldn't *not* tell you. Whether it's real or not, I saw it. I couldn't keep quiet about it. I'm really scared. Please don't get angry at me. I can't handle it. I feel like I'm falling apart."

"I'm not mad, so calm down and tell me what you saw," I said, holding her hand.

"It's the first time I've ever seen anything clearly like this. He strangled her, the woman in the movie. And he put the body in the car and drove a long, long way. It was that Italian car you were driving once. That car, it's his, isn't it?"

"Yes, it's his car," I said. "Is there anything else? Slow down and think it over. Whatever comes to mind, no matter how small, tell me. I want to know."

She shook her head tentatively, twice, three times. Then she breathed deeply. "There's really not much more. The smell of soil. A shovel. Night. Birds chirping. That's about it. He strangled that girl to death, loaded her off somewhere in that car, and buried her. That's all. But—and this is the truly strange part—the whole thing didn't seem vicious or horrible or anything. It didn't even seem like a crime. It was more like a ceremony. It was a quiet thing, between the killer and the victim. But a very strange quiet. Like it was out on the edge of the earth or something."

I closed my eyes. My thoughts wouldn't go anywhere. Objects and events in my head were disintegrating, flying like shrapnel through the dark. I didn't believe what Yuki was saying; I didn't disbelieve what Yuki was saying. I let her words sink in. They weren't fact. They were possibility. Nothing more, nothing less, but the force of the possibility was shattering.

Any semblance of order I had come to know over the last few months was shot. Diffuse, uncertain, but it was order, and it had taken hold. No more.

The possibility exists. And in the moment that I admitted

that, something came to an end. Ever subtly, yet decisively, it was over. But what? I couldn't think further. No, not now. Meanwhile, I found myself alone again. With a thirteen-year-old girl, on a rainy beach, desperately alone.

Yuki squeezed my hand.

How long she held it, I don't know. A hand so small and warm it almost didn't seem real. Her touch was more like a tiny replay from memory. Warm as a memory, but it doesn't lead you anywhere.

"Let's go," I said. "I'll take you home."

I drove her back up to Hakone. Neither of us spoke. When the silence became too oppressive, I put on the stereo. There was music, but I didn't hear it. I concentrated on driving. Hands and feet, shifting gears, steering. The wipers going back and forth, monotonously.

I didn't want to have to see Amé, so I let Yuki out at the bottom of the steps.

"Hey," said Yuki, looking in through the passenger seat window, arms crossed tight and shivering, "you don't have to swallow everything I told you. I just saw it, that's all. Like I said, I don't know if it *really* happened. Please don't hate me. I'd die."

"I don't hate you," I said, coming up with a smile. "And I won't swallow anything, unless it's the truth. It's got to come out some time. The fog's got to pull away. I know that much. If what you say turns out to be true, okay, it just means that I got a glimpse of the truth through you. Don't worry. It's something I have to find out for myself."

"Are you going to see him?"

"Of course. I'll ask him if it's true. There's no other way."

Yuki shrugged. "You're not mad at me?"

"No, I'm not mad at you, of course not," I said. "Why would I be mad at you? You haven't done anything wrong."

"You were such a good guy," she said. "I never met anyone like you."

Why the past tense? I wondered. "And I've never met a girl like you."

"Good-bye," said Yuki. Then she took a good, long look at me. She seemed fidgety. As if she wanted to add something more or hold my hand or kiss me on the cheek.

Nervous images of possibility kept floating into my head all the way home. I made myself focus on the mindless music and tacked my attention to the road ahead. The rain let up just as I exited the Tokyo–Nagoya Expressway, but I didn't have the energy to turn off the wipers until I pulled into my parking space in Shibuya. My head was in a shambles. I had to do something. So I sat there in my parked Subaru, my hands glued to the wheel.

39

I tried to put my thoughts in order.

First question: Should I believe Yuki? I analyzed matters on the level of pure possibility, wiping the field clear of emotional elements as far as I could see. This required no great effort. My feelings had been numbed, as if I'd been stung, from the very beginning. *The possibility exists.* The longer I considered the possibility, the more the possibility moved toward probability. I stood in the kitchen making coffee. Then pouring myself a cup, I retreated with it to my bed. By the time I'd finished it, the probability had become a fair certainty. Yes, it was exactly as Yuki had seen it: Gotanda had murdered Kiki, hauled her body away, and buried it.

How absurd. There was no proof whatsoever. Only the dream of an oversensitive thirteen-year-old girl watching a movie. And yet, somehow, what she said could not be doubted. This was shocking. Still my instincts accepted it fully. Why? How could I be so sure?

I didn't know.

Next question: Why would Gotanda kill Kiki?

I didn't know.

Next question: Did Gotanda also kill Mei? Why? What would make Gotanda want to kill her?

Again I didn't know. I wracked my brains, but couldn't

come up with a single reason why Gotanda would kill either
Kiki or Mei.

There were too many unknowns.

I had to see Gotanda. I had to ask him directly. I reached
for the phone but couldn't bring myself to dial his number. I
set down the receiver, rolled over on the bed, and gazed up
at the ceiling. Gotanda had become a friend. I would never
have guessed how much of a friend. Suppose he did kill Kiki,
he was still my friend. I didn't want to lose him. Not like I'd
already lost so many things in this life. No, I couldn't call
him.

I didn't want to talk to anybody.

I sat, and when the phone rang, I let it ring. If it was
Gotanda, what was I going to say? If it was Yuki, or even
Yumiyoshi, I didn't care. I didn't want to talk to anybody.

Four days, five days, I stayed put and thought. *Why?* I
hardly ate, hardly slept. I didn't drink a drop. I stayed
indoors. I lost touch with my body. With all that had happened to me already, I was still losing. And now here I was,
alone. It was always like this. In some ways, Gotanda and I
were of the same species. Different circumstances, different
thinking, different sensibilities, the same species. We both
kept losing. And now we were losing each other.

I could see Kiki. *What was that all about?* But was Kiki
dead, covered with dirt, in the ground? Like my Kipper?
Ultimately, Kiki had to die. Strange how I couldn't see things
any other way. The skin of my soul was no longer tender. I
tried not to feel anything at all. My resignation was a silent
rain falling over a vast sea. Even loneliness was beyond me.
Everything was taking leave of me, like ciphers in the sand,
blown away on the wind.

So another person had joined the group in that most
bizarre chamber of my world. Four down, two to go. Sooner
or later, bleached white bones ferried to that room via some
impossible architecture. Death's waiting room in downtown
Honolulu, connected to the dark chill lair of the Sheep Man
in a Sapporo hotel, connected to the Sunday morning bed-

room where Gotanda lay with Kiki. Was I losing my mind? Real events, under imaginary circumstances, filtering back, wild, distorted, bizarre. Was there nothing absolute? Was there no . . . reality? Sapporo in the March snow could as easily *not* have been real. Sitting on the beach in Makaha with Dick North had seemed real enough—but a one-armed man cutting bread in perfect slices? And a Honolulu call girl giving me a phone number that I later find in the anteroom to the death chamber Kiki leads me to? Why isn't that real? What could I reasonably admit into evidence without causing my whole world to shake at its foundations?

Was the sickness *in here* or *out there*? Did it matter?

What was the line now? Get in step and dance, so that everyone's impressed. Keeping in step—was that the only reality? Well, dance yourself to the telephone, give your pal Gotanda a ring, and ask him casually: "Did you kill Kiki?"

No way. My hand experienced sudden paralysis. I sat by the phone, numb, shaking, as if I was in a crosswind. Breathing grew difficult. I liked Gotanda, I liked him a lot. He was my only friend, he was part of my life. I understood him.

I tried dialing. I got the wrong number, every time. On the sixth try, I hurled the receiver to the floor.

I never did manage to call. In the end it was Gotanda who showed up at my place.

It was a rainy night. He was wearing a rain hat and the same white trench coat as the night I drove him to Yokohama. The rain was coming down hard, and his hat was dripping. He didn't have an umbrella.

He smiled when he saw me. I smiled back, almost by reflex.

"You look awful," he said. "I called and called but never got an answer. So I decided just to come over. You been under the weather?"

"Under is not the word," I said.

He sized me up. "Well, maybe it's a bad time. I'll come

back when you're feeling better. Sorry to come by unan-
nounced like this."

I shook my head and exhaled. No words came. Gotanda
waited patiently. "I'm not sick or anything," I assured him.
"I just haven't been sleeping or eating. I think I'm okay now.
Anyway I've been wanting to talk to you. Let's go somewhere. I haven't eaten a full meal in ages."

We took the Maserati out into the rainy neon streets.
Gotanda's driving was precise and smooth as ever, but the
car now made me nervous. The deep soundproofed ride cut
a channel through the clamor that rose all around us.

"Where to?" Gotanda asked. "All I care is that it's somewhere quiet where we can talk and get decent food without
running into the Rolex crowd." he said. He looked my way,
but I said nothing. For thirty minutes we drove around, my
eyes focused on the buildings we were passing.

"I can't think of any place," Gotanda tried again. "How
about you? Any ideas?"

"No, me neither." I really couldn't. I was still only half
present.

"Okay, then, why don't we take the opposite approach?"
he said brightly.

"The opposite approach?"

"Someplace noisy and crowded. That way we can relax."

"Okay. Where?"

"Feel like pizza? Let's go to Shakey's."

"I don't mind. I'm not against pizza. But wouldn't they
spot you, going to a place like that?"

Gotanda smiled weakly, like the last glow of a summer
sun between the leaves. "When was the last time you saw
anyone famous in Shakey's, my friend?"

Shakey's was packed with weekend shoppers. Crowded
and noisy. A Dixieland quartet in suspenders and red-and-
white striped shirts were pumping out *The Tiger Rag* to a
raucous college group loud on beer. The smell of pizza was
everywhere. No one paid attention to anyone else.

We placed our order, got a couple drafts, then found a

table under a gaudy imitation Tiffany lamp in the back of the restaurant.

"What did I tell you? Isn't this more like it?" said Gotanda.

I'd never craved pizza before, but the first bite had me thinking it was the best thing I'd ever tasted. I must have been starving. The both of us. We drank and ate and ate and drank. And when the pizza ran out, we each bought another round of beer.

"Great, eh?" belched Gotanda. "I've been wanting a pizza for the last three days. I even dreamed about it, sizzling hot, sliding right out of the oven. In the dream I never get to eat it, though. I just stare at it and drool. That's the whole dream. Nothing else happens. What would Jung say about pizza archetypes?" Gotanda chuckled, then paused. "So what was this that you wanted to talk to me about?"

Now or never, I thought. But come right out with it? Gotanda was thoroughly relaxed, enjoying the evening. I looked at his innocent smile and couldn't bring myself to do it. Not now, at least.

"What's new with you?" I asked. "Work? Your ex-wife?"

"Work's the same," Gotanda said. "Nothing new, nothing good, nothing I want to do. I can yell until my throat gives out, but nobody wants to hear what I have to say. My wife —did you hear that? I still call her my wife after all this time—I've only seen her once since I last saw you. Hey, you ever do the love hotel thing?"

"Almost never."

"I told you she and I have been meeting at love hotels. You know, the more you use those places, it gets to you. They're dark, windows all covered up. The place is only for fucking, so who needs windows, right? All you got is a bathroom and a bed—plus music and TV and a refrigerator—but it's all pretty blank and anonymous and artificial. Actually, very conducive to getting down and doing it. Makes you feel like you're really *doing it*. After a while, though, you feel the claustrophobia, and you begin to sort of hate the place. Still, they're the only refuge we got."

Gotanda took a sip of beer and wiped his mouth with the napkin.

"I can't bring her to my condo. The scandal rags would have a field day if they ever found out. I got no time to go off somewhere. They'd sniff it out too anyway. We've practically sold our privacy by the gram. So we go to these cheesy fuck hotels and . . ." Gotanda looked over at me, then smiled. "Here I go, griping again."

"That's okay. I don't mind listening."

The Dixieland band struck up "Hello Dolly."

"Hey, how about another pizza?" Gotanda asked. "Halve it with you. I don't know what it is with me, but am I starving!"

Soon we were stuffing our faces with one medium anchovy. The college kids kept up their shouting match, but the band had finished their final set. Banjo and trumpet and trombone were packed in their cases, and the musicians left the stage, leaving only the upright piano.

We'd finished the extra pizza, but somehow couldn't take our eyes off the empty stage. Without the music, the voices in the crowd became plastic, almost palpable. Waves of sound solidifying as they pressed toward us, yet broke softly on contact. Rolling up slowly over and over again, striking my consciousness, then retreating. Farther and farther away. Distant waves, crashing against my mind in the distance.

"Why did you kill Kiki?" I asked Gotanda. I didn't mean to ask it. It just slipped out.

He stared at me as if he were looking at something far off. His lips parted slightly. His teeth were white and beautiful. For the longest time, he stared right through me. The surf in my head went on and on, now louder, now fainter. As if all contact with reality was approaching and receding. I remember his graceful fingers neatly folded on the table. When my reality strayed out of contact, they looked like fine craftwork.

Then he smiled, ever so peaceably.

"Did I kill Kiki?" he enunciated slowly.

"Only joking," I hedged.

Gotanda's eyes fell to the table, to his fingers. "No, this isn't a joke. This is very important. I really have to think about it. *Did* I kill Kiki? I have to give this very serious thought."

I stared at him. His mouth was smiling, but his eyes weren't.

"Could there be a reason for you to kill Kiki?" I asked.

"Could there be a reason for me to kill Kiki? I don't even know myself. Did I kill Kiki? Why?"

"Hey, how would I know?" I tried to laugh. "Did you kill Kiki, or didn't you kill Kiki?"

"I said, I'm thinking about it. Did I kill Kiki, or didn't I?"

Gotanda took another sip of beer, set down his glass, and propped his head up on his hand. "I can't be sure. Sounds stupid, doesn't it? But I mean it. I'm not sure. I think, maybe, I tried to strangle Kiki. At my place, I think. Why would I have killed Kiki there? I didn't even want to be alone with her. No good, I can't remember. But anyway, Kiki and I were at my place—I put her body in the car and took her someplace and I buried her. Somewhere in the mountains. I can't be sure if I really did it. I can't believe I'd do a thing like that. I just *feel* as if I might have done it. I can't prove it. I give up. The most critical part's a blank. I'm trying to think if there's any physical evidence. Like a shovel. I'd have to have used a shovel. If I found a shovel, I'd know I did it. Let me try again. I buy a shovel at a garden supply. I use the shovel to dig a hole and bury Kiki. Then I toss the shovel. Okay, where?

"The whole thing's in pieces, like a dream. The story goes this way and that way. It's going nowhere. I have memories of *something*. But are the memories for real? Or are they something I made up later to fit? Something's wrong with me. It's gotten worse since my wife and I split up. I'm tired. I'm really . . . lost."

I said nothing.

After a pause, Gotanda went on. "Well, what's real any-

way? From what point is it all phobia? Or acting? I thought
if I hung around you, I'd get a better grip on things. I
thought so from the first time you asked me about Kiki. Like
maybe you'd clear away this muddle. Open a window and
let some fresh air in." He folded his hands again and peered
down at them. "Let's say I did kill Kiki—what would be the
reason? I liked her. I liked sleeping with her. When I was
down, she and Mei were my only release. So why kill her?"

"Did you kill Mei?"

Gotanda stared at his hands for an aeon, then shook his
head. "No, I don't believe I killed Mei. Thank god, I have an
alibi for that night. The day she was killed, I was at the studio until midnight, then I drove with my manager to Mito.
What a relief. If no one could swear I was at the studio that
night, I'd worry that I killed Mei too. But I still feel responsible for Mei's death. I don't know why. I wasn't there, but it's
like I killed her with my own hands. I have this *feeling* that
she died on account of me."

Another aeon passed while he stared at his fingers.

"Gotanda, you're beat," I said. "That's all. You probably
didn't kill anyone. Kiki just vanished somewhere. When we
were together, she used to disappear like that. It wouldn't be
the first time. You're riding yourself too hard. Don't do it."

"No, it's not like that. Not that simple. I probably did kill
Kiki. I don't think I killed Mei, but, yes, I think I killed Kiki.
The sensation of the air going out of her throat is still in my
fingers. I can still feel the weight of the dirt in the shovel. In
effect, I killed her."

"But why would you kill Kiki? It doesn't make sense."

"No idea," he said. "Maybe an urge to self-destruct. It's
happened before. I get this gap between me Gotanda and me
the actor, and I stand back and actually observe myself doing
shit. I'm on one side of this very deep, dark fault, and then
unconsciously, on the other side, I have this urge to destroy
something. Smash it to bits. A glass. A pencil. A plastic
model. Never happens when other people are around,
though. Only when I'm alone.

"But once, when I was in elementary school, I knocked into this friend of mine, and he fell off a small bluff. I don't know why I did it. But the next thing I knew, he was down there. It wasn't a big fall, so he wasn't hurt too bad. It was supposed to be an accident. I mean, why would I push this friend of mine over the edge on purpose? That's what everyone thought. I wasn't so sure. Then high school, I set fire to these mailboxes. I'd put a burning rag down the slot. Not just once, not even as a prank. It was like I was compelled to do it. Like it was the only thing that'd bring me to my senses. Unconsciously, that was what I thought. But afterwards I would remember the feel of things. I could still feel it in my hands. And I wouldn't be able to wash it off. God, what a horrible life. I don't know how I can stand it."

Gotanda shook his head.

"How do I check if I killed Kiki?" Gotanda went on. "There's no evidence. No corpse. No shovel. No dirt on my trousers. No blisters on my hands. Not that digging a hole is going to give you blisters. I don't even remember where I buried her. Say I went to the police and confessed, who'd believe me? If there's no body, it's not a homicide. She disappeared. That's all I know for sure. There've been times I wanted to tell you, but I just couldn't. I thought it'd wipe out whatever closeness we had. Whenever I'm with you, I feel so relaxed. I never feel the gap. You don't know how precious that is. I don't want to lose a friendship like ours. So I kept putting off telling you, until you asked, like this. I really ought to have come clean."

"Come clean? When there's no evidence you did anything?"

"Evidence isn't the issue. I ought to have told you first. But I *concealed* it. That's the problem."

"C'mon, even if it were true, even if you did kill Kiki, you didn't *mean* to kill her."

He held out his palms, as if he were going to read them. "No. I didn't mean to. I didn't have a reason. I liked her, and in a small way we were friends. We could talk. I could tell her about my wife, and she'd listen, honestly. Why would I want to kill her? But I did, I think, with these hands. Maybe I didn't do it willfully. But I did. I strangled her. But I wasn't strangling *her*, I was strangling my *shadow*. I remember thinking, if only I could choke my shadow off, I'd get some health. Except it wasn't my shadow. It was Kiki.

"*It all took place in that dark world.* You know what I'm talking about? Not here in this one. And it was Kiki who led me there. *Choke me,* Kiki told me. *Go ahead and kill me, it's okay.* She invited me to, allowed me to. I swear, honestly, it happened like that. Without me knowing. Can that happen? It was like a dream. The more I think about it, the more it doesn't feel real. Why would Kiki ask me to kill her?"

I downed the last of my lukewarm beer. A dense layer of cigarette smoke hovered like an ectoplasmic phenomenon.

"Feel like another beer?" I asked him.

"Yeah, I could use one."

I went to the bar and came back with two mugs, which we drank in silence. The turnover at the place was as busy as Akihabara Station at rush hour, customers coming and going constantly. Nobody bothered listening in to our conversation. Nobody even looked at Gotanda.

"What'd I tell you?" Gotanda summoned up a smile as he spoke. "Not a star in sight." Gotanda swished his two-thirds empty glass around like a test tube.

"Let's forget it," I said quietly. "I can forget it. You forget it too."

"You think I can forget it? Easy to say, but you didn't kill her with your own hands."

"Hey, you hear me? There's no evidence you killed Kiki. Stop blaming yourself for something that might not have even happened. Your unconscious is using Kiki's vanishing act as a convenient way to lay a guilt trip on you. Isn't that a possibility?"

"Okay, let's talk possibilities," said Gotanda, laying his palms flat on the table. "I've been doing nothing but considering possibilities lately. All sorts of possibilities. Like the possibility that I'll kill my wife. Am I right? Maybe I'd strangle her if she allowed me to, like Kiki did. Possibilities are like cancer. The more I think about them, the more they multiply, and there's no way to stop them. I'm out of control. I didn't just burn mailboxes. I killed four cats. I used a slingshot and busted the neighbors' window. I couldn't stop doing shit like this. And I never told anyone about it, until this minute. God," he sighed deeply, "it's almost a relief, telling you.

"What goddamn thing am I going to do next? That gap—it's too big, too deep. Professional hazard, huh? The bigger the gap, the more weird the shit I find myself doing. Is it in my genes? God, I'm afraid that I will just kill my wife. I haven't got any control over it. *Because it won't take place in this world.*"

"You worry too much," I said, forcing a smile. "Forget this nonsense about genes. What you need is a break from work. Stop seeing your wife for a while. It's the only way. Throw everything to the wind. Come with me to Hawaii. Lie on the beach, drink piña coladas, swim, get laid. Rent a convertible and cruise around listening to music. And if you still want to worry, you can do that later."

"Not a bad idea," he said, the folds of his eyes crinkling as he smiled. "We'll get us two girls and the four of us can fool around till morning again. That was fun."

Shoveling that good snow. Cuck–koo.

"I can take off any time," I said. "How about you? How long will it take you to finish up what you're doing?"

Gotanda gave me the oddest smile. "You don't understand a thing, do you? There's no such thing as finishing up in my line of work. All you can do is toss the whole thing. And if I do that, you can be sure I'll never work again. I'd be drummed out of the industry, *permanently*. And, I'd lose my wife, *permanently*."

He drained the last of his beer.

"But that's fine. Back-to-nothing is fine. At this point, I'm ready to call it quits. I'm tired. Time I went to Hawaii and

blanked out. Okay, let's scrap it all. Let's go to Hawaii. I can
think things over later. I'll . . . become a regular human
being. Maybe too late, but worth a try. I'll leave everything
up to you. I trust you. Always did, from the time you first
called me up. You seemed like such a decent guy. Like what
I'd always wanted to be."

"No such decent guy here," I protested. "I'm just . . .
keeping in step, dancing along. No meaning to it at all."

Gotanda spread his hands a body-width apart on the
table. "And just where, pray tell, *is* there meaning? Where in
this life of ours?" Then he laughed. "But that's okay. Doesn't
matter anymore. I'm resigned to it. I'll follow your example.
I'll hop around from elevator to elevator. It's not impossible.
I can do anything if I put my mind to it. I'm sharp, handsome, good-natured Gotanda after all. So, okay, Hawaii.
We'll get the tickets tomorrow. First class. It's gotta be first
class. It's in the cards, you know. BMW, Rolex, Azabu, and
first class. We'll leave the day after tomorrow and land on
the same day. Hawaii! I look good in an aloha shirt."

"You'd look good in anything."

"Thanks for tickling what remains of my ego."

Gotanda gave me a good, long look. "You really think
you can forget I killed Kiki?"

"Uh-huh."

"Well, one other thing you don't know about me.
Remember I told you I got thrown in confinement for two
weeks?"

"Yeah."

"That was a lie. I blabbed everything and they let me out
right away. I wasn't scared. I wanted, in some sick way, to
do something gutless. I wanted to hate myself. I'm such a
louse. You didn't know that when you clammed up to save
my face, you also saved my rotten hide. You did something
for me that I wouldn't do for myself—wash away my dirt.
And I was glad, you know. It gave me the chance to finally
be honest with myself. I feel like I've come clean at last.
Man, I bet it wasn't too pleasant to watch."

"Don't worry about it," I said. *It's brought us closer together*, I wanted to say. But I didn't. I decided to wait for a time when the words would mean more. So I just repeated myself, "Don't worry about it."

Gotanda took his rain hat from the back of his chair, checked to see how damp it was, then put it back. "I got a favor to ask you," he said, "as a friend. I'd like another beer, but I don't have it in me to get up and go get one."

"No problem," I said.

I stood up and went up to the bar. There was a line, so it took me a while. By the time I waded back to the table, mugs in hand, Gotanda was gone. Ditto his rain hat. And no Maserati in the parking lot either. Great, I shook my head, just great.

There was nothing I could do. He had disappeared.

4∅

The following afternoon they dredged the Maserati out of Tokyo Bay. As I expected. No surprises. As soon as he disappeared, I saw it coming.

Another corpse. The Rat, Kiki, Mei, Dick North, and now Gotanda. Five. One more to go. What now? Who was the next in line to die? Not Yumiyoshi, I wouldn't be able to bear that. Yumiyoshi was not meant to die. Okay, then Yuki? The kid was thirteen. I couldn't let that happen to her. I was going down the list, as if I were the god of doom, dealing out orders for mortality.

I went down to the Akasaka police station to tell Bookish that I'd been with Gotanda the previous night until right before his death. Somehow I thought it was the right thing to do, though naturally I didn't mention Kiki. That was a closed book. Instead, I talked about how exhausted Gotanda had been, how his loans were piling up, the problems with work, the stresses in his personal life.

Bookish took down what I said. Unlike before, he made simple notes. Which I signed. It didn't take an hour. "People dying left and right around you, eh?" he said. "At this rate, you'll never make friends and influence people. They start hating you, and before you know it, your eyes go and your skin sags. Not a pretty prospect."

Then he heaved a deep sigh.

"Well, anyway, this was a suicide. Open and shut case. Even got witnesses. Still, what a waste. I don't care if he was a movie star, he didn't have to go blitzing a *Maserati* into the Bay, did he? Ordinary Honda Civic or Toyota Corolla would've done the job."

"It was insured."

"No sir, insurance never covers suicides," Bookish reminded me. "Anyway, you can go now. Sorry about your friend. And thanks for taking the trouble to come in," he said as he saw me to the door. "Mei's case isn't settled yet. But the investigation's still going on."

For a long time after, I walked around feeling as if I'd killed Gotanda. I couldn't rid myself of the weight. I went back over all the things we'd talked about that night. If only I'd given him the responses he'd needed to save himself, the two of us might be relaxing on the beach in Maui right now.

No way. Gotanda had made up his mind from the beginning. He'd been thinking about plowing that Maserati into the sea all along. He'd been waiting for an excuse. It was his only exit. He'd already had his hand on the doorknob, the Maserati in his head sinking, the water pouring in, choking him, over and over again.

Mei's death had left me shaken, Dick North's death sad and resigned. But Gotanda's death lay me down in a lead-lined box of despair. Gotanda's death was unsalvageable. Gotanda never really got himself in tune with his inner impulses. He pushed himself as far as he could, to the furthest edge of his awareness—and then right across the line into that dark otherworld.

For a while, the weeklies and TV and sports tabloids feasted on his death. Like beetles on carrion. The headlines alone were enough to make me vomit. I felt like throttling every scandalmonger in town.

I climbed into bed and shut my eyes. *Cuck–koo,* I heard Mei far off in the darkness.

I lay there, hating everything. The deaths were beyond comprehension, the aftertaste sickening. The world of the living was obscene. I was powerless to do anything. People came and went, but once gone, they never came back. My hands smelled of death. *I wouldn't be able to wash it off,* like Gotanda said.

Hey, Sheep Man, is this the way you connect your world? Threading one death to another? You said it might already be too late for me to be happy. I wouldn't have minded that, but why this?

When I was little, I had this science book. There was a section on "What would happen to the world if there was no friction?" Answer: "Everything on earth would fly into space from the centrifugal force of revolution." That was my mood.

41

Three days after Gotanda plowed the Maserati into the sea I called Yuki. To be honest, I didn't want to speak to anyone, but her of all people I *had* to talk to. She was vulnerable and lonely. A child. And I may have been the only person in the world who would hear her out. Then again, more importantly, *Yuki was alive*. And I had a duty to keep her that way. At least, that's what I felt.

Yuki wasn't in Hakone. A groggy Amé answered the phone and said that Yuki had left two days earlier to return to the Akasaka condo.

I called Akasaka. Yuki snatched up the receiver immediately. She must have been right beside the phone.

"It's okay for you to be away from Hakone?" I asked.

"I don't know. But I needed to be alone. Mama's an adult, right? She ought to be all right on her own. I wanted to think about myself. Things like what to do from here on. I think it's time I start to get serious about my life."

"Well, maybe so."

"I saw the papers. That friend of yours, he died, huh?"

"Yes, the Curse of the Maserati. As you warned me."

Yuki did not answer. The silence seeped through the wires. I switched the receiver from the right ear to the left.

"How about a meal?" I asked. "I know you've only been eating junk, right? I haven't been eating too well myself. Let's get ourselves a better class of grub."

"I've got to meet somebody at two, but before that I'm okay."

I looked at the clock. A little past eleven.

"Fine. I'll get ready now. See you in about thirty minutes," I said.

I changed clothes, took a swig of orange juice, pocketed my wallet and keys. I'm off, I thought. Or no? Had I forgotten something? Right, I'm always off. I'd forgotten to shave. I ran over my beard with a razor, then sized myself up in the mirror. Could I still pass for a guy in his twenties? Maybe. Maybe not. But did anybody care? I brushed my teeth again.

Outside it was sunny. Summer coming on. If only the rainy season could be put on hold. Sunglasses on, I drove to Yuki's condo. I rang the bell at the entrance to her building and Yuki came right down. She was wearing a short-sleeve dress and sandals, and carried a shoulder bag.

"You're looking very chic today," I said.

"I told you I had to see someone at two, didn't I?" she replied.

"It suits you, your dress. Very becoming, very adult."

She smiled but said nothing.

It was a bit before twelve, so we had the restaurant to ourselves. We filled up on soup and pasta and sea bass and salad. By the time the tide of salarymen washed in, we were out of there.

"Where to?" I asked.

"Nowhere. Just drive around," she said.

"Antisocial. Waste of gasoline," I said, but Yuki let it drop, pretending not to hear.

Instead she turned on the stereo. Talking Heads, *Fear of Music*. When did I ever put that tape in the deck?

"I decided to get a tutor," she said. "That's who I'm meeting today. I told Papa I wanted to study, and he found her for me. She seems like a real good person. Strange, but seeing that movie made me want to learn."

"What movie? *Unrequited Love?*"

"That's right. Sounds crazy, I know. Even sounds crazy to me. Maybe your friend playing the teacher made me feel like studying. At first, I thought, gimme a break, but I must have gotten hooked. Maybe he did have talent."

"Yeah, he had talent. He could act. If it was fiction. Not reality, if you get what I mean."

"I think so."

"You should have seen him as a dentist. He told me *that* was acting. . . . Anyway, wanting to do something is a good sign. You can't really go on living without it. I think Gotanda would be pleased to hear it."

"Did you see him?"

"I did," I said. "I saw him and we talked. We talked a long time. A very honest talk. And then he died, just like that. He was talking with me, then he gunned the Maserati into the Bay."

"Because of me?"

"No, not because of you." I shook my head slowly. "It's not your fault. It's nobody's fault. People have their own reasons for dying. It might look simple, but it never is. It's just like a root. What's above ground is only a small part of it. But if you start pulling, it keeps coming and coming. The human mind dwells deep in darkness. Only the person himself knows the real reason, and maybe not even then."

He'd been waiting for an excuse. He'd already had his hand on the doorknob.

No, it was nobody's fault after all.

"Still, I know you hate me for it," said Yuki.

"I don't hate you."

"You may not hate me now, but you will later."

"Not now, not later. I don't hate like that."

"Well, maybe not hate, but something's going to go away," she murmured, half to herself. "I just know it."

I glanced over at her. "Strange. Gotanda said the same thing."

"Really?"

"Yeah. He said he had the feeling things were disappearing on him. I don't know what kind of things he meant. But whatever they are, sometime they're going to go. We shift around, so things can't help but go when that happens. They disappear when it's time for them to disappear. And they don't disappear until it's time for them to disappear. Like that dress you got on. In a couple of years, it won't fit you, and you might even think the Talking Heads are moldy oldies. You might not even want to go on drives with me anymore. Can't be helped. As they say, just go with the flow. Don't fight it."

"I'll always like you. That has nothing to do with time."

"Makes me happy to hear that, because I want to think so too," I said. "But to be fair, Yuki, you still don't know much about time. It's better not to go deciding too many things now. People go through changes like you'd never believe."

She was silent. The tape auto-reversed to side B.

Summer. Wherever you looked, the town looked like summer. Cops and high school kids and bus drivers were all in short sleeves. There were even women in no sleeves. And to think not so long ago it had been snowing.

"And you really don't hate me?"

"Of course not," I said. "In this uncertain world, that's about the only thing I'm sure of."

"Absolutely?"

"Absolutely 2,500 percent."

She smiled. "That's what I wanted to hear." Then she asked, "You liked Gotanda, didn't you?"

"I liked him, sure," I said. Suddenly my voice caught. Tears welled up. I barely managed to fight them back and took a deep breath. "Each time we met I liked him more. That doesn't happen very much, especially not at my age."

"Did he kill the woman?"

I scanned the early summer cityscape for a moment. "Who knows? Maybe he did and maybe he didn't."

He'd been waiting for an excuse.

Yuki leaned on her window and looked out, listening to her Talking Heads. She seemed a little more grown-up than when we first met, only two and a half months before.

"What are you going to do now?" asked Yuki.

"Yes, what am I going to do," I said. "I haven't decided. I think I've got to go back to Sapporo. Tomorrow or the day after tomorrow. Lots of loose ends up there."

Yumiyoshi. The Sheep Man. The Dolphin Hotel. A place that I was a part of. Where someone was crying for me. I had to go back to close the circle.

I offered to drive Yuki wherever she had to go. "Heaven knows, I'm free today."

She smiled. "Thanks, but it's okay. It's pretty far; the train'll be faster."

"Did I hear you say thanks?" I said, removing my sunglasses.

"Got any problems with that?"

"Nope."

We were at Yoyogi-Hachiman Station, where she was going to catch the Odakyu Line. Yuki looked at me for ten or fifteen seconds. No identifiable expression on her face, only a gradual change in the gleam of her eyes, the shape of her mouth. Ever so slightly, her lips grew taut, her stare sharp and sassy. Like a slice of summer sunlight refracting in water.

She slammed the door shut and trotted off, not looking back. I watched her receding figure disappear into the crowd. And when she was out of sight, I felt lonely, as if a love affair had just broken up.

I drove back up Omotesando to Aoyama to go shopping at Kinokuniya, but the parking lot was full. Hey, come to think of it, wasn't I going to Sapporo tomorrow or the day after? So I cruised around a bit more, then went home. To my empty apartment. Where I plopped down on the bed and stared up at the ceiling.

They've got a name for this, I thought. *Loss. Bereavement.* Not nice words.

Cuck–koo.

It echoed through the empty space of my home.

42

I had a dream about Kiki. I guess it was a dream. Either that or some act akin to dreaming. What, you may ask, is an "act akin to dreaming"? I don't know either. But it seems it does exist. Like so many other things we have no name for, existing in that limbo beyond the fringes of consciousness.

But let's just call it a dream, plain and simple. The expression is closest to something real for us.

It was near dawn when I had this dream about Kiki.

In the dream as well, it was near dawn.

I'm on the phone. An international call. I've dialed the number that Kiki apparently left me on the windowsill of that room in downtown Honolulu. *Beepbeepbeep beep beepbeep beepbeep* . . . I can hear the phone lines connecting. I'm getting through. Or so I think. The numbers are linking up in order. A brief interval, a short dial tone. I press the receiver to my ear and count the muffled reports. Five, six, seven, eight rings. At the twelfth ring, someone answers. And in that instant, I'm in that room. That big, empty death chamber in downtown Honolulu. It seems to be daytime. Noon, judging from the light pouring straight down through the skylight. Flecks of dust dance in these upright shafts of light, bright as a southern sun and sharp as gashes from a knife. Yet the parts of the room without light are murky and cold. The contrast is remarkable. Like the ocean floor, I'm thinking.

I'm sitting on a sofa there in the room, receiver at my ear. The telephone cord trails away over the floor, across a dark area, through the light, to disappear again into the gloom. A long, long cord. Longer than any I've seen. I've got the phone on my lap and I'm looking around the room.

The furniture in the room is the same as it was. The same pieces in the same places. Bed, table, sofa, chairs, TV, floor lamp. Spaced unnaturally apart. And the room has the same smell as before. Stale and moldy, a shut-in air of disuse. But the six skeletons are gone. Not on the bed, not on the sofa, not in the chair in front of the TV, not at the dining table. They've all disappeared. As have the scraps of food and plates from the table. I set the telephone down on the sofa and stand up. I have a slight headache. The kind you get when there's a high-pitched hum in your ears. I sit back down.

I detect a movement from the farthest chair off in the gloom. I strain my eyes. Someone or something has gotten up and I hear footsteps coming my way. It's Kiki. She appears from out of the darkness, cuts across the light, takes a chair at the dining table. She's wearing the same outfit as before. Blue dress and white shoulder bag.

She sits there, sizing me up. She is quiet, her expression tranquil. She is positioned neither in light nor in darkness, but exactly in between. I'm about to get up and go over to her, but have second thoughts. There's still that slight pain in my temples.

"The skeletons go somewhere?" I ask.

"I suppose," says Kiki with a smile.

"Did you dispose of them?"

"No, they just vanished. Maybe you disposed of them?"

Eyeing the telephone beside me, I press my fingers to my temples.

"What's it mean? Those six skeletons?"

"They're you," says Kiki. "This is your room. Everything here is you. Yourself. Everything."

"My room," I repeat after her. "Well, then, what about the Dolphin Hotel? What's there?"

"That's your place too. Of course. The Sheep Man's there. And I'm here."

The shafts of light do not waver. They are hard, uniform. Only the air vibrates minutely in them. I notice it without really looking.

"I seem to have rooms in a lot of places," I say. "You know, I kept having these dreams. About the Dolphin Hotel. And somebody there, who's crying for me. I had that same dream almost every night. The Dolphin Hotel stretches out long and narrow, and there's someone there, crying for me. I thought it was you. So I knew I had to see you."

"Everyone's crying for you," says Kiki, ever so softly, in a voice to soothe worn nerves. "After all, that whole place is for you. Everyone there cries for you."

"But you were calling me. That's why I went back, to see you. And then from there . . . a lot of things started. Just like before. I met all sorts of folks. People died. But, you did call me, didn't you? It was you who guided me along, wasn't it?"

"It wasn't me. It was you who called yourself. I'm merely a projection. You guided yourself, through me. I'm your phantom dance partner. I'm your shadow. I'm not anything more."

But I wasn't strangling her, I was strangling my shadow. If only I could choke off my shadow, I'd get some health.

"But why would everyone cry for me?"

She doesn't answer. She rises, and with a tapping of footsteps, walks over to stand before me. Then she kneels and reaches out to touch my lips with her fingertips. Her fingers are sleek and smooth. Then she touches my temples.

"We're crying for all the things you can't cry for," whispers Kiki. Slowly, as if to spell it out. "We shed tears for all the things you never let yourself shed tears, we weep for all the things you did not weep."

"Are your ears still . . . like they were?" I'm curious.

"My ears—," she breaks off into a smile. "They're in perfect shape. The same as they were."

"Would you show me your ears again, just one more time?" I ask. "It was an experience like I've never known, as if the whole world was reborn. In that restaurant that time, you knocked me out. I've never forgotten it."

She shakes her head. "Maybe sometime," she says. "But not today. They're not something you can see at any moment. It's something to see only at the right time. That was a right time. Today is not. I'll show you again sometime, when you really need it."

She stands back up and into a vertical shaft of illumination from above. She stays there, her body almost decomposing amid the specks of strong light.

"Tell me, Kiki, are you dead?" I ask.

She spins around in the light to face me.

"Gotanda thinks he killed me," says Kiki.

"Yes, he does. Or he did."

"Maybe he did kill me. For him it's like that. In his mind, he killed me. That's what he needed. If he didn't kill me, he'd still be stuck. Poor man," says Kiki. "But I'm not dead. I just disappeared. I do that. I move into another world, a different world. Like boarding a train running parallel. That's what disappearing is. Don't you see?"

No, I don't, I say.

"It's simple. Watch."

With those words, Kiki walks across the floor, headlong toward the wall. Her pace does not slacken, even on reaching the wall. She is swallowed up into the wall. Her footsteps likewise vanish.

I keep watching the wall where she was swallowed up. It's just a wall. The room is silent. There's only the specks of light sifting through the air. My head throbs. I press my fingers to my temples and keep my eyes on the wall. When I think of it, of that time in Honolulu, she'd vanished into a wall too.

"Well? Simple enough?" I hear Kiki's voice. "Now you try."

"You think I can?"

"I said it's simple, didn't I? Go ahead, give it a try. Walk straight on as you are. Don't stop. Then you'll get to this side. Don't be afraid. There's nothing to be afraid about."

I grab the telephone and stand up, then walk, dragging the cord, straight toward the wall where she disappeared. I get wary as the wall looms up, but I do not slacken my pace. Even as I touch the wall, there is no impact. My body just passes through, as it might a transparent air pocket. Only the air seems to change a bit. I'm still carrying the telephone as I pass through and I'm back in my bedroom, in my own apartment. I sit down on the bed, with the phone on my lap. "Simple," I say. "Very, very simple."

I put the receiver to my ear, but the line is dead.

So went the dream. Or whatever it was.

43

When I got back to the Dolphin Hotel, three female receptionists stood behind the front desk. As ever, they were uniformed in neatly pressed blazers and spotless white blouses. They greeted me with smiles. Yumiyoshi was not among them. Which upset me. Or rather, it tipped over all my hopes. I'd been counting so much on being able to see Yumiyoshi right away that I could hardly pronounce my own name when asked. As a result, the receptionist wavered slightly behind her smile and eyed my credit card suspiciously as she ran a computer check.

I was given a room on the seventeenth floor. I dropped my bag, washed up, and went back down to the lobby. Then I sat on the sofa and pretended to read a magazine, while casting occasional glances at the front desk. Maybe Yumiyoshi was on a break. After forty minutes she still had not shown. Still the same three indistinguishable women with identical hairstyles on duty. After one hour, I gave up.

I went out into town and bought the evening paper. Then I went into a café and read the thing from front to back over a cup of coffee, hoping for some article of interest.

There wasn't. Not a thing about either Gotanda or Mei. Notices of other murders, though, other suicides. As I read, I was hoping Yumiyoshi would be standing behind the counter when I got back to the hotel.

No such luck.

Had she for some unknown reason suddenly vanished? Walked into a wall? I felt a terrible uneasiness. I tried calling her at home; no answer. Finally I telephoned the front desk. Yumiyoshi had taken "a leave of absence." She'd be back on duty the day after next. Brilliant, I thought, why hadn't I called her before I showed up?

I'd worked myself up into such a state that it hadn't entered my mind to do something as obvious as that. What a dummy! And when was the last time I'd called her anyway? Not once since Gotanda died. And who knows when before that. Maybe not since Yuki threw up on the beach. How long ago was that? I'd forgotten about Yumiyoshi. I had no idea what might have happened with her. And things do happen.

I was suddenly shaken. What if Yumiyoshi had disappeared into a wall, and I'd never see her again? Yes, one more corpse to go. I didn't want to think about it. I started hyperventilating. I had trouble breathing. My heart swelled big enough to burst through my chest. Did this mean I was in love with Yumiyoshi? I had to see her face-to-face to know for sure. I called her apartment, over and over, so many times my fingers hurt. No answer.

I couldn't sleep. I lay in my hotel bed, sweating. I switched on the light and looked at the clock. Two o'clock. Three-fifteen. Four-twenty. After that, I gave up. I sat by the window and watched the city grow light to the beating of my heart.

Yumiyoshi, don't leave me alone. I need you. I don't want to be alone anymore. Without you I'll be flung out to the far corners of the universe. Show your face, please, tie me down somewhere. Tie me to this world. I don't want to join the ghosts. I'm just an ordinary guy. I need you.

From six-thirty in the morning I dialed her apartment at half-hour intervals. To no avail.

June in Sapporo is a wonderful time of year. The snow has long since melted, the plains that were frozen tundra a few months earlier are dark and fertile. Life breathes everywhere. The trees are thick with foliage, the leaves sway in the breeze. The sky is high and clear, crisply outlining the clouds. An inspirational season. Yet here I was in my hotel room dialing Yumiyoshi's number like a maniac. She'll be back tomorrow—what was my rush? I must have told myself this every ten minutes. I couldn't wait. Who could guarantee she'd come back tomorrow? I sat by the phone and kept dialing. And then I sprawled out on the bed and stared up at the ceiling.

Here is where the old Dolphin Hotel used to stand. It was the pits of a hotel. Untold others stayed there, stepped in the grooves in the floor, saw the spots on the wall. I sat deep in my chair, feet on the table, eyes closed, picturing the old place. The shape of the front door, the worn-out carpeting, the tarnished brass keys, the corners of window frames thick with dust. I'd walked those halls, opened those doors, entered those rooms.

The old Dolphin Hotel had disappeared. Yet its presence lingered on. Beneath this new intercontinental Dolphin, behind it, within it. I could close my eyes and go in. The *cr-cr-crr-creaking* of the elevator, like an old dog wheezing. It was still here. No one knew, but it was here. This place was my nexus, where everything tied together. This place is here for me, I told myself. Yumiyoshi *had* to come back. All I had to do was sit tight and wait.

I had room service bring up dinner, which I accompanied with a beer from the mini-bar. And at eight o'clock I tried Yumiyoshi's number again. No answer again.

I turned on the TV and watched baseball, with the sound off. It was a lousy game. I didn't want to watch baseball anyway. I wanted to see live human bodies in action. Badminton, water polo, anything would have done as well.

At nine o'clock I tried calling again. This time, she picked up after one ring. At first I couldn't believe she was actually there. I was cut to the quick, a lump of air stuck in my throat. Yumiyoshi was actually there.

"I just got back this minute," said Yumiyoshi, utterly cool. "I went to Tokyo to see relatives. I called your place twice, but nobody answered."

"I'm up here in Sapporo and I've been calling *you* like crazy."

"So we nearly missed each other."

"Nearly missed," was all I could bring myself to say, tightly gripping the receiver and peering at the muted TV screen. Words would not come. I was caught off-guard, impossibly confused.

"Hey, are you there? Hello? Hello?"

"I'm here all right."

"Your voice sounds strange."

"I . . . I'm nervous," I explained. "I've got to see you or I can't talk. I've been on edge all day. I've got to see you."

"I think I can see you tomorrow night," she said after a moment's thought. I could just picture her pushing her glasses up on the bridge of her nose.

Receiver fast to my ear, I lowered myself onto the floor and leaned back against the wall. "Tomorrow's a long way off. I kind of think it'd be better to meet tonight. Right away, in fact."

A negative air came to her voice. Even if that voice hadn't said anything yet, the negative came across. "I'm too tired now. I'm exhausted. I just got back. And since I'm on duty tomorrow morning, tonight I just want to sleep. Tomorrow, after I get off, let's get together. How about that? Or won't you be around tomorrow?"

"No, I'll be here for a while. And I do sympathize with your being tired. Only, honestly, I'm worried. Like maybe by tomorrow you'll have disappeared."

"Disappeared?"

"Disappeared. Vanished."

Yumiyoshi laughed. "I don't disappear so easily. I'm not going anywhere."

"No, it's not like that. You don't understand. We keep moving. And as we do, things around us, well, they disappear. I know I'm not entirely coherent, but that's what worries me. Yumiyoshi, I need you. I mean, I really need you. Like I've never needed anything before. Please don't disappear on me."

Yumiyoshi paused for a moment. "Golly," she said. "I promise. I won't disappear. I'll see you tomorrow. So please just wait until then."

"Okay," I said. I had no choice but to be satisfied—though I wasn't—with her assurances.

"Good night then," she said, and hung up.

I paced around the room, then went up to the lounge on the twenty-sixth floor, the lounge where I'd first seen Yuki. The place was crowded. Two young women were drinking at the bar, both very fashionably dressed, one with beautiful legs. I sat, nursing my vodka tonic, and eyed them with no special intentions. Then I turned my gaze to the night skyline. I pressed my fingers to my temples, though I did not have a headache. Then I felt the shape of my skull, slowly tracing the shape of bone matter beneath the skin, imagining the skeletons of the women at the bar. Skull, vertebrae, sternum, pelvis, arms, legs, joints. Beautiful white bones inside those beautiful legs. Pristine, white as clouds, expressionless. Miss Legs looked my way, undoubtedly aware of my stare. I would have liked to explain. That I wasn't looking at her body. That I was only thinking about her bones!

I had three drinks, then returned to my room. Having reached Yumiyoshi at last, I slept like a dream.

Yumiyoshi showed up at three in the morning. The doorbell rang, I turned on the bedside lamp, and looked at the clock. Then throwing on a bathrobe, I went to the door, innocently, three-quarters asleep. I cracked it open. And there she was, in her light blue uniform blazer. She stepped into the room through the narrow opening, like she always did.

She stood in the middle of the room and breathed deeply. Without a sound she removed her blazer and folded it carefully over the back of the chair. The same as ever.

"Well, I haven't disappeared, have I?" was the first thing she said.

"No, it doesn't look like you've disappeared," came my voice from somewhere. I couldn't quite grasp whether this was actually happening or not.

"People don't disappear so easily," she spoke deliberately.

"You just don't know. Lots of things can happen in this world. You name it."

"Perhaps, but I'm here. I haven't disappeared. You *do* admit that, don't you?"

I glanced around the room and looked Yumiyoshi in the eye. This was real waking reality. "Yes, I admit it. You don't seem to have disappeared. But what brings you to my room at three in the morning?"

"I couldn't sleep," she said. "I went to bed right after you called, but my eyes popped wide open at a little past one and I didn't sleep a wink after that. What you said kind of got to me. So I called a taxi and came here."

"Didn't anyone think it was strange, you showing up at three in the morning?"

"Nobody noticed. Everyone's asleep. The hotel keeps going twenty-four hours, but the only people awake at three A.M. are the front desk and room service. Nobody's hanging around the employees' entrance. And nobody keeps track anyway. You can always say you came to sleep in the sleep room. I've done it plenty of times before."

"You've done this before?"

"Yes, when I couldn't sleep. I come and wander around. I know this sounds strange, but it's very restful. And, well, I like it. No one ever notices. It's not a problem. Of course, if they found me in this room, that's another story. But don't worry, I'll stay until morning and slip out to work. Okay?"

"Of course it's okay by me. What time do you have to be on duty?"

"Eight," she said. "Another five hours."

Yumiyoshi nervously removed her watch and laid it down on the table. Then she straightened her skirt. I sat down on the corner of the bed, having slowly awakened to the circumstances. "So now," said she, "did I hear you say you need me?"

"Like crazy," I said. "I've been all around. I've made a complete revolution. And I've come back to the fact that I need you."

"Like crazy," she reminded me, tugging at the hem of her skirt.

"That's right, like crazy."

"Just where all around have you been?"

"You wouldn't believe it if I told you. I've made it back to reality—that's the important thing. I've come full circle. And I'm still on my feet, dancing."

She looked at me quizzically.

"I can't go into details. Just believe me. I need you. That's very important, to me anyway. Maybe it could be important to you too."

"So what do you want me to do?" said Yumiyoshi, with no change of expression. "Fall into your arms? Be moved to tears? Tell you how wonderful it is to be wanted?"

"No, no, nothing like that," I said quickly, but then couldn't find the right words to go on. As if there were right words. "What can I tell you? I've known it all along and never doubted it. I knew that we would sleep together. Only at first we couldn't. The timing wasn't right. It had to wait until it was right."

"So now I'm supposed to sleep with you? Just like that?"

"I know the argument's short-circuited. And I know it's the worst possible way to convince you. But to be honest, that's what it comes down to. I can't help how the words come out. I mean, with me too, if these were normal circumstances, I'd try to do things in the proper order. I'm not that much of a dud. But this is a very simple thing, and this approach is truer. I know it. Which is why I can't express it any other way. I've always known that we would sleep together. It's decided, it's fact. And we shouldn't go fiddling around with that. That might ruin everything. Honest!"

Yumiyoshi eyed her watch. "You do realize you're not making much sense, don't you?" she said. Then she sighed and began to unbutton her blouse. "Don't look."

I lay back on the bed and gazed up at a corner of the ceiling. There's another world somewhere, but now I'm here, in this one. Yumiyoshi undressed slowly. I could hear soft sounds of fabric against skin, then the sound of folding. Then the sound of her glasses being set down. A very sexy sound. And then she was turning out the bedside lamp and sliding under the covers next to me. As quietly as she'd stolen into my room.

We touched. Her body and mine. Smooth, but with a certain gravity. Yes, this was real. Unlike with Mei. Mei had been a dream, fantasy, illusion. *Cuck–koo.* But Yumiyoshi existed in the real world. Her warmth and weight and vitality were real. I caressed her and held her.

Gotanda's fingers trailing down Kiki's back was also illusion. It was acting, light flickering on a screen, a shadow slipping between one world and another. It was not reality. *Cuck–koo.*

My real fingers were stroking Yumiyoshi's real skin.

Yumiyoshi buried her face in my neck. I felt the touch of her nose. I searched out every part of her body. Shoulder, elbow, wrist, palm, the tips of ten fingers. My fingers explored and my lips kissed. Her breasts, her stomach, her sides and back and legs, each form registered and sealed. I needed to be sure. I ran my fingers over her pubis. I moved down and kissed it. *Cuck–koo.*

We did not speak. We held each other. Her breath was warm and wet. Words that were not words hung in the air. I entered her. I was hard, very hard, and full of desire.

Toward climax, Yumiyoshi bit my arm, enough to draw blood. The pain was real. I held her hips and slowly eased into ejaculation. Ever so slowly, sure not to miss a step.

At seven I woke her. "Yumiyoshi, time to get up," I said.

She opened her eyes and looked at me. Then slid out of bed like a fish and stood naked in the morning light. She seemed full of new life, alive. I propped myself on my pillow and admired her. The body I'd registered and sealed a few hours before.

Yumiyoshi showered and brushed her hair with my brush and got dressed. I watched her put on each article of clothing, the care she took doing up each button. Her blazer was next, then she checked in the mirror for wrinkles. She was very serious about these things. Her attitude said "morning." "My makeup is down in my locker," she announced.

"You're beautiful as you are," I said.

"Thanks. But makeup is a part of the job. I don't have a choice."

I gave Yumiyoshi a hug. It was so good to hold her with her glasses and blazer on.

"You still want me, now that it's morning?" she asked.

"I still want you," I said. "I want you more than I wanted you yesterday."

"I've never had anyone want me so much before."

"No one's ever wanted you?"

"Not the way you do," she said. "It's like being in a nice, warm room. Nice and cozy."

"Well, stay put. There's no reason ever to leave."

"Are *you* going to stay put?"

"Yes, I'm going to stay put."

Yumiyoshi pulled back a bit. "Can I come stay with you again tonight?"

"Absolutely. But aren't the risks too high? Wouldn't it be better if I went to your place or stayed in another hotel?"

"No," she said, "I like it here. This is your place, and it's also my place. I want to make love with you here. That is, if it's all right with you."

"I want to make love with you wherever you like."

"Okay, I'll see you this evening. Here." Then she cracked the door open and slipped away.

I felt happy. Yes, I felt happy. And then I wondered if, maybe, it was time to give up the shoveling habit. Do some writing for myself for a change. Without the deadlines. Something for myself. Not a novel or anything. But something for myself.

44

Yumiyoshi came back at six-thirty. Still in uniform, although her blouse was different. She'd brought a bag with a change of clothes and toiletries and cosmetics.

"I don't know," I said. "They're going to find out some time."

"Don't worry, I'm not careless," she said, then smiled and draped her blazer over the back of a chair.

Then we sat on the sofa and held each other tight.

"I've thought about you all day long," she said. "You know, wouldn't it be wonderful if I could work during the daytime, then sneak into your room at night? We'd spend the night together, then in the morning I'd go straight to work?"

"A home convenient to your workplace," I joked. "Unfortunately I couldn't keep footing the tab to this room. And sooner or later, they'll find out about us."

"Nothing goes smoothly in this world."

"You can say that again."

"But it'd be okay for a few more nights, wouldn't it?"

"I imagine that's what's going to happen."

"Good. I'll be happy with those few days. Let's both stay in this hotel."

Then she undressed, neatly folding each article of clothing. She removed her watch and her glasses, and placed them on the table. Then we enjoyed an hour of lovemaking, until we were both exhausted. No better kind of exhaustion.

"Mmm," was Yumiyoshi's appraisal. Then she snuggled up in my arms for a nap. After a while, I got up, showered, then drank a beer. I sat, admiring Yumiyoshi's sleeping face. She slept so nice.

A little before eight, she awoke, hungry. We ordered a sandwich and pasta au gratin from room service. Meanwhile, she stored her things in the closet, and when the bellhop knocked, she hid in the bathroom.

We ate happily.

"I've been thinking about it all afternoon," I began, picking up from our earlier conversation. "There's nothing for me in Tokyo anymore. I could move up here and look for work."

"You'd live here?"

"That's right, I'd live here," I said.

"I'll rent an apartment and start a new life here. You can come over whenever you want to. You can spend the night if you feel like it. We can try it out like that for a while. But I've got the feeling it's going to work out. It'll bring me back to reality. It'll give you space to relax. And it'll keep us together."

Yumiyoshi smiled and gave me a big kiss. "*Fan*tastic!"

"What comes later, I don't know. But I've got a good feeling about it. Like I said."

"Nobody knows what's going to happen in the future. I'm not worried about that. Right now, it's just fantastic! Oooh, the best kind of fantastic!"

I called room service for a bucket of ice, making Yumiyoshi hide in the bathroom again. And while she was in there, I took out the bottle of vodka and tomato juice I'd bought in town that afternoon and made us two Bloody Marys. No lemon slices or Lea & Perrins, but bloody good enough. We toasted. To us. I switched on the bedside Muzak and punched the Pops channel. Soon we were treated to the lush strains of Mantovani playing "Strangers in the Night."

You didn't hear me making snide comments.

"You think of everything," said Yumiyoshi. "I was just dreaming of a Bloody Mary right about now. How did you know?"

"If you listen carefully, you can hear these things. If you look carefully, you'll see what you're after."

"Words of wisdom?"

"No, just words. A way of life in words."

"You ought to specialize in inspirational writing."

We had three Bloody Marys each. Then we took our clothes off and gently made love again.

At one point, in the middle of our lovemaking, I thought I could hear that old Dolphin Hotel elevator *cr-cr-crr-creaking* up the shaft. Yes, this place was the knot, the node. Here's where it all tied together and I was a part of it all. Here was reality, I didn't have to go further. I was already there. All I had to do was to recover the knot to be connected. It's what I'd been seeking for years. What the Sheep Man held together.

At midnight, we fell asleep.

Yumiyoshi was shaking me. "Wake up," she said urgently. Outside it was dark. My head was half full with the warm sludge of unconsciousness. The bedside light was on. The clock read a little after three.

She was dressed in her hotel uniform, clutching my shoulder, shaking me, looking very serious. My first thought was that her boss had found out about us.

"Wake up. Please, wake up," she said.

"I'm awake," I said. "What is it?"

"Hurry up and get dressed."

I quickly slipped on a T-shirt and jeans and windbreaker, then stepped into my sneakers. It didn't take a minute. Then Yumiyoshi led me by hand to the door, and parted it open a scant two or three centimeters.

"Look," she said. I peeked through the opening. The hallway was pitch black. I couldn't see a thing. The darkness was thick, gelatinous, chill. It seemed so deep that if you stuck out a hand, you'd get sucked in. And then there was that familiar smell of mold, like old paper. A smell that had been brewed in the pit of time.

"It's that darkness again," she said.

I put my arm around her waist and drew her close. "It's nothing to be afraid of," I said. "Don't be scared. Nothing bad is going to happen. This is my world. The first time you ever talked to me was because of this darkness. That's how we got to know each other. Really, it's all right."

And yet I wasn't so sure. In fact, I was terrified out of my skin. Thoroughly unhinged, despite my own calm talk. The fear was palpable, fundamental; it was universal, historical, genetic. For darkness terrifies. It swallows you, warps you, nullifies you. Who alive can possibly profess confidence in darkness? In the dark, you can't *see*. Things can twist, turn, vanish. The essence of darkness—nothingness—covers all.

"It's okay," I was now trying to convince myself. "Nothing to be afraid of."

"So what do we do?" asked Yumiyoshi.

I went and quickly got the penlight and Bic lighter I'd brought just in case this very thing happened.

"We have to go through it together," I said. "I returned to this hotel to see two people. You were one. The other is a guy standing somewhere out there in the dark. He's waiting for me."

"The person who was in that room?"

"Yes."

"I'm scared. I'm *really* scared," said Yumiyoshi, trembling. Who could blame her?

I kissed her on her brow. "Don't be afraid. I'm with you. Give me your hand. If we don't let go, we'll be safe. No matter what happens, we mustn't let go. You understand? We have to stay together." Then we stepped into the corridor.

"Which way do we go?" she asked nervously.

"To the right," I said. "Always to the right."

We shined the light at our feet and walked, slowly, deliberately. As before, the corridor was no longer in the new Dolphin Hotel. The red carpet was worn, the floor sagging, the plaster walls stained with liver spots. It was *like* the old Dolphin Hotel, though it was *not* the old Dolphin Hotel. A little ways on, as before, the corridor turned right. We turned, but now something was different. There was no light ahead, no door leaking candlelight. I switched off my penlight to be certain. No light at all, none.

Yumiyoshi held my hand tightly.

"Where's that door?" I said, my voice sounding dry and dead, hardly my voice at all. "Before when I—"

"Me too. I saw a door somewhere."

We stood there at the turn in the corridor. What happened to the Sheep Man? Was he asleep? Wouldn't he have left the light on? As a beacon? Wasn't that the whole reason he was here? What the hell's going on?

"Let's go back," Yumiyoshi said. "I don't like the darkness. We can try again another time. I don't want to press our luck."

She had a point. I didn't like the darkness either, and I had the foreboding feeling that something had gone awry. Yet I refused to give up.

"Let's keep going," I said. "The guy might need us. That's why we're still tied to this world." I switched the penlight back on. A narrow beam of yellow light pierced the darkness. "Hold on to my hand now. I need to know we're together. But there's nothing to be afraid of. We're staying, we're not going away. We'll get back safe and sound."

Step by step, even more slowly and deliberately, we went forward. The faint scent of Yumiyoshi's hair drifted through the darkness, sweetly pricking my senses. Her hand was small and warm and solid.

And then we saw it. The door to the Sheep Man's room had been left slightly ajar, and through the opening we could feel the old chill, smell the dank odor. I knocked. As before, the knock sounded unnaturally loud. Three times I knocked.

Then we waited. Twenty seconds, thirty seconds. No response. Where is he? What's going on? Don't tell me he died! True, the guy was not looking well the last time we met. He couldn't live forever. He too had to grow old and die. But if he died, who would keep me connected to this world?

I pushed the door open and pulled Yumiyoshi with me into the room. I shined my penlight around. The room had not changed. Old books and papers piled everywhere, a tiny table, and on it the plate used as a candle stand, with a five-centimeter stub of wax on it. I used my Bic to light it.

The Sheep Man was not here.

Had he stepped out for a second?

"Who was this guy?" asked Yumiyoshi.

"The Sheep Man," I said. "He takes care of this world here. He sees that things are tied together, makes sure connections are made. He said he was kind of like a switchboard. He's ages old, and he wears a sheepskin. This is where he's been living. In hiding."

"In hiding from what?"

"From war, civilization, the law, the system, . . . things that aren't Sheep Man-like."

"But he's not here. He's gone."

I nodded. And as I did a huge shadow bowed across the wall. "Yes, he's gone. Even though he's supposed to be here."

We were at the edge of the world. That is, what the ancients considered the edge of the world, where everything spilled over into nothingness. We were there, the two of us, alone. And all around us, a cold, vast void. We held each other's hand more tightly.

"Maybe he's dead," I said.

"How can you say a thing like that in the dark? Think more positively," said Yumiyoshi. "He could be off shopping, right? He probably ran out of candles."

"Or else he's gone to collect his tax refund." Even in the candlelit gloom I could see Yumiyoshi smile. We hugged each other. "You know," I said, "on our days off, let's drive to lots of places."

"Sure," she said.

"I'll ship my Subaru up. It's an old car, but it's a good car. It runs just fine. I like it better than a Maserati. I really do."

"Of course," she said. "Let's go everywhere and see lots of things together."

We embraced a little longer. Then Yumiyoshi stooped to pick up a pamphlet from the pile of papers that was lying at her feet. *Studies in the Varietal Breeding of Yorkshire Sheep.* It was browned with age, covered with dust.

"Everything in this room has to do with sheep," I explained. "In the old Dolphin Hotel, a whole floor was devoted to sheep research. There was this Sheep Professor, who was the father of the hotel manager. And I guess the Sheep Man inherited all this stuff. It's not good for anything anymore. Nobody's ever going to read this stuff. Still, the Sheep Man looks after it."

Yumiyoshi took the penlight from me and leafed through the pamphlet. I was casually observing my own shadow, wondering where the Sheep Man was, when I was suddenly struck by a horrifying realization: I'd let go of Yumiyoshi's hand!

My heart leapt into my throat. I was not ever to let go of her hand. I was fevered and swimming in sweat. I rushed to grab Yumiyoshi by the wrist. *If we don't let go, we'll be safe.* But it was already too late. At the very moment I extended my hand, her body was absorbed into the wall. Just like Kiki had passed through the wall of the death chamber. Just like quicksand. She was gone, she had disappeared, together with the glow of the penlight.

"Yumiyoshi!" I yelled.

No one answered. Silence and cold reigned, the darkness deepened.

"Yumiyoshi!" I yelled again.

"Hey, it's simple," came Yumiyoshi's voice from beyond the wall. "Really simple. You can pass right through the wall."

"No!" I screamed. "Don't be tricked. You think it's simple, but you'll never get back. It's different over there. That's the otherworld. It's not like here."

No answer came from her. Silence filled the room, pressing down as if I were on the ocean floor.

I was overwhelmed by my helplessness, despairing. Yumiyoshi was gone. After all this, I would never be able to reach her again. She was gone.

There was no time to think. What was there to do? I loved her, I couldn't lose her. I followed her into the wall. I found myself passing through a transparent pocket of air.

It was cool as water. Time wavered, sequentiality twisted, gravity lost its force. Memories, old memories, like vapor, wafted up. The degeneration of my flesh accelerated. I passed through the huge, complex knot of my own DNA. The earth expanded, then chilled and contracted. Sheep were submerged in the cave. The sea was one enormous idea, rain falling silently over its vastness. Faceless people stood on the beachhead gazing out to the deep. An endless spool of time unraveled across the sky. A void enveloped the phantom figures and was encompassed by a yet greater void. Flesh melted to the bone and blew away like dust. *Extremely, irrevocably dead,* said someone. *Cuck–koo.* My body decomposed, blew apart—and was whole again.

I emerged through this layer of chaos, naked, in bed. It was dark, but not the lacquer-black darkness I feared. Still, I could not see. I reached out my hand. No one was beside me. I was alone, abandoned, at the edge of the world.

"Yumiyoshi!" I screamed at the top of my lungs. But no sound emerged, except for a dry rasping in my throat. I screamed again. And then I heard a tiny click.

The light had been switched on. Yumiyoshi smiled as she sat on the sofa in her blouse and skirt and shoes. Her light blue blazer was draped over the back of the chair. My hands were clutching the sheets. I slowly relaxed my fingers, feeling the tension drain from my body. I wiped the sweat from my face. I was back on this side. The light filling the room was real light.

"Yumiyoshi," I said hoarsely.

"Yes?"

"Are you really there?"

"Of course, I'm here."

"You didn't disappear?"

"No. People don't disappear so easily."

"It was a dream then."

"I know. I was here all the time, watching you. You were sleeping and dreaming and calling my name. I watched you in the dark. I could see you, you know."

I looked at the clock. A little before four, a little before dawn. The hour when thoughts are deepest. I was cold, my body was stiff. Then it was a dream? The Sheep Man gone, Yumiyoshi disappearing, the pain and despair. But I could remember the touch of Yumiyoshi's hand. The touch was still there within me. More real than this reality.

"Yumiyoshi?"

"Yes?"

"Why are you dressed?"

"I wanted to watch you with my clothes on," she said.

"Mind getting undressed again?" I asked. It was one way to be sure.

"Not at all," she said, removing her clothes and easing under the covers. She was warm and smooth, with the weight of someone real.

"I told you people don't just disappear," she said.

Oh really? I thought as I embraced her. No, anything can happen. This world is more fragile, more tenuous than we could ever know.

Who was skeleton number six then? The Sheep Man? Someone else? Myself? Waiting in that room so dim and distant. Far off, I heard the sound of the old Dolphin Hotel, like a train in the night. The *cr-cr-crr-creaking* of the elevator, going up, up, stopping. Someone walking the halls, someone opening a door, someone closing a door. It was the old Dolphin. I could tell. Because I was part of it. And someone was crying for me. Crying for me because I couldn't cry.

I kissed Yumiyoshi on her eyelids.

She snuggled into the crook of my arm and fell asleep. But I couldn't sleep. It was impossible for my body to sleep. I was as wide awake as a dry well. I held Yumiyoshi tightly, and I cried. I cried inside. I cried for all that I'd lost and all that I'd lose. Yumiyoshi was soft as the ticking of time, her breath leaving a warm, damp spot on my arm. Reality.

Eventually dawn crept up on us. I watched the second hand on the alarm clock going around in real time. Little by little by little, onward.

I knew I would stay.

Seven o'clock came, and summer morning light eased through the window, casting a skewed rectangle on the floor.

"Yumiyoshi," I whispered. "It's morning."